THE
GLITTERING
STRAND

By the same author

Reynardine
Till the Day Goes Down
The Italian Garden

THE
GLITTERING
STRAND

JUDITH LENNOX

St. Martin's Press
New York

Library of Congress Cataloging-in-Publication Data

Lennox, Judith.
The glittering strand / Judith Lennox.
p.   cm.
ISBN 0-312-10469-3
1. Silk industry—France—History—16th century—Fiction.
2. Women slaves—Africa, Northern—Fiction.   3. Kidnapping—Fiction.
I. Title.
PR6062.E63G58   1994
823'.914—dc20   93-44046   CIP

First published in Great Britain by HAMISH HAMILTON LTD.

First U.S. Edition: April 1994
10 9 8 7 6 5 4 3 2 1

CONTENTS

PART I

1586–8

SERVING IN NEW OFFICES

The Christians must needs to the galleys,
to serve in new offices: and they were no
sooner in them, but their garments were
pulled over their ears, and torn from their
backs, and they set to the oars.

266 Christians delivered out of Turkish
captivity: Richard Hakluyt

If I close my eyes, all I see is blue. Blue upon blue, planes of azure, cerulean, lapis. The blue of the sea is flecked with silver, the blue of the sky is unceasing.

At Algiers the pale walls of the houses doubled themselves in the sea, and I had to close my eyes to shut out the hard blue and white. I was sick, then; my eyes hurt. The crescents on the sails of the galleys were scarlet: blood-red part-moons against the midday sky, curling in the breeze.

There are no galleys in the harbour below. Barques and carracks, pinnaces and galleons. More blue: if I half close my eyes I can almost see the *Kingfisher* threading her way through the fidgeting boats. Her pennants are of aquamarine, and my insignia is on the sails. Hearts beat a little faster, breath is caught in the throat at the sight of something beautiful. Did I ever tell you that, Thomas? Did I ever tell you to pause and listen for that collective sigh – of pleasure, of envy, of a scarcely understood pain?

Not that you would have paused and listened. You were always running, weren't you, Thomas? Adjusting ropes, measuring distances, assessing the stars. Always in a hurry, always impatient. As though you knew.

Did I know, that day I set sail from Marseilles? Not at all: I was ten years old and sure of my own destiny. I took with me the blue gown the colour of your eyes, Thomas, the colour of Francesco's eyes. Come to me, Francesco, and let me turn from the harbour and hold you.

I do not wish to see any more. I wish to remember.

The Guardi housekeeper, Marthe, made the blue gown, and Serafina embroidered it herself.

Marthe's eyesight was too poor for such fine work, and Serafina had no mother to labour over a daughter's betrothal gowns. But she liked to embroider, just as she liked to go with her father, or with Monsieur Jacques, or with Angelo, to the warehouse where the silks were stored. Her father would pull out the bright bales of fabric and, showing her the different colours, would say, 'Choose whichever you like, petite. These are your inheritance.'

With Monsieur Jacques it was a little different. His small brown eyes would dart impatiently round the warehouse, his plump brown hand would wipe the sweat from his brow. 'These should have gone already,' he would say despairingly. 'These wars, damn them! Which shall I cut for you, mademoiselle?'

Only Angelo touched the glimmering material as Serafina touched it, with respect, with reverence, letting the jewelled plains and patterns trail slowly through his fingers like sand. Emerald, ochre, gold, and crimson; figured, and damask, and brocade. And Angelo's voice as he held up swathes of fabric. 'The raw silk was brought to France from Persia, Serafina. From Persia to Aleppo, to Scanderoon, and then to Florence, where the workshops of the Corsini made it into cloth. Then it was sent to Livorno, and shipped from Livorno to Marseilles. And now we, the Guardi, will transport it to the great cities of the north.'

Serafina liked Angelo's version best. Angelo was clever and handsome and knew the silk trade as well as anyone, even Franco Guardi, Serafina's father. Angelo was not really a Guardi. He had lived with the Guardi family since before Serafina was born, but he was Serafina's mother's elder brother's illegitimate son. His name was Angelo Desmoines, and when Serafina left Marseilles he was nineteen years old. When she was six Serafina intended to marry Angelo. By the time she was nine, she was wiser.

She chose the blue silk because it was the colour of the sea and the sky. A length for herself, and a length for Rosalie, her doll. Rosalie had a rag body and a wooden head. Later, sitting on a balcony overlooking the harbour, Serafina embroidered silver stars and golden moons all over the bodice of her betrothal gown. Moons and stars for Rosalie also, but in miniature, sparkling on the rich blue silk.

The Guardi house was four storeys high, and almost in the centre of Marseilles, not far from the highway of La Canebière. Serafina's grandfather, who had left Florence for France, had built the house. He had seen the city of Marseilles for what it would become: a gateway to the north, through which, carefully assisted by him, all the glorious treasures of the Levant might flow. Eventually, leaving spices and metal ores to others, he began to specialize in cloth. Kerseys, linens and broadcloth from north to south, silks and grograms and cottons from south to north. Like twin currents in a river, but colluding, not opposing. Guardi pack-horses travelled the valleys of the Rhône, Guardi cogs and roundships sailed the Gulf of Lyons and the Ligurian Sea. If France's civil wars made difficulties for the Guardi, then still they survived. Geography had conveniently isolated Provence, and Serafina heard nothing more than Monsieur Jacques's complaints, saw nothing more than a few more limbless beggars in the back alleys of the city.

Apart from Monsieur Jacques, who was Franco Guardi's factor, there was Monsieur de Coniques, the notary. Monsieur de Coniques drew up the legal documents, made insurance claims for any lost ships, was the final arbiter for any queries concerning merchandise. Franco Guardi addressed his excellent notary as Jehan, but no one else did, because though the notary's family had once been noble, they had left him with nothing more than an old name and a qualification in law from the Sorbonne. Because of this, Franco disregarded Monsieur de Coniques's drinking bouts. Franco Guardi had tremendous respect for an old name, an old family, old money, and quite understood that a man who had lost any one of these might seek to comfort himself occasionally with wine. Jehan de Coniques was thin and dark and clever, and to Serafina he was old. Any man of greater years than Angelo was old. She used to study him – secretly, she thought – wondering what it would be like to lose everything but your name and education.

Marthe, the Guardi housekeeper, had once been Serafina's wet-nurse. She had nursed Serafina's elder brothers too, but they had proved less tenacious, and had died before they were weaned. Marguerite Guardi had died of the smallpox when Serafina was six months old, but Serafina, nursed at Marthe's plump white breast, had suffered only one pock-mark, on her belly, and no fever at all. The single scar remained, but she had no memory, of course, of her mother. Marthe was large and black-haired and bad-tempered, and before her eyes grew dim she had taught Serafina to embroider. Jehan de Coniques taught her Latin, Angelo taught her to know a good silk from a lesser one, the streets and the docks taught her French, her family taught her Italian. She did not know who had taught her her numbers: she thought that she had sucked them in like breast-milk, greedily, hungrily.

On the morning of the day on which she had learned of her betrothal, Serafina had played with the baker's daughter, Lisette.

Lisette was two years older than Serafina, she had dark curls and a small but definite bosom. Serafina silently envied the baker's daughter both the curls and the bosom.

They were making Rosalie a bed in one of the chests in Serafina's bedchamber. Stockings, petticoats, linen and chemises from the chests were strewn on the floor. Rosalie reclined in splendour, her wooden head resting on a lace-edged pillow, a silk coverlet up to her chin.

Lisette, kneeling on the floor, was telling Serafina about the morning at the bakery.

'He tripped over and the bag of flour burst. He was all white! He looked' – Lisette lowered her voice so that Marthe, dozing in a nearby chair, should not hear – 'he looked like Madame Lamotte.'

Serafina giggled. Madame Lamotte was immensely old, wore an orange wig, and far too much face-powder.

Lisette, pulling a face, began to giggle too. Marthe, eyelids twitching, stirred in her chair. Both girls, clamping their hands over their mouths, buried their faces in their skirts and rocked with laughter.

There was the sound of a footfall outside, and the door opened. Marthe's eyelids flickered, Serafina wiped the tears from her cheeks and looked up.

'Papa!'

She was in her father's arms in a moment, small hands grabbing at his travel-stained clothes, dark eyes minutely studying his familiar beloved face for any alterations that the four-month voyage might have made.

Franco was a big man and, for an Italian, fair. Serafina did not resemble him: she was small and dark, like her Provençal mother.

'Sir . . .' Marthe, still hazy with sleep, had struggled out of the chair, and was laboriously curtseying, a great rustling of taffeta and scraping of buckram. 'It's good to see you safely back, sir. Run along now, child.'

This to Lisette, who obediently took to her heels.

'We made Rosalie a bed, Papa.' Serafina, seizing Franco's hand, gestured to the chest. 'See, isn't she comfortable?'

'Very comfortable,' said Franco Guardi, absently. He smiled. 'Come here, petite. I have news for you. And Angelo – and Jehan and Marthe. You must listen, too.'

Angelo and Jehan, who had climbed the stairs to greet their newly returned employer, came into the room.

'When I was in Florence,' said Franco, 'I saw, of course, our old friends the Corsini. I talked to Michele at great length, and found that he was of a mind to marry again. He has chosen his bride. It was an important decision and one in which, I am glad to say, we found ourselves in complete agreement. You are to marry Michele Corsini, Serafina.'

At first, her principal emotion was one of confusion. Marriage was, after all, for grown ladies, for princesses in fairy tales, and not for Serafina Guardi, who had everything she wanted here, in Marseilles. Then, for an instant, she felt fear. Her father had spoken of her as though she were a pawn on a chessboard, a credit-note for barter. Her father wanted to send her away. Why did he want to send her away?

Her eyes stung. Serafina let his large hand slip from her fingers, and she turned away, so that he should not see her face. Stooping, she took the doll out of the wooden chest, and held her tightly.

'Marthe will make you a new gown, Serafina,' added Franco.

'Angelo will take you to the warehouse, and you may choose whichever silk you wish.'

Franco smiled, and touched Rosalie's bald wooden head. He said coaxingly, 'You may sew a gown for your doll also.'

'Rosalie,' said Serafina, reminding him. Her voice hardly shook at all. 'The same silk, Papa?'

Franco beamed. 'Of course, my pet.'

He signalled for Angelo to pour the celebratory wine. Serafina thought of the gown she would make for Rosalie. Blue, with moons and stars on the bodice . . . She took a deep breath and found that she no longer wanted to cry.

She had, of course, known her duty for as long as she could remember. She was, after all, her father's only child, the sole heir of the House of Guardi. Without her there would be no one to ward the house, the ships, the warehouses, or the mule trains and barges that carried silk to the north.

Slowly, Serafina looked round the room. She saw Marthe's expression of pride, Jehan de Coniques's look of utter boredom. And Angelo – in Angelo's dark eyes she saw neither hate, nor resentment, nor anger at a stranger taking what in different circumstances might have belonged to him. Just a brief flicker of acceptance, as though he too had grown wise, and had known this day would come.

A marriage to Michele Corsini need not keep her from Marseilles, from the ships, from the business of silk and lace and linen. A few years spent in Florence, perhaps, but one day she would need to return home.

They raised their glasses to her. A nine-year-old child, saluted by three grown men. A nine-year-old child, to be betrothed the following year to a man the same age as her father. Serafina began to feel very proud.

The next day she picked out the blue silk.

A week later, when the commotion and work caused by Franco Guardi's return had lessened, Angelo took Serafina out for an afternoon in the country.

He did so every month or so, when he had time, when the weather was good. The weather was still very fine – hardly any wind, the sky an unblemished blue. They travelled through the white hills behind Marseilles. Serafina rode her good-tempered mule, Angelo his small Spanish jennet. Serafina wore silk from the Levant and sat on a saddle of Spanish leather, her gloves perfumed with the rare scents of the Indies. But she noticed none of these things: she saw only Angelo ahead, his hair made gold by the sunshine, the feather on his hat bobbing in time with the rhythm of his horse's hooves. Serafina liked to be seen with Angelo. She had noticed how the other girls looked at him.

They stopped in the hills, Angelo helping Serafina down from her mule. In front of them lay Marseilles and the wide blue plain of the Mediterranean; behind them were the hills and the ancient robbers' nest of Les Baux. Serafina had seen Les Baux once, but she would not go there again, for there were ghosts there, ghosts of those thrown to their deaths from the high walls of the fortress. Cruelty for pleasure: the discovery of such a possibility had kept her awake at night.

Angelo spread his cloak on the grass. Serafina sat down, knees hunched up to her chin, watching the butterflies hang almost motionless in the warm air. It was all so still. Covertly, she watched Angelo. The shade of the olive tree dappled his smooth skin, deepening the indentations of mouth and nose, the cleft of his chin. He wore blue doublet and hose, and that blue was also darkened and patterned by the shadows of the olive trees. Serafina's favourite story at that time was the tale of Aucassin and Nicolette. To her, Aucassin was always Angelo: gold-brown locks of hair touching his collar, a smile that said, of all the people in the world, it is you that I wish to be with now. She picked sprigs of rosemary and handed them to Angelo, wanting the world never to change.

Then Angelo, sitting up, his face in shadow, said, 'And how will you like to be a married lady, Serafina?'

She had forgotten Michele Corsini and his tall terracotta house in Florence. 'I will like it very well,' she said idly, rolling on to her stomach. 'But I will not be married for many years. I shall sail to Italy in the spring for my betrothal ceremony, that's all.'

Italy. It gave Serafina great pleasure simply to say the word,

Italy. Her father's visits to the country of his origins were frequent, but Serafina had not yet travelled there.

'A betrothal is as binding as a marriage,' said Angelo, lazily twisting bindweed round the stems of rosemary. 'You must love your betrothed, and no other man.'

Serafina stared at him. Love? Love was for fairy tales, for ballads. Why should she love Messer Corsini, who was an old man, a stranger? She said as much to Angelo, and he grinned, his teeth white against his tanned skin.

'Why else do you marry, if not for love, little Serafina?'

She was nine years old, and she did not fully understand him. She only knew that there was something hidden from her, something important, something talked about only amongst grown-ups. She struggled to disguise her sense of humiliation with arrogance.

'I marry, cousin, because Messer Corsini is a rich and great man. And because he is of good birth.'

Angelo did not stop smiling. He only rose, and, dropping the garland he had woven on top of Serafina's small unkind dark head, walked to the shade of the olive trees.

Guiltily, Serafina scrambled to her feet and ran after him. Taking his hand she whispered, 'Be my friend, Angelo. Please be my friend.'

Her voice trembled on the edge of tears. Angelo turned and adjusted the slipping garland, but his gaze soon returned to the blue sea, to the pattern of tiny islands that clung to the southern coast of France, to the white rims of the breakers that had begun to disturb the smoothness of the water.

'Always your friend, Serafina,' he said, softly. 'What else would I be?'

Her fingers were still threaded through his. Angelo raised Serafina's hand to his mouth and kissed it. Then he stooped and, fleetingly, his lips brushed against hers. His eyes were bright and dark and he was smiling. She could no longer hear the birds: their song was drowned by the drumming of her heart.

There was a small gust of wind, and Serafina saw what she at first thought were a dozen butterflies, tossed by the air currents. But they were not butterflies, she realized almost immediately.

was clever, prosper. The alliance of Serafina Guardi and Michele Corsini would be a business transaction, and she would respect it as such. She would provide her husband with heirs, and he in return would provide her with the necessary male figurehead for her beloved ship: the Guardi cloth-trade.

The business that her grandfather had begun, Serafina's father had greatly expanded. Marseilles had profited by Venice's recent troubles. Venice's wealth had made her vulnerable: to the Turks, to Ragusan pirates, to the envy of other Christian nations. Although the coast of Provence was still plagued by Barbary galleys, treaties between the Sultan of Turkey and the King of France kept the encroachments of Islam to an irritation, rather than a wound.

All this Serafina had known for as long as she could remember. Padding after Monsieur Jacques as he oversaw the loading and unloading of the ships at the docks, standing silently, hands clasped behind her back, at the clerks' desks as they wrote their endless columns of figures. Listening to Angelo itemize the different types of silk, their prices and their countries of origin. Employees must be patient with the pampered only child of their employer.

The Guardi owned both galleys and roundships. The square-rigged roundships carried a larger cargo, but were slow and cumbersome; the galleys, their bows painted white and gold, were slim and swift, like fish. Oriflammes pasted straight against the winds, they would dart from the harbour into the open sea.

The galleys were crewed by slaves and felons: twenty-five banks of rowers, chained to the benches, rowing twenty-five Sisyphean strokes to the minute, until they dropped, or died. Serafina was used to the galleys, but a stranger would scent their foul stench on the wind long before he caught the first glorious sight as they glided into port. The galley-slaves were naked but for their canvas drawers, and their heads were shaven. In port, they were housed in barracks by the harbour, with their own living-quarters and mosque. The Guardi owned an infidel kitchen-porter called Ibrahim. Five times a day, no matter where he was, he would fall to the floor and worship his heathen god.

They were falling leaves, those first unmistakable signs of winter.

From that afternoon Serafina resolved to rid herself of ignorance. Sitting with Marthe one evening, sewing tiny silver stitches in the vast expanse of blue, she made Marthe tell her the secrets of marriage.

She learned that she would not wed Messer Corsini until she was truly a woman – and because she was only a tiny slip of a thing she might not become a woman for many years yet. She learned how babies were begun, and how they were brought into the world. The fear she felt was to do with loss of privacy, the sense of shame because she must endure such intimacies with a stranger. She knew her duty, though. As Marthe spoke, Serafina sewed perfect, small, even stitches, and her needle scarcely paused or shook.

When Marthe had finished, Serafina said, 'Angelo says that I should love Messer Corsini.'

Marthe scowled. 'You should not discuss such things with Monsieur Desmoines, petite. It is not proper. And of course you will love Messer Corsini. He will be your husband.'

Serafina finished off a French knot, resisting the temptation to bite the left-over thread with her teeth.

'I will marry Messer Corsini and bear his children, but I will not love him. He is too old.'

Marthe looked troubled. She shifted her great bulk amid a creaking of buckram, a dry rustle of taffeta. She said sternly, 'You must love no one else, Serafina. Italian men are very jealous of their wives' honour.'

Serafina felt quite impatient with her beloved Marthe. Her marriage to Michele Corsini would not affect her true love – indeed, it would allow it to flourish.

'I love this,' she said, holding out the blue silk. It whispered in shimmering folds and waves to the floor, a web of glittering, covetable strands. Part of it was marked with stars and moons like the wide Mediterranean sky.

A single woman would find it hard to make her way in the man's world of commerce, but a married woman might, if she

The Guardi had soldiers, too, more than fifty of them. It was their job to see that the silks and grograms and mohair travelled north to Arles and Beaucaire and Valence, and then to the fair at Lyons. In turn, broadcloth and kerseys must find their way first to Marseilles, and then to Italy. The Wars of Religion had not made France a safe place for the carrying of gold and precious cloths. Though Monsieur Jacques often cursed the cost of the mercenaries, they were a necessary expense.

Franco Guardi taught his daughter about such things during their last winter in Marseilles. He had realized that their time together had become limited, that he had often been too busy, or simply too long absent from home, to spend much time with Serafina. It pleased him that she took such an interest in business affairs: pleased him also that Angelo and the notary, Jehan, who had often quarrelled, seemed at last to be agreeing better. Her father explained to Serafina the value of employees such as Angelo and Jehan, and told her that one must always treat them with respect. Remembering her former rudeness to Angelo, Serafina blushed and vowed in future always to choose her words with care. She had always been polite to Monsieur de Coniques – it would never have occurred to her to be otherwise.

And yet there was an undercurrent of resentment in the notary that even Serafina was aware of. The resentment was not directed against anyone in particular, but against the world in general. Jehan de Coniques was then still quite young – in his mid-twenties – but the bitterness of dispossession had given him the air of a man twice his age. He tolerated Serafina, as he tolerated all those who were equal to him or above him. This, perhaps, was his difficulty with Angelo – he could not decide Angelo's position in the scheme of things. Angelo was a bastard, yet Angelo was also a close relation of the Guardi family, eating every day at the family dinner-table. Serafina sometimes suspected that Monsieur de Coniques knew that Angelo made fun of him, which Angelo frequently did, behind his back, with Serafina his only audience. He would twist his hat into a lawyer's cap, twist his face into an incongruous mixture of disappointment and pride. My family had three chateaux and a hundred armed men, he would say, and now they haven't as much as a chamber-pot. And Serafina would roll round the floor in giggles, her nine-year-old dignity completely destroyed.

She was happy, that winter. She had become accustomed to the prospect of her betrothal, to welcome it, almost, aware that her future status gave her an added and enjoyable importance in the Guardi household. Even the mistral – at first a fluttering of dry leaves and litter in the gutters, then a gathering of copper-coloured clouds on the horizon, and at last a dreadful, vengeful monster that stole the tiles from the roofs and loosed the ships from their moorings – did not send Serafina scuttling, as in the past, for the comfort of Marthe's lap. She was grown up now: she was to be betrothed. Instead, she peeped from between the closed shutters as the ships were tossed to matchwood, and the baker's house opposite lost most of its roof.

It was not until the evening of her departure to Tuscany that some of her equanimity began to fade. Serafina had felt restless all day, unable to sew or to read, prickly with an irrational but increasing dread. Her father and Marthe were talking: Marthe would not travel to Florence because her eyesight had grown too poor, her health too uncertain, for such a journey. A girl called Mathilde, a nervous, fluttering creature, would accompany Serafina as her nursemaid. They would be away throughout the summer months, because as well as the betrothal, Franco Guardi had business in Florence, Naples and Livorno.

It occurred to Serafina, sitting silently by the window, her doll in her lap, that when she returned, things might be different – *would* be different. She would no longer be a child, but a betrothed woman. Her family would be an unknown old man in Florence.

No. She clenched her hands into fists. Rosalie slipped to the floor unnoticed. The pile of boxes and bags, so neatly packed by Marthe, began to blur. Franco Guardi stood with his back to Serafina, facing the fire. No. *This* is my home, she thought, Serafina Guardi my name. Why should I leave?

'Serafina?'

Her father had turned, and was walking towards her. 'Serafina, what is it, my dear?'

She ground one small heel into the floor. 'I don't want to go,' she mumbled, overcome with a mixture of dread and delight at her insolence.

Her father did not hear her at first, so she repeated herself, lower lip stuck out as though she were still only two years old.

'It's a long journey, my love,' said her father, kindly, 'but we will travel slowly, keeping to the coast. You need not fear the open sea.'

'I don't want to go,' Serafina said, mulishly. 'I want to stay here.'

Her father tried to put his arm round her shoulders, but she pulled away from him, and stared glowering through the window. The sun had not yet set, and she could see the distant forest of masts and prows that crowded the harbour. Some of those masts belonged to the three ships that would set out on the long voyage to Pisa the following morning. The *Gabrielle*, the *Mignon*, and the *Petit Coeur*. The friendly sea suddenly looked forbidding, ominous, an unknown element. The masts, with their sails furled, were like a forest of pikes and swords stabbing the horizon.

Serafina heard her father say, his voice falsely cheerful, 'You will see the land of your forefathers, Serafina. All the lords and ladies of Florence will come to your betrothal ceremony, and when you are married they will call you madonna. You will wear the beautiful gown that Marthe has made for you.'

Next, Serafina thought angrily, he'll promise me a box of comfits and a puppy-dog. 'You are my family,' she said. 'This is my home. Why should I leave it?'

'Because you are a woman,' said Franco, sadly. 'So you must marry.'

Marthe had explained to her the physical side of marriage. She had been frightened then: now, she was angry.

'Aye.' Serafina spun round to face her father. 'I must marry. To get an heir for you in an old man's bed.'

She heard Marthe's hiss of disapproval, and she saw her father's face whiten and grow old. She regretted her words instantly: she could not bear the look of pain on his face. He was always such a happy man, such an – innocent, she might have said, had she understood the word then. Running to him, she uncurled his clenched fists, and wound her fingers through his.

'Forgive me, Father,' she whispered. 'Of course, I am honoured to marry Messer Corsini.'

He still looked troubled. 'This house will always be your home,' said Franco Guardi. 'The Corsini have a great name, but little money. One day, when I am gone, Michele and his sons – your sons – will carry on the business that your grandfather began. You will have to teach them how, Serafina.'

She began to cry then. Her head ached and her skin burned, and she had mislaid her handkerchief, so the tears fell in sparkling drops through her threaded hands, glinting on her bodice like diamonds.

They had to rise early the following morning to sail with the tide. Marthe dressed Serafina in layers of petticoats and a jewelled gown of tight black velvet, as though seeking to smother her with affection. She felt hot and suffocated before she had even left the house.

The weather was fine, the sky a clear bright blue dabbed with only a few puffy clouds. They walked the short distance to the harbour, Serafina's bags carried by servants, including the red-hatted Ibrahim. He sprawled himself on the ground to pray as they left the house, but they had grown used to that, so no one even stopped to stare or curse. Serafina's feet would hardly carry her: had she been a few years younger, her father might have swung her up on his shoulders and carried her thus enthroned through the crowds. But today she wore a bodice of buckram and a small, rigid farthingale, so, even though she felt sick to the stomach, and her legs were almost as lifeless as the bales of linen stowed in the *Gabrielle*'s hold, she made herself walk.

Until Angelo, whom she had not yet seen that morning, appeared. He led by the reins his own pretty jennet, which was saddled and bridled. He stopped in front of Serafina and her father, halfway across the market-square, and bowed, sweeping off his cap, so that his thick hair tumbled, brown and gold, over his face. 'My lady,' he said, and held out his hand.

So Serafina rode to the harbour on a neat Spanish pony, like

any great lady. She passed the butcher's, and the baker's, and the
pastrycook's, and the baskets of fish set out on the quayside:
mullet, dory, bonita, and loup, brightly coloured, glimmering
like silk in the early morning sun. She waved to the people she
had known all the short years of her life, and they waved back,
and curtseyed laughingly, and called her Madonna Corsini and
threw her flowers. Everything seemed unnaturally bright, as
though all the small details of her childhood fought to etch
themselves on her memory for ever. When they reached the
Gabrielle, Serafina accepted Angelo's hand as she dismounted
from his pony. Standing on the quayside, he kissed her on both
cheeks and on her fingers. She walked up the gangway at her
father's side, her black velvet skirts lifted from the dust.

As the galley drew away from the quayside, Serafina stood on
the rambade and waved and called farewell to Marthe, to
Angelo, to all the rest of the gathered House of Guardi. And
then, when the only sound was the beating of the oars and the
murmuring of the sea, and the only sight the cliffs and the
waves, she said farewell again. In her head, that time, she said
goodbye to the tight-packed rows of houses, to the distant white
cliffs, to the butterflies, the winds, and the flowers. But in her
heart, Serafina promised that she would return.

They were to sail close to the coast, putting in frequently to
port. In that way they could buy and sell as they travelled. The
Petit Coeur and the *Mignon* were cogs – small, somewhat
ungainly roundships; but the *Gabrielle* was a two-masted galley,
fully fifty paces long, as glittering and as graceful as a dragonfly.

Serafina stood at the gunwale at first, watching the rhythmic
dip and surge of the oars in the sea. The cold smell of salt
masked the other, less comfortable scents from below, and the
pattern of the oars was a miracle of timing and strength. The
hot sun beat down, and Serafina began almost to envy the
galley-slaves their nakedness: her stiff grown-up gown had begun
to itch round the collar; the rigid buckram, intended to display
her non-existent breasts, dug into her skin. She wanted to scratch
and itch and wriggle, but she stopped herself because she was a
woman, not a child, and she was soon to be an affianced lady.

She watched the comitre come up from the deck and speak to her father; she watched the *Petit Coeur* and the *Mignon* lumber along in the wake of the *Gabrielle*. She let her gaze travel to the land, to the littering of islands that clung to the coastline, and she watched the slow, unnatural lurch of those islands up and down in time with the rhythm of the waves, the rhythm of the oars. Serafina closed her eyes and gripped the carved rail with hot, damp fingers, and then she walked smartly to the poop, and sat down under the covered awning.

She could not believe it: she, who had the sea in her veins, felt seasick. And she still had the headache that had begun yesterday. Serafina thought of calling the idiotic Mathilde and decided against it: it was the nursemaid's first voyage, and she was on her knees in the taverne below, praying to every saint in the litany. The striped silk awning sheltered Serafina from the sun, the dozen or more coloured, tasselled cushions were comfortable to lie on; she soon began to feel a little better. Sprawled on the cushions, her doll in her lap, scratching surreptitiously at her wrists, she found a bracelet of red spots under the tight cuffs. A heat rash, she thought, overcome by a desperate longing for Marthe. Sternly reminding herself that she was almost a grown woman, Serafina made herself sit up straight, her eyes fixed on the horizon.

Because of this, she later believed it was she who first saw the other ship. She knew immediately that it was a galley, though its greater length and narrower bows made the poor *Gabrielle* appear clumsy. As she looked, Serafina heard the comitre call to her father, who was standing by the mainmast. Franco Guardi turned and, sheltering his eyes from the sun, answered, 'She's Venetian, I think – yes. See the pennant.'

Serafina stood up, holding on to the rim of the awning for support, screwing up her own eyes. The new galley, skimming fast towards the Guardi ships from the east, was brightly carved and gilt. If she looked hard enough, Serafina too could see the lion of St Mark's emblazoned on the triangular pennant. She sat down again, dizzy with heat and light and the relentless movement of the waves. She had seen Venetian galleys in Marseilles. They were no novelty. Sitting back on her cushions, Serafina closed her eyes and tried to sleep.

Much later, looking back, it seemed impossible that she had dozed through those last moments of freedom. Someone, something, should have woken her, warned her, torn her from complacency. You should not sleep when your world is about to shatter in splinters about you.

It was the comitre's shout that eventually shook her from slumber, sending her running, like everyone else, to the gunwale. Three further galleys skimmed towards the Guardi ships from the shelter of the islands. The lion of St Mark's had disappeared: from each galley the red crescent of Islam struggled to free itself from the masthead.

Barbary corsairs, from the coast of North Africa. Turkish sea-devils who robbed and enslaved their Christian captives, putting the men to the galleys, forcing the women into harems. Even Serafina had heard whispered tales of their cruelty. The Guardi ships could not outrun them, and they could not outgun the corsairs because they had fast positioned themselves where the French bâtards and coursiers would strike only water.

No one spoke to Serafina during those endless, agonizing moments. No one glanced at her. She was alone, watching, a useless, silent witness to the destruction of her childhood, her future. Every man on board ship was involved in desperate, futile activity. The world had narrowed to the shouting of the comitre, the beating of the oars fifty to the minute, the sound of the whip upon the slaves' backs. And Franco Guardi's voice as he ordered the guns to be readied, and tried to swing the wider, less manoeuvrable French galley broadside to the Turkish boats.

The roundships were boarded first, but any hope that the Turks might take only the cargo soon vanished. Human plunder was every bit as valuable as linens or broadcloth. The Turkish empire had been built and was maintained by Christian labour. Serafina watched, her mal de mer forgotten, as two of the infidel galleys scythed through the water towards the *Gabrielle*, and their guns aimed and fired across the decks. Two men slipped forwards to the wooden boards, their skins stained with a crimson dye.

Serafina did not move: she watched, her sickness abated, her headache providing a drumroll rhythm to the tableau before her. She felt apart from it all, detached. It reminded her of the pageants she had seen in the market-places of Marseilles: dragons slain, monsters beheaded. It was not real, it could not be real. More Turkish arrows hissed through the air. The sailors the arrows struck collapsed to the deck like old rag puppets.

The acrid scent of gunpowder clogged the sky, the crescent moons swelled and stirred on the billowing flags of the Barbary ships. The moons were like those she had embroidered on the bodice of the blue betrothal gown, now safely stowed in the *Gabrielle*'s hold. Where was her father? She could not see him through the smoke, and yet she knew he must come to her soon. Then she would be safe. The Turkish soldiers had gathered on the poop-deck, their loose white robes echoing the movement of the sails, their curved swords catching the high, bright sun. Through the cries and groans and the slap of the waves Serafina heard her father's voice.

He was standing at her side. Franco Guardi's handsome face was blackened with smoke, and he looked distraught. For the first time, Serafina, too, began to feel afraid. Grasping her hands so hard the bones seemed to grind together, Franco said, 'Say you are but seven years old, Serafina. Only seven!'

His agitation disturbed her more than the swords, the gunpowder, the screams. She did not understand then why he asked her to lie about her age. She was not a baby of seven, but ten years old, almost grown-up. But she nodded obediently, and Franco released her hands. Later, she knew that he had meant to save her from the seraglio.

She felt the impact as the Turkish ram scraped against the *Gabrielle*'s prow. The galley shook, and Serafina found herself on her knees, the pile of tasselled and silk-covered cushions scattered around her. She knew that her father had gone, and she was glad, because his disquiet had threatened to infect her. She tucked her doll under one arm and began to pick up the cushions. She had always been a tidy child. Blues here, red there, orange in the corner. Straighten the tassels, smooth the silk so that it gleamed and glowed just like Guardi silk always did. Someone said something, and Serafina turned round and saw a man, bearded and turbaned, beside her. Briefly, she wondered whether she should curtsey. Raising the palm of his hand, the Turk knocked Rosalie from Serafina's arms to the deck. Then he lifted his curved sword so that its tip scraped at the jewelled bodice of her gown.

Serafina's eyes flickered to her doll, to her father, to the corsair. Flung on to the smoky deckplanks, Rosalie's bright blue gown had begun to look grimy, the painstaking embroidery to fray, the small even seams to part. Her smooth wooden face stared up at Serafina, still simpering, her expression unaltered by disaster. Serafina heard her father's shouted curse and, glancing across the deck, she saw him struck across the face with a whip. Franco Guardi, like every other Christian man on the ship, was naked except for his breeches.

She understood then what the Turk wanted, and raised herself slowly to her feet. She had only recently, since her conversation with Marthe, begun to feel ashamed of her body. But she did not tremble or cry, and her hands, as they unhooked the buttons of the gown, were almost steady. She told herself that she was glad to be rid of the wretched thing. She told herself that she would feel so much cooler in her layers of light petticoats.

They put Mathilde and Serafina in the small taverne below decks, where the comitre stored the barrels of wine. Mathilde still wore her gown – they had taken Serafina's only for the pearls sewn on the bodice. The men they put to the oars, releasing those of their own religion. Imprisoned in the darkness of the taverne, it occurred to Serafina that somewhere out there, perhaps only a few feet away, her father, the proud Franco Guardi, was chained to a bench. His hands pulled at the oar, his back took the Turks' whip, his belly received only dry rusks and vinegar. Fear returned tenfold: she would not allow herself to think of him. Instead, Serafina glared at Mathilde, snivelling in the corner, all her prayers ignored. She looked a sight: any dignity she had once possessed had already been destroyed. Serafina despised her for that. She would not let herself become so.

She reserved her immediate anguish for more mundane matters. Since the Turk had taken her gown, she had discovered that her entire body was covered with small red spots. Her chest was patterned pink and white like damask, the crooks of her elbows and knees, her armpits and groin, were red and blotched. Serafina thought of becoming betrothed to Michele Corsini, and looking so. Then she realized that now she would not have to marry Messer Corsini, so she rolled on to a bench, and went to sleep.

After sailing for many hours, they stopped at a small island to take on water. They were hustled off the galleys and on to the shore: the salt water, as Serafina waded to the beach, felt good on her hot, itching limbs. Mathilde, her face swollen with weeping, let herself be led by Serafina off the *Gabrielle* and towards dry land.

Sitting on the sandy beach beside the useless Mathilde, Serafina saw her father for the last time. The sky was a hard enclosing bowl of blue, the island a barren outcrop of rock, its single stream rushing through a green-edged gully. She kept her aching eyes half closed, unable to open them properly even when she saw her father, at the Turks' command, rise.

Between Serafina and the fettered Christian galley-slaves was a large fire, built by the captives. As well as the cooking-pots and utensils there was a single straight rod of iron, half buried in the glowing ashes. One of the purple-robed janissaries motioned Franco Guardi to sit down and extend his bare foot. Then he took the length of red-hot iron and drew it twice across the sole of Franco's foot.

Serafina's hands were threaded over her eyes, to keep out the painful sunlight. But she could still see, through the tiny chinks and diamonds formed between her fingers, what the janissary had drawn on the sole of her father's foot.

He had drawn a cross. Now, Franco Guardi would trample the symbol of his faith into the ground wherever he walked.

A common enough ceremony, to ensure a prosperous voyage.

Her skin itched unbearably. Left alone in the tiny cabin with Mathilde, Serafina wriggled and scratched to her heart's content. Mathilde had reduced herself by weeping almost to catalepsy. Her swollen lips no longer muttered prayers, her rosary had slipped through her fingers to the floor. When she appeared to be sleeping, Serafina pushed the rosary through a gap in the boards. Common sense, not faith, at ten years old. She saw no point in courting the Infidels' wrath.

In spite of the single porthole in the taverne, Serafina lost track of time. They might have been sailing for an hour or for a month. Sometimes it seemed very cold and she shook uncontrollably, convinced that they were sailing north, to the lands of ice and snow and winter. At other times sweat ran down her skin in rivulets, tangling her hair, sticking her petticoats to her poor, aching body.

Eventually a janissary came to take them on deck. At first, Mathilde would not move, but Serafina pulled her and pinched her until she crawled moaning to her feet and shuffled out of the cabin and up the companion-way.

The sunlight stabbed her eyes, the waves caught and reflected the sunlight like glass. Even Marseilles was never so hot, so bright. Serafina did not let Mathilde cling to her, and neither did she let her own trembling knees fail to bear her. Forcing her eyes open, she stared at the city that formed out of the horizon.

Rows and rows of white houses, blue-shadowed and flat-roofed, their green gardens merging out of the distance like moss. On top of the steep hillside an immense fortress; in front of the city, a great mole guarding the harbour. The two protective arms of fortress and breakwater seemed to circle the entire city in their embrace.

Algiers.

Serafina was taken to a small dark cell in the bagnio, and left there alone. She never saw Mathilde again: she was sent to some seraglio, perhaps, to weep and wail and pray.

Because of her small size and tender years, Serafina was deemed to be of little use for the harem. Of little use to anyone, in fact – the dragoman, seeing her sway with exhaustion and unable to answer even the simplest question, shook his head and patted her hand kindly. She could not remember her name for him, let alone her age or place of birth. Thinking she was simple-minded, he sent her off, like all the others, with her blanket and her piece of black bread and bowl of water. She did not flinch when they riveted the iron ring about her ankle; she had no strength left even for fear. As though she might run! Serafina stared, her eyes damp with fever, not tears, through the labyrinth of rooms. She had no strength left to run. She would not know where to run to. She no longer saw one familiar face.

She could not eat the loaf of black bread, but she gulped down the water. Lying on the small pallet allotted to her, she wrapped herself in the blanket, and tried to sleep. Her arms ached for the solace of even the vacuous Rosalie. From the rooms beyond, all the tongues of the known world filtered through her fevered head. French, Spanish, Italian, and other languages she did not recognize. And also the strange lingua franca of the bagnio, a crude mixture of Italian and Spanish that sometimes she found she could almost understand. When she closed her eyes the language of the slaves filtered through her dreams. She spoke in it, thought in it. Indeed, she had forgotten any other tongue.

The bagnio was an immense, stinking dark cave, scuttling with red-capped slaves. The Guardian Pasha and his janissaries flitted through the labyrinth like vast shrouded bats, each with their sugar-loaf hat or turban. They, like Ibrahim in Marseilles, threw themselves to the ground five times a day in prayer. Only here, no one laughed at them, or cursed them.

By the following day Serafina's sickness was at its worst, and it was all she could do to answer the dragoman's call and follow him out of the bagnio. In the strong sunlight she blinked and shivered and stood listlessly while a handful of fellow-captives were gathered around her. They were all women and children – those who were too old, too young, too sickly for the harem. Serafina recognized none of them. But if she looked long enough, sometimes the plump dark woman's face would adopt Marthe's beloved scowl, sometimes the curly-headed girl, clutching a rag comforter, would shape-shift into the baker's daughter at Marseilles. Serafina did not protest at such irrationalities. She was fast discovering that the world is not a rational place.

They were taken to the suk, a seemingly endless covered

market, a forest of tent-poles and hangings. The women were veiled from head to foot, the children darted through the alley-ways like small dark birds, and the rich reis with their jewelled and feathered turbans paraded their pretty young boys. The scents of couscous and sherbet, of spices and bhang, of goat dung and overheated human bodies thickened the hot air. The bright colours of the silks on display reminded Serafina sharply, painfully, of home. Turning her face, she stared instead into the cool darkness of the awnings and the booths. Above the noise of the suk, there was a drumbeat inside her head, and a pain behind her eyes. She walked, chained like the others, sometimes singing a little to herself, sometimes talking. Often, she thought she heard her father's voice. And yet, every time she looked, she could not see him.

In the Bedestan, the slave-market, the captives were peered at and poked and prodded, their mouths opened and their teeth inspected as though they were ageing horses at a fair. Serafina paid her abusers no attention: all her thoughts were concentrated on her father. Papa would come soon, Papa would take his little girl home again. Papa had never failed her. She talked to her father in Latin, she talked to him in French, and sometimes she talked to him in the hateful polyglot language of the bagnios. And when some particularly inquisitive prospective purchaser prodded a little too roughly, Serafina cursed him, extensively and specifically, in the colourful French of the Marseilles docks.

She did not know that she had spoken aloud until she felt a blow across her face that knocked her to the ground. While she lay sprawling in the dust, wondering whether she still possessed all her teeth, she heard the tail end of a vast bolt of laughter, and a voice crying out, 'Little one, you will have to moderate your language, or they will set you to rowing the galleys!'

Serafina hauled herself to her knees. She picked one face out of the blurred, red-hazed mass around her. A giant of a man, both tall and broad, was walking towards her, his face creased with laughter. His skin was dark and seamed, he wore robes and a coloured turban, but his eyes were blue.

'Little one, these gentlemen are your masters, and they do not like to be compared to the vermin of the gutter.'

His voice was reproving, but there was still laughter in those blue eyes. Bowing to the man who had struck her, he held out a hand and pulled Serafina to her feet. She tasted blood in her mouth, and her right eye had already begun to close. He shook his head.

'I have not heard such language for many years,' he said. 'Since I left Marseilles, in fact. And that was more than twenty-five years ago. Not so long for you, I would guess, little one?'

Serafina stared at the dusty, bloodied earth. 'Three days ago – four –' she whispered, and began to cry, not only because it hurt to speak, but because she could not even remember when she had last seen her home.

'Marseilles was my birthplace,' the Frenchman said, gently, and smiled.

Her purchaser talked fast, fluent Marseilles French as she trotted along the gutter beside him, but she understood less and less of what he said. She was fast reaching the point when even pride could no longer bear up her legs.

They had left the Bedestan as soon as the Frenchman had finished his business – namely, the purchase of Serafina and two older women to work in his kitchens. Outside the western gate of the city, the Bab el-Oued, in a clearing dotted with piles of wood and dusty charcoal-sellers, a cavalcade of horses and slaves waited. Shivering in the sunlight, Serafina stared at the houses of the rich, bright with gardens and fountains. Her master turned to mount his horse. Glancing down at Serafina, he paused and frowned.

'Little one,' he said, and beckoned to her.

She could not move. She remained motionless, apathetically waiting another beating. But instead of raising his hand, her master left his horse and crossed the distance between them, tilting Serafina's face between his two palms to the sunlight.

'Little one, you are sick,' he said.

She began to howl again, no longer even despising herself.

'Little one,' he said, studying the rash, gently touching her forehead, 'you have the measles.'

And lifted her on to his own saddle-bow.

*

In another life, in Christendom, Serafina's new master had earned his living as a physician. Trained at the university of Padua, he had practised his art in the great houses of Florence, in the stews of Naples, at the docksides of his birthplace of Marseilles. When, on a voyage from Naples to Malta, his ship was chased and boarded by Algerian corsairs, his trade let him escape the drudgery of the beylik, the living hell of the galley-slave. Islam needed physicians. And when, like so many other Christians, he took the turban, he was able to earn himself a fine house in the fertile ground between Algiers and Oran, and as many horses and slaves as he desired. 'La ilaha illa'llah,' he said. There is no God but Allah. His name had once been Raoul Hérault, but in renouncing his faith he became Kara Ali.

But on the long, hot journey from Algiers Serafina knew none of this. She knew only that her master was a kind man. He found her ointments to cool the heat of the rash, and a draught to let her sleep through the awful, jolting journey. He wrapped a cloth round her head so that her eyes would not ache at the sight of the glaring white salt flats, the smooth shining curves of the sand dunes.

They travelled slowly, keeping close to the coast. They stopped frequently for food and water at the khans, each with their cool courtyard shaded with fountains and trees. At one of the khans Kara Ali fed Serafina sour milk and told her his name. 'And what is your name, little one?' he asked.

'Serafina,' she said, but the familiar syllables seemed strange to her bruised lips. When Kara Ali had himself settled down to eat and drink, she crawled over to the fountain. There was a pool of still water around it: she knelt, intending to wash her face.

She found that she did not recognize the reflection that looked back at her from the shallows. Swollen, staring eyes, bruised, cracked lips, dark hair that straggled anyhow over blotched, tear-stained cheeks.

That was not Serafina Guardi. That was a slave-girl's face.

Kara Ali's house had a courtyard, just like the khans. Serafina lay in the coolness of the courtyard day and night, at first, until her fever abated, and the angry red rash faded from her skin.

During that time she watched and listened, unconsciously preparing to adapt to her new life. She had been stripped, she had been struck, she had had an iron ring riveted around her ankle. Such cruelty had never before been part of her universe. Lying in the courtyard, watching the palm trees furl and unfurl their fronds in the gentle breeze, Serafina began to accept her new vista of the world. If rich clothes brought her humiliation, then she would wear rags; if curses brought her blows, then she would guard her tongue. She smelled the scents of rice and mutton and spices from the kitchen, and she listened to the slaves calling to each other in the lingua franca of the bagnios. She watched veiled female slaves cross the courtyard, carrying baskets or pots on their heads.

When she was well again, she was set to work in the kitchens. She learned from the Spanish cook how to clean the big pots they used for making couscous, how to cut up vegetables and trim meat. These were not tasks she had ever done before, yet she found herself apt at them. She even enjoyed them. If she worked hard enough she need not think of her father, need not see that mocking cross drawn for ever on the sole of his foot. If she exhausted herself by day then she could sleep at night, and not dream that she stood once more on a cool hillside, a garland of bindweed and rosemary on her head. Serafina's fingers were quick and neat, and she began to understand the patois of the kitchens even though she herself scarcely said a word. Nobody struck her if she chopped the peppers carefully and drew water from the well without slopping it over the courtyard. She discovered something that she was to remember for the rest of her life: that hard work is a balm to any hurt.

After she had recovered from her sickness, Serafina did not see her master again for many days. The kitchen-slaves whispered that Kara Ali was a magician – that at night he used his magic to call up the djinn, who, in their turn, taught him sorcery. The djinn, said the cook, had been made by God from out of smokeless fire – unlike man, who was moulded from potter's clay. The djinn were terrible in appearance, and entered a house by cracking the wall from floor to ceiling. When one evening she was sent to take her master sherbet, Serafina expected to find him in conversation with one of these dreadful creatures.

He was, however, alone. The house was a collection of buildings around a central courtyard, the quarters where the physician
worked being on the opposite side of the courtyard to the
kitchens. When he opened the door to Serafina (still carefully
carrying the tray with the glass of sherbet), Kara Ali smiled and
beckoned her inside.

'Well, well, little Serafina,' he said, as she put down the glass
on the table, 'and how do you like my house?'

Looking around, Serafina, who had scarcely used her tongue
for weeks, was silenced. But she managed to splutter, 'I like it
very well, sir,' while her eyes continued to take in the room and
its contents.

It was a large room, high-ceilinged, with small high windows.
Into the far end of the room were built three huge furnaces,
which roared and seethed like the djinn themselves. The orange
glow from the furnaces sketched many other strange objects –
flasks, bottles, and bundles of dry herbs hanging from the rafters.
Most terrible to Serafina were the bones piled in one corner of
the floor, including – and she stepped back a pace or two – a
human skull, blank-eyed and toothless.

And the books! More books than in Franco Guardi's library
in Marseilles, more than in the notary's office. They covered one
entire wall, they were scattered across the large table, some
open, with a quill pen and a piece of paper nearby, others
closed, piled and dusty.

The physician followed her gaze and laughed.

'It is somewhat untidy, isn't it, Serafina? If you wish, you
may bring back a little order. Here is a cloth – dust the covers
and put the books back in the shelves. But be careful, mind.'

She took the cloth from him, and one by one gently dusted
the leather covers of the books, returning them to the shelves.
One of the books was open: a single glance at the picture on the
page, and Serafina gasped in horror.

Kara Ali turned. 'What is it, little one?'

She pointed at the book. 'A djinn, master.'

He glanced down at the open page, and smiled. 'It is not a
djinn at all, Serafina, but an elephant.' Kara Ali drew her closer
to him, and held the book under the candlelight. 'A dram of

ivory from an elephant's tusk alleviates leprosy. A piece of
elephant's hide tied to the body will cure the ague. A miraculous
beast indeed, but not a djinn. This book is the bestiary of Ibn
Bakhtishu', a great physician who lived many years ago. See.'

He turned the pages slowly, showing Serafina the pictures of
the lion, the bear, and the simurgh. The simurgh could pick up
an elephant in its talons.

'It is a pretty book,' said Serafina, studying the pictures.

'It is a very pretty book,' agreed Kara Ali, 'and also a useful
book. It is an account of the beasts and the medicines that may
be obtained from them. This' – he drew over a larger volume,
without pictures – 'is a useful book, too, but my eyes now
struggle to read it.'

'*A Labyrinth of Errant Physicians,*' read Serafina, out loud, and,
as the physician made no answer, she returned to her dusting.

She did not realize that Kara Ali was staring at her. She only
heard him say gently, 'So you can read, little one?'

She nodded, and put another book back on the shelf. Of
course she could read. She could not remember not being able
to read.

'And can you write?'

Serafina nodded again. Monsieur de Coniques himself had
taught her to write, in a clear bold hand.

'And do you know your numbers?'

Numbers had always been like toys to her, something to be
played with, juggled with, enjoyed. 'Yes, sir,' said Serafina.

Kara Ali was frowning. The light from the furnaces drew his
kind old face, sketching every blade of his beard, every line that
age had added to his skin. He said, 'Sit down, Serafina,' and she
did, on a high stool that brought her almost up to his level.

For a few moments he was silent. Then he said, 'I bought you
in the Bedestan, Serafina, for only fifty aspers, because you were
thought to be sickly, simple-minded, and of low birth. But now
you are no longer sick, you are certainly not simple-minded,
and neither are you, I think, of low birth. Tell me about yourself,
child.'

So she told him. She told him about Marseilles, and about the
Guardi cloth-trade. And eventually, to the rush of the furnaces

and the howl of the wind outside, she told Kara Ali about her father.

At the end of it, the physician stood up and drank his sherbet. When he had finished and had replaced the glass on the tray, he said, 'The corsair who captured you will intend to ransom your father back to his family. He must be imprisoned in Algiers. As you should be.'

She did not understand him at first. So Kara Ali explained that to a corsair, a rich captive was like gold. Such a prize would not be wasted on the galleys or allowed to die slaving as a beylik in Algiers, but would be sold back to his family. Using the Jews, perhaps, as an intermediary, or one of the orders of Redemptionist friars.

'If it had been known that you were well born,' said the physician, 'then I could not have bought you for fifty aspers. No – there must have been some mistake. When I next travel to Algiers I will make inquiries concerning your father, and see what can be done. And meanwhile' – he glanced down at the book in front of him – 'meanwhile, you will write for me.'

From that evening, Serafina rediscovered hope. By day she still worked in the kitchen, but in the evening she helped her master. She read to him, she wrote for him, she listed complicated ingredients of complicated potions. She wrote about the elements, the three chemical principles, the archeus and the vulcanus. She wrote about the Philosopher's Stone, that magical artefact that would transform base metal to gold. Often, when her pen still scratched across the paper at midnight, and the roar of the furnaces was the only sound in the entire world, Serafina still expected to see the djinn. But she no longer felt quite so afraid, for she had fixed a limit to the term of her exile. It would take her master so long to travel to Algiers, so long to find her father, so long for them to travel back across the Inland Sea. And then she would be in Marseilles, and she would never, ever leave it again.

Kara Ali left for Algiers just after the end of Ramadan. For a month the entire household had fasted by day, feasted by night, until the world seemed upside down. When the feasting was finished, the physician and his cavalcade rode away, retracing the tracks across the desert that Serafina had made many months before.

She stood in the courtyard each evening, watching the stars in the sky repeat themselves in the fountain. Those same stars were over Marseilles, Kara Ali had told Serafina. The stars that would tell the past and the future, if only we could discover their key. Serafina would gaze at them for a few moments each night, trying to read her fate.

She was in the courtyard when Kara Ali arrived home, many weeks later. The night was dark and cold; she had wrapped a shawl around her shoulders. She heard the commotion as the riders returned, and stood, unable to move, dreading yet longing for news.

'Serafina.'

She turned: the physician stood beside her, his face still marked with the dust of the journey.

'Walk with me a while, little one.'

She followed him obediently out of the courtyard. The gardens round the house were extensive, because the streams that ran from the mountains beyond to the sea had been funnelled and channelled so that plants might grow. Date palms and lemon trees and cyclamen all flourished in the oasis that the water had made.

They walked in silence to a small copse of trees. Olive and eucalyptus, their twisted boughs and grey leaves painted by the moonlight. Serafina had not been there before: she had not seen the small stone hidden beneath the winding branches.

'My daughter,' said Kara Ali softly, pausing in front of the stone. 'Her name was Badr-al-Dujja. That means, Full Moon of the Night. She was ten years old when she died. She had a fever. I did everything I could, I practised all my arts, but I could not save her. It was Allah's will that she should die.'

Serafina looked up at him, and then back down to the small moonlit square of grey stone. She had begun to guess her master's next words before he spoke.

'It has been Allah's will also, little one, to take your father. I inquired in Algiers, and discovered that he died shortly after you arrived in this country. He had a fever – his death was quick. It is often thus, particularly for those of gentle birth. The heat – the change of circumstances . . .'

He let his voice drift away into nothingness. Serafina could hear only the rustle of the leaves, the gentle hiss of the wind. She thought of her father at the dinner-table in Marseilles, she thought of him at the helm of the *Gabrielle*. She thought of him sitting on the shore of some strange island while a cross was branded on the sole of his foot. He had always been such a great part of her life, and yet she had not known the moment of his death.

Kari Ali did not attempt to comfort her with any foolishness about the delights of heaven, whether that of Christianity or Islam. Instead, he touched her head just once and left her there, with the moonlit stone, the shiver of the olive leaves, and the endless stars.

She began then, for a while, to accept her new life. She was a kitchen-slave by day, and her master's secretary by night. She was fortunate (all the other slaves were of the same opinion) in her master, who neither beat her nor starved her. Several of the other slaves had stories of harsher treatment, of the bastinado and the whip. She began, almost, to consider herself fortunate. She had not, like her father, died of a fever in the bagnio. She had not been sent to a harem, as Mathilde presumably had, and neither had she, like the rest of the Guardi crew, to ply the seas for the Infidel. She had food and water and a bed to sleep in.

It was only sometimes, when she woke very early in the morning, long before the rest of the household had stirred, that Serafina felt despair. Most of the time she felt nothing: she existed. She tried to please, because if she did not, she was boxed on the ears. She stole scraps of food because all the other slaves did so; it was natural to a slave to steal. She spoke French to her master, and the language of the slaves in the kitchens, and soon was equally familiar with both.

Yet in the early mornings, when the sky was still dark, and the house still silent, she wept. For her father, for her home, for all that she had lost yet could not name. She cried silently, as she had learned to do everything silently, because attention was undesirable. Eventually, having soaked her pillow with tears, she would fall asleep again as the sun rose over the horizon.

Kara Ali was fast becoming an old man. He could no longer read the smallest print, nor could he jump on and off a horse as once he had been accustomed to. He still worked as a physician, travelling round the country, but his expeditions had become less frequent, and his obsession with his other interests of alchemy and astrology had begun to be all-consuming. Serafina entrusted her well-being to him, and as she began to accept her condition, she found that she cared less about the future. She took life a day at a time, because every day seemed the same, and nothing seemed to matter but survival. Triumphs were a handful of sweets filched from a tray, a mouthful of cool sherbet stolen on a hot day. Pleasure was the occasional visit of a storyteller, the scratch of the pen across paper every evening. Love, if it ever had been important, had ceased to be so. She had lost the object of her infant love.

She could have remained like that for ever, in a limbo in which neither happiness nor unhappiness, anger nor bliss, existed. It was, after all, easier to feel nothing. But one day the following summer, when the sun was as hard as brass and the air so thick you could slice it, Serafina stole a bowl of almonds.

They were good plump almonds, left over from the previous day's meal, unnoticed by anyone else, hidden by Serafina until she was able to be alone. She found a shady bush in the gardens, hid herself in the shadow of the branches, and crunched the almonds one by one, cradling the bowl in her hands. It was a beautiful bowl, glazed a pure deep Mediterranean blue. She did not steal it because she was hungry – it was the luxury of it, and, of course, the smallest of battles won against an unimaginably vast enemy.

The almonds were delicious, crisp and coated in honey. There was sand everywhere that day: it was a constant battle to keep it out of the house, and it gritted Serafina's eyelids and mouth as she ate. She had folded her dusty black robes around her so that she could not be seen through the equally dusty leaves. When she heard the horsemen she merely flicked her djellabah further over her head, buried the blue porcelain bowl in the swathes of cloth, and folded herself up even smaller. Serafina was good at making herself invisible.

She heard one of the riders call for her master, and saw Hassan, the groom, run off to find him. She remained under the bush, eating. A few minutes later, Kara Ali came out of the house followed by a stranger clad in the purple robes and tall hat of the janissary.

'The child is dead,' she heard the physician say. 'She was a sickly creature.'

Serafina chewed, rolling a single nut between finger and thumb, interested. The two men were walking towards the grove of olives and eucalyptus, to the grave where Kara Ali's daughter lay.

'So I regret I cannot help you, my friend,' added the physician. 'She cost me only fifty aspers – I could have made a fat profit.'

The remaining almonds rolled to the ground, but Serafina did not move. Her eyes did not leave the two men as they stood, their backs to her, in front of the tiny grave.

The janissary spread out his hands in a gesture of dismissal. 'No matter. Allah has done what otherwise would have been my duty. God be with you, friend.'

'God be with you.' Kara Ali escorted the janissary back to the house; Serafina bowed her head to her knees, afraid that the questions in her eyes would glare out from her hiding-place like beacons. *She cost me only fifty aspers – I could have made a fat profit.* The words pounded through her head like a drumbeat. She could no longer eat the almonds.

When it was safe to do so, Serafina turned round and watched the janissary ride away, his retinue following in a cloud of dust. Then she heard Kara Ali calling her name.

It was mid-afternoon, and the sun was still bright, the air sleepy. The physician stood in the courtyard beside the fountain. He looked troubled.

'Listen to me carefully, little one,' he said. 'Your name is no longer to be Serafina. You are Badr-al-Dujja, and you have lived here all your days. Forget your home, forget your family

– speak your language only when we are alone together. It will be better so.'

Serafina stared at him. Badr-al-Dujja was her master's daughter's name, not hers. 'Why?' she asked.

He did not answer at first. Then he said, 'Because then you will be safe, little one.'

Safe? Sticky fingers clenching the rim of the blue bowl, Serafina glared round the courtyard at the kitchens, the stables, the rooms with the furnaces. 'I am safe,' she said, obstinately.

Kara Ali did not scold her for her insolence, but shook his head. 'There are those who wish you ill, child,' he said, gently.

She did not understand. Why was she to change her name, to forget her home, her family?

Kara Ali was silent for a moment. The sun, still high in the sky, cast dark shadows, deepening the lines of age on his face.

He said, 'Who will inherit in the event of your father's death, child? Have you brothers?'

Serafina shook her head. She had understood her importance in the House of Guardi since babyhood.

'I have an illegitimate cousin, that's all,' she said. 'But everything will be – is – mine.'

She had not considered that before. That she, now ten years old, was head of the House of Guardi. Then she recalled the unknown Messer Corsini.

'And my husband's, of course,' she added. 'We were sailing to Pisa to celebrate my betrothal to a Florentine lord.'

The physician said, without looking at Serafina, 'And should neither you nor your father survive . . . who will inherit the house and business then?'

She had never before considered such a possibility. 'I don't know.'

Kara Ali beckoned her to sit on the rim of the fountain beside him.

'Little one, the janissary who visited just now offered me a large sum of money to have you put to death. I told him that you had already died of a fever contracted in the bagnios. I showed him my daughter's grave and told him that it was yours.'

Despite the brightness of the day, Serafina felt suddenly cold. Her master had told the janissary that she was dead. The janissary had offered him money to have her killed –

The blue bowl slipped through her fingers and shattered on the paving stones. Serafina no longer asked *why*, she simply accepted Kara Ali's words as one more evidence of a malign world. She could neither move nor speak at first, but eventually she dropped to her knees and began to pick up the broken pieces of pottery. Her fingers were stiff, they could hardly grip the delicate fragments.

When she could speak, she said, 'Then I will be Badr-al-Dujja, Papa.'

She spoke the endearment without thought. But her master only patted her on the head, and said, 'Allah be with you, child,' and went inside the house.

She stayed in the courtyard for a long time, though, after he had gone. The sun gleamed on the ornamental archways, on the thin arcs of water from the fountain, on the damask-petalled roses. The shards of the blue bowl were gathered in Serafina's lap, and she realized for the first time that she had stolen not only for the food, but for the beautiful bowl itself, which she had since destroyed.

She had lost her home, her family, and her language. And a part of her said that it was better so, the same part that had learned to steal and to dissemble, to survive the hour, and not live for the future. That was the easy way, the way without pain.

Yet she had begun also to discover the anger that lay somewhere inside her, buried under layers of compliance and acceptance. They could take everything she owned, everyone she loved, but as long as she remembered it, they could not take her name. It was hers, and one day she would use it again.

'I am Serafina,' she whispered to herself. 'I am Serafina . . .'

PART II

1593

FALLEN INTO
A DESERT PLACE

We consulted together what course to take,
seeing that we were fallen into a desert
place.

The Casting away of the Toby:
Richard Hakluyt

'Faithless Faith,' muttered Thomas Marlowe ecstatically when he had breath to speak again.

It was midday and mid-August, but the unseasonable rain that battered the Greenwich streets went unnoticed in Faith Whitlock's best bedchamber. On the polished oak floor, a farthingale stood like a reproachful ghost of its owner, and from the bed-canopy a battered black hat slipped slowly downwards, pulled by the inevitable force of gravity, cast up there a half-hour before by the equally inevitable force of passion.

Faith Whitlock, pretending pique, said, 'You wouldn't love me if I was faithful, Thomas.'

'True.' Thomas grinned, and caught his hat as it plummeted to the floor. 'And it's a pleasant way to spend a wet afternoon, isn't it, my dear?'

'Averagely so.' Faith, her russet hair fanned over the pillow, allowed herself to smile.

Outside, the rain mixed the calls of the street and the clatter of the nearby docks to a sodden ragbag of sound. Thomas Marlowe, black hair still curled like kale by the rain, his favourite hat cradled on his bare chest, half closed his eyes and let himself dream of his ship.

Four-masted, narrow-beamed, and not top-heavy like Richard Staper's damned *Toby*. Square-rigged, of course, and built of the best English oak. She'd go twice the *Toby*'s speed at half the risk, he'd guarantee it.

Faith, sensing her lover's mental, if not physical absence, moved, and said sharply, 'Lucy may be back soon. And I really must talk to Cook about the dinner for Edward's return tomorrow —'

Thomas rolled over on to his side, propped on one elbow. The black hat tumbled finally and soggily to the floor; Thomas's hand and mouth caressed Faith's full white breasts.

'Lucy and Ned will be another hour at least. Ned will not leave the docks until Lucy has named every ship for him. That boy,' said Thomas, running his palm and then his mouth down to Faith's flat white belly, 'will be a mariner one day. I shall show him the stars next summer. And as for Edward – he can have his collops and Candian wine tomorrow.' He looked up briefly and grinned. '*I* am having mine today.'

Ten minutes later, Faith, mollified, said, 'Did you ask Mr Staper?'

Rain still battered the casement windows. Thomas lay back on his pillow, and scowled. 'I did.' His voice altered in vicious yet accurate imitation of Richard Staper, founder member of the English Levant Company. 'You are a pilot, Mr Marlowe. You are an excellent pilot. You are not a shipbuilder.' The scowl grew blacker. 'He's trying to persuade me to navigate the *Toby*.'

Faith, for the past ten years a merchant's wife, said reasonably, 'Edward says the *Toby*'s a fine ship.'

'The *Toby* is an adequate ship. No more. My ship will be a fine ship – the finest.'

Thomas, stark naked, slid out of the four-poster bed and went to stand by the window, to glower furiously at the rain-soaked docks.

Faith added, 'So you said to Mr Staper . . .?'

'I told him he could scuttle his bloody *Toby* – and that fool of a master he's sending with her.'

Faith, five years Thomas's senior, sighed as she might sigh at her own headstrong small son. 'So Mr Staper,' she said crisply, 'offered you five hundred crowns and the use of a dockyard?'

Thomas, turning, had the grace to look a little sheepish. 'Not exactly.' He shook his head. 'The *Toby* sails with the tide tomorrow morning, Faith, and I'm right about the master. His name's George Goodlay, and he's about my age and blessed with as much sense as your Ned. He's master,' said Thomas, leaving the window, 'because his father did some sort of a favour for Richard

Staper. That's all. He knows less about the sea than you do, my love.'

There was the sound of a door slamming below. 'Lucy,' said Faith, unflustered, piling up her rich red hair on top of her head. 'The docks must have palled for once —'

She broke off. Those were men's boots treading the hall below, not nursemaid's pattens, and no small child's voice was imperiously calling her name. '*Edward,*' whispered Faith and Thomas together, and Thomas, hastily grabbing his breeches and his hat, ran for the stairs.

Too late. They saw each other, he and Edward Whitlock, and if half-laced breeches and a bare chest were not evidence enough, then Thomas's rapid reversal and dive, sword quickly in hand, for the bedchamber window, must have added the final touch.

Faith Whitlock, wishing she had been truer to her name, sat up in her marital bed, witnessing it all. Her lover, sword in his teeth, hat covering his black curls, disappearing rapidly through the mullioned window; her husband, worse-tempered than usual after a long journey, flinging open the bedchamber door, and glaring once, accusingly, at his errant wife, before running off to fetch his pistols. The small sounds of Thomas, enmeshed with ivy, crumbling brick and drainpipes, and then a preposterous explosion of sound as Edward's pistol succeeded in firing into the rain. A '*Jesus*' from Thomas, and an 'If I ever see you in London again I'll shoot your bloody arse off!' from Edward. A sound of falling masonry and tearing leaves, and Faith buried her head in her hands.

Thomas Marlowe set sail from Blackwall as pilot of the *Toby* the following morning.

It gave him small satisfaction, in the weeks that followed, to confirm that he had been right about the *Toby*. The two-hundred-and-fifty-ton merchantman was bound for Livorno, Zante, and Patras in the Morea, her hold crammed with twelve thousand pounds' worth of cargo. The crew were a reasonable enough bunch of men, and Thomas himself, as the ship's owner had said, was an excellent pilot. But the master —

The master, thought Thomas wearily, as they weathered the

gales that hovered round the Straits of Gibraltar, was a fool. The master refused to take anyone else's advice – even Thomas's own excellent advice. The master wore puffed breeches and a French ruff in the middle of a sub-tropical storm. The master, in short, would have been an ornament at Whitehall, but on the decks of a small, fragile wooden ship was a damnable liability. Thomas, who had not slept for forty-eight hours, was sorely tempted to tap the master forcefully on his neatly trimmed curls so that the rest of them might be permitted to get on uninterrupted with the job in hand. Only the calm good sense of William Williams, ship's carpenter, prevented him.

'When he comes round, he'll clap you in irons, and insist on piloting the hulk himself. Then we'll all be singing choruses with the mermaids.' The carpenter turned towards Thomas. 'Unless you were thinking of making sure that he never came round?'

'The thought had crossed my mind.' Thomas's clenched fist struck the wooden wall of the pilot's cabin. 'It'd make little difference if I were clapped in irons, Will. Our precious Mr Goodlay doesn't take heed of a word I say.'

'Aye.' William Williams shook his head. The ship lurched violently: Thomas's cross-staff and sand-glass rolled off the table. Thomas caught the glass before it hit the floor, picked up his hat and headed for the half-deck.

George Goodlay stood by the mizzen-mast, one embroidered glove gripping a beribboned cane, the other curled around the mast itself. Crop-headed, with a small pointed beard, he wore quilted crimson velvet, and a jewelled and plumed hat.

Thomas, making superhuman efforts to be tactful, nodded a bow and said, 'I think we may be a little off course, sir.'

He had to shout to make himself heard over the clamour of the wind and the rain.

The master, without troubling to turn, said, 'Your responsibility, surely, Mr Marlowe.'

Thomas struggled to keep his temper. George Goodlay's curls were glued to his head with the rain; the brim of his hat and the lace of his ruff had both collapsed. The occasional bolts of lightning showed his skin to be an interesting shade of green.

'We're being blown too far south, sir – and we're sailing too close to the coast. You'll have to bring her round.'

A particularly large wave drenched George Goodlay's velvet and Thomas's linen and broadcloth. When he had retrieved his hat, the master focused disdainful grey eyes on Thomas.

'*Have* to, Mr Marlowe? You forget who is master of the ship, sir.'

Thomas resisted the urge to hit him. 'And you forget who is pilot,' he hissed and, extracting his own hat from out of the rigging, stumped back below decks.

The storm began to lessen that evening. By then, the only dry things on the *Toby* were the precious bales of Hampshire and Devonshire kerseys, the dozen taffeta-trimmed hats, the six dozen holland shirts, and the crates of tin that crammed the hold. Every man's hair was matted and tangled with salt; every man's eyes were red-rimmed with wind and exhaustion.

Thomas Marlowe did not yet sleep, however. On deck, his arms spread along the gunwale, he watched a copper sun paste itself over the sea as his tired brain continued to assess their course.

They were too far south and too close to the coast. They had sighted Mount Bujeo two days past, therefore they had sailed past, not through, the Straits, yesterday. Which put them somewhere off the Barbary coast, to the south of Cape Espartel. They should keep away from the coast and its treacherous tides and sandbanks, and head back for the Straits.

Instead of which, taking advantage of a fair wind, they were to bear sails all night in the incorrect expectation of making up lost time. The livid sun disappeared below the horizon as Thomas Marlowe groaned and buried his head in his hands. If he could only have explained to George Goodlay that to him, the astrolabe and cross-staff were merely servants. If he could only have explained that he felt the course of the tides, the pattern of coast and sea in his blood. Then the man might have understood, instead of seeing him as some brassy little upstart who needed to be put in his place. But any conversation with George Goodlay instantly reduced Thomas from a fairly reasonable adult to an insolent schoolboy. William Williams, unlettered, untutored William Williams, had better success with the master. But even William Williams had not been able to persuade George Goodlay, on Thomas's instructions, to abandon what Thomas knew to be a disastrous course.

Disaster struck about an hour and a half before dawn. Thomas slept where he had stood, curled up like a baby on the bridge, one hand still loosely gripping the brim of the battered felt hat. He was awake before the lookout had realized what was happening, jerked into consciousness by the appalling scrape and shudder that vibrated through the wooden timbers as the *Toby* ran on to the sandbank.

He was on his feet and at the gunwale as the lookout called, 'Man the decks! We're aground!' Turning, Thomas saw George Goodlay, his face still muddled with sleep, climb up from the Great Cabin to the foredeck. Thomas's hand gripped slowly round the hilt of his knife, but he did not speak. It was too late for speech: waves battered against the fragile wooden hull, the unknown coast of Barbary glittered like the land of Cockaigne, just out of reach.

Thomas heard the ship's carpenter mutter in his ear, 'Jesus Christ,' and he saw him furtively cross himself. The master had fallen to his knees, his head bowed in prayer.

Thomas crossed the deck, and said with heavy politeness, 'Shall we cut the mainmast, sir?'

George Goodlay's eyes focused, and he rose unsteadily to his feet. 'My fault,' said the master. 'God forgive me . . .' And then any pity Thomas felt for inexperience, for lack of instinct, disappeared as Goodlay added, 'No, Mr Marlowe, we shall not cut the mainmast. We will launch the ship's boat.'

Thomas's teeth were clenched so hard that they ached. 'The ship will overturn, sir,' he said tightly. 'She's too top-heavy with the masts and sails up. The boat will take a dozen – a dozen and a half –'

There was a shout from below decks. 'She's taking on water!' someone called, and Thomas felt the rhythm of the ship alter, as the *Toby* became heavy with the weight of the sea that forced its way into the hull.

He did not wait to ask any more: other hands as well as his own supported the tall mainmast as the ship's carpenter sawed through its circumference. Too late, too late – the words rattled through Thomas's head in time with the crashing of the waves, the rasp of the saw. And he was right: as they lowered the mast to the decks, the hull of the ship, weakened by the force of water inside and out, began to tear in half.

Thomas found himself high up in the shrouds of the foremast. Many of the rest of the ship's company were also there, though some who had been trapped on the afterdeck fought for their lives in the waves. Thick green water crashed across the bows: they were, thought Thomas, about a half-mile from shore. Someone began to sing the twelfth Psalm. 'Help, Lord, for good and godly men,' muttered Thomas Marlowe to himself as he secured his knife to his belt and stuffed his hat inside his shirt. And then all was reduced to chaos as the foremast, crippled by the weight of the men and the strength of the sea, fell, tumbling them all into the water.

If drowning men recall the past as the salt water forces into their nostrils, their eyelids, their mouths, then Thomas Marlowe would have seen Greenwich, the docks, the sea. The years at the grammar school that had lifted him from the mediocrity of his birth, making him pilot, rather than bosun, the succession of pretty girls, of various ages, colourings, and temperaments, that had brightened his life since he was fourteen or so. His more profitable recent years, sailing for the Levant Company. But most of all, the ship, *his* ship, that as yet existed only in his head, but that he would build, must build, some day.

Afterwards, he always thought that it was the ship that had kept him forcing his way out of the imprisoning green cage, pitting his own violence against a greater master. But his head finally pierced the glassy mirror of the waves, and his lungs found air, and his strong, muscular arms automatically began the lengthy fight for life, and the coast.

It was partially swimming, and partially simply being pushed by the overmastering strength of the sea. Eventually Thomas could think of nothing but the clawing of the water through his palms, the great gulp of air he must take as his head dipped and pulled out of the water. When, after what seemed like hours of struggle, his knees struck sand, he could not walk, but crawled to the sea-strand, as weak as any infant.

He did not know how long he lay there, sprawled like an ungainly starfish, head half buried in the white, powdery sand. He did not know whether he slept or lost consciousness, but he was aware, with a weak, vestigial flutter of triumph, that he had cheated death.

At last he became aware of the sun, beating down on his uncovered head, drying his hair into black, salt-encrusted corkscrews, burning the skin on the back of his neck. With difficulty, he rolled over on to his back, his limbs weak and shaking as though with a fever. The back of his shirt and breeches were dry; Thomas lay with one arm flung across his eyes, and with his other hand he took out his sodden felt hat from inside his shirt.

Eventually he sat up. Shading his eyes, he looked out to sea. At first, he could not see the *Toby*. Thomas had drifted leewards, and had washed up on a small cove bracketed by rocks. Then he saw the remains of the *Toby*'s hull, wedged by the weight of the sand, and the mizzen-mast rising from the waves, as fragile as a straw. He had had his reservations about the *Toby*, but he felt as though he were being forced to watch a friend's slow and untimely death. Thomas climbed unsteadily to his feet.

Both the sea and the coastline were already littered with detritus from the shipwreck. Ropes and sails, timbers and spars, and all the pathetic debris of everyday life. Cups and bottles and barrels and kerchiefs, flung up on an alien shore to lie on the strand mingled with strange coloured pebbles and exotic shells. Thomas, stumbling slowly along the water's edge, saw a book, its pages reduced to pulp by the waves, and a hogshead of ale, the stopper loosened, contents dribbling fast into the sand. His eyes were dragged to a heavier, easily recognizable shape, bobbing out near unreachable rocks, and then suddenly, at his feet, there was a velvet hat, plumes ripped and swallowed by a greedy sea, pearl clasp still in place.

Shutting his eyes, turning, Thomas was noisily and thoroughly sick. When he had finished emptying the salt-soaked contents of

his stomach over the Barbary coast, he found that his head had
cleared, and his limbs felt a little more cooperative. He was
alive, that was what mattered. He must assess his position, look
to the future.

He thought himself to be on the Atlantic coast of North
Africa, somewhere between Tangier and the corsair ports of
Sallee and Rabat. Well, then, he would head north, away from
the dark unknown kingdom of Prester John, back towards the
Inland Sea. But first he must find out whether he was the *Toby*'s
only survivor.

Thomas began to scramble up one of the arms of rock that
surrounded the bay. The rock was black and sharp and tore at
his hands and feet. He remembered that he had kicked off his
shoes in the swim from the *Toby*, but he was thankful that he
had kept his hat. The heat of the sun was intense.

When he had almost reached the summit of the spar of rock,
Thomas paused to gather his breath. A metallic glitter that
caught and magnified the sun's rays a hundred times jabbed at
his eyes. Clambering along, he saw a small wooden chest, hurled
by the waves and caught by a rock, jammed in one of the black
crevices. From a hole in the side of the chest there dripped a
small trickle of gold coins that fell slowly, one by one, into the
rock pool below.

Gold belonging to the Levant Company, to grease a few
palms, oil a few wheels. A hundred crowns or more, locked in
the master's cabin until the ship should put into port at Livorno,
Zante, or the Morea. The *Toby* would not see Livorno, Zante,
or the Morea now.

Grimly, Thomas set his mouth and resumed his climb. For
the first time he became aware of sounds other than the crashing
of the sea on the rocks, the shore. Men's voices. Through a cleft
in the rocks he saw the next bay, a broad span of white sand. He
recognized William Williams the carpenter, and about a dozen
others. He was about to stand up, to wave his hat in the air and
shout, when he stopped, frozen with possibility.

A hundred crowns or more. Lost, apparently, in the shipwreck
of the *Toby*.

Thomas could not breathe, he felt as though the sea still

pushed its way into his lungs. If he hailed his shipmates, then he would return with them, eventually and with luck, to London, to be a pilot of the Levant Company.

If he did not hail his shipmates . . .

A hundred crowns would allow him to begin to build his ship. A hundred crowns and some convenient freeport where no questions would be asked.

There was really no decision to be made. The rest of them would manage just as well without him. 'Help, Lord, for good and godly men', whispered Thomas to himself, as he began to scoop the gold from the rock pool into the crown of his hat.

His journey was easy enough at first.

Against his original instincts, Thomas walked inland, beneath the protective covering of tamarisks and pine trees. His bare feet trod white sand and dead pine needles. His muscles ached with their battering from the waves, but he felt ridiculously light-hearted. He was alive: he was not now flotsam, to be washed up white and bloated on the unfriendly Barbary coast. He had taken a water-bottle and a doublet from the wreckage of the *Toby*. In the shelter of the trees he unpicked the doublet's quilting, replacing the wadding with gold coins.

The forest thinned out to scrubland, and the sun beat down from the sky like a gleaming brass gong. Thomas reckoned it mid-afternoon. He had seen not a soul since he had left his shipmates on the beach, but he was glad that he had no company except the insects and lizards. His dress marked him out as a European, his lack of horse or camel, and of any weapon other than a knife, made him most men's inferior. Even his skin was not a Berber's skin: he could already feel the back of his neck, the uncovered parts of his arms and feet, begin to scorch in the heat.

He considered the distance he must travel to the coast, and his scanty knowledge of the kingdom of Morocco. Ships of the Barbary Company had traded with Morocco since 1585; Thomas himself had safely docked several times at Sallee. But English slaves worked Berber lands and ships; the nomadic tribes of the desert knew no laws but their own. But then, thought Thomas happily, recently he had narrowly missed both being drowned and being shot.

He travelled until nightfall, eating nothing more than date roots and olives. When it was dark, he curled himself under an olive tree and slept, the familiar stars looking down at him.

Thomas was woken the following morning by someone shouting at him. Incomprehensible words, like a monkey in a menagerie, like an idiot child. Only it was neither a monkey nor a child: he knew that as soon as thought started functioning, from the foot that nudged his head, the sword that scraped his belly.

Thomas's eyes were suddenly open very wide. He saw a man, the owner of both the sword and the boot, wearing ragged, dirty robes that had perhaps once been white. The man stank, and he was grinning.

Sitting up, Thomas also found his most pleasing smile, the one he used for the richest ship-owners, the prettiest women. He then searched for a placatory phrase in all the languages he had even the slightest acquaintance with, and meanwhile checked that his dagger was still tucked into his belt. Neither the smile nor the words seemed very successful: the nudge became a kick, the sword pressed a little harder until it drew blood.

It was early morning. The sun bounced on the horizon, the thin grass was soaked with dew. Thomas's aggressor was not a particularly large man, and there was a very useful-looking horse tethered to an olive tree nearby. Thomas wanted the horse, and he wanted the water-bottles that he could see hanging from the saddle. As he stood, still smiling, he let one hand fold round the hilt of his dagger.

He had no chance to use the knife, however. Thomas felt something cold sear the burnt skin on the back of his neck, and then a hand grabbed his wrist and forced his fingers apart. He had not even time to count them before their feet and fists battered him into unconsciousness.

They had taken his knife, his hat, and his handkerchief, but not, thank God, his doublet. When Thomas awoke, the sun was high in the sky, and he was still on his back in the same olive grove.

Slowly, painfully, he opened his swollen eyelids, squinting at the hard disc of the sun. He knew that there was blood on his face and neck, already dried to powder by the heat, and that his limbs, bruised by the sea the previous day, had been battered almost to a pulp.

He was surrounded by men, women and ragged children. The blurred figures shifted and shimmered in the sun. Some moth-eaten mules, several overburdened camels, and a flock of sheep grazed round the edges of the olive grove. Thomas tried to sit up.

His hands and feet were tied, and his wrists were also tethered fast to the tree-trunk. Thomas, unable to stop himself, groaned.

He received a kick in the belly that made him double up in pain, and then the ropes that bound his feet were cut and he was hauled upright. He saw that the caravan was beginning to assemble. The camels had been roped together and the panniers were being loaded on to the mules. He wondered what particular treat fate had reserved for an aggressive ship's pilot who had been foolish enough to let himself be washed up on the Barbary coast. He wondered why they had let him remain alive.

He found out soon enough. He was to be a beast of burden, like the camels, the mules, the horses. Thomas's shoulders were laden, his roped hands linked to someone's bridle, and a whip put to his back to start him on the long road south.

He knew that they were journeying south, but he soon lost track of the hour, the day. He did not think they were heading for Rabat or Sallee because they were travelling towards the mountains. The land had become more arid, the occasional patches of lush vegetation less frequent.

He was given enough water and enough food – dates and olives and a little bread – to keep him alive and useful to them. If his limbs had not been strengthened by the years at sea, then he would have collapsed on the second day of the trek, and would have been left to die where he had fallen. As it was, it was hard, but no harder than weathering a gale.

They travelled slowly, covering, Thomas thought, about three miles a day. After a while the movement of one step in front of the other became purely mechanical, and he hardly noticed the weight of the pack on his back. If he kept up with the rest of the straggling caravan, they did not beat him. At midday they sheltered as best they could from the full glare of the sun; at night Thomas slept under the stars while his captors laughed and quarrelled and smoked kif in their black goathair tents. If he had time to think, it was to know that he must be patient and conserve his energy and wait for the right moment.

He lost count of the days that he had travelled – a fortnight, he thought, perhaps three weeks. The voyage of the *Toby*, the shipwreck, had become a painless memory, but with the fading of that event, some of Thomas's old impatience began to return. He had not been put on this earth to be a beast of burden for a disorganized group of Berber nomads. He had been put here to build a ship, and to sail that ship to any part of the earth worth trading with. He had the money now – he had taken off his shirt to cover his head and the back of his neck, and the weighted doublet beat clammily against his naked back – and all that was left to him was to find the right place, organize the carpenters, choose the wood. He could do all that: he longed to do all that.

The right moment came, as he had expected it to, at night. Tethered to a tree, Thomas watched and waited. The night sky illuminated the scene before him: he could see the nomads, their robes palely drawn by the moonlight, and he could smell the heavy sweet scent of kif. That was good, a point in his favour. He could see the water-bottles that he had helped fill from a stream, piled up outside the tent. Even better.

Thomas's blue eyes cast about in the darkness to find the third thing that might make escape possible. A sharp stone: sweet Lord, let there be a sharp stone nearby. And there was – his heart, usually so steady, began to bounce and flutter, and he could hardly restrain himself from crowing with delight. Silently, using one foot, he began to draw the stone towards him.

He had the stone behind his back and wedged in the tree-trunk within a few minutes. He began to saw away at the strands of rope, his gaze fixed all the time on the black tents. Sometimes the stone scraped at his raw, blistered wrists, but he kept on until he felt the bonds loosen and break.

Still he must be patient. As with navigating, inaction could be just as important as action. The smoke from the tent had begun to make even Thomas feel light-headed: much more and he, too, would cease to care about anything. Turning his head away, taking in mouthfuls of fresh air, Thomas's eyes focused on the perimeter of the encampment, and he blinked.

At first he could hardly believe what he thought he saw: a drug-induced dream, surely, an illusion conjured from the darkness by the hemp they smoked in the tent. Then, gloriously, he did believe, and his whole body began to tauten in anticipation.

They were not alone. There were others out there, scarcely visible, like black ghosts in the moonlight. Thomas could see camels, tall and white, richly caparisoned, pale exotic phantasms. The dim light caught the swirl of a robe, the steel of a sword or dagger.

Raiders, riding to steal what goods and beasts Thomas's captors possessed. Thomas's God, the God of shipwrights and cocky London self-made men, had been generous again. Glancing back swiftly to the Berber tents, Thomas heard the muted lazy laughter, saw that some of the nomads had begun to close their eyes.

It was a matter of catching the wind, taking the tide, and none knew better than he how to grasp at even the feeblest straws offered by opportunity. Very slowly, Thomas drew up his legs in front of him, and fisted his hands by his sides. He would take one of the water-bottles first, and a knife if he could see one. Then he would make for the mountains, and freedom.

He made his move as the raiding tribe broke through the perimeter of the oasis. He had seized two water-bottles before the Berbers had realized what was happening, and then he was running, his bare heels burning the ground, a short curving knife in his hand, before the first swords clashed.

He began to walk at dawn the following day. He was aware that not far behind him were the Berbers and the raiders: Thomas had no wish to be found by either. The lack of ropes or burden, the freedom from mocking voices and the ever-present smell of camel dung, made him feel light-headed with joy. Singing to himself, knocking the undergrowth aside with a stick, Thomas Marlowe began the long walk back to his destiny.

The only difficulty was that he had no idea where he was heading. Morocco seemed littered with people he had to avoid, but barren of anywhere where he might expect sanctuary. The land was growing steadily more arid, the soil giving way to sand, the small oases of trees a rarity. He decided to continue to head south, for no better reason than that to head north might force him back across the path of the Berber nomads.

The heat grew more intense as he travelled, and clouds of insects feasted on his flesh. Resting at midday beneath a group of palm trees, scratching at the swollen scarlet bites, Thomas saw a flash of blue, brighter than the blue of the sky. A kingfisher, he thought, knowing that this was neither the country nor the habitat of the kingfisher. But in his mind's eye Thomas could see the boat, *his* boat, masts silhouetted like palm fronds against a Mediterranean sky, the name emblazoned on her bows. The *Kingfisher*, her blue pennants pulled taut by the wind, as fleet and as graceful as her namesake. *He* would name her now, not some damned begrudging patron. '*Kingfisher,*' shouted Thomas to the mosquitoes and the wide African sky. 'I name you the *Kingfisher!*'

But by the following day, Thomas was forced to consider whether he had not escaped one enemy for a more deadly one. He had found no sign of human habitation, and he had only an inch of water left in his flask. The country had become more difficult, and although the mountains themselves looked temptingly cool, try as he might, he never seemed to get closer to them. Thomas's tired brain pictured cascades of icy water, shaded groves of trees. Stopping briefly in the feeble shelter of some rocks, he found that if he closed his eyes, he could feel the rush of water, hear the rustle of leaves. But waking, looking round him, there was only the distorting gleam of the heat, and a nest of tiny snakes hiding, like him, from the pitiless eye of the sun. His lips were cracked and peeling, his eyelids blistered and swollen. The weight of the gold-filled doublet was worse than the pack that the Berbers had made him bear: it dragged him down, it slowed his feet.

Thomas began to lose track of day and night. He walked a little, rested a little, no longer able to keep to any pattern. Every limb ached. The need for water became all-engrossing; he had filled his flask from a small muddy trickle in a sun-baked gully, but he had only a few mouthfuls left. He had not eaten for days, but he no longer felt hungry. He needed water, ice-cold, crystal-clear water.

But the desert seemed to be everywhere, rolling waves of sand interrupted by outcrops of rock. His skin was made raw and bleeding by insect bites and sunburn, and the rocks scorched his fingers if he touched them in his search for shelter. The dryness of the air, the sand, the sky, tormented him.

Eventually, he could walk no more. He could see not a flicker of green, not a drop of water; sky and sand shaded from yellow to livid red, to a glaring white. A few drowsy flies floated up from the sand as Thomas rolled into a shadowed crevice between rock and desert. If he had had the strength, he would have taken off the doublet, because its weight was killing him. Laying the tattered remains of his shirt over his face, muttering a little to himself, Thomas Marlowe closed his eyes.

He thought of his family, of his parents, dead of the plague many years past, of his elder brother, who had had the good sense to save himself some money and buy a tavern in South-wark. Robert was not dying in a foreign desert because Robert was not argumentative, obstinate and obsessed. He thought of Faith, with her long russet hair, and her creamy, freckled flesh. He liked big, generous, uncomplicated women. He thought of all his voyages, ten years of them now, and he thought of the doomed *Toby*. He no longer thought of the *Kingfisher*; the *Kingfisher* had killed him. He thought he was on board ship, and he could hear the wind in the sails, feel the cool sea-spray against his face.

The stars, drops of crystal against the blackest velvet, indicated change, decision, an end to contentment.

Later, in his house, as he spoke of the degrees of fire and the hierarchy of colour, the physician considered the nature of contentment. Happiness was a fragile thing: he had found and lost it many times in as many years, but contentment was perhaps a little more durable. Contentment came with age, with loss of expectation, with a narrowing and settling of boundaries.

Kara Ali was old now, almost seventy. He would no longer use his curative pills or draughts for himself: only the ones that killed pain, or brought sleep. He would not resist death when it came. He found that he did not dread death. He had changed his nationality and his religion, had lost one identity and found another. He had always had the immense solace of his profession and his learning, yet that learning had failed him when he had most needed it. He had buried a beloved wife. He had lost one daughter, and found another.

Serafina. The name took the physician almost by surprise; he found that he had ceased to think of her as Serafina. She was Badr-al-Dujja, and sometimes he forgot that the first child of that name was long dead and buried under the eucalyptus trees in the garden. Serafina passed for an Arab girl just as well as his own mixed race daughter had. Dark hair, dark eyes; sometimes it was as though his own child had been taken away from him and returned ten years later in the Bedestan in Algiers.

Tonight, though, when usually he felt nothing but content watching her sitting across the table writing for him, the physician felt a flicker of unease. She was no longer a child, but a woman of fully fifteen years. Kara Ali studied the girl as she wrote, her head bent over the paper. She was small for her age and neatly formed. She moved silently, quickly, like some small bird. Turn your head and there would be Serafina behind you, and you would have heard nothing more than the flutter of the breeze, a stirring of dust. Her skin was a smooth deep olive after six years on the Barbary coast, her demeanour all that a father could ask for. Why then did he feel unease? Because the change, the decision that the stars had indicated, was to do with Badr-al-Dujja – *no*: Serafina?

'Papa?'

She looked up, pen poised over the paper, brows raised. Kara Ali felt his heart contract a little, and he sat down, hiding the pain, ignoring the warning flutter in his breast.

Change, decision, and an end to contentment. These did not

apply to himself: he had outlived such things. They applied to
the child that fate had given him. Since the janissary had called
so many years ago, they had had no more unexpected visits. Yet
he had been careful to keep her out of sight, never to allow her
to ride with him to Algiers. She had not seemed discontented
with that, yet – could he find a husband for a woman who
should not exist? She might be Badr-al-Dujja for any passing
visitor, yet a closer acquaintance might, Kara Ali feared, betray
the deception.

The fires in the furnaces had almost died. He could no longer
stoke them himself, yet he did not want to send for Hassan. The
Philosopher's Stone could wait for a more auspicious night. He
made himself smile.

'It is late, little one. Go to bed.'

He watched her wipe the pen and lay it beside the inkwell,
sprinkling sand over the paper. Her features were neat and
precise, and her eyes were always secretive. He knew that she
told no one, not even he, what she truly felt.

And he, too, had secrets. He touched her hand as she passed,
and listened for the light patter of her feet as she crossed the
courtyard. He must let her choose, he thought, soon, before his
own feeble health made it too late. To choose her own destiny
Serafina must know the cruel patterns of the past. He had played
at being God too long. The stars worked their patterns: soon he
would know when to speak, what to say.

All knowledge is a drop from his ocean, all wisdom a handful
of dust from his stream, all time an hour from his life.

Thomas was on board ship. All those other events of the past
weeks he must have dreamed, because he was travelling, and he
could feel the rocking motion of the waves. Up and down, up
and down, slung in a particularly uncomfortable hammock.

Thomas seemed to drift in and out of consciousness for some
time, but when he thought he was awake, he was always on
board ship. It was nice to be sailing again: water dripped into his
mouth, and he sucked at it feebly; something cool soothed the
heat of his tortured skin. The noises were wrong, though: he
could not hear the crack of the sails, nor the patter of men's feet

on wooden decks. And there was an overpowering smell of – he could not quite remember what – but it was certainly neither pitch nor salt.

Eventually, however, the motion stopped. Thomas became aware of hands hauling him out of his hammock, and then, again, the sensation he had longed for these past few days. Ice-cold water was trickling into his mouth: he spluttered, choked, and opened his eyes.

When at last he managed to focus, he knew that he was in heaven. Not only was there water, but there sat beside him the most beautiful woman he had ever seen.

She was fair-skinned and dark-eyed. She wore no veil, like so many of the women of these parts, so Thomas could clearly see the curving red lips, the long, straight nose, the dark oblique eyes that were fringed with black. He could also see black coils of hair under a silver scarf. Her silk robe moulded against a well-formed, curving body, her jewellery – gold, silver, amber and cornelian – drew his eyes to the narrow columns of her neck, her wrists, her ankles. Thomas swallowed, and she dripped more water into his mouth from the sponge she held in her hand.

Slowly, his mind began to work again. He was in a tent, and beyond the tent, through the half-draped awning, he could see more tents, a long string of camels, people gathered around cooking-fires, all silhouetted against the dying desert sun. The sensation of being on board ship – now nothing more than a confusing memory – must have been the motion of a camel. Which also accounted for the smell: yes, he must have been travelling in the side-pannier of a camel.

So, he had been found by these people, and – he looked down at himself – his hands and feet were not bound. The brief glance downwards told him something else as well. He was being tended by the most beautiful woman in the world, and he was naked. Too exhausted to do anything but accept his situation, and not overburdened with modesty anyway, Thomas Marlowe's only thought was for his doublet. Attempting to sit up, he began, wildly and inefficiently, to gesticulate in the region of his chest.

'Your doublet?' said the lady, coolly, in Spanish. 'I have it
here for you.'

She placed the doublet carefully in his hands. He tested the
weight of it and heard her say, 'Your gold is safe. The holes you
made have been repaired.'

It was true: neat stitches had rejoined the seams he had split.
He managed to mumble his thanks in adequate Spanish, and
take the cup that the woman held out to him.

As he drank, Thomas continued to inspect his surroundings.
The tent was made of leather, and he was lying on cushions on
the floor. The walls and awnings were hung with coloured silks
that shimmered like an uncertain rainbow; the cushions were
jewelled, embroidered, tasselled. The light from the brass lamp
that swung from one of the cross-pieces of the tent picked out
the stones sewn into the cushions, the dull rich patina of the
silks. The woman's skin had that same close fine texture, and her
tightly bound hair shone like jet. It was months since Thomas
had made his hasty exit from Faith Whitlock's bedchamber.

Feeling a familiar stirring of the flesh, he pulled a nearby cloth
over himself. The woman did not speak; she merely clapped her
hands, and the curtain that covered the awning shivered.

A Negro slave-girl entered, carrying a tray of food. Thomas
sat up as the girl put down the tray on the cushions beside him
and left the tent.

Dates, figs, honey and sherbet. Thomas's appetite had begun
to return, his exhaustion to lessen. He ate greedily, and when
he had finished, the Negro girl returned to take the tray
away.

He heard the other woman say, 'So, Señor —?'

'Marlowe. Thomas Marlowe,' he said hastily, rising and nodding his head in a bow.

'So, Señor Marlowe. You have eaten, you have drunk, your
bites and your burns have been attended to. Is there anything
else that you need?'

He was conscious of a restless feeling in the pit of his stomach.
There were other appetites besides the one for food and drink.
The piece of silk was knotted rather inadequately round his
waist, his brain did not seem to be functioning properly. He

managed to say, 'I would be honoured to know who you are – and where we are going . . .'

The woman smiled calmly. 'My name is Jamila. You are travelling, Señor Marlowe, in a camel caravan escorted by my people, the Tuareg. We are taking salt and gold dust and black slaves to the Spanish presidio of Oran, and then continuing to the city of Algiers. Does that suit you, Señor Marlowe?'

She was seated on a pile of cushions in one corner of the tent. He managed to mutter a reply. Algiers suited him very well: from Algiers he could travel to Italy or to France.

'Good,' said Jamila, and patted the cushion beside her.

Thomas could not move. He watched Jamila draw back the silver scarf that covered her head. Slowly, her white hands began to loosen the great black plaits of hair.

That same calm smile.

'My Spanish is not good, I am afraid. I have picked up a little of the language in Algiers and Oran. You know how it is . . . Perhaps I should have said, Señor Marlowe, is there anything else that you *desire*?'

Thomas discovered that he would have to pay for his supper.

It was six weeks before Allah found Kara Ali the right words, the right time.

He had, in return for having cured a sick child, been given a copy of Ptolemy's *Geographica*. Beautifully bound, showing all the lands of the known earth, it lay open on the table in the room with the furnaces. Serafina was studying it.

Kara Ali was reminded quite suddenly of that night six years ago, when he had shown her the simurgh, the lion, the elephant. The memory was like a blow to the chest, as though someone had knotted their fists together and struck him in the ribs. He knew that tonight he must speak.

He waited until she had found the map of the Inland Sea. Then he said, 'We are here, Serafina, between Oran and Algiers. And there' – his pointing finger traced the path across the Mediterranean to the southern coast of France – 'there is Marseilles. Your birthplace. Your home.'

He chose the word *home* quite deliberately. She looked up at him, but her eyes, as usual, masked any possibility of pain. 'Yours too, Papa.'

He shook his head. 'No. France ceased to be my home when I took the turban. I am a Moslem now. This is my country.'

He had never before, in her years in his house, asked her to make that choice. But now he said, carefully, 'This could be your country also, daughter.'

She did not answer him. He knew that of all her gifts, her instinct for calculation was the greatest, that the same skill she used in accounting she used now, to assess advantages and disadvantages.

As he had too, many years ago, when offered the same choice. It was only later that it had come to mean a little more to him. He said, 'You need not decide now, little one. I offer you a choice.'

She still watched him, waiting. He had moved away from the table, had gone to stand beneath the small square window. There were stars in the sky, speckling the blackness.

'I have to tell you about the death of your father,' he said.

He saw emotion then, quickly masked.

'My father?' Serafina plaited her small slender hands together. 'My father died of a fever in the bagnio in Algiers.'

She said it automatically, like a litany, as though it meant nothing to her. Kara Ali sighed. He was aware of an utter weariness. 'It is true,' he said gently, 'that your father died in the bagnio, but it is not true that he died of a fever. I told you that because you were a child, and because I had begun, even then, to love you. Now you are a woman – and now I see my own death approaching – I believe that I must tell you the truth.'

She had not moved. The lamplight gleamed on the dark wings of her hair, and on the gauzy veil that covered her head. There was no kind way of saying what he had to say.

'Your father did not die of a fever, he was put to death. The same person who intended your death, intended your father's also and, in his case, succeeded. The corsair who captured your father's ships was offered a large sum of money to have his most valuable hostages put to death.'

She was silent for a long moment. Then she said, stiffly, 'Tell me the manner of his death.'

It was what the physician had most dreaded. But he told her, simply and honestly, because he knew it was her due. By the time he had finished, he thought he had seen her form another layer of the protective shell she had fashioned round herself.

'Little one,' he said, when he had finished, 'I tell you this not to distress you, but to offer you a choice – a true choice. If you become a Moslem I will give you your freedom and find you a good husband, and leave you what little wealth I can. It will only be a little: under Islamic law I have no possessions. However, you may, if you choose, return to France. But I believe you will be in danger if you do so, just as I believed six years ago that you were in danger. I think' – he paused, weighing his words – 'I think that the danger to you may come from France.'

She was staring at him, brows creased. 'How, Papa?' she said, sharply.

He sat down. He no longer wanted to see the stars.

'I have had many years to think about this. After your father was taken to Algiers, the agents of the corsair would have contacted your family in Marseilles. They would have demanded a ransom, which should have been paid. It was not paid, however; instead, I believe that money was sent to ensure that both you and your father never returned to Marseilles. I think you should consider, little one, who might profit by your father's death.'

The gauze veil had slipped backwards off her head, her wide dark eyes were staring at him. He knew that she was calculating again, listing each member of the Guardi household in turn and coolly assessing their possible culpability. He loved her because he believed that under the reserve was something else, something that history had not yet allowed to blossom.

'No,' she said, at last, and frowned. 'No. It is mine now – all of it . . .' Serafina rose, replacing her veil. She said, quite simply, 'It is mine, Papa. I must go back to Marseilles.'

That was all. He had, Kara Ali realized, never expected that she would find the decision difficult. Because of that knowledge, he did not even feel sorrow. She had been lent to him for a while, that was all, and he thanked Allah for the gift of those years.

'It will not be easy,' he said. 'We must be careful. We will wait for the stars to tell us what to do.'

The scheming of the stars brought Kara Ali a visitor the following week. The physician knew that he was a Tuareg warrior from the veil that covered all but the eyes and the patch of blue-dyed skin surrounding them.

He found out what his visitor wanted of him over a glass of milk and a handful of dates in the coolness of the courtyard. A bad fall from a horse, and the broken bone in a boy's leg would not set. He had treated these people before; he knew the slow enormous caravan that each year brought gold dust and salt and slaves from the black heart of Africa to Oran and Algiers.

Kara Ali rode out in the late afternoon attended by Hassan and Ahmed and the tall Tuareg warrior. His bones had ached all day, and there was still that nagging intermittent flutter of the heart to remind him of his own unfinished obligations. He smiled a little as he wondered which heaven waited for him. He rather hoped for the heaven of Islam, which promised him houris and a sexual pleasure that would last for a hundred years.

The caravanserai was a courtyard surrounded by rooms with stables underneath. Goats, mules, sheep and camels added their clamour to the chatter of the people: Bedouin and Tuareg, and their dusty blue-black slaves. The smell of couscous, of camel-dung fires, and of jostling people and animals was overpowering. In the gathering darkness of one of the rooms, the physician set the boy's leg and left a draught to let the child sleep. He was tired, his hands began to tremble even as he tied the final bandage. There was music and feasting in the courtyard below. Letting Ahmed gather up his belongings, Kara Ali left the room.

While he ate — mutton, pigeon stewed with almonds, semolina and rice — the darkness of the distant desert and mountains became complete. The light from the fires and the swaying brass lamps flickered on the gold and silver bangles of the dancers, on their long, loose dark hair, on their black, glittering eyes. The music of drum and tambourine and pipe half hid another familiar, more urgent beat. But he was too old for such things, thought Kara Ali. Far too old.

Had he been twenty, or thirty, or forty, he might have loved one of these women. The faces of the Tuareg women were unveiled, lit and shaped by the firelight, patterned by shadows from the swinging brass lamps. They were beautiful women, tall and strong and graceful, fair-skinned and dark-eyed, and the customs of their tribe allowed them as many lovers as they wished. Kara Ali's gaze moved from the dancers to a woman seated across the fire. A man stood beside her: they did not touch, but they looked as though they belonged to each other. No: he frowned, watching, and then understanding. The man belonged to the woman, that was it. The man was not a Tuareg, because his dark curling hair was uncovered by a blue veil, his skin free of the warriors' dye. The woman possessed the kind of strong, definite beauty that would have made her appear plain at fifteen, yet quite breathtaking at twenty-five. That could be Serafina's sort of beauty, thought the physician, taking the stones out of a handful of dates. Men did not trouble to look twice at her now – but in a few years . . . in a few years she would truly be Badr-al-Dujja, Full Moon of the Night. If she had been his blood-daughter, then he would have found a good husband for Serafina tomorrow. Beauty would give her power, Kara Ali thought, finishing the dates and carefully picking up the stones. Sometimes he wondered what she would do if she had power.

Date-stones gripped in his palm, the physician rose and slowly walked to the boundaries of the caravanserai. He was tired, as though he, like the Bedouin and their Tuareg escort, had journeyed across mountains and desert. He tired easily these days.

Out in the wilderness, as the sound of feasting and music and dancing faded to insignificance, Kara Ali threw the date-stones to the bare earth so that they might feed weary travellers in years to come. He, too, had travelled many miles, but he would travel no more. He looked up, as he always did, to the stars.

A meeting, they said. As he grew older, the messages of the heavens grew a little clearer. Even so, he knew that he only understood a fraction of what was written there. Wiser men than he would unlock their secrets, if Allah wished it.

A meeting, though. Turning, Kara Ali walked back to the caravanserai.

★

By the time he took his place in the courtyard again, the dancing had finished and the fighting had begun. The Tuareg fought with two-edged swords, daggers, and leather shields. Had this not been merely an entertainment, they would have ridden white war-camels and carried lances.

As it was, the physician found some pleasure in watching the swordsmanship. In their different way, the men were as graceful as the dancing-girls. Blue veils swirled in the firelight, copper skins gleamed with sweat. Kara Ali accepted a cup of mint tea and felt no regret in knowing that he was too old for such sport.

He had begun to doze when the curly-haired man stood up to fight. The physician's heavy eyes focused again as one of the Tuareg warriors won his third fight in succession, and the crowd howled their appreciation. The victorious warrior – sword still in hand, eyes bright with pride – looked round for another challenger. And watching, Kara Ali saw – a flick of an eyelid, the graceful movement of a hand – the Tuareg woman send her unveiled lover into the square of sand in the centre of the courtyard.

His drowsiness had retreated, and the physician sat up, chin cradled in his hands. At first, Kara Ali had thought the man a half-caste, of mixed Arab and Negro race, which would account for the curling hair. But no, the new challenger was fair-skinned, blue-eyed, of middle height, unlike the tall, graceful Tuareg warriors. Italian, perhaps? Or even – Kara Ali frowned at the effort of memory – Irish?

Whatever race he was, he was competent with a sword. Both the European and the Tuareg carried a short sword and a dagger, but the Tuareg's dagger was strapped to his left wrist, the European's to his waist. The Tuareg's eyes gleamed darkly in anticipation of pleasure through the blue recesses of his veil as the two men circled in the small square of sand, waiting for the best moment to move. A flick of a sword, no more than a moving line of light in the darkness, and the fight had begun.

It did not take long, though, for the physician to realize that this fight was to be a little different to the others. All the previous bouts had been a clever, breathtaking display of the skill of the lords of the desert – terrifying and magnificent, yes, but a display nevertheless. But this – and Kara Ali's heart fluttered again at the repeated clash of steel on steel, the pounding of feet on packed sand – was something more than display.

He knew the cause of it, of course. She had not moved throughout the evening: the Tuareg woman sat, heavy with silk and gold, her profile drawn from the shadows. She owned the European, the Tuareg wished to own her. The Tuareg might treat their women with a respect unequalled in the Arab world, but man's need for ownership was deeper than custom. The men fought as two rutting boars fight, as two great stags fight, antlers locked.

Kara Ali would have put his money on the Tuareg, had he not seen the expression on the European's face. He thought he had rarely seen such determination, such – obstinacy. That man knew he was fighting for his life, for a possibility of a future. And he was unhampered by any notions of gentlemanly conduct. He fought like a gutter-dweller fights, like a dockhand fights. Kara Ali's heart began to flutter again as excitement stirred in his breast. He was reminded of Marseilles, of the dark alleyways where even he had to learn to fight for his life. A meeting, the stars had said.

First blood to the Tuareg, however. A dagger cut the length of the European's forearm, a black line against a tanned skin. The wounded man did not even wince, though. It was like that in the heat of battle, the pain would come later. Blood dripped down the bare arm, fouling the tip of his dagger. The Tuareg were stamping and calling to cheer on their own man; the Bedouin women had added their own strange wailing to the noise. They called like that when they sent their men into battle, and they loosened their hair, and swayed and shook their heavy bracelets. Only the Tuareg woman was motionless, as though she were carved in stone.

The Tuareg took the next blow, a swordcut to the ribs. The night had begun to cool rapidly, but Kara Ali could see the sweat running in rivulets from the fighters' bodies. The European's foot hooked round the Tuareg's leg, and both men fell to the ground, dust rising in great clouds to make the fires spit and spark.

They had both lost their swords and shields, and they rolled, clothing and skin dyed ochre by the sand, daggers gripped in their palms. Then even Kara Ali cried out as he saw the European, his fingers soaked with sweat and blood, lose grip of his dagger. It slipped and slithered from his fingers like a snake, and then the Tuareg's dagger was resting against the curly-headed man's throat.

'Sweet Jesus,' Kara Ali heard him whisper, in the sudden silence of the courtyard. *English*, thought the physician, leaning forward, he is an Englishman.

And then the Tuareg woman called out in her own language, 'He is mine, Hanif.'

The knife slipped a little, scratching the Englishman's throat. The silence seemed almost tangible. Very slowly, the Tuareg rose, and spat on the sand, and walked away.

Kara Ali attended to the Tuareg first, because he was the victor, and besides, the wound was more severe. Then, filled with what curiosity age had left him, he went to the Englishman.

He was in the Tuareg woman's tent, but he was alone, for which Kara Ali was thankful. He had a bowl of water and some rags, and was attempting to clean the cut on his arm when the physician appeared.

'You will be so good as to allow me to do that,' said Kara Ali, in French.

He saw that he was understood, and resented. He added, 'I am a physician, friend. It is my job to repair the foolishness of others. You will forgive me if I do not speak your language, but my English is poor. French, Italian, Arabic, even the Hamitic language of these people – but English . . . my poor tongue has never been able to master it.'

Sitting cross-legged on the floor, he took the bowl and the rags from the Englishman, and began to bathe the wound. It was a long, deep cut, but properly dressed, it would heal well. He saw the anger in the Englishman's blue eyes begin to lessen as he worked, efficiently and quietly.

At length, Kara Ali said, 'The stars told me of a meeting, my friend. See, the heavens announced your presence to me.'

'The stars,' said the Englishman scornfully, 'tell north from south, the winter solstice from the summer. That is all. That is everything.'

Tearing a length of cotton into a strip, Kara Ali said gently, 'You do not believe that they show us our future?'

'They allow us to *make* our future. If we do not take heed of them, then we find ourselves at the bottom of the ocean, or battered by rocks. They do not tell us – our fate.'

'No?' The physician's heart had begun to beat unevenly again; he made himself breathe steadily, and his hands, winding the bandage around the damaged arm, did not shake. 'You are a mariner, then, Mr –?'

'Marlowe. Thomas Marlowe. Yes, sir, I am a mariner. I am a pilot, and I do not believe that if I sail too far from the Inland Sea I will fall from the corners of the world, and neither do I believe that those pinpricks of light in the sky can predict my future. But I thank you, sir' – looking down at the completed bandage – 'for your trouble.'

The Englishman, rising first, had to help Kara Ali to his feet. The physician, leaning on Thomas Marlowe's shoulder in the half darkness of the tent, knew that the stars made only half the pattern: Allah and man the rest.

'I would like you to return with me to my own house for a night, Mr Marlowe,' he said. 'I have a request to make of you.'

Because the physician had cured a child of her tribe, the Tuareg woman did not refuse Kara Ali's request that Thomas Marlowe accompany him home. She was not pleased, though; Kara Ali saw that in the small pursing movement of her lips, her hand's tight gesture of dismissal.

Back in the silence of his house, Kara Ali took Thomas Marlowe to the room with the furnaces and the books. The furnaces were cold, so Ahmed lit the brass lamps before retiring to sit in the courtyard outside the door.

The physician was tired, but he had not finished his night's work. He said, briskly, 'Tell me your story, Mr Marlowe. Tell me how an English pilot comes to be travelling through the mountains with a Tuareg caravan.'

'I was shipwrecked.' The Englishman, who had dressed in

breeches, shirt and a quilted doublet, looked up briefly from the
Mercator map that the physician had spread out on the table in
front of him. 'Off the Barbary coast – here, I think.' Thomas
Marlowe pointed to a corner of the page. 'Approximately four
months ago. We ran aground on a sandbank.'

Kara Ali raised his eyebrows. 'And you ship's pilot, Mr Marlowe?'

'A pilot,' Thomas Marlowe said stiffly, 'however good, can recommend a course, but he cannot force the master to take it. Sadly.'

Kara Ali, easing himself on to a stool, watched his visitor.
'And then, Mr Marlowe?'

'And then – I found no other survivors, so I began to make
my way to some sort of port. But I was taken by a group of
nomads, who used me as a beast of burden. I managed to escape
from them, but lost myself, I'm afraid, in the desert. I'm used to
seas of water, sir, not sand. I thought I would die, but the
Tuareg found me and took me with them.'

The pilot's eyes had not left the map while he had spoken.
Kara Ali thought he could detect true love there, even an obsession. He said, 'And what now, Mr Marlowe? Are you happy
to travel with the Tuareg for the rest of your days?'

He had the man's full attention now. The blue eyes were
angry again, and disdainful.

'Certainly not. I have work to do.'

'What sort of work, Mr Marlowe?'

Carefully, the young man refolded the map. 'I'm going to
build a ship . . .' he said.

The physician did not speak immediately, for his heart had
begun to pound again. He could feel life trickling away like
sand through his fingers, and he knew that he must struggle to
keep the final grains safe for a little longer in the folds of his
palm. So he watched Thomas Marlowe for a while, noting the
hooked nose, the firm mouth, the proud clever face. And the
hands, marked with the callouses of many years' honest labour.
And then he spoke.

'I have a story to tell you, Mr Marlowe. And a proposition to
make.'

★

When he had finished, the Englishman said, 'Oran to Cartagena? In a *rowing-boat*? I might die in the process!'

'So you might, Mr Marlowe.' Kara Ali folded his robes around his aching limbs. 'But I thought that you said you were a good navigator.'

'The best.' Marlowe's hands were fisted, the Mercator map forgotten. 'But even I, dear sir, cannot foresee the future. A storm might spring up when we are ten leagues out of port – especially at this time of year – the Inland Sea is notorious –'

Anger had stiffened every sinew of his body. If he had been younger, thought Kara Ali happily, then the pilot would have hit him. But he had the protection of age, so he said, 'You have not asked me about payment, Mr Marlowe.'

'Payment?' Marlowe swung round. 'I've escaped death a dozen times in the past six months. What can you possibly offer to make me wish to court it again?'

'I could offer you gold, of course,' said Kara Ali softly. 'To help build your boat. Or – or I could offer you your freedom.'

The Englishman smiled tightly. 'I have gold,' he said. 'And I have my freedom.'

Kara Ali shook his head. 'I don't think so.'

Again, he was glad of his advancing years. He saw fury spark the blue eyes like a furnace, and then the anger was veiled as the eyelids dropped.

'A pleasant sort of slavery,' said Kara Ali meditatively, recalling the beauty of the Tuareg woman. 'Yet slavery nevertheless. But' – the physician's eyes met those of Thomas Marlowe – 'if Islam were to find out about your skills as a pilot, then you would spend your years navigating corsair galleys out of Algiers. Good pilots are always in short supply on the Barbary coast.'

The threat was there, well-veiled, but unmistakable. Kara Ali added, softly, 'Think, Mr Marlowe – I offer you a chance to escape the spider's web that fate has woven for you. Or that you have woven for yourself, if you prefer.'

He saw the pilot stare at him, the anger gone, replaced by understanding, even, perhaps, by shame. Then as the Englishman nodded in assent, Kara Ali called for Ahmed to wake Serafina.

PART III

1594

THE DESIRE OF GOLD

The Desire of gold will answer many
objections.
Sir Walter Raleigh's discovery of Guiana:
Richard Hakluyt

She had packed her bag and changed her clothes before she met the English pilot.

He was in the room where they ate, waiting for her and Kara Ali. She saw the small twitch of his mouth as he glanced at her, and heard him say, 'I thought you said a *daughter*, sir?'

She did not trouble to answer.

Kara Ali said mildly, 'Serafina, this is Mr Thomas Marlowe, who will take you back to Marseilles.' He turned to the pilot. 'A man and a woman sailing a fishing boat would be thought a strange thing in this country, Mr Marlowe. A man and a boy will be rather more acceptable.'

'But not in doublet and hose,' said Serafina, glancing briefly at the Englishman.

She had never liked the English, and she would make no exception for this man. He was of medium height, stocky, with curling black hair and a tanned, arrogant face. All the English were arrogant. Years ago they had owned great tracts of land in France, but they had lost them all, through conceit and stupidity.

Serafina's uncovered cropped hair and boy's tunic and loose trousers felt curiously light, but she said calmly, 'He must wear a robe, mustn't he, Papa?'

Kara Ali nodded, and Serafina saw Thomas Marlowe's eyes flash with impatience.

But, as Ahmed ran for a spare robe, the pilot said only, 'I will need a lodestone, sir. Do you have one?'

Kara Ali not only possessed a lodestone, he also had maps and an astrolabe. Serafina watched the man who had been her owner and her father for the past six years, and she saw that his movements had grown slow, the colour of his skin had bleached.

She had offered to stay to the end, and he had refused her. She knew that she had made the right decision: if she faltered at the thought of crossing the sea in a small boat with a stranger, then she only had to think of an iron brand drawing a cross on the sole of a foot. She had begun to dream of that again these past few weeks, since the physician had told her the manner of her father's death. By day, she had still been Badr-al-Dujja, a dutiful Moslem slave-girl; by night her true name pounded through her head in rhythm with the beating of the waves against a corsair's ship, the wailing of the captives in the bagnio at Algiers. The cutting of her hair, the discarding of the clothes she had almost accepted as her own, created in her a small kernel of excitement.

She took the physician's hand, though, as they stood in the darkness of the courtyard, the horses saddled and laden beside them. She found that there was nothing she could say, no words that would be adequate. Kara Ali said softly, 'Allah be with you, little one,' and then she mounted the horse and rode away from him for ever.

The Englishman made no allowance for her age or her sex on the ride from the physician's house to the coast. He intended to set sail before dawn, he said, before the fishermen awoke and saw that one of their boats was missing. One of Mr Marlowe's arms was bandaged, but that did not seem to make any difference to his progress. On horseback he was not graceful, like the Bedouin who often called at the physician's house, nor elegant, as Angelo had been. He merely drove the creature to the limit of its capabilities, no further, and seemed to expect her to do the same.

They reached the coast within a remarkably short time, unloading the horses and hiding them under a cluster of date palms. Ahmed would collect them the following day. The night sky was still black, but Serafina could find her way to the sea in darkness. They had been here often, she and Kara Ali, ostensibly to buy fish, or to tend the sick; in reality — in reality, she thought, to see the sea. To know that same blue expanse of water touched Africa, Italy, France. Grabbing the Englishman's sleeve, Serafina guided him down to the beach.

The fishing boats, sails furled, bobbed in the water like white petals cast on a pond. Tartanes, feluccas, chebecks, single- or two-masted, most of them, their triangular sails furled and lashed in place. Moonlight drew the thin graceful spars, the low fragile hulls. The pilot, tramping through the shallows with Serafina at his side, inspected each boat in turn, running his short calloused hands round the bows, scowling. Then, 'This one,' he said.

He chose the tartane because it had only one mast, and two sails. He did not think he could manage any more single-handed: he had already discounted the girl as incapable of offering any assistance. She looked more like twelve than sixteen, with arms and legs like sticks and no concessions to womanhood that he had been able to distinguish. She said nothing as he offered to help her on board, just primly took his hand and hauled herself over the gunwale.

Thomas saw the first pink strands of sunlight as he lifted the anchor and began to unknot the sails. But he felt at home suddenly, more so than he had felt since the *Toby*'s foremast had snapped, sending them all into the waves. Letting the sails unfurl, he used an oar to push the tartane further out to sea. The fishermen would be here soon, gathering the nets that were strung like spiders' webs all over the beach. The sails began to collect the breeze and use it, tugging the tiny craft across the surface of the water. The girl was sitting at the stern of the boat, knees together, bags piled in front of her. Serafina, he thought, as he adjusted the sails to catch the freshening wind. What a bloody silly name.

He thought he heard the fishermen shout as he left the currents of the coast and headed into open sea. He shook his fist at all those who had tried to impede him, filled with joy at his escape from a land that could have kept him for ever. He glanced at Serafina, alone at the stern, expecting to see some mirrored emotion in her face. But there was nothing, her features were shuttered, her dark eyes watched only the horizon.

Thomas discovered over the course of the day that the boat and the girl had something in common.

They were both bitches. The tartane was a bitch because the two sails and the lack of a decent rudder made her the devil to steer. The girl was a bitch in a rather more subtle way.

He had thought at first that her silence was due to shyness, or modesty. He knew that she was of Italian origin, but of French birth, and that she had spent the last six years in slavery. He had thought that perhaps she found the lack of a scarf to cover her head or robes to hide her body embarrassing. Not that there was anything to hide but, attempting to act the gentleman, he offered her his own robe when they were far enough out of port to make it no longer necessary. But she merely looked at him as though he were a plague-carrier, and said, 'No thank you, Mr Marlowe', and continued to stare, hands folded, out to sea. He realized then that she did not speak because she did not think him worth speaking to.

He thought that with the right wind they could reach the coast of Spain within a few days. Towards the end of the second day, the wind began to trouble him: not the direction of it, which was southerly, just what he wanted, but there was a freshness that made him think a storm was likely. Thomas dozed intermittently that evening, jerking awake whenever the breeze jabbed fiercely at the sails, searching, when the sky cleared, for the stars that would guide his way.

In the early hours of the morning he could no longer only feel the storm in his bones, he could see it in the thickening waves, hear it in the beating of the sails. He found the girl first, curled up at the stern, and tied the rope round her waist before she woke.

Once roused, he had to clamp his hand over her mouth and shout to get her to listen.

'There's a storm coming – I'm tying us both to the mast. Here's a bucket to bale out with –'

Knotting the other end of the rope, Thomas left Serafina angry-eyed by the mast. He furled the sails within a few moments, fighting against the might of the wind to lash them to the yards. His only hope was that the tiny tartane might bounce and skim like a walnut shell on the water. He could not steer her.

In half an hour, with everything possible tied up or battened down, Thomas was on his knees beside Serafina, and both were baling out. The storm came in great savage gusts followed by short periods of calm. In the calm, Thomas, fighting the exhaustion of two sleepless nights, talked to keep himself awake.

About the *Kingfisher*, of course. He told Neptune – for Serafina certainly was not listening – about the *Kingfisher*. Four masts, square-rigged with topgallants, a narrow beakhead and a spritsail. Thick green water swirled in the bottom of the tartane. Thomas, his shirt reduced to rags, the bandage flapping from his arm like a pennant, scooped out the invading sea with a hollow gourd. Long in the keel, a narrow hull, and not too high-sided. That was where most of them went wrong, giving them those high pretty walls, decorated with gilt and ornaments and all sorts of other damned things that were no use at all in foul weather. The *Kingfisher* would be a beauty, but the beauty would be in her line, in her purpose.

The wind picked up again, and even Thomas could no longer speak. He took the bucket from Serafina, still on her knees, and looped it to the mast. Just in time – a wave took the boat and twisted it into the air, and Thomas felt the entire craft begin to lurch over to the side.

He had only one weapon to stop it capsizing: his own weight. That he threw himself backwards was instinctive, without thought. That the girl came with him, landing head-first on the low wooden gunwale, was because he had had the foresight to rope them together.

The boat stayed upright, and Thomas became aware of two things. That there was light on the horizon, and that Serafina lay draped across him like a rag-doll, completely still.

The breath began to return to his body. Serafina's eyes were closed, and a small trickle of red ran from her temple down the side of her face. Her clothes, like Thomas's, were completely soaked: the thin white muslin moulded to her body, showing him the small, previously unnoticed curves and hollows. She had thin bones, like a bird's, but her chest was not flat, as he had previously thought, and nor were her hips narrow like a boy's. Her skin, chilled by sea-water, felt like satin. Her cropped hair clung to her eyes and mouth: gently, Thomas brushed it aside.

He felt the pulse in her neck to reassure himself that she was still alive, and then, moving carefully, laid her in the shelter of the hull. The storm had begun to lessen, but Thomas still worked hard, baling out the huge wave that had almost capsized them, tying down ropes, checking sails. When he had assured himself that the tartane was as seaworthy as it would ever be, he returned to Serafina.

Her eyes were still closed, the blood a scarlet stream against her white skin. Thomas, kneeling beside her, began to tear his despised muslin robe into strips.

The cut was short and deep and high up near her hairline. She must have caught the edge of the gunwale with her brow. Thomas's own clothes clung cold and heavy to his body, but he worked swiftly and carefully, mopping up the mess and tying the makeshift bandage round her forehead. When he had finished, he shook Serafina's shoulder gently and said her name.

Her lids fluttered, so he hauled her upright, his arm around her, her narrow back resting on his chest. Water dripped from his eyelashes and his hair, and he would have sold his soul for some aqua vitae, but of course the old renegade would have had none of that. Her body was warm and heavy against his. He did not want to move, but he said her name again, and touched her cheek, and noticed, for the first time, that there was land on the horizon.

He felt, as he always did on such occasions, a tremendous surge of emotion. It had not occurred to him that she might feel the same, though; he thought it was the navigator in him, not the exile.

'Look, Serafina,' he said gently, seeking to rouse her. 'Land.'

He saw her dark eyes open and focus on the jagged orange-pink line of the horizon. He had thought her a hard little bitch; it was, therefore, with some consternation that Thomas Marlowe, pilot of the English Levant Company, watched his passenger begin to cry.

They beached the tartane on a small, rock-strewn bay, leaving her to be battered to splinters by the next high tide. Serafina, her muscles weak and her head throbbing, let the Englishman help her out of the hull and on to the sandy cove that he believed to be part of the southern coast of Spain.

Sitting on a rock, Serafina fought hard to recover her composure. She had not thought it would be like this: this rush of longing, and misery, and joy.

Her vision was blurred as she watched the Englishman unload the fishing boat. She found that, little as she liked Thomas Marlowe, she respected his skill and his strength, and the tenacity that had made him keep the tartane afloat. She despised her own tears, her own lack of strength.

She had six long years to make up for when she returned to Marseilles, six years with no Guardi to judge the silk, or test the wind, or look to the future. The thought that there might be nothing left when she returned home, that everything she had once possessed might have crumbled to dust, dispersed by the wind, was unendurable, one of her worst nightmares.

It was over a week later that, sheltering from a spring downpour in a roadside tavern, Serafina talked to the Englishman about his ambitions. Thomas Marlowe had not thought she had listened to what he had said in the tartane during the storm, but she had. She knew she had a life to rebuild, and for that she needed gold and men and ships. So she had stored up his words, as though they were a stolen handful of rice, or a fine blue bowl, to be kept for future use.

Although they had bought good horses, their journey was slow. The early spring weather was uncertain, the roads uniformly poor. Because of the bandits that infested the land, they travelled simply and with no show of wealth. Increasingly, Serafina found that images of home bunched around her, like badly stacked cards in a pack.

Riding through the rain, or lying wakeful in bed in the early hours of the morning, she told herself that it would all be the same. That the years in Africa, almost half her lifetime, would cease to be of importance. That she would be Serafina Guardi again, not Badr-al-Dujja, nor some nameless stable-boy. That there would be Marthe, bad-tempered and black-gowned, unable to believe that her child had returned to her. And Angelo, as tall and as handsome as ever, the Aucassin of her girlhood fantasies, would smile and kiss her again. It would all be the same, she told herself, knowing that there would be one important, terrible difference. Then, meticulously as always, Serafina would adjust her clothing to keep out the rain, or pull the blankets over her head, and shut out all recollection of her father.

She was still dressed as a boy: it was simpler that way, Mr Marlowe had said, handing her clothes bought from a village market-place. She had seen the sense in it, and had pulled the cap over her cropped dark hair without argument. When they rode, their silence was dictated both by speed and by antipathy.

But the Englishman had something she wanted. Today, beaten by endless rain and a bitter wind from the mountains of Spain, they had retreated in the early evening to the warmth of an inn.

When she had eaten sufficient and her clothes had begun to dry in the heat of the fire, Serafina said, 'And you, Mr Marlowe? What will you do when we reach Marseilles?

She judged him to be a little mellowed by the ale, but not yet mellow enough to send her upstairs and play dice with the assortment of ruffians in the corner of the taproom.

'Me?' Thomas ran his short square hands through his damp hair, and cut himself the end off the loaf of bread. 'I'll be making up for lost time. I seem to have lost six months in doing nothing very useful.'

He would take his leave of her when he had returned her to her family in Marseilles. That was the agreement that Thomas Marlowe and Kara Ali had made.

Serafina said, apparently incurious, 'You are a sailor, aren't you, Mr Marlowe?'

'A pilot.'

Serafina noticed the by now familiar gleam of interest in his eyes as the Englishman slit the bread in two with his knife.

He added, 'I've sailed other people's ships for the past ten years. I wish to sail my own now.'

'The *Kingfisher?*'

He stared at her. If Angelo had always been the prince of her fairy-tale imaginings, then in appearance Thomas Marlowe, with his dark, muscular frame, was the antithesis of that image. She was interested in his ambitions, nothing else.

She heard him chuckle, and saw him shake his head.

'You were listening. On the tartane.'

'Was I not intended to? Do Englishmen commonly talk to themselves, Mr Marlowe?'

He shrugged. 'It's no secret, I suppose.' The hard ride had worked off some of his energy, making him more approachable. 'Look. I'll show you what I'm going to do.'

He began to draw, his finger dipped in ale, on the scuffed table-top. The noise of the crowded taproom faded as the Englishman drew two ships – just sketches, swiftly drawn but instantly recognizable. He pointed to the first sketch.

'This is a galley. This, I should imagine, is what you were sailing when you were taken by the corsair. What the corsair sailed also.'

She nodded. The images of the battle were still there, but she had learned to keep them remote and distant, as though part of another person's life.

'The Infidels' ship was different to ours,' she said. 'Longer – thinner.'

He almost looked pleased with her. 'Which is why they won. Why you, Serafina, spent six years in slavery on the Barbary coast. They would have run up to you broadside to broadside and you wouldn't have had a chance to turn. And because you couldn't turn, you couldn't use your ordnance.'

One short, ale-stained finger rested on the stern of the galley. Serafina remembered the corsair's cannon, firing across the bows, and the *Gabrielle*'s bâtards, impotently pointing out to sea.

'This,' continued Thomas, pointing to the second sketch, 'is a roundship. Or cog, or nave – whatever you wish to call it. A fine little boat for carrying cargo, but even less use than a galley when faced with a hungry corsair. Top-heavy, unstable, and with as much speed as a snail.'

She nodded again. Two cogs, the *Mignon* and the *Petit Coeur*. 'We were carrying the cloth in roundships,' she said, smoothing her short hair back behind her ears. 'To Italy.'

'Yes. Slowly and at considerable risk.'

The two ale-drawn images had begun to fade already, dried by the heat of the fire. Thomas Marlowe began to sketch again. Another ship grew out of the battered pine.

'Now this – this is the ship that I intend to build. Look, Serafina. Gunports all along her sides, so it doesn't matter a damn which way she's facing. Twice the speed of the roundship, more manoeuvrable than the galley. And she can put out to sea at any time of year – again, unlike the galley.'

'The *Kingfisher*,' Serafina said as the Englishman waved to the tapboy to refill his tankard.

Her clothes, boy's clothes, were almost dry now. 'Will you build her in England?' she asked.

He shook his head. Briefly his eyes avoided meeting hers. 'No. It would be . . . unsuitable, for me to go back to England just now.'

She watched him in silence for a while. 'Then where, Mr Marlowe?'

'Anywhere!' he said, putting down the cup on the table, gesturing wide with his free hand. 'Spain – France – Italy – whoever'll have me. The damned Barbary coast, if necessary. Or' – rubbing his chin – 'perhaps not.'

Thomas Marlowe, Kara Ali had said, had had a Tuareg paramour.

Serafina said, 'Build the ship for me, Mr Marlowe.'

He stared at her for a moment, and then he began to laugh. 'For you? My dear –'

'Spain, Mr Marlowe?' Serafina, her hands folded in her lap, studied him coolly. 'Spain is England's enemy. Would you build ships for Spain's second armada?'

She saw the flare of anger in his blue eyes.

'I will build the ship for no one but myself!' he said.

'You have money then?'

'God, you've a curiosity inappropriate to your size. Yes, my dear, I have money. Enough to start, if not to finish. When I'm halfway there someone will have the sense to see what she's worth.'

The sketch of the ship still glistened on the bare boards.

'I have a cloth-carrying company in Marseilles,' said Serafina.

Her eyes were lidded, her face half hidden by the encroaching shadows of the evening. 'We will need ships.'

He did not look grateful, only exasperated. 'One,' he said, itemizing the numbers on his fingers, 'little girls do not own cloth-trades. Their fathers do. Their brothers do —'

'My father died in the bagnio in Algiers. I have no brothers. The business is mine.'

He went on as though she had not spoken. 'Two, whatever ships you lost six years ago will have been replaced long since. If your company still survives. Three' — he silenced her protests with a wave of his hand — 'three, the *Kingfisher* will not be used for trotting round the coast. She is to be a sea-going ship. An *ocean*-going ship. Not some barge for ferrying woollen caps and ladies' stockings.'

Serafina remembered the silk warehouse in Marseilles, and felt, for a moment, an anger to match his own.

'So you'll look for three-headed monsters in the Indies, Mr Marlowe, or fairies' gold in the New World?'

He glared at her. 'Not at all. Trade — on a scale you couldn't even conceive of. Now go to bed, child.' A pair of dice nestled in the palm of his hand. 'I've a mind to increase my fortune.'

She rose, because she was accustomed to obedience. She had slid a piece of bread into her pocket, to eat in the privacy and silence of her room, and she had planted the idea in Thomas Marlowe's rebellious head. For now, that was enough.

That France was a country at civil war became increasingly obvious the deeper Thomas and Serafina rode into Provence. The cancer that had gnawed at Paris and the north had at last infected the south, so that the cities of the Mediterranean coast increasingly displayed a loyalty to themselves, and not to their changing, changeable kings.

The unavoidable legacies of civil war — suspicion, violence, and hunger — scarred the heathlands of lavender and rosemary, the whitewashed villages that huddled next to the sea. Savoyard troops, as well as innumerable French Catholic and Huguenot factions, had trampled beautiful Provence into a uniform mire of political and religious strife. Four years previously, Charles de

Casaulx had seized the Hôtel de Ville, and in doing so had begun a period of dictatorship. As the wars had progressed, and Henri IV's grasp on his inheritance became more firm, Marseilles had found herself increasingly isolated, until she was forced to call on Spain: for grain, for armaments, for soldiers and galleys.

Thomas Marlowe felt the unease creep into his belly the closer they came to Marseilles. If it had not been for the wretched girl who rode beside him, he would have taken ship from Cartagena or Valencia to Italy, and avoided Henri of Navarre's troubled kingdom altogether.

They reached Marseilles in the early summer, riding down from the high white cliffs, entering the gates to a chorus of inquisitive questions from an officious captain of the guard. Having given his nationality as Genoese, and his business as a sail-maker, and having addressed a silent Serafina as Giovanni, and given a host of increasingly imaginative answers to increasingly irritating questions, Thomas was finally allowed to ride out into the early afternoon sunlight.

It was a feast-day: hautboy and tambour, viol and flute shrieked in the glaring oppressive heat. He saw Serafina blink and bow her head at the noise and the light. Thomas, however, felt his heart lighten at the prospect of casting off the last and most ludicrous of his shackles. Soon he would no longer have to play the incongruous role of nursemaid, soon he would be free to use the gift the sea had so providentially bestowed on him.

Because of the festival, they had to dismount and leave their horses at an inn, before pushing their way on foot through the crowded streets. Thomas had hold of Serafina's elbow: masked figures jostled them, satyrs, and maenads, and two-headed beasts. Serafina had hardly spoken a word all day. She had shown neither fear nor happiness, but had simply closed in on herself, hardly troubling to reply when Thomas spoke. Not that he cared: he could smell the scent of salt and fish and pitch in the air, see a distant tangle of masts against a blue sky whenever they were released from the dark narrow alleyways and into the open squares.

Marseilles was a possibility. The question of where to build his ship had occupied Thomas since the conversation in the tavern. Serafina had, annoyingly, been right. He would not build the *Kingfisher* in Spain, to be used in a second armada against his country; neither would he make ships for the Ottoman empire, because to do so would be to lose, like Kara Ali, his name, his religion, his independence. At the same time, to return to England to build a ship financed with stolen Levant Company money would be, to say the least, tactless. There was also the hot-tempered Edward Whitlock. No, thought Thomas, the *Kingfisher* would be his, from her naming in the deserts of North Africa to the moment she skimmed through the waves, her hold heavy with coral, silks, and spices. He would carry freight for others, but he would not relinquish ownership.

Marseilles – Thomas sniffed the warm salty air as he let Serafina lead him through the streets – Marseilles might do. Marseilles had dockyards, timber and supplies of linen for sails. Marseilles was a centre of trade, a pivot point between the Levant and the north.

But there was a tension, an expectation of violence, in the hot, crowded streets. Thomas, whose only concern with politics was in how it affected trade, found that he kept his palm on the hilt of his knife, his footsteps away from the darkest doorways, the loneliest alleys. A silk-capped merchant tried to push his way through the crowds on horseback, and Thomas heard the unconcealed curses, saw the jostling of the crowd, the ugly expressions on the faces of the men. He was glad of the anonymity of his broadcloth and leather.

They emerged from a narrow alleyway into a wide square, and Thomas saw Serafina's eyes widen: with the great shining plain of the sky and the sea, with recollection.

He followed the direction of her gaze: across the square, beyond the stalls selling ribbons and comfits and ale, beyond the dancers and the jugglers, the sailors and their sweethearts. He saw a house, four storeys high, taller and wider than its neighbours, dominating one side of the square.

The Guardi house, presumably, and for the first time it occurred to Thomas that the Guardi were not mere pedlars, shunting the odd bale of cloth up and down the coast. Around the windows of the four-storeyed house were chevrons and

fleur-de-lys and diamonds, every one of them etched in gold-leaf
on the plaster-work. The entire front fascia sparkled in the
bright sunshine, as though the house were made of gold. Thomas
was reminded of princes' palaces in Venice. An outward show
of wealth, designed to impress and to demonstrate power.

He felt Serafina wriggle from his grasp like a fish, twisting
round the stalls and the street-sellers, winding through the jugglers and dancers and water-carriers and onion-sellers. He saw
her reach the steps of the golden house, and he waited for her to
run up and beat her fist on the door, for the tedious scenes of
Latin grief and joy to begin. He began to walk after her.

Thomas kept his eyes fixed on the small figure at the bottom
of the steps as he forced his way through the crowded market-
square. Serafina did not move, he could not understand why she
did not move. This was Marseilles, that house was surely her
home. The old renegade, Kara Ali, had blackmailed Thomas to
take her here. Yet when he reached her side, she had not climbed
the steps, she just stood there looking, for a long moment,
completely lost.

She did not speak until he said her name. Then, 'It's changed,'
she said. 'All changed –'

Thomas damped down the impatience that rose in him.
'You've been away a long time,' he said, kindly. He had seen, to
his surprise, fear in those opaque dark eyes, something he had
not yet encountered in her, not even on the sea voyage. He took
Serafina's small fisted hand in his in an attempt at comfort.

She pulled away from him as though his touch had stung her.
He saw her glance wildly about, and then she said, 'The baker –'
and began to walk away from the shuttered house. Crossly,
Thomas followed her.

'My dear girl,' he exclaimed, impatiently.

'I want to talk to the baker first,' she called back. 'Monsieur
Caillot is an old friend.'

More pushing and shoving through Marseilles's hot, bad-
tempered crowds. Someone thrust a bunch of lavender into
Thomas's face: Thomas, who had expected his freedom by now,
irritably pushed it away. He followed Serafina into the nearby
baker's shop.

The smell of bread and rolls and pâtisserie was delightful, but they had dined a half-hour before in the tavern. He watched Serafina greet the baker, and saw not a flicker of recognition on the broad red face. How could there be? With her short hair and breeches she would bear little resemblance to the infant who had sailed from Provence many years before. He thought that Serafina had recovered herself, her eyes were masked, invulnerable again. Soon she would find the courage to walk up the steps of her home. As they chattered away in fast Marseilles French, Thomas soon stopped listening. A girl, seventeen or so, sidled out from the bakery beyond, and began to pile loaves on the counter. Her firm breasts spilled out of her gown, her curly hair was lightened with flour. Every so often her eyes would flicker in Thomas's direction. Thomas smiled and nodded his head in a bow.

He had no time for any closer acquaintance, though, for he saw, to his utter amazement, Serafina lean forward and slide a loaf inside her jacket as the baker turned to address his daughter. Then she walked out of the shop, as cool as anything, leaving Thomas gaping like a fish.

The loaf was still warm against her skin, the sun beat down on her uncovered head. She made for the docks, because they were still the same. She heard the Englishman running after her, but she did not turn round.

He caught up with her as she sat down on a barrel, the sea glittering, flecked and frosted, just behind her. She could see that he was angry.

'And what the *hell* did you do that for?'

She did not know what he meant at first. The baker's words jangled through her head in rhythm with the music from the square; she did not wish to speak to Thomas Marlowe.

'*That,*' he said impatiently, pointing to the loaf.

It was still cradled like a baby inside her jacket. She could not imagine why he was making such a fuss. She had taken the loaf because there had been the opportunity to take the loaf.

'I thought we might be hungry later,' she said, wanting his silence.

He was not silent.'Hungry?' he said. 'Why should we be hungry? If we are hungry, then we have gold a-plenty to buy us food. Why risk getting us both thrown in some damned foreign gaol for the sake of a loaf of bread that neither of us needs?'

'He didn't see me,' she said scornfully. In one small swift movement she took the loaf from her jacket and dropped it into the sea below. She heard the pilot's hiss of exasperation, and saw him turn and walk away from her, running his fingers through his short curls. Serafina watched the loaf bob and then sink below the water, and wished that she could do the same.

She had, in the end, lacked the courage to introduce herself. The baker had not recognized her. Neither had his daughter, her playmate of childhood days. The baker had said, on being asked about that gilt, gaudy house, 'He's done a damn sight better for himself than that fool Franco ever did.'

He's done a damn sight better for himself than that fool Franco ever did. Franco was her father. *He* was Angelo.

'Serafina.'

She looked up on hearing her name, but at first could hardly recognize the Englishman, let alone answer him. The baker had said other things, but she would not let herself think of them yet.

She felt something pushed into her hands. She had not realized until she tasted the aqua vitae that she was shaking, trembling as though it were midwinter and not a bright summer day.

'Tell me,' said Thomas Marlowe.

She stared at him. She knew that he simply wanted his inconvenient duty discharged, that he resented this final, un-expected delay. She could see fragments of bread in the water below, not yet eaten by the seagulls.

The Englishman said, 'Your father is dead. You knew that. What of your mother – sisters – grandparents?'

She had never explained to him what she meant by *family*. Family was Franco and Marthe and Jehan and Monsieur Jacques and bales of silk to be transported under Guardi banners from Naples to Lyons. He seemed to expect an answer, though.

'My mother died when I was a child.' Serafina found she had

to force the words out. 'I had a nurse, Marthe. And a cousin, Angelo, who helped my father. And there was a notary called Jehan de Coniques, and a factor – Monsieur Jacques. No brothers, no sisters.'

'The notary – the factor –' The Englishman's voice was kind, he had knelt on the cobbles in front of her. 'Where are they?'

She did not even look at him. 'The baker said that things have been difficult here. That the people have grown to hate the merchants.'

She saw him glance back towards the square, to the milling, ragged crowds, to the house that glittered with gold-leaf. Her palms rested on her dirty breeches. She was quick, normally, understanding the first time things were explained to her, but she did not understand this. But some sort of answer was required, or she knew that the Englishman would haul her up the steps of that changed yet familiar house, and force her to a confrontation she did not wish anyone to witness.

So she told Thomas Marlowe, in words that were small and hard and did not show any duplicity, that the baker had said that times had been hard. That her family had been forced to sell. That the Guardi company did not exist any more. That there was nothing left.

William Williams, once ship's carpenter on board the unfortunate *Toby*, had, like his fellow-seaman the pilot, found the last few months trying. He was a Catholic, and although he was also an amiable, unaggressive man, his Catholicism was fixed, immutable, something that responded neither to persuasion nor threat.

On his eventual return to London, William Williams had found England no longer a safe haven for him. Someone – inspired by conviction, greed, or simple spite – had talked. Someone had noted his infrequent attendances at the Protestant church, someone had seen him in the company of a recusant priest, someone had caught the unfashionable flavour of his sort of religion. Whatever the cause, William Williams had found it advisable to return to sea within a fortnight of his homecoming.

His travels had taken him, eventually, to Marseilles. In Marseilles, it was quite acceptable to be a Catholic. Marseilles might have become enmeshed in the sour tragedy of civil war, but, despite superficial appearances, much of that war was concerned with the ownership of power and wealth, not religion. The dangers of Marseilles were different to, and much less predictable than, those of London. In Marseilles, a man could sit in a dock-side tavern and sip his ale, and not have to fear the tap of cold fingers on his shoulder, the knock on his door at night. Here, the danger was of being caught up in someone else's quarrel, of finding a knife in your back because a stranger had taken a dislike to the expression on your face, the cut of your clothes.

Few men chose to pick a quarrel with William Williams, however. William was six feet of placid Welsh brawn, his muscles hardened by his trade, his head still clear after four pints of ale. He neither feared nor enjoyed fighting: he did not need the release of tension that other men seemed to find in conflict, but he was perfectly capable of defending himself, if necessary. There would be a fight tonight – the ship's carpenter would have bet the contents of his purse on that – but William Williams had no intention of taking part in it. There would be a fight because it was hot, and a feast-day, and Marseilles was constantly spoiling for a fight. The war, the conspicuous wealth of the merchants, provided an excuse, that was all. During his three-week sojourn at the port, the ship's carpenter had seen one merchant dragged off his horse and beaten to death by the crowd, others who refused to leave their doors without an armed retinue.

No merchant, however, would have entered this tavern. There were taverns like this in London, in Dieppe, in Livorno, places where any seaman would feel instantly at home, and anyone else know instantly that they did not belong. There was a trio of pretty serving-wenches, a choleric tapster, and a card-school that William strongly suspected of foul play. He could almost have been in Greenwich.

The fight, thought William, as he raised his tankard for the prettiest serving-wench to refill it, would begin with the card-school. The ship's carpenter's French was poor, but tone of voice and gesture were the same in any language. The card-school had recently been enlarged to include a fifth. That fifth, wearing a battered quilted doublet and an equally battered black felt hat, had his back to William Williams. He was reminded of someone, but he could not yet think of whom. The newcomer would not be a Marseillais, he would be a foreigner, and the Marseillais would fleece him. Sometimes there was a scuffle, at other times the innocent wisely accepted his losses. Occasionally, guessed William Williams, there was a body dumped in the cool secret waters of the docks, late at night.

He thought the hour to be about ten o'clock. The festival still roared and whirled through the town, and the tavern was so full the doors could not be closed. William Williams raised his tankard in glad farewell to France, and saw the fifth card-player also rise, his cards neatly fanned face-down on the table. The man was not going to accept his losses meekly. Instead, he was addressing his fellow-players, the words so low and over-polite that the ship's carpenter could make out none of them. But again, there was that nagging itch of recognition. The fifth card-player – all aggressive stance and well-chosen words, his palm a half-inch away from his knife – definitely reminded William Williams of someone.

Thomas Marlowe. William Williams recalled the navigator as the card-players found their daggers, and table, cards and ale flew into the air. That man reminded William of Thomas Marlowe, pilot of the *Toby*. But Thomas, along with almost forty others, had drowned on the Barbary coast. They had buried none of the corpses they had later found, but they had salvaged some of the cargo. They had been forced to.

William found, almost to his surprise, that he too was standing, and that his dagger was in his hand. Half the tavern seemed to have already joined in the fuss, but a small space had miraculously cleared now amid the straw and litter. Thomas Marlowe had always been an aggressive little bastard. But Thomas Marlowe was dead.

By now, everyone in the tavern had a knife or a sword in their hand, or their fingers were curled into fists. One of the serving-wenches was hitting someone over the head with an ale-flagon. The fifth card-player's knife sank into his adversary's stomach, who swayed, his fingers threaded over the wound, before he toppled to the ground. Reminding himself that Thomas Marlowe had drowned, the ship's carpenter still found himself wading across the room.

The card-players' friend was undoubtedly dead: they undoubtedly wanted revenge. William Williams dispatched one of them with a huge and well-placed fist; the other two had flung themselves on top of the man who looked like Thomas Marlowe. By the time William hauled the two of them off and booted them the length of the room, even Thomas's long-dead and long-suffering mother would have found it difficult to recognize her son.

William Williams did, however. He took the two sides of the battered doublet in his hands, lugged the *Toby*'s pilot to his feet, and dragged him through the open doors of the tavern. And then, outside in the street, hidden in the darkness of a doorway, he dusted the navigator down, set him on his feet, and said, 'Thomas. Welcome to France.'

Only that morning, it had all seemed so easy. She would ride through the walls of Marseilles, down La Canebière, and up to the door of her home. And there they would be: Marthe, and Angelo, and Monsieur Jacques, and Monsieur de Coniques.

The events of the past repeated themselves over and over again in Serafina's aching head as she slid silently out of the tavern and through Marseilles's dark busy streets. Her father's announcement of her betrothal, the winter of preparation, the journey. And Angelo, always Angelo. Angelo at the dinner-table, his handsome face shuttered as her father made his announcement; Angelo on the hillside, placing a garland of rosemary and bindweed on her head. Once, she had wanted to marry Angelo. Angelo had lifted her on to his Spanish jennet, Angelo had ridden ahead of her, a single feather nodding on his scarlet cap. *Always your friend*, Angelo had said, kissing her. *What else would I be?*

Only Angelo and Monsieur de Coniques remained now. The baker had told her that Marthe had died within a year of her capture, and that Monsieur Jacques had left the Guardi long ago.

But there was much worse. She had lied to Thomas Marlowe

later, at the quayside. The company had not been sold. The company thrived and it was Angelo's. And Angelo was neither a caretaker nor a purchaser. He was an inheritor.

The baker had told her that in the afternoon, terrible words over the comforting smells of flour and salt and new bread. He had then said, *He's done a damn sight better for himself than that fool Franco ever did.*

Thus the glittering gold-leaf on the house. *Her* house.

The house still shone even in the night. The sconces on the walls caught the sheen of it; it glistened in the distant light of the candles in the square. It was quiet outside the Guardi house, a small oasis of silence in the fevered noise of the city. Serafina's head throbbed, her eyes hurt, as they once had at Algiers. There were other voices, too, apart from the baker's. Kara Ali's said, *I think you should consider, little one, who might profit by your father's death.*

She sat down on the lowest step, her aching head resting against the cool iron railing. She did not know why she had come here. The masked faces in the square seemed creatures of nightmare; she had spent too long away from the clamour of the city. Did she intend to confront Angelo? To say, 'Give it back, it is mine'? To which he, supposedly, would reply, 'Take it, I have looked after it for you, chérie'?

She was almost too tired to care. It was late in the evening, and she had travelled for months. Her hair was tangled and sour-smelling, her clothes felt stiff with dirt and sweat. She had not yet grieved for Marthe, she had not yet, in truth, grieved for her father. She had expected to do that here, at home.

She was not aware that her eyelids had closed, that time had passed, until she heard the voices in the street. When she woke, Serafina saw that there were two men standing under the light of the sconces on the opposite wall. One was young and handsome, with dark curling hair to his shoulders, a red cap and a slashed and quilted doublet. The other was Angelo.

The Angelo of her recollection, of her dreams. His dark gold hair curled beneath a feathered hat, his short blue cloak was slung carelessly over a white silk shirt. He carried a filigreed rapier, a jewelled dagger. He had not changed at all.

Serafina heard the stranger say, 'There, a pretty boy left like a bale of silk for our collection. Broaden your mind a little, my dear – taste *that* for a night.'

And Angelo, casting one short, endless glance, said, 'Dieu, Pietro – I'd as soon sleep with my mare. At least she only stinks of horse-shit.'

His face felt like someone had danced a jig on it. When he had emptied enough salt water over himself to be able to see and think clearly, Thomas looked at the ship's carpenter, and said, '*Will*. Christ – how did you –?'

'A different route to you, I think, my friend.' The Welshman grinned. 'I thought you were picking coral along with our late lamented master.'

'The injudicious Mr Goodlay?' Thomas shook his head, and winced.

'So you've not been back to England?' The carpenter's eyes were interested, speculative.

Thomas avoided them. 'No. You, Will?'

'For a while. But I was not made welcome.'

He said no more, and after a few moments Thomas realized the subject was closed. 'The others –' the pilot said, recalling the *Toby*, smashed to matchwood on unfriendly black rocks.

'A dozen survived.' They had begun to walk along the harbourside, so that the tavern was soon only a pinpoint of light in the distance. 'It was bad, Thomas. The Moroccans made us salvage the wreck, and then they threw us into prison in Fez. Two of us died of the bloody flux there. The rest got home – eventually.'

Thomas rubbed his chin thoughtfully. William Williams was, he reminded himself, an excellent ship's carpenter. 'What'll you do now, Will?'

Williams glanced back to the tavern and grinned again. 'Leave Marseilles,' he said. 'I've heard Livorno's a friendly place.'

Thomas wished he had not drunk, wished he had not fought. Then he might have thought a little clearer. Livorno was a freeport, a city of Duke Ferdinand of Tuscany's creation. There were dockyards and men and trade to be found at Livorno.

'When?' Thomas asked.

'Tomorrow. I'm setting sail tomorrow. On board a nice little cog called the *Louise*.'

Thomas had begun to smile, with difficulty, even before William added, 'I'm sure there'd be room for a navigator.' And then he recalled the wretched girl, so he made his arrangements, and ran back through Marseilles to the tavern.

Serafina finished dressing only a few moments before the English pilot beat upon her door. She steeled herself then: no sign of injury, no sign of pain.

They must have both gawped at each other, though, as he flung open the door and came into the room. She, because his face looked as though it had been used as a battering ram; he, because she was wearing a gown.

Serafina found her tongue first. 'A pleasant evening, Mr Marlowe?'

She saw him scowl.

'Useful,' he said and, glancing round the room, added, 'You've packed.'

She nodded, made herself smile. 'I'm leaving tomorrow, Mr Marlowe. I'm going to live with my nurse. You remember – Marthe.'

His blackened eyes returned slowly to her. He had not looked at her like that before. 'Good,' he said absently. He did not, she thought with satisfaction, even question the lie.

'So you may go,' she added, making herself clear.

'Ah.' He seemed about to quarrel, to show resentment at being dismissed so lightly, but he said nothing. Instead, surprising her, he swept his hat from his head as he took her hand and kissed it. 'Your servant, mademoiselle,' said Thomas Marlowe in farewell, and left her.

The room seemed achingly empty when he had gone. But the music from the square below had grown louder, as though every cracked flute and badly tuned viol had gathered together in Marseilles that night. Odd words, phrases, filtered up from the crowds and through the open window. All the nationalities of the known world collected in Marseilles, all the tongues of

Christendom drifted through the evening air. But Serafina knew a different language, and it was a phrase from the lingua franca of the bagnios that pounded through her head in rhythm with the music of the dance, the laughter of the streets. *Todo mangiado*, they had said in Algiers, in Oran. *Todo mangiado*.

Slowly, she rose from the bed and went to the window. She had bought the gown in the market with the last of the gold the physician had given her, because she did not ever want another man to look at her as Angelo had looked at her. Reflected in those judicious dark eyes she had been nothing, nothing at all. A creature of no name, no country, no sex.

The people in the square below had formed a dance: long lines of it twisted like a serpent, as far as the eye could see. She did not know where she would go, what she would do. She was a stranger in her own country, she was disinherited.

Todo mangiado. Lost beyond recall.

PART IV

1594−5

A COMMODIOUS HAVEN

The Duke hath a Commodious haven at Ligorno a Citty newly built and fortified, but the Florentines have no Traffick at Sea, but have their goods exported by forraine merchants, who likewise bring them victuals and other necessaryes.

Itinerary: Fynes Moryson

On the coast of Tuscany lay the port of Livorno. Once a fever-town, lost in insect-infested marshes, Cosimo de Medici had built the harbour at Livorno, and his son Ferdinand, Duke of Tuscany, had declared the town a freeport.

Livorno had flourished; at Livorno you could buy and sell anything. Grain, silk, linen, gold, silver, and, of course, people. Livorno had its bagnios, just as Algiers did, and Livorno had its galleys, crewed by both Moslem and Christian slaves. Contra-band cargo – guns, saltpetre, or shot – could be bought or sold at Livorno, and so could the profits of piracy. The new trading companies of the north needed Livorno, a convenient halfway point between the Atlantic and the Levant. All the nations of Christendom gathered at the docksides, a noisy, quar-relsome, undisciplined market-place of skills and strength. Greeks and Corsicans, English and Dutch, crewed the merchant vessels that sailed the Mediterranean.

In the November of 1594, the sky was a pure deep blue, the sun glittered cold on the tiled roofs, and on the pale green marshes bordering the coast. The dockyards were busy in winter, refitting both galleys and roundships, building new vessels to replace those sunk in storms or lost to the corsair. Barrels of pitch, coils of rope, sacks of hemp and bales of linen were stocked in the warehouses and quaysides. The sun caught the gilded prows of the galleys, the furled sails and rigging of the caravels, galleasses and cogs, as they gently rose and fell on the swelling sea. There was the sound of saw and hammer, the smell of pitch and burning coal. The docks were crowded with men: carpenters and rope-makers, sail-makers and blacksmiths, caulkers and coopers.

On one of the dry docks, the keel, sternpost, and ground timbers of a galleon were laid out like the sun-bleached skeleton of a fish. Not far from the unfinished ship, William Williams bent over a section of wood, saw in hand. At his side, his apprentice, an olive-skinned, curly-headed lad of fifteen or so, fidgeted with set-square and measure on the flagstones.

When, after an uneventful voyage from Marseilles, Thomas Marlowe had shown him the plans for the galleon, William Williams, fifteen years a sailor, and longer a craftsman, had been able to recognize the *Kingfisher*'s potential. A less understanding man might have laughed at the naked enthusiasm on the younger man's face, a less imaginative man might have disregarded inspiration and intuition, and questioned youth, lack of experience, lack of connections. To himself, William had merely briefly questioned the gold that Thomas's battered quilted doublet had contained; but only briefly, because the ways of God were mysterious. Five months ago, their first evening in Livorno had been spent poring over plans in a dockside tavern; since then, William had not regretted the decision he had made that night. Shipbuilding was the only trade he knew, and if he could no longer work in the country of his birth, well then, he would work in Italy for one of his countrymen.

Progress on the ship had been pleasing, if unspectacular. It had taken time for Thomas to gather together the best carpenters, the best blacksmiths, but in this he had been patient, refusing to accept the second-rate. William himself had found a promising, if tiresome, young apprentice in Cristofano – the boy had the faults of every lad of his years: excessive energy, an overactive tongue, and an inability to concentrate if within half a league of a pretty woman. But he was apt and intelligent, and not afraid of hard work.

Straightening up from the plank of wood, William spat on his hands, and waited for Thomas, now threading his way through the clutter, to join him.

'*April*,' said the pilot, tearing off his hat and throwing it to the ground. '*April*, God damn it –'

'Ah.' William Williams threw a few more coals on to the brazier: despite the colour of the sky and the brightness of the sun, the air was bitterly cold. Cristofano grinned and, after a well-aimed kick from William, began to measure out the next section of rib.

Thomas's eyes, the deep blue of the Inland Sea in summer, glittered angrily. His breath clouded the air as he spoke.

'I said to him, how can you build a ship without wood? The man's supposed to be a wood-merchant, for Christ's sake.'

'There are other wood-merchants.' William, who had known Thomas, his perfectionism and his temper for some time now, looked at the pilot doubtfully. 'What did he say?'

Thomas's voice hissed in unkind imitation. 'He said, I cannot make the trees grow, Messer Marlowe. Only the good Lord himself can do that.'

He glared across the burning coals at William, throwing out his hands in a gesture of exasperation. 'To which I blasphemed, he exclaimed in pious horror, I swore, he sent for his servants –'

'– and they threw you out of the house,' finished William, calmly.

Cristofano, a talented but not altogether tactful youth, snorted. There was a flagon of wine warming at the edge of the brazier. Thomas, glowering, took it between his gloved hands, and sat down on a nearby barrel.

'Something like that,' he acknowledged ruefully. 'The man was no bloody use to me, anyway.'

The carpenter said nothing, but went back to his apprentice and his saw, leaving Thomas to drink away some of his bad temper. Thomas possessed unlimited energy, but a horribly limited store of patience. He was right, though, you could not build a ship without wood, even a ship as economical and beautiful as the *Kingfisher*.

It was an ever-present, nagging problem, the shortage of wood, the one canker on the smooth unblemished prospect that Livorno had offered. Planing a section of the strong Tuscan oak necessary for the best merchant ships, checking the measurements that Cristofano had made, William knew that the pilot's anxiety was not misplaced. A shortage of oak for shipbuilding had plagued Tuscany for many years. Lack of good-quality wood could sink a ship, both literally and figuratively. A ship devoured wood with consummate greed. The keel, keelson, ground timbers and ribs – more than a hundred of them – might each be over a foot and a half in width. Delays in construction meant that valuable contracts were lost, schedules were not met, unnecessary fees and wages were paid while men and docks stood idle. You could not borrow money on the strength of a ship that was half built, on timber-yards that were empty. And William Williams guessed that Thomas had not money enough – whatever its source – to cover unexpected delays.

He watched Thomas rise to his feet, the bottle put aside, the ill-humour vanished as quickly as it had appeared.

'You're right, Will. There are other wood-merchants.' The pilot retrieved his hat, plonked it on top of his untidy curls, and let his gaze rest on the nearby raw timber outline of his ship. 'And I'll visit every damn one of them, if necessary.'

In December the merchant Jacopo Capriani returned, after many delays caused by sickness and the poor condition of the roads, to his home town of Pisa. His journey had begun almost nine months before: an elaborate, carefully planned odyssey endured for the sole purpose of making money.

Messer Capriani traded in semi-precious stones and fancy goods. Coral and amber and antelope's tears; silken gew-gaws from the hot south of Italy. In Naples he bought cockades and ribbons, braid and silk knots, fripperies for the gentlemen and ladies of Italy and France. He travelled by land, the finery packed into panniers on mule trains from Naples to Marseilles, returning to Pisa, a convenient halfway point, for four or five months of each year. In every town or city he knew the merchants or their factors or agents. He would visit the trading fairs, and the houses of the richest families, spreading out his goods like a treasure map in front of them. But he would also stop in the smallest village, the poorest hamlet. A few lire, a couple of sous for a ribbon did no harm to the balance sheet; an extra coin or two weighted the coffers just a little bit more.

Messer Capriani owned a house in Pisa, and smaller dwellings in Marseilles and Naples. Between those cities, he stayed in whatever inns and hostelries the open road offered. Never the best – the purpose of the odyssey was to make money, not to spend it – but not the worst, either, because a merchant needed to present a confident face to the world. His house in Pisa was a decent size – not ostentatious; Messer Capriani disliked ostentation – but sufficiently large to take him and his household in reasonable comfort.

He was a widower: his wife, whom he could barely remember, having died many years before whilst failing to produce their first child. Since then, Jacopo Capriani had seen no reason to marry again, but had taken what pleasure he needed in the arms of Pisa's less expensive courtesans. He was long finished with that, though: it was years since he had lain with a woman. He had servants enough to feed him and clothe him and care for him during his occasional bouts of swamp fever; he had no wish to endure a wife's nonsensical prattle over the dinner-table.

Messer Capriani had not travelled alone, of course. He had taken cooks because his stomach was delicate, and maidservants because he was of an age when a comfortable bed and well-aired clothes were important. And he had taken an armed guard because the roads were bad and his cargo was valuable. And three clerks to keep track of all the complicated transactions.

One of Messer Capriani's clerks was, unusually, a woman. Her name was Serafina.

In a tavern in Livorno, Thomas Marlowe was celebrating. The six months since he had arrived in Italy had been characterized by an uneven, halting progress, a mixture of frustration and exhilaration that would have been exhausting to a less energetic man. Thomas, however, had thrived on the rapid succession of setbacks and triumphs, battling against lack of imagination or lack of commitment in others with a fervour only comprehensible to those who, like him, had dragged themselves up from mediocrity.

The nearness of his dream had given him the resilience, and sometimes, the patience, to endure countless obstacles. The shortage of wood had been the most worrying of those obstacles, resolved only today after a fortnight spent scouring the dockyards and streets of Pisa and Livorno. Now, assisted by William

Williams, the apprentice Cristofano, and a number of other men involved in the construction of the *Kingfisher*, Thomas was celebrating his success.

'The best Tuscan oak, and enough to take us through to the spring at least,' he finished triumphantly, and emptied his third tankard of ale.

Cristofano, elegantly gangling in linen shirt and multicoloured hose, stood on the bench and shouted for the potboy. Rufus, the one-eyed Scots blacksmith and a man of few words, spat on the floor.

William Williams, always practical, said softly, 'The price?'

Thomas grimaced and shook his head. 'Too much, of course. With half the shipwrights in Italy desperate for wood, I could hardly expect a bargain.' His voice was low, barely audible over the chatter and occasional shriek of conversation in the tavern. 'I had no choice, Will. To keep men idle costs money.'

They both drank for a moment, silent. It was a saint's day, and the dockside tavern was crowded. Outside, an unpleasant grey sleet blurred the outline of the ships; inside, the crush of people made the low-ceilinged room overheated.

'Your inheritance —' began William, and Thomas grinned. A convenient term, coined some months ago, to describe the golden driftwood that more than a year ago the sea and the wreck of the *Toby* had bestowed on him.

Thomas, who had drunk enough not to care too much, said lightly, 'There's not a lot of it left.'

His head had begun to feel pleasantly blurred, and the glow of relief he had felt on finding a new source of wood had not yet left him. Finding the gold, Thomas now realized, had been only the first step. The rest of it was organization, and luck, and bloody hard work. The long trail from the wreck of the *Toby* on the Barbary coast to his arrival last summer in Livorno seemed insignificant now, important only as a means, not an end. He knew that tomorrow he must begin again to worry about money, to plan against the ever-present possibility that the *Kingfisher* would remain impotent, an unplanked hull on an Italian dockside.

'I'll begin looking for contracts,' said Thomas, staring into his empty glass. 'But I'll not sell her, Will. I'll keep control.' Thomas recalled the slender, graceful shape that was growing from the dry dock. 'When the merchants see her, they'll be queuing up to hire her,' he added, with the confidence only four pints of ale can give. 'You'll see. I'll start calling on them tomorrow.'

William grinned, his broad face lightening. 'Aye,' he said. 'If you can walk.'

Thomas had risen to his feet, clapped his hat on his head. 'A call of nature,' he said, enunciating the words with care. He found that he felt particularly pleased with himself, and knew that he had not realized the extent of his worries until he had resolved them.

There had been a very pretty chambermaid in the wood-merchant's house. It occurred to Thomas, weaving his way through the throng, that he might call there again later that night. He had lived, he considered, like a monk since his arrival in Livorno – since he had sailed from North Africa, in fact. He had admired the elegant madonnas as they sat at their upstairs windows, and had then recalled Faith Whitlock and the legendary jealousy of Italian husbands. He had not been able to afford the courtesans, and he had no wish to buy himself a present of the pox from a dockside whore. He was recalling optimistically the wood-merchant's chambermaid's thick fair hair when someone upended a flagon of wine over his shirt-front.

Thomas saw a thin, arrogant face, voluminous black robes, and a narrow-bladed knife held against his own soaking shirt. He heard French curses, liberally mixed with complaints about his own carelessness. The tip of the knife, which shook a little, was rather too close for comfort. Made unusually tolerant by relief and alcohol, Thomas managed a conciliatory smile, and extended his hands in a gesture of apology.

'A thousand pardons. My mistake, of course.'

The owner of the knife was, Thomas realized, even more drunk than he. There was a short pause, in which Thomas made ready to reach for his own dagger and call for his men, and then the other man muttered, 'You should learn to look where you are going.'

Thomas gently pushed aside the knife. He felt unusually

magnanimous, at peace with the world. Bowing, he said, 'Let me buy you another pint of claret to make amends, Monsieur – ?'

'– de Coniques,' said the stranger, reluctantly.

The flicker of recollection struck Thomas as he took the empty flagon from the stranger's hand, and called for the tapster to refill it. But it was not until he was outside and alone and breathing in the cold, sleet-edged air, that he remembered.

The girl Serafina, whom he had escorted from the North African coast to Marseilles for the renegade physician, Kara Ali. In Marseilles, she had stolen a loaf from a baker's shop and, sitting on a barrel at the dockside, had told him about her family. The cousin, the factor, and the notary. The notary had been called Jehan de Coniques. And that man, that boorish, aggressive drunkard, had worn notary's robes.

Thomas had scarcely thought of Serafina Guardi since he had left her in Marseilles – no, since he had been *dismissed* by her in Marseilles. He thought of her now, though, and found that he recalled with unexpected vividness that last night, the only time of their acquaintance when he had seen her dressed in a gown. For most of their journey from North Africa to France, he had scarcely thought of Serafina as female – she had been a child, a slave, sometimes even a stable-boy. But on the night before Thomas had sailed for Livorno, she had worn a dark, severe gown, and she had done something clever with her short hair, and he had experienced again that unsought but indisputable interest that had caught at him only once before, on the tartane. In the tartane it had been the feel of her, draped over him, defenceless; in Marseilles, all defences had been up and bristling, warning him off. But, surprised himself at his own understanding, he had recognized passion in those insouciant dark eyes, and some sort of scarcely contained emotion

Still, he had been glad to be rid of her. Turning away from the waterfront, adjusting his sticky, sour-smelling clothing, Thomas admitted to himself that the incident with the loaf had shocked him. Not because of the value of the thing – God knew, he had stolen gold worth several hundred times the price of a loaf of bread – but because of the ease, the casualness, with which she had taken it. As though you took something not from need, but simply because it was there, and you had the opportunity.

Monsieur de Coniques, though. Thomas stared out to sea, at the chill mist that wreathed the darkening ships, at the hazed reflections of the flares in the blurred water. If that man had been Serafina's Monsieur de Coniques, then he was still a notary, even if he no longer worked for the Guardi.

Thomas, who had the sort of curiosity that takes men across oceans, returned to the tavern.

The notary was still there, curled up in a corner with the flagon of claret Thomas had bought for him.

'Jehan,' said Thomas, and the man looked up.

Thomas sat on the bench opposite, knowing immediately from the notary's expression that his instinct had been correct. The tavern was still busy: elbows jolted Thomas's back, and the air was thick with smoke from the fire. This corner was quiet enough, though, guarded by raw brick wall on two sides, lit by a single candle on the table-top. Thomas placed a second bottle of wine between himself and the Frenchman. He would satisfy his curiosity and leave, he told himself. The fellow reminded him of some grotesque black insect, all dry rustling fabric and loose grey skin.

'I know your master,' said Thomas easily. 'Franco Guardi.'

His eyes did not leave the other man's face. He guessed Jehan de Coniques to be somewhere in his mid-thirties, ten or so years older than he. The Frenchman's face was marked by bitterness, furrows seaming his skin from the corners of his eyes to his cheekbones, from the narrow chiselled nostrils to the wine-blackened lips. Thomas almost said, 'I met Franco Guardi's daughter a few months ago.'

But something held him back, and the notary, not looking up from his cup, muttered, 'Franco's dead. The company's Angelo's now.'

Angelo, thought Thomas with a further effort of recollection, had been Serafina's illegitimate cousin. He took another mouthful of wine. Jehan de Coniques was as drunk as a sow: he must be confused. The Guardi business did not belong to Serafina's cousin Angelo, because the Guardi business no longer existed. He knew that because Serafina herself had told him so, sitting on the dockside at Marseilles.

'Franco's dead?' said Thomas, pretending mild surprise. 'There was a daughter, wasn't there?'

Briefly, he had the notary's attention. Grey eyes that away from alcohol would have been sharp and clever, glanced up at him, studying him for the first time.

'The girl's dead, too,' said Jehan de Coniques. His voice was rasping and dry. 'Died the same time as her father.'

'Oh.' Thomas refilled both cups. 'The plague?'

'No. Damned Algerian corsairs,' said the notary and, wiping his mouth on the back of his sleeve, sniggered.

The hairs on the back of Thomas's neck stood upright. He knew suddenly that something was wrong, that something always had been wrong, and that, stupidly, he had failed to acknowledge it. But he made his voice remain easy, normal.

'Then the business was sold?'

'No.' Irritably, Jehan de Coniques raised his cup to his mouth. 'I said, *Angelo* owns it. Angelo owns everything.'

Thomas's hand, curled round his cup, clenched. So Serafina had lied to him that day in Marseilles. The Guardi company still existed, the Guardi company, realized Thomas, remembering the golden house, flourished. Earlier, in the Spanish tavern, Serafina had told him that it was all hers, that she was the sole beneficiary of her father's death. Yet she had refused to climb the steps of her own house. She had lied to him, motivelessly and deliberately, and to Thomas's surprise, the knowledge of her deception angered him.

'The girl had a nurse, didn't she?' asked Thomas, burrowing like a mole in matters best left alone. 'Marthe –'

'Dead too. Died the day she learned her precious Serafina wasn't going to come back.' Jehan de Coniques peered into his empty glass and, grinning, added, 'Angelo's a clever bastard.'

So she had lied more than once. *I'm going to live with my nurse*, Serafina had said in Marseilles, hardly bothering to glance at him. And the nurse, Marthe, was long dead. Thomas, watching the notary, felt his skin prickle and grow cold. He had seen at last with glaring certainty what was wrong, what had always been wrong. Serafina – and her father – should have been ransomed. Someone – charming cousin Angelo, for instance – should have paid Guardi money to release them from their captivity. But no one had, and instead, Serafina had been left to moulder for six years on the North African coast, while her father, according to Kara Ali, had died in the bagnio.

The noise of the tavern had become an irritating irrelevancy. Thomas's mind raced. He had wasted three months of his life on that girl, and yet he knew now that he had only understood a tiny part of the game she played. Serafina had lied comprehensively to him; Serafina had not stayed in Marseilles with her nurse, and the Guardi company had not ceased to trade. She had merely fed him the bait he was most likely to accept and he, poor fish, had swallowed it. Muddled with anger and distance and alcohol, Thomas said, 'The girl – Franco's daughter – why was she travelling? Surely she should have been at home?'

The notary shifted in his seat with a rustle of stained taffeta. 'Serafina was to be married. She was travelling to Italy to become betrothed to Michele Corsini. Franco Guardi bought silk from the Corsini workshops, of course.'

Jehan de Coniques had slumped in his chair, his eyes half closed. Thomas saw pieces scattered around him like a child's puzzle, and he struggled to discover what pattern they made. He knew, with the same deep sense of unease that told him of a coming storm, that Serafina had lied, and that it was all wrong. So Serafina had been sailing from France to Italy to be married. A child of – what? – nine or ten, travelling across the sea to become betrothed to some rich Tuscan lordling. And how mighty convenient for cousin Angelo that the corsair had taken the Guardi ship . . .

Too convenient. Another possibility struck Thomas as though he had been hit by a wave of icy water. He said carefully, 'So the corsair took the Guardi ships before Franco's daughter was betrothed?'

'Before she was betrothed,' repeated the notary. The light from the single candle on the table dug pits and hollows into his skin. 'I told you he was a clever bastard . . .'

Thomas took one rapid indrawn breath. Jehan de Coniques's eye-sockets were cavernous, his smile fixed, teeth bared. He looked, thought Thomas, staring at him, as though Death was already tapping prematurely at his shoulder, peeling the flesh away to show the skull beneath.

'Who are you?' said the notary, suddenly. There was a gleam of intelligence, of suspicion, behind the blurred grey gaze. 'Are you a clever bastard too?'

Thomas shook his head. He did not feel in the least clever, only fooled and foolish. 'Just a mariner. A navigator.' He was surprised to find that his own hand was unsteady as he raised the bottle of wine to his mouth.

'She was an arrogant little bitch,' added the notary unexpectedly. He sniggered again, and looked up at Thomas. 'Thought herself better than the rest of us. I expect a few nights in the seraglio showed her what she was really good for.'

Thomas's head jerked up. Jehan de Coniques's eyes were filled with a hollow laughter. Thomas was swamped by an almost physical disgust: the appearance of the notary, the dawning realization of the web of deceit and betrayal that Kara Ali had involved him in, nauseated him.

Finding that he was losing the last vestiges of his self-control, Thomas rose, nodding a bow to the notary. He did not return to his colleagues, but walked instead to the dockside, to breathe in the clean damp night air.

Numbers, cool rows of figures in a ledger, were a solace, a remedy for pain. Serafina, sitting alone in the accounting-room of Jacopo Capriani's Pisan house late one night, wrote the final figure and sprinkled sand on the paper.

When the ink was dry she closed the book, and went to draw the curtains. Pausing for a moment in front of the window, Serafina could see the town of Pisa, and before it her own reflection in the darkened glass. Both wavered slightly, made imperfect by the minute flaws and uneven thickness of the glass. But she could distinguish shining dark hair under a modest headdress, a plain grey gown outlining a small but curving body.

No longer a slave, nor a stable-boy. Her skin was a smooth golden-brown after a summer spent travelling, her eyes were still black pools, expressionless. No one looked at her now as Angelo had looked at her. She had lost everything once: what little she had clawed back she would not let anyone take from her. She would not let them close enough to try.

She had begun as a maidservant to Messer Capriani, hiring herself to him at the fair at Marseilles the previous summer. She, who had served in Kara Ali's kitchens for many years, had found the work easy enough; but soon, remembering Kara Ali, she had made sure that the merchant had found out that she could read and write. She had taken a few letters for him when one of his clerks had been sick. The clerk had been a fool, she had discovered mistakes in Messer Capriani's precious account-books and, innocently pointing out the errors to her employer, had found herself relieved of housework, and sitting on a clerk's stool in the counting-house. Her languages had been useful, too. She had passed herself off as French to the merchant and his household, but her additional knowledge of Latin, Italian, and Arabic had ensured her a more comfortable life than she otherwise might have expected. There were some things that no one, however lucky, could take from you.

For it had been luck, blind, arbitrary luck that had given the future to Angelo and taken it from Serafina. Angelo had always been an opportunist. Luck had placed the galley *Gabrielle* in the path of the corsair. By the time he received the ransom demand, Angelo would have already controlled the day-to-day running of the company for some months. He would have enjoyed that, would have taken pleasure in it, perhaps even discovered he could do some things better than Franco Guardi. Then, heaven-sent, fate had presented him with the opportunity to continue running the company for ever. He had, simply, to ensure that Franco and his daughter never returned from North Africa. To the corsairs' eventual ransom demand he would have replied simply, 'No, kill them.' And sent money, no doubt, to guarantee the success of his request. To anyone who asked, Angelo would simply have said that the Infidel had killed Franco and Serafina Guardi, or that they had died of a fever in the bagnios of

Algiers. Sometimes Serafina thought she could understand
Angelo, indeed, could almost sympathize with him. So would
she take whatever favourable opportunities fate presented to her.
It was only that, in her case, fate had not been quite so generous.

She had been glad to leave Marseilles last summer, glad to
journey to the country she had first set sail for almost eight years
before. If she thought of the past at all, Serafina thought of it
almost idly, without resentment or bitterness. As in Algiers, she
did not consider the future. The future was dead and buried; the
future was with Angelo and his bright gold house in Marseilles.
She had no part in that future.

Her home now was with Messer Capriani and his account-
books. There were two other clerks in Messer Capriani's
counting-house: Bastien and Amadeo. Amadeo would have been
good at his job if he had neglected his appearance and the
serving-maids long enough to do some work; Bastien, she quickly
realized, altered the figures in the ledger-book and pocketed the
difference. When Serafina had worked in the kitchens both
Bastien and Amadeo had taken a certain, limited interest in her;
as a clerk, though, she was a peculiarity, an oddity that must be
treated with caution. A female clerk was a symptom of Messer
Capriani's approaching senility. In the counting-house Bastien
and Amadeo threw paper darts and made jokes about their
employer. Serafina sat at her desk and thought only of numbers.

Still, Serafina recognized with reluctant amusement that the
legacies of childhood had not completely left her. If she ever felt
anything approaching passion, it was when she looked at Messer
Capriani's ledger-books. The waste of it, the failure to make
what was merely a respectable living into a wealthy one.

To begin with, he should have bought a ship. Slowly drawing
the thick curtains across the glass, Serafina recalled the English
pilot, sketching in ale on the rough wood of a table. Jacopo
Capriani's journeys on horseback, laden with panniers, were
wasteful, exhausting and inefficient. A well-armed ship would
have completed the journeys in half the time. And the goods the
merchant traded in! Messer Capriani knew every family of note,
every merchant in every port from Marseilles to Naples. He
could have traded in spices, in silver, in silk . . . Instead, he sold

fripperies. Serafina recalled the English pilot again, his voice dry with sarcasm. *The* Kingfisher *will not be some barge for ferrying woollen caps and ladies' stockings.* Jacopo Capriani chose to trade in silk cockades and amber ear-drops.

Leaving the counting-house, taking the ledgers, Serafina found Messer Capriani in his withdrawing-room, a bundle of ribbons and thread on the table in front of him. It was a cold night, yet no candles were lit, and only a feeble fire fluttered in the grate. The merchant wore thick brown velvet robes, and a threadbare over-mantle trimmed with fur. Curtseying, Serafina placed the ledger-books on the table.

The tangle of silk and satin and velvet beside the books caught the dull orange glow of the fire, twisting it into endless, beautiful golden patterns. The ribbon seemed incongruous, an almost immoral, seductive sight in the shabby room.

Messer Capriani held the books at arm's length to read them, his watery eyes narrowed. Turning the pages slowly, he muttered, 'It seems satisfactory, madonna.'

Which was Serafina's cue to make a second curtsey and leave, her duties done for the day. But what was satisfactory to Messer Capriani was, she found, increasingly unsatisfactory to her. She wondered, briefly, if Angelo had felt like this, watching her father. Those beautiful coils of ribbon and braid on the table might not belong to her, but she still cared about them. She heard herself say, 'You could charge more for the scarlet ribbon than the crimson. Then you would make an extra thousand lire a year.'

Messer Capriani did not even bother to glance at her. 'I purchased them for the same price in Naples,' he said, taking a handkerchief from his sleeve and wiping his nose. 'Why should I charge more for the scarlet?'

She resisted an immediate feeling of defeat. 'Because it looks better,' she said patiently. Serafina drew a crimson and a scarlet ribbon from the tangle on the table, enjoying the coolness of the smooth fabric against her wrists. Briefly, the merchant glanced across at her.

'They are both red,' he said, dismissively. 'Crimson, scarlet – what does it matter? If I make them pay more for the scarlet, then the ladies will only buy crimson.'

He was not a fool, Serafina thought, he simply had no imagination. 'Look,' she said.

She unpinned her headdress and let her dark hair, now shoulder length, fall to either side of her face. Threading the crimson through one side of the heavy folds of hair, and the scarlet through the other, Serafina moved towards the fire, so that the merchant could see. It was late: there was only the gentle flickering of the flames in the coals, the rustle of Messer Capriani's heavy robes as he turned to look. She stood still as the merchant walked around her, studying the effect of scarlet silk against her gleaming dark hair. She felt his fingers briefly touch her beribboned head, but she did not move. He was estimating his property's worth, her own worth, just as they had in the Bedestan of Algiers.

'The scarlet is better, isn't it?' she said.

The merchant nodded. 'It is better, madonna.' And then, reaching for a pen and a ledger-book, flicking over the pages, Jacopo Capriani began to alter the figure in the column.

A shortage of money, and an even more pressing shortage of materials, forced Thomas to ride to Pisa, a dozen miles north of Livorno, in February. He took the apprentice Cristofano: his own grasp of Italian was good, but there was still the occasional situation that left him tiresomely fumbling for words. Cristofano, a Pisan by birth, knew the name and disposition of every inhabitant of the town. Cristofano, not yet sixteen years old, also knew the best taverns, the most compliant courtesans. Thomas, however, doggedly resolved to reserve such things for when they had cause to celebrate.

The weather was foul, a depressing mixture of sleet and snow. An appropriate backdrop for the gloomy conclusion he had already reached: that he would need to pledge himself to spend a year or two ferrying fripperies round the Mediterranean coast in exchange for the finance to complete his ship.

In Pisa, Thomas avoided the expensive palazzos fronting the Arno, guessing that such houses would need a letter of introduction to allow him across the threshold. He needed to find a merchant who intended to be rich, not one who was rich already.

He found merchants a-plenty, but they were an uninspired, penny-pinching lot, who saw excitement as a few pence more on a yard of lace, adventure as a day's ride to Lucca. Thomas had money enough to be going on with – his own needs were few, and he had already purchased many of the materials necessary for the ship – but he knew that he must find a sponsor before the *Kingfisher* was launched. Fitting out a ship for sailing was expensive, and you could not trade with empty pockets.

The icy rain dribbled down the back of Thomas's neck and trailed off the brim of his hat. The weather reminded him of London in March, but he had only to look up at the graceful, painted façades of the houses, and at the darkened shadows of the women hidden behind the window-glass to know that he was a thousand miles from London. The town seemed a uniform yellow-ochre colour, washed almost grey by the dark winter skies. Cristofano had begun to complain about his empty belly; Thomas gave him a clip round the ear and headed for yet another merchant's house.

They were made to wait for a quarter of an hour in a freezing cold hall, dripping water over the tiles. Bored, Cristofano sat down on a carved chest and sketched with the tip of his finger on a nearby misted window-pane. There was no fire in the grate. Thomas's breath clouded the air. It was a decent-sized house, mustard yellow plaster like the rest of Pisa, but with an air of decay, of neglect. The rushes scattered in the hallway were not clean, and there was dust gathered in the angles of the stairway. Cristofano, in reply to Thomas's question, whispered that Messer Capriani was elderly and unmarried. There was, then, no woman to check the work of the servants, to halt the chill ugliness of the house. Thomas, feeling no great optimism about the visit, leaned against a wall and yawned.

He had almost closed his eyes, when he saw her. He caught a glimpse of a small, slender girl in grey, her arms full of books. He watched first because he thought she might be pretty, and then because he found that he knew her.

Serafina. Thomas was on his feet and across the hallway as the manservant ran downstairs to tell him that Messer Capriani was awaiting him. He had just time to focus on her small.

heart-shaped face, and to hear her say, 'He won't help you, you know. He travels himself. With *donkeys*,' before he followed the servant up the stairs and through the darkened passageways.

Irritatingly, she was right. If ever a merchant had needed a ship, then that merchant was Jacopo Capriani. Yet Messer Capriani, as Serafina had said, preferred donkeys.

He left Cristofano downstairs, his empty belly forgotten at the sight of Serafina. Thomas had wanted to clip the youth round the ear again when Cristofano had risen to his feet and trailed after the girl like a dog chasing a bitch in season.

Messer Capriani received Thomas in an upstairs withdrawing-room. The fireplace had an inefficient draught: the curtains, which might once have been good, were blackened with smoke. The room was sparsely furnished and cold, despite the smoky fire. Messer Capriani, like his house, also possessed an air of neglect. He was, thought Thomas, as he made his bow, well into his sixties. He was tall and gaunt, and his hair straggled in transparent wisps from underneath his lappeted cap. His dark velvet robes seemed a size too big for him, his yellow skin had begun to shrink back into the bones of his face.

'Messer Marlowe.' The merchant, seated behind a large, ugly desk, nodded his head towards Thomas. 'What can I do for you?'

He began to explain, in words he had already used half a dozen times that day, about the *Kingfisher*, about the wonderful opportunity he was offering to the fortunate Messer Capriani. But he felt that he was not as convincing as usual, because half his mind was still preoccupied with the discovery of Serafina, dressed sedately in grey, carrying ledger-books. She had looked as he had last seen her in Marseilles: a plain dark gown, hair in two smooth wings behind her ears. Even the expression on her face, the tone of her voice, had been the same. Assured, detached, contained. Speaking not an unnecessary word, giving not a glance more than the minimum demanded by courtesy. If he had not expected to be kissed on both cheeks, then he found himself resenting the fact that she had not even smiled. Thomas wondered, briefly, how she had come here.

'– so many problems with shipping, Messer Marlowe. Gales – corsairs – I believe the land-route to be more reliable.'

Thomas began again, with a considerable effort at patience, explaining that his ship would be well defended against corsairs, that she could put to sea at all times of the year, that she would make any journey in a fraction of the time it took the merchant and his mules to travel muddy, bandit-infested roads. But Messer Capriani had already picked up his pen and begun to write again. Thomas wanted to shake him, to force him to see that by using the *Kingfisher* he could double his profits within a year.

But the merchant, smiling a small, irritating smile, added, 'And I do not believe in advancing money on projects that may never be finished, Messer Marlowe. That has never been my way.' So Thomas, tasting the gall of defeat yet again that day, sketched an inadequate bow, clamped his hat on his head, and left the room.

He passed Serafina on the stairs, trying to shake off the persistent Cristofano. She said nothing to Thomas: she looked at him as though he were a stranger. No – not even that. A servant, once in her employ, now superfluous to requirement. He received her brief, mocking glance, he felt his temper ignite, and he heard himself say, 'I met a friend of yours. Jehan de Coniques. If you want to know what he told me, you'll find me at the tavern in the Via di Santa Caterina.' Then, hauling the apprentice out with him, Thomas left the merchant's house.

The tavern was half empty, the miserable weather keeping many people in their houses. Thomas, who had spent twelve hours pounding the streets that day, parted thankfully from Cristofano and went upstairs to change out of his wet clothes.

He had almost forgotten Serafina. Almost, but not quite: her image had been at the back of his mind throughout the long, frustrating day. He had regretted the impulse that had led him to tell her of his meeting with Jehan de Coniques almost as soon as he had spoken, and since had managed to persuade himself, as the hours went on, that Serafina would disregard his invitation.

In that he had been mistaken, however. He saw her as soon as he opened the door, seated on a stool by the fireplace in his room, eyes fixed on neither the door nor the flames, but on the blank wall opposite.

She rose as Thomas entered the room.

'I hope you will forgive me, Mr Marlowe. The tapster said that I could wait here. I asked the maidservant to build up the fire.'

She was wearing the same dark grey gown he had seen her in that morning. The sober colour, trimmed with a plain white collar, emphasized the darkness of her hair and eyes, cast shadows on her smooth skin. She looked very young, and with the hem of her gown and her uncovered hair dampened by the rain, almost as defenceless as she had appeared on the tartane.

Thomas pulled off his soaking cloak and hat, and flung them on top of a nearby chest. He said, 'Sit down. Have you eaten?'

Sitting back on the stool, she nodded. He did not quite believe her. He was not hungry himself: what he needed was drink, and plenty of it, to cancel the chill that the day's tedious round had brought him. Opening the door, Thomas called for wine.

His clothes were soaked through, so he pulled off his doublet and slung it over the back of a chair, and stood close enough to the fire to dry his shirt and breeches. He heard Serafina say, 'Did you find your sponsor, Mr Marlowe?'

Thomas shook his head. The potboy had arrived, with a bottle of wine and two glasses.

'It seems that the merchants of Pisa either have ships a-plenty or that they prefer, like your employer, mules. Their ships are small, ill-repaired and poorly armed, of course, but they appear content with them.'

He had poured out the wine. Thomas offered a cup to Serafina, who shook her head.

The slight rush of warmth from the wine was no compensation for a useless day spent tramping about a dreary town. Thomas said, 'When I left you in Marseilles, you told me that you were going to your nurse, Marthe. Yet I find you in Pisa working for Messer Capriani.'

Serafina, seated on the stool again, did not stir. 'Marthe is dead.'

'I know. The notary told me. She died years ago, while you

were in Algiers.' Thomas ran his hands through his hair, shaking off some of the drops of rain. 'Why did you lie to me?'

Serafina shrugged. 'I told you what you wanted to hear. You had done what Kara Ali asked of you.'

The fleeting illusion of defencelessness had gone, replaced by the more familiar arrogance. Thomas felt an unreasonable anger rising in him. The room was small and cramped, her physical closeness unsettled him, intensifying his irritation.

'What he *asked* of me . . . You make it sound as though the cunning old bastard politely requested me to escort his former slave to Marseilles. It wasn't quite like that, though, was it, Serafina? A touch of blackmail from him, followed by a speedy dismissal from you as soon as you had no further use of me.'

She looked up at him, one side of her face bathed in gold by the firelight. 'You wished to leave Marseilles. I let you leave. What would you have preferred, Mr Marlowe?'

He thought, *trust*, but he did not say it. Instead, he said, 'Honesty.'

She almost smiled. 'A luxury item indeed, Mr Marlowe.'

He let out his breath in a hiss of exasperation, and refilled his glass. 'You were my responsibility.'

'Only until we reached Marseilles. That was the arrangement. Besides, I did not come here to discuss the past. You told me, Mr Marlowe, that you had met Monsieur de Coniques.'

Thomas, drinking, had noticed the flicker of interest in her dark eyes, quickly hidden. 'I met him purely by chance in a dockside tavern in Livorno, a few months ago,' he said. 'I should imagine that Monsieur de Coniques spends a lot of time in taverns. I am building my ship in Livorno.'

She nodded. 'The *Kingfisher*.'

He had, suddenly, a wish to provoke some sort of reaction in her. She could have owned the place, sitting there as cool and unmoved as any plaster madonna, not a single hair out of place, a smile touching the corners of her curved red lips.

'Monsieur de Coniques was as drunk as a lord and careless with his words,' said Thomas, leaning against the wall, watching her. 'But what he told me was quite interesting. You lied to me twice, didn't you, Serafina? About Marthe, and about the Guardi company. It isn't finished, is it? In fact the Guardi are doing rather well for themselves – only under slightly different management.'

She whispered, 'Angelo.'

'That's right. Your Monsieur de Coniques now works for Angelo. Personally, if I were cousin Angelo, I'd make sure a few convenient corsairs put paid to Monsieur de Coniques as soon as possible. In fact, I'm surprised he wasn't dispatched on the galley with the rest of you to begin with.'

The effect of his words took Thomas by surprise. He saw Serafina's eyes widen, her skin blanch. Recovering herself quickly, she said, 'He was needed in Marseilles to help Angelo look after the business while my father was away. My father had no reason to take him with us to Italy.'

'Not your father,' said Thomas, impatiently. '*Angelo*. That notary's a bloody liability to him.'

She was staring at him blankly. 'He couldn't –' she said, incoherently. 'Angelo didn't –'

There were other lies, other omissions, a whole catalogue of them. Thomas had had time to think that afternoon: time spent waiting in draughty ante-rooms, knocking on unreceptive doors. He said, cruelly, 'Let's not waste time discussing the unpleasant Monsieur de Coniques. Tell me something of the other members of your delightful family. Your father, for instance. When did he die? And how?'

His aim was entirely deliberate. But Serafina smoothed back her wet hair, and said, 'My father died in the bagnio in Algiers – soon after we were taken there –'

'Of the plague?' said Thomas, innocently. 'Of the sweating-sickness? Or of the bastinado?'

He saw her eyes close for a second, her head bow. Rising, she covered her face with her hands and turned, so that her back was to him. For a moment Thomas almost felt ashamed of himself.

'You knew, didn't you?' he said softly. 'Before you went to Marseilles. You knew that your father had been deliberately put to death by his own kin. That was why you didn't just run up to the house and knock on the door. That was why you let no one know that you were alive. By the way, why did you survive? Why didn't the corsair reserve the same treatment for you?'

He watched her hands slide slowly downwards, and heard her say, 'They intended to. But my master protected me.'

'Christ.' The air in the room had become thick and warm with the heat of the fire. Putting down his glass, Thomas forced open the stiff window-latch, and took a deep breath of fresh air.

From behind him, the small, cold voice said, 'I didn't tell you because you did not need to know. What happened in the past is none of your business, Mr Marlowe.'

She was an arrogant little bitch, the notary had said, and he had been right. Thomas knew that the blood had risen to his face. His shirt still clung damply to his back.

Turning back to Serafina, he said, 'So your father signed his own death-warrant by leaving the company to Angelo.'

'No.' She had recovered herself a little, her voice was stronger. 'Never. My father would never have left Angelo the company. Angelo was illegitimate. Everything was left to me and my husband, and then to our children. That was why I was to marry, Mr Marlowe. To provide my father with an heir. But in Marseilles – in Marseilles the baker told me that Angelo had *inherited* the company.'

Which explained the survival of the notary, of course. A demonic partnership: one to rewrite Franco Guardi's will, the other to make the more exotic arrangements, such as the precise timing of the corsair ship. Thomas suddenly thought of Serafina as she must have looked all those years ago; a child, setting off to an unknown country to marry a stranger.

'It seems – precarious,' he said. 'Your father was gambling on your survival – your safety. You would not have had children for years.'

She stared at him, her eyes a clear dark brown, almost black. 'My father wasn't an old man, Mr Marlowe. He was in his early forties. He thought he would live for ever, I suppose. As we all do.'

In the silence, there was only the crackle of the fire, the noise from the taproom below. 'You should have trusted me,' said Thomas, eventually. He knew that she was right, that it was none of his business, and yet he felt what even he recognized to be an unreasonable bitterness. 'You should have told me the truth, Serafina. Didn't it occur to you that you were putting both of us in danger?'

'In danger?' Serafina's eyes flashed scornfully. 'I ceased to exist eight years ago, Mr Marlowe. How could I be in danger?'

Thomas had put aside the wine cup. 'You might have been recognized,' he said, struggling to keep his temper. 'You didn't think that the man who arranged your death once would baulk at arranging it a second time, did you?'

She shivered. She was still standing, the tension of her whole body scarcely restrained. 'Angelo didn't *arrange* what happened,' she said. Her voice was taut, as though she was fighting for breath. 'He was lucky, that's all. We were in the wrong place at the wrong time, and he made use of it. He was always an opportunist.'

He realized then that though she might have guessed long ago Angelo's involvement in her capture and her father's death, she had not yet understood everything.

'Not lucky,' he said, evenly. 'Clever. That's what your loyal notary told me. *Angelo's a clever bastard.*'

He saw her shake her head, her eyes glazed. No, he thought angrily: it was not that she did not understand, it was that she did not wish to accept the truth. Consciously or unconsciously Serafina was refusing to acknowledge what common sense should have told her years ago. And he knew, suddenly, why she did not wish to acknowledge that truth.

His realization sickened him. He thought, such a rational, practical creature, and yet she, too, had her sticking-point, her unreasonable obsession.

'What were you going to do?' he whispered, his eyes fixed on her small, furious face, her rigidly clenched fists. 'Walk into the house and say *I'm back* and hope everything would be just the same?'

He saw from her face that was exactly what she had intended to do. He almost laughed. He had misread her completely, for an empty-hearted, cold little thing, yet she, too, had her irrational passions. He said, wonderingly, 'And when you saw the house – when you spoke to that damned baker – you realized that things had changed, didn't you? You couldn't be mistress of the House of Guardi, so you contented yourself with stealing a loaf of bread instead –'

He caught her hand before she could strike his face. Her fingers were clawed, like a cat's and her wrist had a surprising strength. She wriggled violently, but he pinioned her arms to her sides.

'Didn't you realize? Did you really think that it had all been luck? How does it feel, my dear Serafina, to know that cousin Angelo arranged the whole thing in the first place? How far out of port were you before the corsair came? And how sensible of cousin Angelo to get you safely out of the way before you had a chance to marry –'

He yelled then, because she had bent her head and bitten his wrist. He shouted, 'You were in love with him, weren't you! Christ, you still are! And he betrayed you!' and she twisted in his arms, and they both fell on the bed, he on top of her.

Thomas did not move immediately. There was blood dribbling down his wrist, and his heart was pounding. Her small, heart-shaped face was beneath his; he could see the thin scar from the gunwale of the tartane white against her hairline, and feel the movement of her body as she struggled for breath. His need for her was suddenly unbearable. Thomas bent his head and kissed her.

He had closed his eyes and lost himself when, curving like a fish, she brought up her knee and struck him, just where it hurt. Thomas found himself on the floor, sobbing with pain and fury. Serafina was already at the doorway. 'Bitch!' yelled Thomas, as the door slammed behind her.

When she did eventually sleep that night, it was to dream again the worst dream. She was sitting on the white sand, the sky was also white, and the sun was a scarlet disc in the sky. Her father was there, and she had to watch as the purple-robed janissary, his back to her, tied him to a pole and began to beat the soles of his feet. The whip sliced through the air like a knife, her father's pale skin was patterned with crimson crosses. Serafina could not move, could say nothing; she just sat there, watching.

Only tonight, the dream was a little different. When the janissary turned, the whip upraised for the next stroke, Serafina saw the face beneath the white turban. It was Angelo's.

She could see his thick, dark gold hair, his black, almond-shaped eyes. His skin was tanned, and a small smile curled the corners of his mouth. She could not scream, could not move, could not breathe. When, eventually, she managed to force open her eyes, Serafina found that, despite the coldness of the night, her skin was drenched with sweat. She sat up, hands fumbling feebly for the tinder. The candle took an age to light, and in the darkness she still expected to see Angelo crouched purple-gowned by the bed, his eyes dark and laughing.

When the candle had finally lit, she made herself look round the room. It was the same, she told herself, just the same. The now familiar objects – the high, narrow bed, the heavy curtains, the plain chest that held her few clothes. The sweat had chilled on her skin, and Serafina began to shudder violently. With difficulty she climbed out of bed, the coverlet wrapped around her shoulders, and went to the window.

The sky had cleared, and a frost outlined the distant tower and duomo. Her heart had begun to slow, but she could still see Angelo's face clearly through the darkened glass. He was smiling, as he had smiled the day she had set sail from Marseilles. He had smiled, and his dark eyes had been bright, and he had kissed her hand. And he had intended, all the time, that neither she nor her father would return. She had not allowed herself to acknowledge what was obvious: that it had been too opportune to be merely a convenient stroke of fate. Tonight, the Englishman had forced her to see what she could hardly bear to see, and now she struggled to keep her reason. *You were in love with him, and he betrayed you,* Thomas Marlowe had said, and in that he had been right. If ten-year-old children were capable of that sort of love, then once she had loved Angelo.

And if she wished to survive, then she must force herself to accept the truth. Since Marseilles, since Angelo had looked at her and despised her, she had not felt truly alive. She had gone through the motions of living, had found herself a roof over her head and food in her belly when all she might have expected was the gutter. But she had not lived. Now she thought for the first time that out of pain might grow the sour seed of revenge, and a reason for living.

Angelo had formed his intention, presumably, when her father had announced her betrothal. He had not been lucky, he had been clever. *A clever bastard.* He had won the notary to his side during that last long winter; he would have needed Jehan de Coniques' help in arranging the legal side of things. Taut with weariness, her eyes shut and every muscle aching, Serafina leaned her head against the cool glass pane, thinking.

Yet Angelo had not succeeded in everything. The thought came to her like a single silvery fish swimming through murky waters, that in one thing Angelo had failed, and did not yet know that he had failed. She was still alive.

Her breathing had calmed. Angelo had once taken everything from her – her family, her home, her name – but she had already begun to claw a little back. She had a roof over her head, and food in her belly. And Thomas had been mistaken – she loved no one. Angelo's betrayal had killed the capacity, the desire, for love. She had cast away her fetters: she was free.

But there were different sorts of freedom. This house was not hers, her security was dependent on the whim of a querulous old man. If Jacopo Capriani died, or if he listened to convention and banned her from the counting-house, then again, she would have nothing. Hers was not the sort of freedom that Angelo had stolen for himself. However much she might want to fight for what was rightfully hers, the bitter truth was that she had nothing to fight with. She was disarmed, powerless, doubly so because she was a woman. She had only the advantages of Angelo's ignorance of her survival, and her own vengeful, haunted heart.

John Keane, agent of the English Levant Company, arrived in Livorno that spring with a set of chessmen, a newly strung lute, and a small three-masted galleon, somewhat the worse for wear.

The ship bore the arms of the Levant Company. At sea, beneath the red cross of England that only the company's ships had a right to bear, a sea-beast writhing beneath a galleon in full sail unfurled from the masthead, announcing England's intention to the world. Now, at last, the air was still, and all the flags drooped listlessly. John Keane, however, sending his exhausted crew to their beds or to the ale-house, remained on deck alone.

He was in his mid-thirties, a tall, mild-looking man, his straight brown hair already beginning to thin and grey at the temples. His eyes were a light, short-sighted blue-grey, framed with a mesh of small lines, and his skin tanned red-ochre from the voyage from London.

It took John Keane a full hour on board the ship to conclude that although the *Garland*'s petals were a little bruised, she might be repaired sufficiently eventually to continue her voyage to Aleppo. Standing on the deck, surveying torn sails and cracked spars, John Keane recalled the storm that had enveloped them in the Tyrrhenian Sea. They had become separated from the convoy, and for a while John, battered by wind and rain, had thought that they would lose the ship. But in the end, he and his crew and God had triumphed, and they had landed their cargo of cloth, tin and Yarmouth herring in Livorno. The convoy had been bound for Scanderoon, the trading port of Aleppo. Letters would have to be written, he thought, explanations sent.

John Keane had been an agent of the Levant Company for more than ten years now, joining not long after Queen Elizabeth had granted the company its Royal Charter. *For trading with the dominions of the Grand Signior*, the charter had said, and ships bearing the royal arms of England had since sailed to Scanderoon, to Smyrna, and to the Sublime Porte itself. They had been successful and exciting years – dangerous, too, for the established Mediterranean powers had resented the intrusion of the brash newcomer England. France, for so long Islam's sole ally in Christendom, had made difficulties wherever possible. Venice, her strength for more than a decade in decline, saw the English traders as yet another obstacle to the recovery of her former glory. Spain, smarting from the humiliation of her armada, welcomed any excuse for retaliation. As for Islam itself,

John Keane knew that he would never feel anything but an outsider in that most foreign of worlds.

The Tuscan port of Livorno offered a convenient and inexpensive stopping-place en route to the Levant. In Livorno the English, specialists in the carrying-trade, sold linens and kerseys, bought raw silk and brocade. Livorno had other specialities – stolen goods, slaves, and an ever-changing, and frequently openly criminal population. John Keane knew Livorno almost as well as he knew his birthplace of Rotherhithe. He no longer stopped to stare at the ladies tottering in their high wooden pantoffles, nor at the bravos escorting painted courtesans. He knew Livorno for what it was: a vibrant, violent melting-pot, a rendezvous for traders from all corners of the Mediterranean. Lading and storage were pleasingly cheap, and there were merchants a-plenty from Genoa and Lucca to purchase cargo. You could trade with Spain and Provence as well; the only people you might not openly trade with were the Barbary corsairs. Englishmen who traded with corsairs would, if Tuscany discovered them, find themselves rowing Medici galleys. John Keane, who liked to strum a lute and play chess, and who had a close, if somewhat frustrated, understanding with a lady in London, frowned, and turned to look again at the broken spars.

A voice from the dockside below called, 'I can give you the name of a good carpenter!'

The language was English, the voice young and friendly. John Keane, peering over the gunwale, saw a dark, stocky man, his curling black hair covered with a hat of Spanish felt.

'I've no shortage of carpenters.' John rested his arms on the gunwale. 'A kind offer, though, Mr –?'

'Marlowe. Thomas Marlowe.' The dark-haired man swept off his hat and bowed. 'Don't you remember me, Mr Keane?'

John Keane, whose agile brain compensated for poor eyesight, squinted.

'The *Flying Heart*,' shouted Thomas Marlowe. 'The *Michael*. And, I regret, the *Toby*.'

The master of the *Garland* squinted even harder. 'The *Toby* was lost off the Barbary coast eighteen months ago,' he called down. 'Only a handful of her crew returned –'

He watched, his vision gradually clarifying, as the other man swung himself on to the gangway and up to the deck of the *Garland*.

John's frown slowly cleared, and he said, 'Yes. Thomas Marlowe. You sailed with the company as pilot.'

Thomas Marlowe bowed again.

John Keane added, 'We thought you were dead.'

'Not dead, as you see, Mr Keane.' Thomas grinned expansively. 'Dragged from the deep, disgorged to the wilderness, and eventually washed up in Tuscany. And now I'm building a ship, rather than sailing one.' He stared at the splintered surfaces of the *Garland*, and added pointedly, 'You should see her, Mr Keane.'

John Keane, not a stupid man, searched for a wine-bottle and two cups while he gathered himself time to think. When he reappeared on deck, he said, 'Who are you building your ship for, Mr Marlowe?'

'Myself.' The pilot's eyes were a clear, untroubled blue as he added calmly, 'I had a bit of luck at cards. You can win yourself a fortune here if you're lucky.'

The wine was poured out: John handed a cup to Thomas Marlowe.

They drank a little, and then the pilot said, as John had guessed he might, 'Only I've not had so much luck recently. And timber's damned expensive. I really think you should come and look at my ship, Mr Keane. This hulk won't make it to the end of the century.'

John Keane, raising his cup, agreed.

Business was, for a while, quiescent in the Pisan house because the merchant Jacopo Capriani was ill.

It was not a new illness, but one that had gnawed at him for years. He knew the cause of it – the swamps that fringed the coast of prosperous Tuscany – and he had come to recognize the symptoms that preceded each bout of wrestling with his own personal devil. The painful drumming behind the eyes, the feeling of unreality, the uniquely colourful nightmares. And then the rising fever, the shuddering of his tortured, aching limbs, the nausea. A long time ago his wife had nursed him: more recently his housekeeper had tended him during these bouts, but she had died a year past. Messer Capriani refused to pay for a physician. This time, he told himself, as he took to his bed, he would struggle with his demon alone.

He lost track of day and night. Outside it was spring, which was when marsh fever most often took him, but Jacopo Capriani did not notice the blue skies, the unfurling leaves. He thought sometimes, fretfully, of his work, but he had no strength to go to the counting-house or the office. He did not trust either Amadeo or Bastien, and the fever magnified his distrust. He slept fitfully, dreaming bright and hideous dreams in which ribbons rotted in warehouses, goods tumbled from panniers down mountainsides. He called out in those dreams, and did not know that he had done so.

He knew neither the time nor the day when he felt something cool pressed against his aching head. Opening his eyes, he could at first only see darkness. The darkness of the grave, waiting for him, already open. He could not breathe, he could already feel the earth falling upon his withered, feeble body.

He heard a voice say, 'Messer Capriani. You must drink this,' and he felt himself raised on pillows and a cup put to his lips. He drank, because he thought it was his mother talking to him, and he was a child again. When he had taken a few mouthfuls, he lay back and went to sleep.

When the merchant next awoke, it was day, and he was not alone. It had not been his mother who fed him, but Serafina, the girl he had hired as a chambermaid in Marseilles. She was sitting by the bed, his ledger-books piled on the chest beside her. He had thought her a plain little thing at first, but now he found her appearance restful.

'I came to show you the figures, so that you wouldn't worry,' she said. She had a pleasant voice, low and soothing. 'You should have some more to drink, signor, then you will soon be well again.'

He drank deep from the cup she offered him, not minding the slightly bitter taste of the liquid. He wondered weakly whether she meant to poison him, and decided that she had nothing to gain. He had taken her on as a chambermaid, and he had since let her work in his counting-house because she had the best head for figures he had discovered in anyone, man or woman.

As time passed, he found that he did not mind her presence at his sickbed because she did not chatter or giggle like most women, she simply sat there, her profile carved against the sunlight.

Jacopo Capriani also found, when eventually he drifted off to sleep again, that Serafina's face figured sometimes in his dreams.

She went to the merchant twice a day with the ledger-books, staying a little longer each time. The fever had eased now, but Messer Capriani was still very weak. Privately, Serafina thought that he would have died if she had not gone to him that night. She did not want him to die: Jacopo Capriani was her only security. If he died, she would be homeless again. She had made the merchant take an infusion of Kara Ali's prescription that had allowed him to sleep, and from that time he had begun slowly to recover his strength.

Tonight, she read to him from the ledger-books, showing him the pages occasionally when he asked. Messer Capriani was propped up on pillows, his face yellow against the white linen. The rest of the house was quiet, the kitchen cleaned and tidied for the morning, the clerks and errand-boys drinking in some tavern.

She finished reading, and closed the book. Serafina put the ledgers aside and sat, still and quiet. Outside, the sky was darkening, washing the roofs and domes with terracotta.

After a while she became aware that Messer Capriani was not asleep. He was awake, and the small dark eyes under the red nightcap were watching her. She did not move, did not speak, but under the plain gown her heart began to beat more quickly. Eventually, she let her hand slide from her lap and on to the coverlet.

'I must go now,' she said, softly.

She felt his fingers clutch at hers; she could feel the dry paperiness of his skin, the lack of flesh to cover the bones.

'Not yet,' he whispered.

★

The merchant's recovery was slow, punctuated by small relapses and smaller improvements.

It was natural, therefore, that the twice-daily studying of the ledger-books should expand into a more general conversation about the health of the business, natural too that Serafina's duties should begin to include purchasing as well as accounting. Messer Capriani had begun to trust her, a privilege he extended to neither of his other clerks. It occurred to Serafina that it was fortunate for her that Amadeo was a wastrel, and Bastien a thief.

At the end of June, Serafina travelled to Livorno with a servant, choosing braid and frills from the incoming vessels. It irked her that she could not buy silk, because the ships had begun to bring in the first few bales. Soon, almost every ship that docked at Livorno would be carrying silk or buying it. The next time she went to Livorno she bought a couple of lengths of silk with her own carefully hoarded wages. One she sold at an impressive profit to another merchant, the other she made into a gown for herself. She showed the profit to Messer Capriani and he, his brow furrowing while his eyes lit up, agreed that they could, perhaps, begin to buy the occasional length.

At Livorno's quayside, running her fingers through cloth that was turquoise and lime, figured and silver-threaded, Serafina began to feel the beginnings of excitement, the beginnings of a wonderful possibility. She was careful to let none of her passion show on her face, however. She merely finished the gown she had begun to sew, and took even more care with the ledger-books.

It was natural also that the studying of the ledger-books should increasingly take place over a meal. After all, Messer Capriani still had to spend much of the day resting, and it was more suitable that he should meet his clerk in his dining-room than his bedchamber. Besides, Serafina herself had begun to take an interest in the kitchens. She had the knack of knowing what the merchant's delicate stomach could most easily digest, the knack of searching out the best morsels the market-place had to offer. Sometimes she cooked a meal herself, gently spiced eastern dishes that tempted the most feeble appetite. Jacopo Capriani laughed and said that he did not know how he had managed without her. It became a joke between them that she was as useful to him as a wife.

They were dining one evening – quails stuffed with almonds accompanied by a honeyed Tuscan wine – when Serafina introduced the subject of transport again. 'The mule train –' she began hesitantly, cutting the flesh of the bird into small pieces. 'When will it leave?'

The merchant belched and wiped his mouth on his napkin. 'It should already have gone,' he said, frowning. 'I usually set out in May.'

'For Naples?' She knew already, of course; it was simply a matter of looking back through the purchase-book, of studying Messer Capriani's odysseys through the lists of items and rows of figures.

'Naples first.' The merchant sipped his wine. His hand shook as he lifted the glass: he had not yet regained full control over his muscles.

Serafina voiced what she knew to be on Messer Capriani's mind. 'It is a difficult journey, signor. The roads are poor and the heat would not be good for you.'

He said nothing, only dabbed at the corners of his mouth where the wine had begun to trickle down his chin. She knew that since the sickness his fear of death had increased.

'You must take care of yourself, Messer Capriani. You were very ill.'

Her food was all cut up into small segments. Neatly, Serafina speared a piece of quail and lifted it to her mouth. Her eyes were lowered, avoiding the merchant's.

'Bastien is not to be trusted; Amadeo is clever enough, but he will not put his mind to his work. It is a pity you are not a man, my dear! Then we could send you in my place.'

Raising her face, Serafina let her smile answer his own. Then she said sadly, 'I could not travel to Naples for you, Messer Capriani. It is too far.'

'Aye.' Putting down his knife, the merchant chewed noisily.

'But perhaps,' said Serafina carefully, 'you need not go to Naples at all this year. I can travel to Livorno for you.'

Messer Capriani frowned. He had drunk two glasses of wine,

and his taffeta cap had begun to slip over his forehead. He said peevishly, 'Naples has the best ribbons and braid, my dear. Livorno has not the choice.'

They ate in silence. Then Serafina said, 'I suppose you might have to purchase a little differently this year.'

No one, listening to her gentle voice, could have guessed how important the merchant's answer was to her. But Messer Capriani merely laughed again. 'Your precious silks! I thought a length or so might satisfy you. Still,' he added, peering across the table, his small eyes narrowing, 'that gown does suit you very well, Serafina. Very well.'

She had worn the new gown for the first time that night. It was a deep amber gold that brought out the warmth of her skin, the sheen of her hair. The neck was low, Italian fashion, and the trim of cream-coloured lace made shadowed patterns on her breast.

'I could buy you silk,' she said, putting aside her plate. 'If you tell me what you want.'

Between them, the candles flickered in the small breeze from the window. Serafina rose to draw the curtains. She did not think she had ever wanted anything more than she wanted him to agree, to say yes, to allow her to begin to practise again the trade she had been born to.

She did not know that the merchant had also risen and stood behind her until he spoke.

'What I *want* –' he said.

His voice was hoarse and unsteady. Serafina's fists clenched, the nails pressing into her palms, but she did not turn or speak. She could smell the dry mustiness of Messer Capriani's robes, hear the unsteadiness of his breathing. She knew suddenly that if she remained still, said nothing, he would touch her. She began to see, a sweet sharp stab of realization, the significance of such contact. Eventually she felt a hand stroke the nape of her neck and slowly move across her shoulder.

'I've a good eye for silk,' Serafina said, keeping her voice even. 'I once worked for a silk-merchant.'

The merchant's hand lingered on her shoulder. She felt his fingers trace down towards the rim of her bodice, brushing against the trailing lace. She was trembling, she was afraid. No man had ever touched her like this. It frightened her to permit such intimacy, to give away a part of herself. She feared that any familiarity would make her vulnerable again.

And yet, along with the fear, there was also excitement. The excitement had nothing to do with the clumsy physical contact, and everything to do with the realization that she had, after all, some kind of power. There were more ways than one of getting what you wanted, and yet until now she had not considered the most obvious way. Messer Capriani's other hand had slipped round her waist, kneading the smooth silk that covered her flat stomach. Serafina's fear dissolved, and she began to feel a precarious triumph. She *did* have something to bargain with. Angelo had been wrong. This man wanted her.

And Thomas Marlowe had also wanted her. She had seen it in his eyes, back in the tavern in the Via di Santa Caterina. Serafina heard Jacopo Capriani groan as his fingers slid beneath her bodice and cupped her breast. She remembered Thomas Marlowe and that forced, stolen kiss, and with the recollection she felt her own heart begin to flutter a little, her own breath become taut. She felt awkward, clumsy: she knew suddenly that she had been mistaken in being so brusque with the English pilot. She had not understood the extent of her ignorance, or the usefulness of such knowledge until now. She heard the wheezing breath, felt the bony fingers clutch at her nipple, and realized that she knew nothing of what men wanted, nothing of what they did. She, who had studied so much, was ignorant of the only thing that might give her power. She could not move or speak; she stood quite still until the merchant, his forehead sheened with perspiration and his eyes glazed, let her go.

'I think it would be useful for me to buy a little silk, don't you, Messer Capriani?' she said at last.

Turning, smiling, Serafina saw him nod.

PART V

1595

O MY LITTLE HEART!

This wimpled, whining, purblind, wayward boy,
This senior-junior, giant-dwarf, Dan Cupid;
Regent of love-rhymes, lord of folded arms,
The anointed sovereign of sighs and groans,
Liege of all loiterers and malcontents,
Dread prince of plackets, king of codpieces,
Sole imperator and great general
Of trotting paritors: O my little heart!
   Love's Labour's Lost: William Shakespeare

Thomas Marlowe, conferring inside the almost completed hull of the *Kingfisher*, received the information that he had a visitor with initial impatience.

Then: 'She's wearing a yellow dress and a pair of those wooden shoes,' added Rufus the blacksmith, peering down the ladder, and Thomas, pushing his untidy hair into some sort of order, began to feel a little more curious.

It was, he found, Serafina. He recognized her as soon as he saw her, despite the veil that swung over her face and, as Rufus had said, the yellow gown and wooden pantoffles. Only the gown wasn't really yellow, it was a muted golden colour, and Serafina even managed to appear graceful in the high-soled footgear, a fashion that Thomas had hitherto only found ridiculous.

A small hammering of his heart, and Thomas jumped down to the dockside. The sun was high in a clear blue sky, the air thick, heavy and shimmering. Flies swarmed on the marshes that bordered Livorno, straying into the town, aggravating tempers already shortened by the unremittingly hot weather. Pitch refused to set in the heat, timbers warped and cracked if not continuously dampened and covered. Serafina, though, cool in light silk, appeared untouched by the sun or the insects.

'Mr Marlowe.' She stepped forward from the clutter of barrels and planks. 'How pleasant.'

Thomas grinned. 'When I return from having discovered the North-West Passage, laden with gold and spices, you will say, "Mr Marlowe. How pleasant."' He made his bow. 'I am honoured, Mademoiselle Guardi. What brings you to Livorno?'

He used the more formal address without thinking. She was

no longer Serafina, slave, stable-boy, or clerk, she had become a
beautiful and elegant woman. She had thrown back her light
veil, and the gown that Rufus had called yellow shimmered and
gleamed in the bright sunlight, a rich silk that flattered the fine
texture of her skin, the velvety darkness of her eyes. They had
parted on disastrous terms almost five months ago; he had
behaved appallingly then. But there was no sign of reproach or
resentment in those unfathomable eyes, only a distant but typical
glitter of amusement.

'Trade, Mr Marlowe,' she said. 'What else?'

She began to walk alongside the hull of the *Kingfisher*. Brushing away the flies that continuously buzzed around his head,
Thomas, perspiring and overheated in his light shirt and breeches,
noted the neat arrangement of Serafina's hair, the perfect order
of her dress. Even on the long ride from Valencia to Marseilles,
he recalled, she had never to him looked dirty or untidy.

She said, 'Messer Capriani has not been well, so he has entrusted me with some of his purchasing.' Serafina added one of
her rare smiles. 'Not gold or spices, though, Mr Marlowe. Silk.'

They reached the prow of the *Kingfisher*, stopping beneath where
the beakhead and figurehead would one day jut out over the waves.

Running one slender finger along the seasoned oak, Serafina
said, 'It takes a while to build a ship, doesn't it, Mr Marlowe?
How long is it since you arrived in Livorno?'

Her voice was mild, the question one of polite interest.
Thomas scowled.

'Almost a year, damn it,' he said, thumping one fist against
the stout wooden wall. 'It should have been quicker ... But
we've had trouble with supplies – and I haven't been able to
employ as many men as I would have liked ...'

His voice trailed away, lost in the glittering sunlit harbour.
He had summed up, in a couple of phrases, the frustrations that
had nagged him for months, the difficulties that had obsessed
him, day and night, awake and dreaming. In his worst nightmares he imagined the *Kingfisher* for ever incomplete, through
lack of money, through the constant battle to keep the best
craftsmen, to find the best materials. And that would be worse
than if she had never been begun.

Thomas took a deep breath. 'The planking's almost finished, so we'll be caulking her soon. And I've got my eye on some English oak for the masts.'

'She's going to be a fine ship,' said Serafina gently.

He had almost forgotten that she was there. Almost, but not quite: there was a scent of patchouli in the windless air, a rustle of silk. If he had discovered his own dreams to be patched with nightmare, then how had Serafina, with her disconnected past, found the months in Tuscany?

But she spoke before he could find the words. She had flicked the veil over her face again, and her voice drifted to him through the protective layer of muslin, above the clatter and clamour of the docks.

'I'm staying in the Palazzo Sacchetti, Mr Marlowe,' she said. 'Perhaps you'll dine with me tonight. We have a great deal to talk about. Trade, for instance.'

The Palazzo Sacchetti did not live up to the grandeur of its name. Small and slightly crumbling, the house crouched in one of the warrens of twisting streets behind the docks. Thomas, twitching the plume of his hat into place before knocking at the front door, noted that the murals, faded in the heat, had not been repainted, that many of the louvred shutters were in bad repair.

The palazzo did not belong to Messer Capriani, Serafina explained later over corn-fed chicken and rice and light red wine. Messer Capriani merely had leave to use the house whenever he was in Livorno.

Thomas, his mouth full of chicken and rice, could only mumble his reply. They had talked of the weather, of the politics of Tuscany, of food and land prices. Finishing his third glass of wine, Thomas found that he had begun, for the first time in many months, to relax a little. He had not realized how far the problems with the ship had preoccupied him until he had permitted himself this unexpected evening off.

The chicken was cleared away, and replaced by bowls of almonds and fruit. Thomas, picking up the strands of an earlier conversation, said, 'Silk. I didn't know that Messer Capriani was a silk-merchant.'

A look of genuine irritation puckered Serafina's smooth brow. 'Cockades,' she said. 'Knots. *Antelope's tears.*' And to Thomas's blank stare, Serafina added scornfully, 'Bezoar, my dear pilot. Found in antelopes' stomachs. It is believed to cure snake-bites.'

She looked, thought Thomas with a grin, as though she would have liked to introduce a large asp to the unfortunate merchant. 'There's always a market for such fripperies,' said Thomas, enjoying himself.

'There's a better market for silk.'

Serafina rose and drew the curtains. Her lips were still pursed, her eyes hard. 'The finest silk from the Levant comes to Livorno. There are silk-workshops in Florence, and Pisa and Siena. Messer Capriani knows every merchant, every wealthy family, from Naples to Marseilles. And he sells them *antelope's tears.*'

She was speaking to herself, thought Thomas, not to him. Her voice was bitter.

'Silk, spices, gold,' said Thomas, mildly. 'They are what we fight over nowadays in the Inland Sea, Serafina. No more armadas, no more crusades against the Infidel, no more great conquests of territory. Even the Sultan himself is drawing in his horns. It's become a different sort of battle. Perhaps Messer Capriani is happy trundling his mules and his cockades along the Ligurian coast.'

'Happy?' Serafina swung round. 'Would you be happy with that, Thomas? *Ferrying woollen caps and ladies' stockings?*'

He knew that she did not refer to Messer Capriani's ambitions. He realized both that her ambition matched his, and that she had at last addressed him by his forename. Finishing a peach and placing the stone in the centre of his plate, Thomas said slowly, 'No. I would not be happy with that. There are greater seas than this, Serafina, and they are what I intend to cross.'

'The North-West Passage?'

Thomas smiled. A faster passage to the Indies was the Holy Grail that every merchant adventurer sought. 'God willing. But I may be obliged to ferry whatever I can get paid for – for a while, at least. I hope not. I can manage at the moment – just.'

The fire had retreated again, her eyes were cool, almost affectionate. 'Don't the merchants recognize the value of your ship?' she said.

'Some do.' Thomas thought of his lengthy negotiations with John Keane. 'Some do only too well.'

Serafina said nothing, only waited attentively for him to continue. His wine-glass had been refilled; Thomas cradled it between his short, square fingers.

'I've been talking to an agent of the English Levant Company. I was pilot for the company for many years. The agent – his name's John Keane – has made me an offer.'

There was a short silence. Thomas drained half of his cup of wine in one gulp. 'Keane is making difficulties. He'd like to *buy* the *Kingfisher*, you see, Serafina. And buy me with it, of course. If I'm not very careful, I'll never get out of this damned sea.'

'So what will you do?'

They had both finished eating. The candles were lit, picking out the faded finery of the room: the frayed tapestries fluttering on the walls, the chipped, fragile glassware.

Thomas shrugged. 'Try and keep going for a while longer, until I find a more compliant patron.' He rose, and stood by the fireplace, one elbow resting on the chimney-piece. 'I've borrowed a bit – won a little at dice.'

Serafina smoothed down the folds of her silk gown. 'What did the Levant Company offer you?'

It was hot in the small dining-chamber. Thomas, remembering long-drawn-out discussions with John Keane that had left him scarcely capable of civility, said bitterly, 'To advance me sufficient money to finish the ship. But piecemeal, paying each bill, each wage-packet as it falls due. A few ducats when I need to buy wood, a few more to pay the men. It would be better for the Levant Company – a smaller outlay of capital at any one time – but humiliating for me. It would take away my freedom. It would mean that I would have to account to the company for every penny spent. It would give Keane the last word in the choice of men and materials. And he will inevitably incline to economy rather than quality, because he is answerable to his own masters in London. But also –' He stopped, leaving the most bitter pill to the last.

'*Also?*' prompted Serafina, with a lift of her eyebrows.

'Also, the Levant Company would have the right to charter the *Kingfisher* for the first five years after she's launched.'

It was an altogether thoroughly unpalatable offer, and, Thomas knew, intended to be so. Five years was too long; Drake had sailed round the world in two. Thomas had already begun to feel the itch of inactivity, the itch of being landbound. Five years peddling company goods around the confines of the Mediterranean would feel like a prison sentence. As a boy, he had stood on the dockside at Greenwich and watched the ships from the Indies unload their cargo. Gold and silver, china, silks, black-skinned princes from countries as yet unseen and unnamed, exotic birds and animals. The sense of excitement he had felt then had never left him. It drove him still: it was the fuel that made him labour, and scheme, and steal.

Thomas knew that John Keane was deliberately making things difficult, because John Keane wanted to own the *Kingfisher*. Keane had sufficient vision and intelligence to see the potential of Thomas's ship. And Keane needed the *Kingfisher* to replace the failing *Garland*.

'I'm trying to persuade Messer Capriani to charter a ship,' said Serafina.

Thomas's gaze fixed suddenly on the carved marble of the fireplace, on the overweight cherubs and goddesses that twined themselves around the barley-sugar pillars. He saw for one glorious moment the possibilities, and then, almost as immediately, the drawbacks.

'Come into the withdrawing-room.'

Thomas followed Serafina into the withdrawing-room. The room was dark, the candles unlit, but it was a little cooler, and more airy. He watched as Serafina took a taper and lit the candles from those standing on the dining-table. One by one they flared into small golden life, illuminating her face, bathing the smooth skin of her neck and bosom.

'It would still shackle me to the Mediterranean,' said Thomas, at last. 'And besides, I made the same suggestion to Messer Capriani in the spring. As you know.'

Watching her, Thomas remembered the frail, hidebound old man. He remembered seeing Serafina on the stairs of the house in Pisa, he remembered later that day, when he had kissed her. He had never before wanted a woman as he had wanted Serafina

Guardi then. She fascinated him, and he did not know why. He had known prettier women, wealthier women, much more amiable women. Yet she dragged him unknowingly to her, so that he squirmed in her disinterested vortex.

'Messer Capriani,' said Serafina coolly, 'has begun to give me more responsibilities. I've bought a little silk for him – I'm selling it in Pisa and Lucca. It's too late for the mule train to leave this year. I think that eventually I will be able to persuade him to use shipping. It really would be so much more profitable. And less exhausting. As I told you, Messer Capriani has not been well.'

To Thomas's unvoiced question, she added, 'Swamp fever. He has it every year or so. It weakens him greatly.'

She had lit every candle; light washed the walls of the room. Thomas could see the murals painted high up close to the ceiling, the endless woven lines of classical dancers and musicians, naked every one of them.

'Perhaps you should consider talking to Messer Capriani again,' said Serafina.

Some of the dancers, like the marble cupids, were intertwined with each other. Men and women, women and women, women and animals. Thomas, looking slowly back at Serafina, said, 'I hadn't thought of you as a merchant.'

She smiled. He thought that he could count on the fingers of one hand the number of times he had seen her smile, and yet her whole face lightened when she did so. 'It is in my blood,' she said.

Thomas thought of Angelo and the notary Jehan de Coniques, and what Serafina had lost, through someone else's design.

'I have been bought and sold myself, Thomas,' she said softly, voicing his thoughts. 'Why should I not also buy and sell?'

He knew then, with a brief cold icing of the skin on the back of his neck, that however much the months in Italy had outwardly changed Serafina, she had not forgotten the past. He put down his glass; he no longer wanted to drink.

Serafina added, 'Do you know how the Algerian merchants choose Christian women for the seraglio, Thomas? The women are dressed and veiled, of course, in accordance with Islamic law, and they are hidden behind a screen. But there are gaps in the screen, and gaps also in the captives' clothing. So that the merchants may tell for themselves whether their prospective purchases are truly virgin, you see.'

She paused. 'I was never sold to the seraglio, Thomas. Fate, and my master, saved me from that. But in Algiers I learned a little more about buying and selling.'

His gaze flickered to the wall-frieze and then back to Serafina. She still wore the shimmering amber silk, yet in his mind's eye Thomas saw her dressed in loose robes like the Tuareg women had worn, half hidden behind a carved ivory screen. He became aware that his shirt clung to his back with sweat, that he was possessed by an old familiar hunger. He had put that hunger out of his mind since he had seen her in Pisa, and it had repaid him by returning now, unexpectedly, in double quantity. As if in a dream, he saw Serafina put aside the taper and come towards him.

'We are alike, you and I,' she said softly. 'You will have your ship, I will have my silk. Perhaps one day you'll build a ship for me, Thomas.'

Her hand rested on his arm; he could feel the warmth of her palm through his shirt. His fingers tentatively traced her shoulders, his thumbs followed the curve of her neck. The house had grown silent, the walls of the room constricted, as though only the two of them existed. He felt her hand slide round his waist, and he bent his head and kissed her hair, her forehead, the small white scar sketched along her hairline. Her hair had the fineness of the silk she coveted. A small band of pearls fixed the smooth coils in place: carefully, Thomas loosened them so that her dark locks fell in a single shining wave to her shoulders.

It would have been enough, almost, to feel the cool texture of her skin against his mouth, to let her unbound hair trail through his outspread fingers. But he knew, then, by the pressure of her fingers on his back, by the way she lifted her face, that it was not enough for her. So he let himself begin to trace out the old paths, aware all the time of a frightening newness, an undiscovered country, aware too that he had wanted this for months, since, perhaps, he had crossed the Mediterranean with her.

He, who had first lain with a woman when he was sixteen, found himself sailing across unfamiliar seas. She felt small and fragile within his arms, and yet, when he briefly opened his own eyes, he could see the heat in hers, feel, too, the strength of her small roving hands. It was he who eased her gown from her shoulders so that he could kiss the hollows and shadows of her skin; but she who unlaced her bodice so that the two silken halves parted to show him the treasure they contained.

She had sunk to the ground, her gown a cloud of golden silk around her, and Thomas knelt in front of her. The candlelight drew for him her smooth rounded breasts, unexpectedly heavy for so small a frame, and, cupping them in his hands, he laid his face between them. Her skin was warm and soft like the peach he had eaten only a half-hour before; gently squeezing her nipples between forefinger and thumb, he half expected sweet juice to trail out into his mouth. He heard her small indrawn breath as he ran the palms of his hands over her flat belly, and then untied the ribbons attaching her bodice to her skirt.

He watched her as she lay back on the floor, the silk rustling in folds and curves around her. Afterwards, that small dry rustling sound would always be Serafina for him: Serafina of the straight, graceful limbs, flat belly and rounded breasts, lying back in a bed made from the riches of the East. His lungs were filled with the scent of the patchouli she wore to perfume her skin, her body was gilt with the reflection of candlelight and silk. She was a goddess of the East, and he would have crossed oceans for her, navigated uncharted waters. He moved aside the last of her petticoats and let his hands trace the path from her navel to the small but inviting forest that flourished between her legs.

Because he was a perfectionist, Thomas did not hurry. He knew that it was best when you both took your pleasure together, and for that he knew also that he must be patient. But Serafina was not hard to please: he saw her dark, watchful eyes finally close, her lips open a little. He felt the taut muscles of her body relax as his fingers caressed the black silky hair. Then, when her thighs had parted for him, he lowered himself on top of her and let her pull him inside.

It was not, after all, as difficult as she had feared. She had been nervous that evening, had drunk more wine than she was accustomed to. And yet she knew now that the wine had not been necessary, that her untutored body learned quickly what to do.

Nor, this time, did she experience the vulnerability she had earlier felt with Jacopo Capriani. To make love to Thomas Marlowe which, when the idea had first occurred to her, had seemed so necessary yet so frightening, was not in the end daunting. To feel his arms around her, the warmth of his mouth against hers, seemed entirely right. It was a comfort, a reward, perhaps, for years of solitariness.

When they made love a second time she heard herself cry out a single word of endearment that she believed lost in the tangled sheets, the hot, perfumed night. And yet, had he heard, she would not have drawn the word back even if she could.

Tomorrow she would put love and all its entrancing, deceitful web aside again. But tonight, she would allow herself, for just a little while, to be ensnared by its delightful, glittering strands.

She was gone when he woke up the following morning, his head thick with red wine and a long night.

Watching the sunlight filtering through the bed-curtains, Thomas recollected the events of the previous night, and made no sense of them. Serafina Guardi was undoubtedly a bitch, but she had also been – to his surprise – undoubtedly a virgin. He had assumed that her years in Barbary had relieved her of that particular commodity. He was glad, though, that fate had kept her from the seraglio. No Sultan of any taste would ever have let her go.

He knew, of course, why he had made love to her. It would have been almost impossible to have chosen otherwise. Somehow, during their irregular meetings over the last eighteen months, Serafina had progressed from being an irritation, to a fascination, to an obsession. His own motives were obvious. Her image had seared itself to his inner eyelid, her voice, her presence, she had locked into his soul. What he did not understand was why she had made love to him.

She had made it perfectly plain on their last meeting that she had found his clumsy advances repellent. He had taunted her with the curious fusion of love and hatred she felt for her cousin Angelo, and she had treated him with the contempt he had undoubtedly deserved. And yet last night she had welcomed him, encouraged him, embraced him. Indeed, it had been she who had touched him first, she who had unlaced her gown for him.

They had gone to bed at last, and made love for a second time there. He remembered the soft cloud of her hair against his face, the look in her eyes when she wanted him to please her. He knew that he had murmured endearments to her, and that once, joyously, she had allowed herself to utter a single word of love. He did not underestimate the significance of that single word: her past would not have permitted her the easy voicing of affection. Yet it did not surprise him that her side of the bed was empty that morning, that her pillow and half of the sheets had been smoothed into place, so that no imprint of her body remained. But every time he closed his eyes, Thomas saw the sheen of her honey-coloured skin, her dark, hungry eyes.

From an upper window in the house on the Via S. Domenico, Jacopo Capriani watched Serafina return to Pisa in the early evening.

She had ridden to Livorno three days before with the clerk Amadeo, to buy silks and ribbons from the newly unloaded ships. But Amadeo had returned alone the previous day. Messer Capriani had thought he would scold Serafina, but then, when he saw her riding down the dusty street, he knew that he would not.

The house had been empty without her. There was no point in going to the counting-house when Serafina was not there to smile and nod her head, no point in sitting down at the table to eat without Serafina opposite him, making a simple meal into a banquet. Often in the last few weeks, he had thought he must be ill again, because he had the restlessness of fever, the interrupted and colourful dreams. But his forehead had been cool, his heart-beat normal. He had realized, eventually, that certain feelings he had thought stifled by years of disuse were not dead, only buried. He told no one about this, of course, partially because there was no one to tell, and partially because he knew how they would laugh at him. He did not laugh, however, except occasionally, in unexpected delight. She had made him feel like a young man again, tasting spring for an unexpected second time.

Now, when he could not sleep at night, it was not because of the discomforts of old age or sickness, but because of Serafina. She did not even possess the sort of looks he generally admired, but there was something in her eyes, in her smile, in her soft silky skin that made him forget the preconceptions of a lifetime. In the withdrawing-room, Jacopo Capriani waited for her to come to him, to tell him of the goods she had bought, to let him kiss her, and then to ease her gown from her shoulders so that he could touch her breasts. He expected no more; he had asked for no more. She had already given him a joy he had never thought to experience again.

There was no knock at his door, though, and when he heard her bedchamber door close, Jacopo was seized by unformed, inexpressible fears. He found himself walking from the withdrawing-room window to Serafina's bedchamber door on the upper floor without thought, as though his actions were no longer his to control.

He was reassured, though, when he knocked and called out, and she answered immediately. Opening the door, Jacopo saw that Serafina was standing in front of the window, backed by the setting sun that filtered through the translucent curtains. Her shoulders were gleaming and naked, her dark hair trailed down her back. There was a towel loosely knotted round her breasts, and a large bowl of water stood on another towel behind her.

The merchant's heart had begun to beat very fast. She said, 'Shut the door,' and he obeyed with difficulty, his muscles scarcely capable of movement. When he turned back, he saw that she had let the towel fall to the floor and was walking naked back to the wash-basin.

He understood then that he was to be allowed more than even his dreams had permitted him. He watched, his breath knotted in his throat, as she picked up the sponge, and squeezed the water over her breasts, her belly, her buttocks. The dying sun gilded her small perfect body, shadowing her skin with a rosy gold, glittering on the moving, mirroring water in the bowl.

When she had washed and dried herself, she came to him and led him to the bed. The tips of her long dark locks clung damply to her back, her cheeks were stained with pink. Taking Jacopo Capriani's hand in hers, she let it trace the contours of her body, and then made him wait no more.

In the bed she practised all that Thomas Marlowe had taught her. The actions were the same, she even used some of the Englishman's words, and yet she felt as though she was watching herself from a distance performing some jerky, meaningless dance. What had seemed so easy, so right, with Thomas, now was hollow, a laborious, degrading forcing of mind and muscle. As the merchant's mouth sought hers, as his fingers dug into her flesh, she knew that tears lined her lids and gathered in the corners of her eyes. Angrily, Serafina fought back the thought that she was a puppet, and Angelo still working the strings.

The warm wind twisted the gauzy curtains, illuminating the couple on the bed with the pink rays of the setting sun. Taut skin and slack, smooth limbs and wrinkled, performing rituals as old as mankind itself.

Throughout the continuing hot weather, Thomas had slept on board the *Kingfisher*. It was airless in the cramped rooms of his lodgings, and besides, valuable tools and materials frequently had to be left on board ship. He slept lightly on one of the half-finished decks; Rufus the blacksmith snored behind the foremast, William Williams and the youth Cristofano dozed somewhere in the hold below.

It was too hot to sleep well, so Thomas, lying on his back, his head cradled on his hands, lay open-eyed, studying the comforting patterns of the stars. The renegade physician had seen the future there, but Thomas saw nothing other than a reminder of the voyages he was impatient to make. Those same heavens watched over the Indies, Cathay, the Americas. His need to see those lands was sometimes overwhelming, as though he, like his unfinished *Kingfisher*, was both pinioned and caged.

But a different obsession had increasingly consumed him in the last fortnight. Sometimes Thomas found it hard to believe that that one extraordinary night had ever happened; at other times the memory of it swamped him, so that the simplest action became mechanical, unsupported by coherent thought. Since that night at the Palazzo Sacchetti, Thomas had seen or heard nothing of Serafina. He had not expected to, and neither had he made any attempt to contact her himself. Yet the days – and worse, the nights – seemed filled with constant reminders of her. The sight of a yellow gown would set his heart beating at twice its usual speed, the scent of patchouli drifting from one of the packages of spices unladen from the Levant would make his body ache with memory. He told himself that such folly would not last. But Serafina seemed to have imprinted herself on every part of him, as though he were damascened with her like the silk she coveted.

Opening his eyes, hot with a desire that had quickly become habitual, Thomas saw that the sky had begun to lighten, that a wash of orange covered the darkness. For one confused moment he thought that it was dawn, and then, immediately following, he knew that he had only recently heard the church bells chime midnight.

He was on his feet, pulling his shirt over his head and shouting to the others before he had even voiced to himself the awful truth. The orange sky signified nothing other than what any dry, overheated dockyard most dreaded. A fire.

He had jumped down to the quayside, Cristofano at his heels and William Williams running behind him, as he pinpointed the source of the flames. The timberyard: Thomas swore hopelessly, and ran with renewed speed towards where his wood was stacked; the wood that he had begged for, bargained for, sold his soul for.

By the time they reached the timber-yard, half the population of Livorno seemed to be there also. All the tongues of the globe called to each other: buckets of water were passed from white hands to black, black to brown. The slaves from the bagnio were there, still fettered, working to save the wood to build the galleys that they would be forced to row. Sparks soared into the

air, the red light of the flames reduced all faces, black and white
alike, to a tortured darkness. Thomas, ducking through the crowds
with the boy Cristofano in his wake, felt the heat hit him like a solid
wall as he ran further into the timber-yard. The heavy bolts of
wood had caught alight like paper, dried by two months of
drought and the fierce Tuscan sun. If he had been able to cry at what
Thomas knew might be the funeral pyre of all his dreams, then the
tears would have turned to vapour before they left his eyes.

He sent the apprentice back to fetch more water. Then, cursing
his lack of gloves, Thomas began to drag an untouched timber
from the smouldering pile. He felt the load lighten suddenly,
and saw William Williams, his hands wrapped in his leather
apron, lift the other end of the beam. Through the hiss of steam
as water caught charred wood, through the cries of slaves
scorched by the darting flames, Thomas and the carpenter began
to haul the timber to the comparative safety of the dockside.

He knew, of course, that it could all be futile. He knew that
any moment a fireball might roar out of the gathering inferno
and engulf the timber-yard, the docks, the town itself. And if
the arsenal caught fire, then Livorno would simply sink back
into the swamps from which the Medici had raised it.

Thomas worked doggedly, unaware that the skin on his face
had begun to peel, disregarding the pain in his hands. Rufus was
hauling a huge oak-beam single-handedly out of the periphery
of the fire: sparks danced golden in the air as the wood dragged
along the ground. Cristofano's naked torso and face were blackened with soot, so that he looked indistinguishable from the
slaves from the bagnio. Thomas could smell, through the acrid
scent of soaked, charred timber, his own scorched hair and skin.

He knew that they had won when the circle of people around
the timber-yard began to constrict, trapping the flames as though
they were a myriad small creatures ensnared by the plough. But
by that time, Thomas understood that he had lost.

They had saved a dozen beams out of a stock of fifty. They
had lost the precious English oak that he had bought for masts
and spars. Overnight, the price of timber would treble: overnight, the bigger concerns – the trading companies, the sea-
princes – would have priority to buy what little timber was left.

Thomas, sitting on the edge of the quayside, staring at the sea, hardly noticed the pain of the burns. The pain in his heart was much worse, for it represented the death of his dreams.

The merchant Jacopo Capriani and his entourage had ridden north, to visit the city of Lucca.

Messer Capriani took, as always, his clerks Amadeo and Bastien, his errand-boys and armed guard. The clerk Serafina came too – but no: she could no longer be called a clerk, she had become something more than that. Amadeo and Bastien still sniggered to each other in private, but there was the sting of defeat behind their laughter. The maidservants and errand-boys answered Serafina's call as quickly as they answered Messer Capriani's – not because she was overbearing or officious, but because there was a look in her cool dark eyes, a timbre in her pleasant voice, that made obedience natural. When the merchant inspected the goods unladen from the ships, or newly completed in the workshops, Serafina went with him. Sometimes, though, she visited the market-places alone, leaving Messer Capriani dozing in a chair in the fly-ridden heat.

In Lucca, Messer Capriani and Serafina paid calls to the great palazzos. While Messer Capriani discussed prices with his customers, Serafina laid out ribbons and braid and silk and cockades on a suitable table, and later noted the purchases in a ledger-book. In the luxurious ante-room of a palazzo belonging to the banker Galeazzo Merli, the rich colours shimmered in the heavy afternoon heat: ochres and purples and crimsons, echoing the carved golden stone surrounding the open windows, the intricate patterns of the tapestries that hung limply in the windless air.

If the merchant had not made his usual odyssey this year, then business was still reasonably good. Customers appreciated the wider choice of items, the brighter colours, the finer quality of Messer Capriani's wares. Meticulously, Serafina added the finishing touches to an enticing display of finery, and tried not to be sick.

Always honest with herself, she knew that her nausea was caused neither by swamp fever nor by tainted food. She was sick because she was frightened. She, who had been bought and sold, who had crossed the Mediterranean in a fishing boat, trembled at the thought of what she must do next. Her eyes darted restlessly around the room, fixing briefly on the candelabra, the carved and inlaid chests, the wide, polished wood floor scattered with rugs. Through the window she could see Messer Merli's exquisite formal garden, still and heat-soaked, powdered with dust. As she smoothed creases from the silk, her hands were not quite steady, her hair had glued itself in small twisting curls to her forehead. Over and over again she had told herself not to be foolish: she had not been afraid when she had lost her virginity to the Englishman, she had not been afraid when she had taken the merchant to her bed. Why then, when all she needed was a small but well-timed display of emotion, did her heart rattle against her ribs, and her stomach squeeze like a swimming jelly-fish?

That morning, Madonna Merli, Galeazzo's wife, had chosen her purchases from Messer Capriani's wares. Madonna Merli, younger than Serafina, had been dark and plain and rather plump; her maid, whose bulk and demeanour had reminded Serafina abruptly of Marthe, had accompanied her throughout. Madonna Merli had bought figured silks and the scarlet ribbons that sold so well. Messer Merli, more than twice the age of his wife, had not been present while she made her choice. He did, however, now accompany his mistress, Costanza.

Retreating respectfully to the window, trying to steady her fluttering heart, Serafina watched the courtesan through lowered lids. She was between thirty and forty, and not beautiful, exactly, but her profile was strong and well formed. She had an aura of calmness that Messer Merli's infant bride had lacked, a dignity that kept her movements slow and measured, her grey eyes ironic. Costanza was, Messer Capriani had earlier whispered to Serafina, a Venetian by birth, but she had lived profitably in Lucca for twenty years now.

'My dear –' Galeazzo Merli, eyeing Serafina with interest, led the courtesan forward. The merchant remained courteously in the background, but Serafina knew without looking that his eyes, as well as those of the banker, were on her, hungrily studying her skin, her face, her body.

She had given Jacopo Capriani a taste of youth and pleasure again, but she had recently, by careful arrangement, withdrawn that gift. She had not slept with Messer Capriani for over a week now: the lack of privacy afforded by the open road and the necessity of staying in other people's houses had made such things difficult. All Serafina had had to do was to make the difficult impossible, by sharing her bedchamber with a maid, or by suffering a well-timed headache. Not because it disgusted her to sleep with Messer Capriani, but because it was time that the merchant paid for his pleasures. He was too old for the hunger to last long; she knew that she must be sure of gaining what she wanted before desire dulled to indifference.

She had thought it out so carefully, and it had all seemed quite simple. Yet now the broad, well-furnished room had become constricted and airless, and there was that same suffocating sense of futility she had endured in the merchant's arms, when her body had no longer seemed to belong to her, but to some other, older master. The grip of the nausea intensified, and her fingers knotted together, so that she wanted to fist her hands and chew them like a baby. Serafina made herself look out of the window to the garden below, to where the crosses and triangles of green grass were intersected by paths of red, dusty earth. She could feel the merchant's eyes burning on her turned head, and for a moment she hated him with a pure, cold hatred she had not known she possessed. Thomas had looked at her like that: with longing, with hunger. A few weeks ago, in the Palazzo Sacchetti, she had seen herself reflected in Thomas Marlowe's blue eyes as something beautiful, something desirable. Something of worth.

No – she must not think of Thomas. Thomas was not, could not be part of the future she had begun to create for herself. Thomas was nothing to her, and she was nothing to Thomas. For Thomas, she had been nothing more than a pleasant way of passing the night, an enjoyable distraction from day-to-day worries. The night in the Palazzo Sacchetti had been insignificant; it had simply served a purpose.

But still she shook as though she had an ague. The voices of Messer Merli and Costanza blurred into the background; almost choking, Serafina mumbled her excuses and ran out of the room and into the garden.

She knew that the merchant would still be watching her from an upstairs window. Careless for once, Serafina sat down on the low wall that surrounded the fountain and balled her fingers into fists, pressing them against her eyes. In spite of the heat, she was shivering like the dusty grey leaves of the eucalyptus. The sky was an intense, hazy blue, and she could smell the sharp scent of the orange and lemon trees in their terracotta pots. Suddenly she was back at Kara Ali's house again, in the courtyard with the archways and fountains, where the bitter fragrance of lemon was made captive by the windless air. The shards of the blue pot were at her feet, her face and hair were covered by a veil. The memory calmed her; she knew again why she was here. For the loss of those years, for the loss of her family and her inheritance. Dropping her hands from her face, Serafina straightened and turned towards the fountain. The fine spray caught against her cheeks, painting tears where she had been able to find none. At last she heard the merchant's footsteps on the path.

'She has chosen all dark colours, would you believe? I would have thought such a creature would have taken yellows and reds.'

Serafina said nothing. Her face, lowered, was turned away.

'Perhaps you should help me price them . . .' began Messer Capriani, uncertainly.

'I think I should go –' Her voice was low, unsteady.

The merchant said, 'I did not mean that you must go to work immediately, Serafina. If you are unwell perhaps you should sit out here a little longer.'

The sickness she had felt had retreated now. 'I mean,' she whispered, 'that I should leave your service, Messer Capriani.'

She did not look, but she knew that he had sat down on the wall beside her. She could hear the rustle of his robes and smell, through the scents of orange and lemon and eucalyptus, the indefinable scent of old age.

'Why should you go?' Beneath the false overlay of jollity, there was panic in the merchant's voice. 'The business needs you, Serafina. Who else has such an eye for silk?'

She shook her head. 'I cannot stay,' she said, sadly, and slowly turned her face.

Her eyes were red because she had rubbed them, her cheeks damp with the spray of the fountain. It was enough: the merchant caught her hands between his two old, dry ones.

'My dear Serafina. You should not cry. What troubles you?'

She took one sharp, wobbling breath, and dropped her face. 'I have been so happy working for you, Messer Capriani. But I must not stay any longer. What has happened between us – I am afraid . . .'

She let her voice drift away on the small warm breeze that twisted briefly round the dry earth and glazed leaves.

Reclaiming one of her hands, she wiped her face dry with her fingers and said, with an apparent effort at resolution, 'I have not been feeling well, Messer Capriani. There are sicknesses a woman is prone to if she lies with a man.'

Even then, spelt out quite bluntly, it took him a while to understand. But eventually, she felt his hand tighten in hers, and heard his rapid indrawn breath.

She waited until the confusion in his eyes had been replaced first by realization, and then by pride, and then she said, 'I will not bear a bastard in your house, Jacopo. I would not shame you so.'

She did not move. She became aware that her hands had clenched again, that a trickle of sweat ran down between her breasts. But she felt excitement now, not nausea. She had offered him a choice between lust and common sense, and she knew that the weighting in her favour was not heavy. She thought that if she stood, if she moved so much as a muscle, she might lose him and the opportunity he represented for ever. So she remained still, trusting in the proximity of her flesh, the scent of her perfumed skin.

'I will find another home for your son,' she said softly.

She knew immediately that she had chosen her words well. There was lust and there was pride, and there was the dizzying, aching desire to recapture the youth that Jacopo Capriani had believed for ever lost. There was the inevitable human need to fight back against the dank odour of the grave that old age and fever had conjured. When Messer Capriani took her hand, and raised it to his lips, Serafina knew that she had won.

When they went back into the house, the courtesan Costanza was making ready to leave. As she bowed her head to Serafina and the merchant, the silk scarf she wore slipped, and for the first time Serafina clearly saw the left side of her face.

On the right side of her face Costanza's complexion was still perfect, thick and waxen and creamy like a magnolia, with no trace as yet of the passing years. But on the left side – and Serafina began to shiver again – placed there deliberately by some angry or possessive lover, was a thin curved scar the length of her jaw that destroyed her perfection for ever, and announced to the world both her profession and her punishment.

The worst of the burns had blistered when, a few days later, Thomas Marlowe reached Pisa.

Not a man to dwell on misfortune, he had occupied the days following the fire by inspecting his remaining stocks of wood, by methodically visiting every timber-merchant in Livorno, and equally methodically accepting the critical nature of his situation. He had no money, and no materials, and an unfinished ship. He had debts and men to pay and dock space to rent. Unless a miracle happened soon, the *Kingfisher* might never sail.

Not much of a believer in miracles, Thomas had ridden through the night to Pisa. Rarely given to self-analysis, he did not waste time trying to unravel the unaccustomed tangle of his emotions. He should have been feeling despair: he knew that if Capriani made him an offer, he would be bound to sail the Mediterranean for years to come. But it was not despair that he experienced that night: instead, Thomas found that he felt incongruously cheerful. Throughout the long ride the thought that he would see Serafina again – even if only across a bargaining table – cheered him. Arriving in Pisa, Thomas found a tavern to look after his horse, and walked to Messer Capriani's house.

Inside, he was greeted not by the merchant, but by Serafina herself. She was dressed in the same gown she had worn when

Thomas had first visited Pisa: grey, with a demure white collar and long tight sleeves. But this time there was a gold pendant round her neck, and jewels in her ears and on her fingers. The sober shade of the material contrasted with the slight colour in her cheeks, and the gold of the pendant echoed the bloom of her skin.

Thomas bowed, and swept off his hat. 'Mademoiselle Guardi.'

Serafina held out her hand for him to kiss.

He followed her into a small parlour. There were two chairs and a rickety table, and the sunlight from the window jewelled the dusty surfaces and cobwebbed corners. 'Have you heard about the fire in Livorno's shipyard?' he asked.

Serafina nodded. 'Yes. Most annoying.' She shook her head, crossly. 'If only I had bought wood . . .'

He stared at her, uncertain for a moment whether to feel anger or amusement. Then he shut the door behind him, tossed his hat on the table, and gave a small crow of laughter.

'Unfortunately, I *had* bought wood. Most of it is now fit only for charcoal. The timber-merchants are adding a nought to all their former prices.'

He saw that she was staring at his hands. 'I apologize for my appearance,' said Thomas, raising his reddened, blistered palms. 'And for my unexpected haircut. We saved – a little.'

'Does it hurt?'

She was standing in front of the window: he could see Messer Capriani's small, tired terrace garden beyond. 'It doesn't hurt at all,' he said, with honesty. 'Not now.'

Serafina motioned him to sit down. Filling a glass with wine, Serafina handed it to Thomas.

'I take it this is a business call, then, Mr Marlowe.'

He felt a little of his old irritation return at her deliberate coolness. He had noticed how her eyes avoided his.

'Because of the fire?' Thomas took a few mouthfuls of wine. 'Yes. I find myself in a rather difficult situation. You indicated when we last met that you might be able to help me.'

When we last met. For a moment Thomas was no longer in the small, dusty parlour, but back in the faded grandeur of the Palazzo Sacchetti.

Serafina did not answer immediately. Her hands were knotted together on her lap; her dark eyes looked anywhere but at him.

'I feel sure that we can come to some arrangement, Mr Marlowe.'

He knew that she was deliberately walling herself off from him and from what friendship he might want to offer her. A technique she had, presumably, perfected in her years on the Barbary coast. But he had crossed that wall once, when, in the Palazzo Sacchetti, she had murmured that single endearment to him. Because of that memory, he managed to keep his voice as light, as practical, as hers.

'The *Kingfisher* is not yet complete, and I've no timber to finish the work. No money to buy any, either. It would be worth Messer Capriani's while to finance the *Kingfisher*'s completion – she'll be a lovely ship.'

'Of course.' The grey folds of Serafina's gown draped gracefully around her. 'I've never doubted that, Mr Marlowe.'

'Thomas.' There were too many memories that made her insistent use of his surname ridiculous or insulting. She spoke the truth, though: she had always treated his enterprise with utter seriousness.

'If you wish. Thomas.' Her voice shook slightly: but her hand, as she rang the bell on the table beside her, was steady. He wanted to shake her, or to embrace her. Anything to break through the ice.

A servant appeared to refill the glasses and offer Thomas biscuits. Serafina spoke to him briefly, too softly for Thomas to hear, and the man lowered the blinds, shutting out some of the harsh midday sunlight. Again, thought Thomas, half amused, it was as though she owned the place. He had once tried to picture Serafina in the bagnio in Algiers, and had failed, because it was impossible to imagine her taking orders from anyone.

When the servant had gone, she added, 'I'm sure we can come to some mutually agreeable arrangement. I will be able to offer you more acceptable terms than the Levant Company, I feel certain.'

He noticed, through the pleasant wave of relief that flowed over him, her natural, autocratic use of the personal pronoun.

Messer Capriani, thought Thomas, his amusement increasing, might not exist. He realized that along with desire, he had acquired a respect for Serafina, a respect for the cool, hard intellect she possessed.

Thomas raised his glass. 'To trade, then, my dear Serafina.'

'To silk.' Her glass, half full, trapped the remaining sunlight in the prism of its amber light. 'To the day when my name shall head the greatest silk trading company in Europe.'

'We should marry,' Thomas heard himself say.

The words were out before he could draw them back, called thoughtlessly from heart to tongue. He saw her cup pause, the wine in it swaying like a miniature sea.

'Marry?' said Serafina. She laughed, a sound as brittle as glass. Her eyes met his at last, and Thomas glimpsed in them an uneasy mixture of pride and defiance. 'Marry? A woman cannot have two husbands, Mr Marlowe. Even Islam does not permit that.'

It must have taken only a fraction of a second for Thomas Marlowe to understand her fully, but it seemed like an hour. He stared at her, and for the first time he began to question the significance of the jewels, of the servant, of her use of that small yet critical word, *I*.

'I married Messer Capriani yesterday morning.'

Thomas did not shout, or break his glass, or draw his sword. His temper, usually so easily ignited, remained quiescent. Serafina sat there, small and proud, her muscles rigid, her features unmoving. The colour that had momentarily flooded her face had retreated, leaving her somewhat paler than usual.

He managed to say, drily, 'Congratulations.'

'Thank you, Mr Marlowe.' He saw her relax a little, and reach for a pen and paper from the table. 'Perhaps we should begin to discuss terms for the completion of the *Kingfisher*.'

Thomas did not answer. He rose and went to the window, running a finger along the dust-filled slats of the wooden shutters. His thoughts tumbled, badly organized at first, but then slotting into place with appalling finesse. He said carefully, 'You haven't drunk your wine, Madonna Capriani. And I have forgotten the toast you proposed.'

He hadn't forgotten, of course. When she did not reply, he said idly, his back still turned to her, 'To the day when your name shall head the greatest trading company in Europe . . . What name had you in mind, Serafina? You've had quite a few names, after all. Badr-al-Dujja – Giovanni – and now Capriani. But I think you'll still want the name of Guardi to fly from the banners, won't you?'

She said nothing. Swinging round, he saw that her curved red lips were set, her eyes were dark and hard. Thomas's burnt hands had begun to throb; suddenly he felt the weariness of a night in the saddle, of the months of struggle.

Exhaustion gave an unkind clarity to his thoughts. He said, 'It's Angelo, isn't it? You intend to get it all back from Angelo. That's why you took service with the merchant – that's why you've married him. That's why you are persuading Messer Capriani to trade in silk, so that you can compete with Angelo. Antelope's tears just won't do, will they, Serafina? And that's why' – and Thomas found that a small hard ball of anger had begun to form in his stomach – 'that's why you want the *Kingfisher*. You can't destroy cousin Angelo with *mules*, after all.'

She did not deny it. She simply opened out her palms in a gesture not of apology, but of acceptance, and said, 'It is mine.'

'What will you do, Serafina?' Thomas was staring at her. His voice was choked, starved of air. 'Stab Angelo in the back as he sleeps at night?'

The colour had ebbed from her face, and her eyes were blank, black, like a doll's. 'I won't kill him. I won't need to. I'll ruin him. That's all.'

Her brittle voice stabbed at him. 'So for Angelo you'll bed an ailing old man?' Thomas stared at her. 'No, you bedded him before you married, didn't you? A taste of honey for the poor old bastard, was it, so that he'd offer you his name and his fortune in return for a bit of company at night? My God, he's sixty-five – seventy – and you're –'

'Seventeen,' she said. Her eyes burned with an ice-cold fire. 'Do you think that makes any difference, Thomas?'

He scarcely heard her. 'And me?' he said. His voice was

shaking slightly. 'Where did I come into it?' Suddenly he understood it all, and he found himself laughing, a sound utterly devoid of humour. 'A bit of practice. That's what I was for, Serafina, wasn't I?'

The ball of anger had gathered meteorically, making ready to soar into a different, darker abyss, one Thomas found that he did not want to see. But he made himself say, '*That* was why you made love to me.'

Her eyes lowered at last. Her hand reached out towards the bell, but he was there before she could touch it, her fragile wrist gripped by his blistered fingers.

He welcomed the pain, it enabled him to say, 'Tell the truth for once, Serafina. You let me seduce you because you wanted to be rid of your virginity.'

Her lids raised, her eyes met his. The pupil was hardly distinguishable from the iris. 'I needed to learn,' she said softly. 'I could not have done it without you, Thomas.'

The frailty of her body seemed inappropriate to her ruthlessness, to the strength of her purpose. There was a terrible temptation to crush the slender wrist in his grasp, to squeeze until bone turned to powder, until she cried to him for the mercy he wanted to beg from her.

But he managed to stop himself and, dropping her arm and walking from the room, merely said, 'Then damn you and your buying and selling to hell. I'll have no part of it.'

They had married two days previously, as soon as they had returned from Lucca: a furtive, hurried ceremony because Messer Capriani had been afraid that he might lose his suddenly bashful bride. Standing beside her bridegroom in the dusty, draughty withdrawing-room, Serafina had recalled those long-ago preparations for the betrothal that had never taken place. She would have married Messer Corsini in white, with her hair down, all of Florence decked out in their finery to watch them. To wed the merchant she wore the amber gown she had sewn herself, with the clerk Amadeo and a young Jesuit from the duomo as the only witnesses. She had still worn her hair down, though, despite the merchant's pathetic pride in her loss of virginity.

She had felt little more at the wedding ceremony than irritation at the interruption to her true business of trade. The triumph, and the disquiet, had begun later. She knew the reason for the triumph: now she was no longer either a slave or a servant, but the wife of a respected and successful merchant. The disquiet was less easy to pinpoint. She told herself that she had no reason to feel uneasy, that she had merely made a bargain. Her body, her beauty, in return for financial security. Such bargains were struck every time a bride let her future husband place his ring on her finger.

The nausea had returned in the evening, when Messer Capriani, prompted by her suggestion, but believing himself to be the instigator of the idea, had drawn up a new will. He had left everything to the fictitious child in her belly. Serafina had had to put aside her red wine, leaving it untasted, because the sour smell made her heart pound and her stomach contract. When, later, the merchant had taken her to his bed, she had found that she felt well again, almost able to welcome the embrace that made her marriage valid.

Unlike the nausea, the frightening sense of unreality had not returned. Nor had the nightmares: her sleep was deep and dreamless. Lying in bed on the first morning of her married life, watching the sun filter through the dusty rose-coloured bedcurtains, Serafina had told herself that things were settled now, she had a place, a name, an inheritance. Unwed, she had been nothing more than a serving-maid foolish enough to sleep with her master. Marriage to Jacopo Capriani – marriage to an ailing old man – was essential to her survival. She did not worry about the non-existent child – if Jacopo Capriani's enfeebled loins could not produce an heir, then she, for one, would not yet grieve. With the medical skills that she had learned from Kara Ali, she could surely keep Jacopo alive for a few years yet. There was no room for a brat in the future she had begun to create, and she did not, like many other women, feel any particular affection for babies. She would counterfeit an early miscarriage when her time of the month – never a very regular occurrence – next came. She was the merchant's legally wedded wife; as long as she kept him happy, and as long as he lived for a few more

years, then she had nothing to fear. She would make his business
thrive, and his house would be more comfortable than it had
been for decades. Like any wife, her happiness was dependent
upon the happiness of her husband.

And yet, after the English pilot had gone, Serafina's unease
returned. She told herself that her regret was for the loss of the
ship, for the loss of Thomas Marlowe's *Kingfisher*. She had
always sensed the importance of Thomas's dream, and recently
she had begun to see the *Kingfisher* through the Englishman's
eyes. She needed Thomas Marlowe. She needed his ship, and she
needed the pilot himself, who could navigate a cockle-shell across
the wide expanse of the Inland Sea.

If only he had not asked her to marry him. The memory of
the scene in the parlour made the blood rise to Serafina's skin,
burning her face. She told herself that her anger was with
Thomas, for complicating a situation that should have been
simple, for squandering a bargain that would have been to both
their advantages. And yet she knew, if she was honest, that her
anger was with herself as well. She had mishandled something
of importance to her, and in doing so she had lost both the
Kingfisher and the English pilot.

For Thomas had understood her. He had traced the tracks of
her intention with horrible accuracy, and had known himself
used. *A bit of practice. That's what I was for.* The memory of the
expression on Thomas's face made the nausea return again. A
cold icing of sweat gathered on Serafina's forehead while her
heart beat like a recruiting-sergeant's drum. Flinging open the
shutters to breathe in the hot, still air, she told herself once more
that it did not matter, that the Englishman had had his pleasure,
that it was a simple matter of trade.

John Keane, now comfortably ensconced in a tall thin house in
the centre of Livorno, had also been expecting a visit from
Thomas Marlowe. He had witnessed the burning of the timber-
yard from the top storey of his house: a few moments salvaged
from a fevered hour spent rushing up and down stairs with his
manservant Antonio, carrying his most precious possessions to
the safety of the street. When he had seen the fire retreat, the

colours muting from golden to amber to a dark, glowing pink, they had re-enacted the whole process in reverse, but at a different pace. The house was safe, the *Garland* and the company's warehouses were safe. John Keane had known himself to be a fortunate man on a night when many had been ruined beyond recovery.

He had heard whispers, inaccurate and ill-matched at first, then increasingly coherent, concerning the fate of his countrymen in Livorno. He had heard, eventually, that Thomas Marlowe's unfinished *Kingfisher* had survived the inferno, but that the materials bought to complete her had not. So he had waited, customarily patient.

He had not expected the knock on the door to be at midnight, though, when the servant had just begun to light the candles in the bedchamber. John himself, yawning, finished wrapping his lute in a length of red velvet.

He called Antonio to show the visitor upstairs and, running his hands through his thinning, greying hair, rose and nodded as the pilot entered the room.

'Sir.' Marlowe bowed. 'My apologies for calling on you at such an unreasonable hour.'

John Keane made polite disclaimers concerning the necessity for apologies but checked nevertheless for the whereabouts of his sword. The pilot's clothes were covered in dust, and though his words were civil, the tone of his voice struggled to remain so.

'A drink, Mr Marlowe?'

They drank red wine to the smell of sea-salt that filtered through the open window, and the disapproving clatterings of Antonio in the kitchen below.

Thomas Marlowe, draining his glass before John had emptied half of his, said, 'I've come to offer you the *Kingfisher*, Mr Keane. On the terms we have discussed already, more or less.'

Keane put down his own glass. 'The fire must have hurt you badly,' he said, studying the pilot.

'The fire?' For a moment Thomas stared at him with incomprehension. Keane noticed that the blue eyes were red-rimmed, the tangled black curls singed.

Marlowe's confusion was momentary. 'Of course, the fire. Yes – the fire hurt me a great deal. It has made my chronic financial problems acute, which is why I come to you, Mr Keane. To remedy the hurt.'

Keane nodded. Aware of a small but unmistakable feeling of triumph, he picked up the pen on the table and, sitting down, began to write. 'I will have to ratify the agreement when my superior arrives with the next company convoy. But I'm sure there will be no difficulty. The terms as we discussed, then, Mr Marlowe?'

'The terms as we discussed. With one proviso.'

Keane turned, pen in hand. The wildness that had prompted him to look for his sword had gone from the pilot's eyes; they were masked now by a clear cold calculation.

'I will choose the materials, Mr Keane. I will not compromise on that. I will sink her now rather than have some corsair sink her later because you have chosen to economize on cannon or suchlike.'

A demanding, if not unexpected, proviso. The pen still rested in John Keane's hand.

'I assure you, Mr Marlowe,' he said, carefully, 'that I take the threat of corsairs as seriously as you do.'

'Aye. I don't doubt it.' Marlowe laughed unpleasantly. 'After all, you're not above playing the part of the corsair if it will bring you a little extra profit.'

Keane shrugged. 'I cannot deny that. Neither are we above selling the Turk Cornish tin so that Islam may cast itself bronze ordnance. No, Mr Marlowe, I am not above such things. It is trade, that's all.'

'The word *trade* seems to cover an interestingly diverse variety of sins.' Thomas Marlowe, at Keane's gesture of assent, refilled his glass, drank heavily, and then looked up to the agent. 'Tuscany will not tolerate the company's excesses for much longer, Mr Keane. They might have invited you here in the first place, but they will not continue to turn a blind eye to piracy.'

John Keane, having returned the pen to the inkwell, folded his hands together. He said softly, 'Do you think that Duke Ferdinand's objections are to our supposed acts of piracy, Mr

Marlowe, or to our successful trading? The Mediterranean is an increasingly crowded pond, the prizes of the Levant and the Indies are increasingly great. We northerners have the ships, the sailors – the navigators. Venice is a failing power, France has struggled since the civil wars. Spain is governed by an obsessed, ageing King. There has been peace in the Mediterranean for twenty years now. Peace of a sort. The times have never been better for us.'

Thomas Marlowe did not immediately reply. Keane watched as he walked slowly round the room, past the lute, the chess set, the books.

'Yet you are a civilized man, sir. Doesn't it trouble you that the Levant Company arms the Turk, and plunders the ships of Christendom?'

Keane thought, then, that Thomas Marlowe had grown up a little since he had last spoken to him. He guessed Marlowe to be in his mid-twenties, about ten years younger than he, and with the half-formed morality of a younger man.

'It troubles me – a little,' he said. 'Our government burns at the stake those who consider themselves Christians . . . and has beheaded a Queen who also considered herself Christian . . . These things have happened in my lifetime – in both our lifetimes – Mr Marlowe. I find the complexities of dogma beyond me. That is why I am a merchant, not a theologian. I will, however, do whatever is necessary for the success of the company. That is how I – and my family – and my country – will survive.'

He looked up at the younger man, meeting the angry blue gaze. 'You, too, are a survivor, after all, Mr Marlowe. And I suspect that, like me, you will do almost anything to remain so.'

And Thomas did not, as John Keane knew he might, reach for his sword. Because Thomas Marlowe, as well as being a survivor, was also, like Keane himself, an intelligent, civilized man.

He had thought long enough. John Keane added softly, 'I agree to your proviso, Mr Marlowe. You may choose the men and materials to complete your ship.'

PART VI

1595

THE SMELL OF GAYNE

The smell of gayne is sweete, though it come of Dung.

Itinerary: Fynes Moryson

Serafina spent the first two months of her married life sweeping out the dustier corners of Jacopo Capriani's property. She engaged new servants: a woman to cook and supervise the maids, a new clerk to replace the dishonest Bastien. Sometimes she threw an apron over her own gown and beat decades of dust from the carpets and hangings; equally as often she kept to the counting-house, supervising clever but feckless Amadeo. In the evenings she devoted herself to the entertainment of Messer Capriani.

Only her health seemed, inconveniently, to have let her down. She was still sometimes attacked by nausea, and at other times, most frequently in the afternoon, she was overcome with a weariness so great that if she closed her eyes she would sleep where she sat. Serafina fought off both the exhaustion and the sickness, hiding them from husband and servants alike. It seemed ironic that her health, which apart from that single bout of measles in Algiers had always been excellent, should desert her as soon as her life began to improve.

Still, the antelope's tears were slowly transmuting to silk, and Jacopo, diverted temporarily from the business of making money, was increasingly content to leave the routine responsibilities of house and business to one who longed for power, however mundane. Pisa was not Marseilles; Jacopo Capriani's villa did not compare with the home Angelo had stolen from her, but she had discovered an exciting sense of progression, of being drawn slowly but inevitably towards a destiny she was herself creating. For the first time since the corsair ship had robbed her of the most fundamental human dignities, she had taken control of her own life, shaping it and moulding it like clay with her own strong hands.

It is mine, she had said to Thomas Marlowe, and she would know no peace of mind until she had seized back everything she had lost. The house, the company, the name. She would possess them all again: she had armed herself with the means to do so, she had discovered in herself the will and the strength. That was what allowed her to endure Jacopo's complaints and demands, that was what allowed her to ignore the whispers of the servants, the staring in the streets.

She had considered the ways that a man might be ruined. Financially, there were the disastrous agencies of storm or fire, over which only God had control. But there were slower, more insidious methods that a clever businessman – or woman – might employ. Direct competition, undercutting of prices, acquisition of either customer or wholesaler. To be able to compete on Angelo's grounds, she must avoid the percentages payable to Italian shipping agencies. She must purchase in markets further afield than Livorno, she must buy in bulk, and distribute her cargo quickly and reliably. She must sail to the Levant. To ruin Angelo, she had concluded furiously, she needed the *Kingfisher*.

But both Thomas Marlowe and his ship had disappeared completely from her life. For the first time, as she watched the motes of dust dance in the newly swept corners, as she checked the neat rows of Roman numerals in the ledger-books, Serafina experienced regret. But only for the ship, for the Englishman's glorious, half-finished *Kingfisher*.

And Angelo? To ruin your enemy, you must study him closely, understanding intimately every detail of his talents, his faults, his ambitions. Angelo had never sought happiness, Serafina understood that now. He had had other gods, and sometimes, in the unforgiving silence of the early mornings, Serafina thought that she, too, had come to know those gods over the passing years, and that their names were ambition, and power, and security.

They shared the same stars, she and Angelo. November births both of them, and the scorpion's venomous tail was already curling, making ready to strike.

In Livorno, walking along the busy dockside, John Keane was

more than happy with his two most recent purchases. The re-employment of Thomas Marlowe by the Levant Company had meant not only the continued construction of the *Kingfisher*, but also the efficient restoration of the damaged *Garland*. Marlowe had happily agreed to supervise the repair of the older ship, and to lend Keane his carpenters and shipwrights while the *Kingfisher* waited for timber. No – not happily. Happy was not a word that John Keane would have applied to Thomas Marlowe just now. Energetic and hard-working: yes. But not happy. Rather – foul-tempered.

Keane put his new employee's prickliness down to his loss of independence. Understandable enough: Thomas wanted to discover new lands, to sail uncharted seas. He wanted to sail to the Indies, the Americas, Cathay, in a ship he had designed, built, and navigated himself. The cage that John Keane had helped build for him would be to the benefit of the Levant Company, but it was a cage nevertheless. Marlowe's restlessness was almost tangible, kept barely under control by hard work and heavy drinking. Sometimes, John found himself waiting, nerves steeled, for the inevitable breaking-point.

Halting level with the *Garland* and squinting up to the deck, John picked out the pilot from the huddle of men on board. Cupping his hands round his mouth, he called, 'Thomas Marlowe! How goes it?'

Through the blur of myopia, he saw a dark head detach itself from the cluster round the mizzen-mast. Thomas, elbows resting on the gunwale, shouted down, 'The deckplanks are all sound, and William's repaired the yards on the mizzen. Come and see.'

John Keane climbed the gangway to the deck of the *Garland*. The deck was solid underfoot now, not splintered as it had been after the storm, and the masts and spars stood strong and proud, ready to take the weight of the wind in the sails. Thomas had been correct when he had said that the *Garland* would not see the end of the century. But she should now see another year or two.

On the foredeck, his narrowed eyes inspecting the ship, John Keane said, 'You've done a good job, Thomas.'

The pilot shrugged. He wore canvas breeches and a filthy

linen shirt, and his eyes were a bright clear blue in a skin burned brown by the Tuscan sun. 'Keep your congratulations for William Williams. He's a damn good carpenter.'

'Of course.' Keane's short-sighted light eyes registered curiosity. 'He sailed with you on the *Toby*, didn't he?'

Thomas nodded. 'And went down with her, too. We were lucky.'

There was an acid inflection in the pilot's voice that seemed to bely the meaning of the word, *lucky.*

John Keane said gently, 'All of Livorno's looking for timber for masts. You'll get it. It will just take time. Meanwhile –' He hesitated.

Thomas said, 'Meanwhile, let me take the *Garland* to Zante. I'll get you a good price for your tin, John. And the voyage would be a proving-ground for the old thing.' He patted the *Garland*'s mainmast affectionately.

John Keane shook his head. 'I've a different diversion in mind, Thomas. I was going to suggest that what you need is beautiful women – fine wine – the most carefully cooked delicacies plucked from the Mediterranean Sea. In other words, the representatives of the Levant Company have received an invitation to a banquet at the house of a respected Lucchese banker.'

Thomas was staring at him, and John Keane could not quite read the expression on the pilot's face. Then he saw the younger man groan and shake his head.

'Fat Italian matrons, snivelling infants attempting to sing, and overcooked octopus. I've been to these affairs before, John. I'd rather sit on the deck of my half-finished ship with a pack of cards and a pint of cheap red wine.'

'Exactly,' said John crisply. Leaving the pilot, he began to walk back towards the gangway. 'As you have done each evening for the last eight weeks. I have an invitation to Messer Merli's house in Lucca on Friday evening. The company does business with Messer Merli. I have to be there. And so' – he looked back as he stepped off the gangway – 'do you.'

In the end, the banquet was even more appalling than he had expected it to be.

There were jugglers, and conjurors, and a fire-eater, and a monkey that disgraced itself by biting Messer Merli's ankle. Messer Merli jabbed at it with his rapier, but the monkey, who had not, like his adversary, consumed a great deal of claret, fled unscathed and shrieking up one of the curtains and refused to come down all evening.

There was a dwarf who produced silk flowers from improbable places such as candles and nectarines and ladies' bosoms. And inevitably, there was a small collection of overweight infants, all fathered by Galeazzo Merli, performing a mime accompanied by a bevy of shrieking madrigal singers. When the fattest and plainest child seated itself, complete with trident, on a papier-mâché scallop-shell, a distinct rending noise could be heard, and Thomas buried his head in his hands and groaned.

By then he had seen her, of course. It was no surprise to Thomas that the Caprianis were in Lucca that night: they were merchants, too, part of the same small, tight community that he and John Keane also belonged to. Thomas had known as soon as Keane had issued his unwanted invitation that Serafina might be there. He had caught sight of her as he entered the Great Chamber, ensconced with her ageing husband and a fawning group of fellow-merchants in one corner of the room. Her small straight back was encased in some peculiar brownish material, her dark hair threaded with ribbons and pearls as elaborately as a galleon's rigging. He had not approached her then, because he had known himself incapable of merely bowing and saying coolly, *Buona sera, Madonna Capriani*. He would have wished her publicly to the devil in front of all this appalling congregation and that, Thomas had recently acquired the sense to realize, just would not do.

Serafina had been pleased but surprised to receive the invitation from Galeazzo Merli. Pleased, because the invitation would afford her the social recognition she so desperately needed, but surprised that the banker should think the Caprianis worthy of his notice.

She understood his motives, however, as soon as she was reintroduced to him, standing beside the carved marble fireplace of his sparkling Great Chamber. Galeazzo Merli's plump white hands clutched her own fingers just a little too long, and his eyes, roaming greedily over her face and figure, lingered an unreasonable length of time at her bosom.

Serafina remained composed, however. She had learned better than to reject out of hand even that sort of interest. And Jacopo, grumbling about the heat, did not notice. It was just that, she thought as Messer Merli finally released her and she stepped thankfully into the crowds, she felt particularly unwell tonight. Nerves, she told herself. She would have to make up one of Kara Ali's tisanes. Her head ached with the light from the ranks of candelabra, and her stomach was performing somersaults.

She had persuaded Jacopo to quit the comfort of Pisa for a tavern in Lucca because she had realized how useful this banquet could be to her. Serafina took a deep breath, and flicked her fan to and fro. The music had changed from a saltarello to a pavane: sweet and cool and calm. She began to feel better, to recall just how far she had travelled. The rich colours of the silks and brocades mingled into one glorious pattern of purple, of turquoise, of amber and cerise. She was here, she reminded herself, mingling with princes and merchants, breaking bread with them in one of Lucca's most splendid villas. Only two years previously she had been enslaved.

She heard Jacopo, beside her, mutter, 'There aren't any chairs,' and she felt for a moment a wave of almost intolerable irritation.

But she managed to conceal her temper, and smile, and say, 'Of course there are, my dear. I will go and find you one myself.'

Later, in the banqueting-hall, Thomas stared at food that was lavish and improbable. Poultry in a purple sauce, calves' heads sprinkled with basil, and peacocks, their glorious tails fanned out stiffly behind them. Plates of minced chicken in gelatine, sweetbreads, and an enormous glazed roast boar. Sturgeon, bowls of almond soup, and fish in a silver sauce. Platters of fish formed of a pine-seed paste; sugar boats with sugar mariners and sugar sails, swimming on a gilt marchpane sea. The device of the

Merli family was everywhere: on the silver-ware, the plates, the
napkins, shivering in gelatine in the scarlet and emerald jellies.

Thomas ate a little and drank a lot, and found someone to
talk shipping with, and someone else who knew Greenwich.
John Keane did the business talk, Thomas knew he hadn't an
ounce of the required charm or patience in him that night. The
room was tall and broad, the windows hung with swathes of
heavy fabric, the walls decorated with trompe l'oeil paintings of
hunting-dogs at fences, full-bosomed maidens pausing at garden
gates. Thomas refused to let his gaze wander round the hall,
knowing that it would alight inevitably on that small dark head,
trimmed with pearls and ribbons. Every now and then, though,
he heard her laugh, a sound like a tinkling silver bell, designed
to charm and not a yardstick of amusement. Gritting his teeth,
he was only thankful that the clamour of music and conversation,
the size of the chamber, kept that clear cold little voice from his
ears.

We should marry.

Marry? A woman cannot have two husbands, Mr Marlowe.

And if there had been a single reason why he had passed every
night of the last two months drinking red wine and playing
one-and-twenty, then that brief interchange encompassed it. If he
was alone, if he was idle, those words rattled repeatedly through
his skull, emphasizing over and over again his foolishness, her de-
tachment.

He did not know, he could not understand, why he had said,
We should marry. All he knew was that he had never before
made a fool of himself quite so effectively.

Since that fiasco Thomas had occupied himself with both the
Garland and the *Kingfisher*. John Keane had kept his word:
Thomas had found himself choosing the men and materials for
both ships. Work kept both anger and regret at bay: he was
increasingly impatient to see the completion of the *Kingfisher*, to
be at sea again, doing what he had been born to do. Yet the
galleon's construction was still agonizingly slow. Thomas
doubted if she would sail before the year was out and, so far,
John Keane had refused to let him take the *Garland* to Zante.
Meanwhile, Thomas endured this banquet, looking at any face

but hers, gazing at any woman but her. He kept his eyes averted from where Serafina sat, unaware and uncaring of his presence. Thomas did not intend to compound his former errors, but as he drank glass after glass, he knew that his resolution was fading. He wanted to hear her voice, to see his own reflection in those dark uninterested eyes. He wanted her to acknowledge that he existed.

'Dear Galeazzo,' said a soft voice from across the table, 'will be looking for a third wife before the year is out.'

Thomas glanced at the speaker, a Pisan merchant opposite him, and then looked up to the dais where the Merlis sat. Madonna Merli, her face pale, had risen and was walking from the room, helped by her nurse. Galeazzo Merli's plate and mouth were full of bright green jelly.

'She'll present him with another fat son and drop dead of exhaustion. But I don't think Galeazzo will be broken-hearted, do you, Messer Marlowe? After all, it can't exactly have been a love-match.'

Thomas scowled. Madonna Merli was indeed plain, short and plump, her body now distorted by pregnancy, her sallowness emphasized by an unfortunate yellow gown. Galeazzo Merli, her husband, was about twenty-five years older than his bride. That was nothing, thought Thomas grimly. Jacopo Capriani must be fifty years older than his bride. The thought of them in bed together sickened him.

The Pisan's voice jerked him back to the banqueting-hall.

'You've a cargo stranded in Livorno, I hear, Messer Marlowe.'

Thomas made himself focus on the Pisan. He was young, about Thomas's age, dressed in turquoise velvet with slashings and panes of scarlet. The wings of his doublet were encrusted with jewels, the ruff round his neck and frills at his wrists were of silver lace. A lovelock, trimmed with a green silk ribbon, bobbed against his cheek. Thomas, who had felt unusually resplendent in a black sleeveless doublet and white silk shirt, despised him on sight.

'Not exactly stranded. Delayed, shall we say, Messer –?'

'Tommaso di Credi,' said the Pisan, smiling to display startlingly white teeth. 'I am Messer Tommaso di Credi.'

He bobbed his head in a bow, and the cluster of scarlet feathers on his cap quivered. He looked, thought Thomas sourly, like a cockerel.

'If the goods you trade are of interest to me, Messer Marlowe, I may be able to save your warehouse charges.'

Thomas drained his glass. 'The *Garland* carried herring, tin and cloth,' he said. 'We've sold the herring already and, as you know, warehousing in Livorno is cheap. We're in no hurry to dispose of the tin and cloth.'

Not exactly true, because goods idle in a warehouse were the next best thing to a loss. Which, of course, the Italian knew.

'I could make you an offer, Messer Marlowe. Warehoused cloth tends to collect mildew rather than a profit. And I would give you a good price for the tin.'

'I'll get a better price in the Levant.' Thomas forced himself to relax, to smile. 'The *Garland*'s cargo won't be warehoused much longer, Messer di Credi. She's ready to sail. I intend to take her to Zante in the next couple of weeks.'

For a moment, as she turned to talk to her neighbour, Thomas could see Serafina clearly. The material of her gown, which he had at first thought to be a dull brown, was really nothing so ordinary. It gleamed in the candlelight, intensifying the golden glow of her skin, the slight pink bloom on her cheeks. She even seemed to have put on a little weight. Marriage agrees with her, thought Thomas angrily, seizing the wine-flagon from the centre of the table.

He had not been sufficiently circumspect. The irritating Italian, following his gaze, said, 'A beauty, I would agree, Messer Marlowe. But then there are so many beauties present tonight. Perhaps one must except dear Galeazzo's young wife, but then her attractions were presumably of a more financial nature . . . But his mistress, despite her unfortunate accident, is quite as captivating as the little Madonna Capriani, wouldn't you agree?'

Thomas followed Messer di Credi's graceful flick of the hand. He did not at first know what the merchant meant by *accident*, but then as he studied the pale-skinned, dark-haired woman, she turned, and he saw the ugly indentation in her skin, drawn carefully the length of her jaw.

'Her name is Costanza,' said the Italian, softly. 'But unless you intend to make a great deal of money on your next voyage, I would suggest that you only dream of her. She has an apartment in Lucca, and a house in Pisa, both courtesy of Galeazzo Merli.'

The wine was beginning to go to Thomas's head, taking the edge off his anger. Then anger returned triplefold, and he clenched the bevelled stem of his glass as he heard Tommaso di Credi add, 'Of course, if you are looking for a quick profit then perhaps you should take up a wager. I could wager you that your splintered hulk will sink before she reaches the Levant, but that would be predictable – and dull. There is another wager about. *Much* more entertaining. I have laid ten ducats on it myself already. It concerns the fetching young Madonna Capriani –'

'The profits from silk,' said the merchant Marco Datini, owner of several of the biggest silk-workshops in Pisa, 'grow less and less each year. One wonders whether it is worth troubling oneself.'

It was almost midnight, and Galeazzo Merli's guests had left the banqueting chamber to return to the Great Chamber. In adjacent ante-rooms, trays of sugar fantasies and bowls of bitter cherries had been placed on the tables. Servants wove their way through the crowds, carrying trays of empty glasses. The monkey, shivering on the curtain rail, bared its teeth and gums in an evil grin at anyone who came near it. Serafina, standing beside her seated husband, accepted a glass of wine from Messer Datini, and listened attentively to the conversation.

'My dear Marco' – a Frenchman in a peascod doublet and Venetian trunk-hose shook his head – 'there are profits to be made in silk as in everything else. Many grow rich on the stuff.'

In the centre of the room couples danced to the music of spinet and cittern. The graceful folds of the women's dresses, the rich fabrics of the men's doublets and jerkins trembled and swayed in the golden candlelight. Serafina had danced already: with Messer Datini, with the Frenchman Philippe Moreau, and with a banker's steward called Gianfranco. She had not danced with her husband Jacopo because Jacopo was cross and tired, and wanted to go home. And she had not danced with the Englishman Thomas Marlowe, whom she had recognized in the Merli banqueting-hall hours before, because the Englishman had not asked her.

'I blame the French, myself,' said Marco, maliciously, 'for the problems with the silk trade. Those Frenchmen who have not lost everything in their foolish, foolish wars, have done remarkably well during the last few years.'

'Provence has done well,' agreed Philippe. He had a long, thin face, with a flat nose like a horse's. On his head he wore a baggy velvet cap trimmed with a straggling goose feather that hung down past his jaw. The goose feather was a rather grubby white. 'Intermittently, at least. I'll charter ships round the Cape rather than send my goods through Provence.'

Jacopo Capriani broke wind, closed his eyes, and went to sleep. Three viols and a consort of recorders took the centre of the room. Serafina's fan clicked neatly, impatiently, open as conversation, temporarily drowned, faltered. She, too, wanted to sit down. She, too, wanted a breath of fresh air, and freedom from the tightly boned stays that suffocated her. Above all, she wanted to be away from the dreadful smells of fish and rosewater and hot spiced wine that issued through the double doors of the banqueting-chamber.

But she refused to allow herself to retreat, like many of the ladies, to the Merlis' cool downstairs parlour. She could not allow a small but persistent stomach upset to distract her from the fascinating businesses of silk, and shipping, and politics.

Jacopo began to snore reverberatingly. Serafina said, with a smile and a flick of her fan, 'Why not Provence, Monsieur Moreau? Silk has always been carried through Provence to the north. Surely it is much quicker and safer to travel through France than to sail round the Cape.'

Philippe, turning to Serafina, smiled, and inclined his head in a bow. 'I no longer transport silk through Provence, madame, because Provence has become corrupt.' He frowned. 'You look pale, Madame Capriani – you must permit me to find you a chair.'

She had bit her lips and rubbed red lead into her skin before going out that night, but, catching sight of herself in one of the palazzo's huge casement windows, Serafina had seen a quaking, ghostly reflection, as fleeting and insubstantial as the autumn winds that teased the dying leaves in the garden.

She refused to retire like some old matron, though. She knew what would happen then — the men would close ranks, shut her out, exclude her from any useful conversation. And it had been far too much effort to come here, far too much trouble battling against Jacopo's natural tightfistedness and dislike of society, to allow that to happen.

She spread open her fan. 'It is a little hot in here, Monsieur Moreau. And so noisy. Perhaps we could continue our conversation on one of the balconies.'

Several balconies jutted out from the Great Hall over the sunken terrace garden. The silk merchant offered Serafina his arm. 'I would be delighted, madonna. But, your husband —'

Jacopo's mouth was open, his chin lost in the withered folds of his neck.

'— is unconcerned, I think you would agree, Messer Datini.'

Out in the cooler air of the balcony, away from the chatter and the music, she began to feel better. The September night was still warm: below her, Serafina could see the fountain where Jacopo had proposed to her. The drops of water caught and fractured the golden light that streamed from the balconies, stitching them like jewels on to the velvet darkness.

Gianfranco, a banker's steward, went with them to the balcony. He was a young man, in his early twenties, and he gazed at Serafina with a dog-like devotion.

'Provence,' said Marco, picking up the threads of the earlier conversation, 'could not, in the end, avoid being caught up in the tragedy of civil war. Four years ago, Madonna Capriani, the city of Marseilles declared herself independent of the nation of France. Henri of Navarre is not yet strong enough to assert his authority there. Charles de Casaulx governs in Marseilles, madonna, not the Bourbon king. Such — uncertainties — are not good for business.'

She knew much of this already, of course, from her own stay

in Marseilles the previous year. But she kept her face innocent of knowledge, because innocence was, so often, useful. It encouraged people to talk.

'Consequently, madame, there is fraud, peculation, usury. Too many bribes to be paid to too many people. It costs more to take goods through Marseilles and to Lyons than to ship them round the coast and sell them directly in the north. Bribery cuts into profit, you see, Madame Capriani.'

The Frenchman Philippe Moreau, also a silk merchant, spoke now. 'There isn't an honest man left in Provence. I myself am a Parisian, madame.'

Marco nodded in agreement. 'And there are the wars, too, of course. Both Spain and Savoy are still meddling in French affairs – particularly in Provence. If your husband wishes to sell silk to the north, tell him to transport his goods by sea, not land. Avoid Toulon. Avoid Marseilles.'

'Especially Marseilles.' The voice was new, the Italian English-accented. Serafina had not heard the door to the balcony open, but she had known he would come. She had known he would speak to her. It had only been a matter of time.

Thomas Marlowe wore a black doublet and hose, and a wide-sleeved silk shirt. Serafina found that she was more accustomed to him in broadcloth and linen, that the unaccustomed finery made him look older, less approachable. He had not abandoned the familiar battered black hat, though: but it looked like a crow amongst a field of peacocks and birds-of-paradise.

'Marseilles is full of rogues and vagabonds, isn't it, madonna?'

She knew from the slight slurring of his words that Thomas Marlowe was drunk. Turning and facing the English pilot, Serafina's eyes met those too-familiar blue ones.

'Rogues and vagabonds indeed, Mr Marlowe.' She flicked the carved ivory segments of her fan to and fro. 'Like England.'

His bow was perfunctory. His eyes, intense with an amusement that irritated her, and some other, less comfortable emotion, studied her carefully. She was glad she had worn the bronze shot silk, glad she had bought the red lead.

She said, deliberately, 'Have you found a sponsor for your ship, Mr Marlowe?'

The door had swung partially shut, sealing them off from the music and laughter. Thomas's expression did not alter. 'The English Levant Company,' he said, evenly.

'Dear me, Mr Marlowe.' Serafina was conscious of a curious mixture of satisfaction and resentment. 'It seems you have sold your soul after all.'

For a few seconds there was silence. Then, raising his voice, Thomas Marlowe said, 'But how rude of me. My apologies for interrupting a fascinating conversation, gentlemen. You see, Madonna Capriani has a particular interest in Marseilles. She has acquaintances there. Don't you, my dear?'

'Really?' The Frenchman looked at Serafina with renewed interest. 'As I said, I am a Parisian, madame, but I have known Marseilles well for many years. May I ask the name of your acquaintance?'

Her throat, her lips, had become dry. The muffled notes of music from the Great Chamber had become an irritation, and Serafina's stomach lurched. She had hardly eaten that evening, but now she was forced to take a gulp of wine to steady herself.

Ignoring Thomas Marlowe, turning back to the Frenchman, Serafina said, 'I knew the Guardi. But it was a long time ago.'

She glanced quickly through the half-open door to the Great Chamber. Not far away, the courtesan Costanza was dancing with Messer Merli. As she moved, graceful and dignified, the candlelight deepened the scar along her jaw, delineating it like a dark thread on pale silk. Jacopo, thank God, was still asleep.

'Angelo,' said the English pilot, loudly and happily. 'Madonna Capriani's friend is called Angelo. A dear and faithful friend is such a blessing, don't you think, sirs? Perhaps the gentleman here has some news about your dear friend Angelo, madonna.'

She needed to know, but not in this way, not with Jacopo seated only a few yards distant, and Thomas Marlowe, the only man in Tuscany who had known her too long and too well, watching her. Digging her nails into her palms, disregarding the cold sweat that had begun to trickle between buckram and skin, Serafina's fan snapped shut.

'The Guardi?' Philippe frowned, and absently twisted the long feather that drooped from his hat. 'I know Angelo Guardi a little. We've done business together once or twice. And Gian-franco here makes purchases from the Guardi, I believe. They were from Florence originally, of course. It always was a very respectable business, but Angelo Guardi's made it more than that. I would guess him to be one of the wealthiest men in Provence.'

'Herrings?' said Thomas Marlowe, vaguely. 'Does the gentleman trade in herrings? Or tin? Or – let me see – *antelope's tears?*'

'Cloth, sir,' said Philippe, coldly. 'The Guardi have always specialized in cloth.' He turned back to Serafina, and smiled. 'Although – they say things have been a little difficult for Messer Guardi recently. Marseilles is politically isolated, so it has been hard for the cloth-merchants to transport their goods to the north. Monsieur de Casaulx has not been a friend to the merchants, especially the wealthier ones. Some say he has encouraged the jealousy of the people.'

In Marseilles, the crowds had jostled the rich merchants, who had ridden the streets fully armed, hedged by a bodyguard. Serafina could recall the febrile heat of Marseilles in May, the almost tangible tension of the town. She had been afraid then.

Yet the Frenchman's words made her heart beat faster, but with hope, not fear. *They say things have been a little difficult for Messer Guardi recently.* Was it possible that Angelo, too, struggled against the tides of history?

The Englishman was staring at Serafina, the amusement gone from his eyes. But she needed to know. Her hand clenched the fan so hard she thought the fragile ivory might break.

Addressing Monsieur Moreau, Serafina said, 'Is there talk of bankruptcy, monsieur? For the Guardi?'

The Frenchman chuckled, and absently twisted the tip of his dangling goose-feather.

'Are you hoping for a cheap purchase, madame? Will the Capriani spread their wings from Naples to London?'

She heard Thomas Marlowe laugh, a raw, ugly sound. Serafina lowered her eyes to disguise the almost unbearable compound of hope, excitement, and anger that threatened to overwhelm her. She said, 'My husband's trade is modest as yet, monsieur. We deal in silk goods – ribbons, trimmings, cockades, that sort of thing. Only a little silk. Though yes, Jacopo and I do hope to build that side of the business up.'

Messer Datini's expression was a mixture of admiration and amusement. 'Then you must buy a ship, madonna. Every silk-merchant of note has a whole fleet of ships. You must buy a ship of the northern type – not a galley. A galley would not take you round the Cape.'

The Englishman, much too close to Serafina's shoulder, said, 'Madonna Capriani and I have already discussed shipping, haven't we? Shall we tell the gentlemen about our conversation, madonna? Or' – and he had taken hold of her hand, his fingers trapping hers – 'shall we dance?'

Messer Datini glared at the pilot. 'I don't think,' he said, coldly, 'that Madonna Capriani wants to dance. She is tired.'

Serafina saw that Thomas Marlowe was about to speak, and she interrupted him. She did not trust him: his tongue was loosened too far already by alcohol and temper.

'Thank you, Messer Datini,' she said, calmly, 'but I am quite happy to dance with Messer Marlowe. I am not tired now, and besides, we are old acquaintances.'

He had not let go of her hand. Thomas's fingers gripped hers, hard, and Serafina found herself led from the balcony to the dance floor. Back in the Great Chamber, the light that suffused the room now seemed sulphurous, not golden, a brimstone shade that aged and corrupted the dancers. She knew that she had lied to the Italian silk-merchant. She did not think that she had ever felt so tired. Her feet were heavy and clumsy, but she forced herself to follow the thoughtless, predestined pattern of the dance, to accept the guidance of Thomas's hand at her waist, or touching her fingertips. He was not clumsy, he did not dance like a drunken oaf: he was there when the dance required him, absent but waiting for her when the steps required her to move independently of him. She felt, when in the course of the pavane he held her, safe. She wanted to rest her head against his shoulder, and sleep. She wanted to cry and be comforted.

And then, halfway through the dance, when the whisper of citarron and spinet still possessed the room, he stopped in the centre of the floor, holding her.

'You *are* tired,' he said, softly. 'Why didn't you say so?'

She forced herself to smile. 'You gave me no choice, Mr Marlowe. You wanted to talk about *trade*.'

He did not reply. He touched the tips of his fingers to her cheek, and they came away red. 'You shouldn't put that stuff on your face,' he said.

Her anger was with his habitual need to interfere in her life. She pulled away from him, no longer wanting his touch.

'What I do is none of your business, Mr Marlowe,' she hissed. 'If I wish to paint myself all the colours of the rainbow, then I will do so!'

Paused in the centre of the room, a single still hub in the wheel of the dance, it was for a moment as though only they existed, as though everyone else – Jacopo, the Merlis, the merchants, even Angelo himself – had become unimportant, ceasing to exist.

Then: 'Bankside whores used red lead, and it kills them.' Thomas's expression was an infuriating mixture of arrogance and concern. 'Besides, you don't need it.'

Above them, the monkey was leaping from curtain rail to curtain rail, its raucous squawk mocking the gentility of the music. Thomas Marlowe had compared her to a whore, but Serafina found to her surprise that she still remained there, that she had not yet turned from him and left him standing alone on the dance floor.

'You sell your skill, Mr Marlowe,' she said, coldly and deliberately. 'Your ability to read the stars, or to steer a ship. I sell my charm, my wit – yes, and my face and my body. They wouldn't believe me if I offered anything else, you see. If they did believe me, they would hate me. So I offer myself, as currency, in exchange for information.'

She was looking up at him, the heat in her eyes chilled, every muscle taut. But the Englishman only smiled.

'Then let me give you a piece of information you may not yet have received, madonna. It's quite interesting, I'm sure you'll agree.'

Her eyes, though they did not leave his, could not refrain from forming a question.

Thomas Marlowe said gently, 'They are laying bets, you know. As to whether your senile bridegroom will manage to impregnate you before the year is out.'

Thomas left the Palazzo Merli shortly afterwards, the mark of Serafina's hand still imprinted like a flattened pink star on his cheek.

He had been too drunk to stop her that time, but not sufficiently drunk, thank God, to make the mistake of retaliating. People had stared and muttered and giggled, but no more than that. The lady's charming husband still snored, and Thomas had made a speedy and unregretted exit.

The piazza was empty except for two figures, unrecognizable in the darkness, walking ahead of him. Cradling a half-empty bottle of aqua vitae against his chest, turning up the collar of his doublet to keep out the light rain that had begun to fall, Thomas began to walk back to his tavern.

He felt sickened with himself, sickened with Italy, and he wanted nothing more than to shake the dust of Tuscany from the soles of his shoes, and see only the blue, endless sea. He ached with inaction: he told himself that it was the confinement to land that gnawed at his limited patience, blowing up small setbacks and betrayals out of all proportion.

The rain was still light, and the gentlemen ahead of him had reached the far corner of the square. No: not *gentlemen*. Thomas felt his gullet rise as he recognized one of the walkers ahead from his turquoise velvet doublet and scarlet-feathered hat. Tommaso di Credi, the Pisan merchant who had offered that particularly distasteful wager. Which he, doubly offensive, had later repeated to Serafina.

There was a sour taste in his mouth, but Thomas quickened his pace until he was almost running across the soaking paving-stones. Something long at breaking-point had snapped inside him, and he needed an outlet for his anger. There were two of them, he thought, but all these Italian bravos were as effete as hell, relying more on their tongues than their fists and swords to defend them. He wanted to cut the lovelock from that scented hair, grind that powdered skin into the dust.

Thomas Marlowe, the incandescent flames of war and revenge burning in his blue eyes, found the most arrant insult in his entire Italian vocabulary, and hurled it indiscriminately after his quarry.

Later, the courtesan Costanza, who had walked from the Merli palazzo alone, saw the figure huddled in a doorway on the far side of the square.

The night was dark, but the gentle rain was refreshing after the heavy heat of summer. Costanza wore a gauze scarf over her head and around her shoulders, to protect her hair from the rain. The scarf was silver, a present from Galeazzo. In Venice, the courtesans had been obliged to wear a yellow scarf, so that everyone might know their trade. Costanza had never regretted leaving Venice.

She considered passing the huddled figure by on the other side of the square, but rejected the idea. She found that she recognized the man: he had been at Galeazzo's banquet. She could see only damp black curls and a battered felt hat, flung a few feet away from its owner, but she knew it was the English-man who had arrived with the Levant Company agent, Mr Keane. The drunken Englishman whose face the little Capriani had slapped in front of an audience of a hundred.

She was still cautious, though; the years and the company she kept had taught her to be cautious. She did not guess the English-man to be capable of the worst sort of indiscriminate violence, but she made sure not to go within an arm's length of him, and to keep her fingers resting on the stiletto dagger that she always kept hidden in the folds of her gown. But when she was close enough to see by the light of the flare, she realized that the Englishman's immobility was not, as she had thought, solely due to drunkenness.

His eyes were closed, his doublet and breeches scuffed and torn with mud. And down the side of his face, trickling from the matted hair to the well-shaped mouth, there was a thin trail of blood.

She used the silver scarf without a thought for its price or the identity of its donor. Dabbing gently at the Englishman's temple,

Costanza began to speak, very softly and almost to herself. She spoke in Italian, because English was such an awkward language, and she had never grasped more than the most rudimentary understanding of it.

When, after a few moments, the Englishman's eyelids began to flicker, Costanza noticed the bottle lying on its belly on the stones nearby. Lifting it, she sniffed at the aqua vitae, then held the dregs to the man's mouth until he swallowed and coughed, and a little life began to return to his hazed eyes.

She waited until he appeared to have recovered his senses, and then, looking pointedly at the empty bottle, she said, 'If you wish it, there's better company than that.'

The Englishman's eyes finally focused on her face. He had nice eyes: a clear deep blue. She had noticed them earlier at the palazzo.

'I've no money,' he said, in Italian.

She did not flinch at his unpardonable rudeness. She neither courted it nor welcomed it, but she had learned long since to live with it. 'I'm offering you company, my friend,' she said, coolly. 'Nothing more.'

The blue eyes lidded then, and the mouth twisted, and she thought that he was going to refuse her. But he only said, 'Why?'

There were many flattering, dishonest answers to that, but she gave him the honest one.

'Because the evening was dull. Damnably dull. And if you were sober enough, you might be interesting to talk to.'

She heard him laugh, though he winced and muffled the sound quickly in the folds of his doublet. But at last he rose unsteadily, and walked slowly alongside her into the darkness.

Forty weeks. It took forty weeks to make a baby.

Thomas Marlowe had said, *They're laying bets, you know. On whether your senile bridegroom will manage to impregnate you.* And she had slapped his face and walked away from him across the marble floor.

Messer Merli himself had escorted Serafina from the Great Chamber. Alone with her for a few moments, he had proceeded to make his own insulting offer. She had gazed at him, filled with an ice-cold, uncontrollable anger, and had said, 'There must be some limit, don't you think, Messer Merli, to the number of old men I must sleep with?' Then she had turned on her heel and woken Jacopo and left the palazzo.

Later, in the silence and the darkness, she had briefly regretted her reply. There were more sensible ways of rejecting a powerful man's unwanted attentions. But almost immediately, she forgot Galeazzo Merli, unable to avoid the nightmare that Thomas's words had plunged her into.

For there, in the Palazzo Merli, in the single still centre of the dance, Serafina had realized the truth. Like shards from a shattered pot, the fragments had fitted inescapably together, making hideous sense of her last few months.

She was pregnant. There, with all Tuscany around her and her husband snoring in a chair, she had known that she was pregnant. And that had been why she had struck the English pilot. Because she was pregnant, trapped once again by her sex, enslaved by the feebleness of her body. She had hated Thomas for that. For being a man, for not having to fear the consequences, or pay the price.

Walking back from the Merli palazzo to the cheap tavern in which Jacopo had taken rooms, Serafina had known that those idle, gossiping fools had won their wager already. She had not endured her monthly ailment since her marriage. Not since – and now she sat up in bed, staring wide-eyed at the darkness – not since four – no, six – weeks before her marriage.

And her gowns had become tight, particularly around the bodice. And she had felt *sick*. Figures jangled discordantly in Serafina's head, their significance almost unbearable, their answer always coming to the same appalling total. It took forty weeks to make a baby, but to work out the date of birth, you had to know the date of conception. Kneeling up in the bed with Jacopo snoring beside her, Serafina tried to remember when she had first felt sick.

It had been at the Palazzo Merli, of course, in that same dreadful garden with the damned lemon trees and the fountain. That summer, in the garden, pregnancy had been nothing but a useful lie: an irresistible confirmation of virility to an ageing husband. Now it was a reality, something that must instantly destroy the hope she had so newly discovered.

A baby had no part in her scheme of things: babies were messy, ugly, and inconvenient. Babies made you ill, babies often killed you. Pregnancy would make her look like Madonna Merli, pale and hollow-eyed, her body distorted into grotesque. Pregnancy made women unacceptable, an object of sympathy at best, an object of ridicule unless they shuttered themselves behind curtained windows. Pregnancy made women sexless and witless, barred them irretrievably from the men's world that Serafina had had the audacity to think she might enter. Pregnant, in childbed, or breastfeeding, she could not fight Angelo, she could not take back what was owed to her. Nature, she thought bitterly, intended to imprison her in a way that even slavery had spared her.

And yet there was another, sourer, twist to this tale. Had Jacopo not been at her side, Serafina thought she would have thrown a lifetime's caution to the wind, and fisted her hands and screamed.

Jacopo had proposed to her in Messer Merli's garden. Which meant that she had been pregnant on her wedding day. Which meant – and Serafina's hands clenched in fury and despair – that either man, Thomas Marlowe or Jacopo Capriani, might be her baby's father.

Three days later, the Levant Company galleon *Garland* set sail for the island of Zante in the Ionian Sea. She carried tin and cloth, to be exchanged in Zante for currants. A comparatively short journey, less than half the distance to Aleppo, but if the little ship could avoid jealous Frenchmen and Venetians, corsairs of every nationality, and the ever-present dangers of wind and storm, a potentially profitable one.

Apart from the cargo, the hold of the *Garland* was filled with wine and oil, bacon and beef, and salt and beans. They could have put into port for supplies, clinging to coast and island for much of the voyage, but there would be tolls to be paid for that privilege, which would inevitably sap profit. Besides, frequent dockings would slow their progress, and the master of the *Garland* intended the voyage to be a speedy one.

It had taken Thomas a full day and a great deal of patient argument to persuade John Keane to allow him to take the *Garland* to Zante. Keane was waiting for the arrival of the next convoy of company ships from London; it was against company policy for ships to sail alone. The *Garland*'s cargo was safe in a warehouse in Livorno, why risk venturing in solitude across the open sea? But, as Thomas had known he must, Keane eventually agreed that yes: the voyage to Zante was comparatively short, and yes: there was little money to be made in warehoused cargo. And yes: Thomas could probably sail to Zante and back before the next Levant Company ships reached Livorno.

Privately, John Keane had perhaps thought it wise to give way to the pilot on this issue. Thomas had ridden back to Livorno from Lucca with a black eye and a colourful collection of cuts and bruises. Thomas had been as taut as a bowspring since he had agreed to work for the Levant Company in exchange for the financing of the *Kingfisher*. And the fact that Marlowe had offered to leave his beloved *Kingfisher* in other hands for a few weeks spoke most eloquently of all. Keane wanted the ship and he wanted the man, and he was prepared to relax a few rules to keep them both. Besides, the pilot was right: if the voyage was successful, then the *Garland* could be sailing back to London with a profitable cargo of currants before winter.

The *Kingfisher* was left in the capable charge of John Keane, who stayed on dry land to await the coming of the convoy. Thomas took both William Williams and William's apprentice, Cristofano, who needed the edifying experience of a few weeks at sea. Thomas himself achieved rapid promotion to the rank of master. John Keane, standing on the harbour wall at Livorno as he watched the *Garland* become no more than a nub of black on the horizon, prayed that he had made the right decision.

Thomas Marlowe had no such doubts. It had been necessary for him to leave Tuscany: he had had no choice in the matter. Landbound, he had known himself to be teetering on the edge of something unforgivable, an edge which he had almost tumbled over during that memorable evening in Lucca. Successfully threading his way through the Straits of Messina and entering the Ionian Sea, he was too busy by day for his black thoughts to preoccupy him for long. Standing on the foredeck of the *Garland* with the glorious cerulean blue bowl of the Ionian Sea spread out in front of him, he knew that this time he had followed his instincts correctly. Back in Italy, he had begun to hate even the *Kingfisher*, to fear that when he had bought his future with the wreckage of the *Toby*, he had been deceived, and instead, gaining nothing but disillusionment, had only returned himself to the masters he had so recently left.

By night, things were different, though. By night, pictures formed easily out of a moonlit sea, and Thomas knew that this voyage was merely a hiatus, a brief respite from a muddled present. Alone, leaning against the gunwale, the only sound the gentle flicking of the sails and the creaking of the *Garland*'s timbers, Thomas knew that though the cuts and bruises he had received from the fight in Lucca (a satisfying but ultimately self-defeating experience) might have dimmed, nothing else had changed. He was still bound for the next five years to the Levant Company; and there was still Serafina.

The empty sea around him offered no escape from the all too vivid memory of his conversation with the courtesan Costanza. Gathering him up from the streets, she had taken Thomas back to her Lucchese lodgings: nicely furnished in a stylish, but not over-extravagant manner, untenanted except for one maid and a page-boy. Costanza had provided Thomas with water and linen to bathe his physical wounds, and company as a balm to the blows his pride had endured. She had been kind and intelligent and uninquisitive, and it had been that very gift of un-inquisitiveness that had caused him to continue to act like a fool. Drunk, and suffering from a rather hard knock on the head, he had proceeded to make the undignified error of unburdening himself to the courtesan. For that self-indulgence he had been justly rewarded: Costanza had listened, calmly and dispassion-ately, and had then analysed the nature of his emotions. He had tried, and failed, to dismiss her words as nonsense. One sentence of hers, particularly, stubbornly refused to fade from memory. *It is quite simple, Mr Marlowe — you are in love with her.*

Thomas closed his eyes, pushed his hands through his hair. He remembered that he had laughed at first, and then he had grown angry. Not with Costanza, who had only confronted him with what he had not allowed himself to see, but with fate, for casting him in such a ridiculous role. He had thought himself in love before — with Faith Whitlock, with a flower-seller from St Paul's, with a serving-wench in his brother's tavern. But that, although a heady mixture of liking and lust, had not amounted to love. He had chosen then, he had pursued and had generally conquered, enjoying the consequences.

But there had been little choice or enjoyment in his relations with Serafina. She was a heartless bitch whose limited capacity for affection had been wasted long ago on an over-indulgent papa and a charming, immoral cousin. Her ambitions were solely concerned with revenge and repossession, and to those ends she would use anything and anyone in any way she thought best. She seemed to have no interest in what Thomas had been brought up to think of as the normal feminine preoccupations of home and family. He did not judge her for that: he knew that he certainly had no right to, for his own ambitions, his own methods, had been almost as ruthless as hers. It was the simple lack of choice that had made him so angry. He recognized that he had been unable to keep away from Serafina: he had half expected to see her at the banquet in Lucca and, finding her there, he had not had sense enough to leave without speaking to her. Earlier, in the summer, at the Palazzo Sacchetti, Serafina had simply clicked her fingers and he had run to her. He did not like to see himself cast in the role of puppy-dog.

Cursing himself, Thomas gazed out at the wide, dark sea. Then, abruptly forgetting both Serafina and the Levant Company, he straightened up, his eyes straining to focus on the dim shape forming from the empty plane of the horizon. He thought it was a phantasm at first, a sea-mirage, a shimmering of silver and opal and grey. Then he knew that the *Garland* was no longer alone.

The Ionian Sea was unpredictable, capable of sudden storm

and vicious wind. But it was not the anger of the gods that Thomas feared: frowning, trying to make sense of that dim, distant shape, he knew that man-made dangers troubled him more. From the *Garland*'s masthead, the royal arms of England swirled over a red cross, announcing England's intentions to the world. In these waters there were many who would see the insignia of the Levant Company as a target, a justifiable objective. The French, the Spaniards, the Venetians, even Tuscany herself had learned to resent England's recent success in the Levant. And pirates of every nation – from Barbary, from Ragusa, from the myriad tiny and nameless islands cluttering the coasts of Greece – would recognize the Levant Company's flag as a potential prize. He had everything to fear from envy and opportunism, everything to fear from that unidentifiable flicker on that horizon.

The vague shape enlarged, coalescing into ghostly outline. Moving silently, Thomas extinguished the candle in his lantern between finger and thumb, knowing that such actions were futile, that the moon above lit the *Garland*, too, more lucidly than any torchlight. Thomas did not move from the bridge, however: he waited, knowing that the precise moment when he should call his men to open the gunports, ready the cannon, had not yet come.

But as the distant ship shifted silently into clarity, he thought that any action, fight or flight, might be futile. Staring at the apparition fast materializing out of the sea and the night, for a moment Thomas forgot everything, and only gazed, silenced.

For she was beautiful. She was a galleon, four-masted, graceful and elegant, a glorious ghostly swan to his squat duckling of a *Garland*. The moonlight traced her yards and masts with silver, and fired to gold her carved and gilded bridge. She was everything the *Kingfisher* should be, would be, one day.

And she was French. Thomas saw a single moonlit flicker of a fleur-de-lys in the darkness before, unaccountably, the ship turned about and, apparently uninterested, sailed away. And then the sweat cooled to ice on his brow, and there was nothing other than the gulls overhead and the fish in the sea below.

★

By autumn, Livorno's docks had begun to quieten, and the flow of silk from the East to dry up. But by that time, Serafina Capriani had amassed a small but exquisite selection of bales, all carefully stored in a warehouse in Pisa.

She had been careful to hide her pregnancy from the world. No matter how nauseated she felt, she still choked down a respectable amount of food; no matter how tired she was she still talked, and smiled, and if necessary danced, until midnight. If she laced her gowns tightly the small swelling of her belly was easily hidden. She tried, as far as possible, to ignore this latest, burgeoning imprisonment, persuading Jacopo to maintain his silence about her pregnancy, which Jacopo, perhaps also fearing ridicule, did.

She chose every length of silk herself, she travelled to Livorno and Florence, inspecting cloth, examining bales of raw silk. Sometimes Jacopo accompanied her; increasingly often there was only the clerk Amadeo at her side, while Jacopo concerned himself with beads and baubles, tassels and ribbons. Amadeo, whom she had alternately charmed and harassed since her marriage, had become an asset, rather than the liability he had once been. Much the same age as Serafina, his attitude towards her had become one almost of affection, tempered by a considerable respect for her skill and her tongue. With Amadeo, Serafina tramped round docks, warehouses and workshops, her purse locked and guarded beneath the conveniently capacious folds of her gown. She had had to endure questioning glances, and whistles and jeers. And propositions, and being told, quite bluntly, that her place was in the kitchens or on her back, in bed. She ate when she could, where she could, and slept, exhausted, as soon as her head touched the pillow. She kept meticulous accounts, inspected the clerks' work when they least expected it, made uncomfortable journeys on bad-tempered ponies, accompanied by insufficient guards. She might still be Jacopo's precious pearl, but Jacopo would not pay to have the pearl properly guarded.

The banker's steward, the handsome, adoring Gianfranco of Messer Merli's Lucchese banquet, poured wine and covertly studied his visitor.

She was small and slim and dark-eyed. Those dark eyes were particularly fascinating, because they were slightly slanting and opaque. They looked round the small upstairs withdrawing-room and at the banker's steward with an entirely equal lack of interest. Gianfranco did not know why opaque black eyes should be fascinating, but they were.

When he had received notice of this visit, Gianfranco had expected to see the old man, not his wife. Jacopo Capriani had used the services of Gianfranco's master's bank for many years now; the merchant was quite well known in Pisa. Gianfranco, like everyone else, had laughed when he had heard of Jacopo Capriani's marriage, and he, like the rest, had prophesied a brash young strumpet who would leap into bed with the first passable manservant she saw as soon as her husband's back was turned.

Yet at Galeazzo Merli's banquet, Gianfranco had learned that Madonna Capriani was neither brash nor a strumpet. Instead, she was the most circumspect, refined, quiet little thing. It was a pleasure to watch her small neat hands unfold lengths of silk on the table, a pleasure to hear her low, gentle voice apologizing for, and explaining the nature of her intrusion.

For she had come to sell to the banker's steward, not to borrow money from him. It was Gianfranco's responsibility to feed and clothe the banker's entire vast household: young and ambitious, it was something he sought to do both efficiently and economically. Placing a glass of wine on the table beside the silk, ignoring the clerk Madonna Capriani had brought with her, Gianfranco perched himself on the table edge and gave himself up to the twin pleasures of watching and listening.

'– the cloth-of-gold is from Florence, the damask from the Levant. We have, as you know, ribbons and lace to match.'

Madonna Capriani held out the fabric for Gianfranco to touch. The silk was blue: but the simple description *blue* was not enough. It was azure, ultramarine, cerulean, mauve, turquoise. There were a thousand shades in that one clinging, shimmering length of fabric.

'We will order ribbons and braid, of course, madonna.' The banker's steward let the length of cloth trail slowly back to the table-top. 'As is usual. But the silk . . .' As Gianfranco's voice trickled into silence, his fingers stroked the length of material one last time.

'Ah.' She said no more, only the single word that was almost a sigh, as she began to fold cloth, wind ribbons.

'They are fine fabrics, madonna,' said the steward, hastily, seizing a rippling length of turquoise and holding it up to the light. 'An excellent selection. But . . .' Gianfranco hesitated.

The clerk leapt forward to take the silk from his hands, and Madonna Capriani said, 'You are concerned, perhaps, as to whether we would be able to fulfil a contract?'

Her voice was so soft, Gianfranco could hardly hear her. 'Madonna – I –'

'It is quite understandable, sir. Please allow me to try and reassure you.'

Madonna Capriani's hands, ringed and gloved, were folded neatly in front of her. Her gown was of a rich crimson cut velvet, trimmed with lace. The velvet came from Alexandretta, guessed the steward, who knew about these things, and the lace from Bruges.

'We cannot buy direct from Scanderoon, it is true, at present. But we can travel to Naples, and Florence, and Livorno, to buy from the workshops there. Next spring we hope to employ some artisans of our own. Until then – I can offer you a good price, sir, if you will contract to buy your silk from the Capriani for the next year or two.'

She named a figure which made the steward's eyes brighten, and the clerk hastily suppress a squawk. The price was good, the silk of the highest quality: Gianfranco was almost tempted to accept her.

'And perhaps we should recall what Messer Datini said about the Guardi, your present suppliers.'

Surprised, Gianfranco watched Madonna Capriani leave the table and walk to the window. The sunlight washed over her skin, made glints of gold in those unfathomable dark eyes.

He said, truthfully, 'We have bought cloth from the Guardi for many years now, madonna. They have never given us cause for complaint.'

'Of course not.' She smiled, a delightful twisting of the corners

of her mouth. 'The Guardi are a large and well-respected company whose main concern is in carrying silk to the north, linens
and broadcloth to the south. But, as Messer Datini pointed out,
Marseilles is isolated at present. Its land-routes are dangerous, its
merchants threatened by their unruly countrymen. By Monsieur
de Casaulx himself, perhaps. These are troubled times in Marseilles, sir. Not all businesses can survive such troubled times.'

She was hinting, Gianfranco knew, at the possibility of
bankruptcy. It was not an unrealistic possibility: changes of
government, the affairs of kings, could destroy a successful business
within months, weeks even. Even the most enterprising cloth-
merchant could be ruined by the loss of a single consignment of
goods, to corsairs or brigands, to tempest or flood. But though
one half of Gianfranco's brain might be concerned with the
security of the Guardi company, the other was utterly distracted
with Madonna Capriani's neat little figure. Gianfranco, preoccupied, became aware that the Capriani clerk was glaring at
him.

'Also, consider, sir, that the Guardi's finest fabrics will travel –
as ambassadors, if you like – to Paris, or Bruges, or London.
You might consider, perhaps, whether the Guardi can offer you
their best.'

She paused for a moment, and then she gestured towards the
lengths of silk and ribbon strewn on the table. 'That is *our* best,'
she said. 'We have nothing of lesser quality. As you know, until
recently we have only traded in trimmings and semi-precious
stones. But my husband hopes to expand the business in the
future, to make use of his many valuable contacts. I'm sure,' and
the dark eyes for a moment met Gianfranco's own, 'that your
master would approve.'

'Oh, no doubt. No doubt. And the fabric is excellent, as I
said.' Gianfranco, collecting himself, hesitated again, and struggled to find the most suitable words. 'There is one other small
reservation –'

Madonna Capriani, who had sat down again, looked up enquir-
ingly. Gianfranco found that his mouth was dry.

'It is just that – I'm not sure if –'

For the second time, his words disintegrated to nothingness.

He thought himself incomprehensible, but Madonna Capriani said slowly, 'You are not sure whether your master would approve of your trading with a woman?'

He could only redden and nod his head. Unfeminine, the banker would say. Unnatural.

Another short, painful silence. Madonna Capriani's small hands worked together, her heavy eyelids dropped.

'My husband could not be here today, sir, but let me assure you that he holds the reins of the company firmly in his grasp. After all' – and she smiled, so that her whole face lit up in the most delightful way – 'you would not expect me to deal with figures, would you, sir? I have a poor head for figures, as Amadeo will tell you.'

The clerk blushed scarlet and mumbled something.

'My husband,' added Madonna Capriani, the laughter gone and replaced by a touching sorrow, 'simply entrusts me with the task of visiting customers' houses. I hope you do not find this unsuitable. Or' – the black eyelashes dipped, the small mouth trembled slightly – 'offensive.'

'Not at all!' Gianfranco almost sank to one knee, almost kissed her hand. 'Marriage is a partnership, after all, madonna. Please forgive me if I appeared insulting – it was not my intention, I assure you.'

He watched her take a sip of wine. Her eyes seemed slightly misted, and her voice was not quite steady. 'Then –?'

'Then I shall recommend my employer to sign the contract I will draw up with you.' The words were out before he had fully considered their consequences, but Gianfranco found that he did not care. He patted the fragile shoulder comfortingly. 'For a year to begin with, but the contract can be extended if you satisfy. As I am sure you will.'

The young Madonna Capriani, tears dabbed from the corners of her eyes, left shortly afterwards. The banker's steward watched from a window as the youth Amadeo helped the small veiled figure on to her waiting horse. He smiled a little to himself, looking forward to future business.

He would have been surprised, perhaps, had he seen the expression in the eyes beneath the veil. Triumph, so that they burned, dark and bright.

PART VII

1595

COMPASSED WITH DANGER

Being thus compassed with danger on every side, some of the ships did take in their sails and there lay adrift.

Third voyage of Frobisher for the discovery of Cathay: Richard Hakluyt

'Zante,' said Thomas Marlowe, softly.

Shimmering on the horizon, a haze of azure and emerald and lavender announced the *Garland's* approach to the island of Zante, Flower of the Levant. A tiny, fertile green mound of olive groves and wild vineyards, Zante was a precious jewel in the dominions of Venice, a treasure to be jealously guarded.

'Zante,' agreed William Williams, shading his eyes from the sun as he scanned the horizon. And, 'Venetians.'

Thomas followed the direction of the ship's carpenter's gaze, and cursed. Conjured from the quivering air like some unwanted and fabulous sea-monster, a galley skimmed over the waves towards the *Garland*.

The youth Cristofano, elbows bunched on the gunwale, stood on William's other side. 'We could outrun them,' he said, hopefully.

'I doubt it. They don't need the wind.' Thomas, his narrowed eyes focused on the galley, frowned. The island was already almost lost behind the flickering lion-emblazoned pennants and streamers. 'Besides. I've two dozen crates of tin to sell. I've no wish to cart them all back to Livorno.'

William Williams said nothing, but Thomas himself had already noted how the clear late afternoon sunlight bounced off the burnished helmets of the Venetian soldiers. The faint feeling of unease that had possessed him for days now had magnified suddenly. He could pinpoint the start of that unease, though he had voiced it to no one, not even to William Williams. The French ship, the moonlit vessel that had appeared over the horizon, and looked at him, and then disappeared.

'I think,' added Thomas, slowly, 'that I'll give them the benefit of the doubt. After all, their swords aren't actually drawn yet. We'll smile nicely and invite them aboard for a glass of canary. Cristofano, go and find yourself a decent doublet. William, take – let me see – the master-gunner and one other and keep well out of sight.'

William said softly, 'Samuel? He's a mad-brained fellow. You're expecting trouble?'

Thomas had already turned from the gunwale. No need to mention ghost ships in the night: that galley, skimming over the sea like some elongated water-insect, was trouble enough. It could sink them, or board them, or confiscate their goods, or throw the lot of them in some stinking Greek gaol. And he really had no alternative but to take his chance.

He said, softly, 'Venice is on the defensive these days. She has no reason to love the Levant Company. Our ships have plundered hers before now.'

The galley had drawn closer. From the foredeck of the *Garland* they could see the Venetian soldiers, cooped like a box of chess pieces on the poop-deck.

Cristofano squeaked, 'A doublet? Why?'

Thomas smiled, and turned from the gunwale. 'Because, my dear Cristofano, those gentlemen are about to demand permission to board. If their intentions are honourable, I would rather like to have my beautiful foot-page serving the wine in order to make a good impression. And if they are dishonourable, then I'd like my turbulent master-gunner hidden and ready to surprise them all if I have to fight for my life. I don't know which it is to be, you see. In half an hour's time, I might be lying on the sea-bottom with my throat cut, or, on the other hand, I might be on my way to a delightful evening at the Venetian agent's palace in Zakynthos. Now, go and get that bloody doublet on.'

It proved to be the second option. Boarding the ship, the occupants of the galley inspected the hold of the *Garland* with a thoroughness that surprised even Thomas. Wearing an embroidered doublet over an equally impressive shirt, Thomas felt his face ache with the strain of smiling as he offered refreshments to the galley's master. Cristofano, fetching in scarlet silk, poured the wine. The master apologized in heavily accented Italian, explaining that some vessels, regretfully, tried to avoid paying duties. When his men had finished searching the galleon, the master rose and bowed, and suggested that the *Garland* follow the galley into the port of Zakynthos.

So the plain little *Garland* followed the glittering galley into port. The master of the galley stayed on the foredeck of the *Garland* throughout, of course, politely pointing out the manifold beauties of Zante as they rounded the island. The mountains to the north-west, the sheltered coves and beaches, the pine forests and flower-filled hillsides. Zante glistened in the heat like a beautiful gem as they rounded the headland and came within sight of the port of Zakynthos.

Ships crowded the sheltered harbour with its backdrop of Venetian-style churches and palazzi. Fishing boats, galleys, and roundships, their sails furled, their pennants drooping in the quiet air, while they laded and unladed their cargoes. Caiques and barques, laudi and polaccas, small craft, most of them, that made even the *Garland* look big and lumbering.

It was only after they had docked at Zakynthos, and the master of the Venetian galley had made his generous invitation to Thomas and his crew, and the *Garland* had finally fallen silent, that William Williams, the master-gunner, and the master-gunner's mate emerged from beneath the coils of rope heaped in the boatswain's stores.

Triple-storeyed and with a shallow-pitched roof, the Venetian governor's palace sprawled over the town of Zakynthos like a great bleached toad, oil-lamps already gleaming golden-eyed in the small shuttered windows. It was early evening: in the harbour the setting sun had washed the ships with orange. Blue-black shadows painted themselves on the hills and olive groves that circled the town. Inside the palace Thomas bowed and offered greetings to the Venetian governor, and took in the large, opulent portego the width of the house, the scent of sandalwood and patchouli, the statues and tapestries and carved cedarwood chests that cluttered every corner of the room.

The governor's name was Hieronymo Carcandella, and he

was, Thomas guessed, a roughly equal mixture of Greek and Venetian. Dark-eyed and balding, Messer Carcandella wore a collection of multicoloured robes, none of them particularly clean. After greeting Thomas and his boatswain with effusion, and Cristofano with undisguised interest, he sent the *Garland*'s crew away to some far corner of the house to get drunk on cheap wine.

'I regret the intrusion of my men on to your ship, gentlemen,' said the Venetian governor, gesturing with a grubby sleeve for Thomas to sit down in an overstuffed chair. 'I'm sure you understand that, dealing with honest men like yourselves, such a visit is purely a formality. But we have had – incidents – where cargo has been hidden in order to avoid paying duty.'

He clicked fat fingers, and a servant appeared with wine.

'Duty –' said Thomas, thoughtfully, and Messer Carcandello shook his head.

'– can be discussed tomorrow, don't you agree, signor?' The wide, sweat-soaked face settled into folds and creases approximating a smile. 'I regret that your company's factor cannot be with us tonight. He has a fever. Our climate does not suit him. So perhaps you will be kind enough to tolerate my poor company.'

Thomas, drinking malmsey wine, made suitable noises of mingled regret and delight. The climate of Zante was notoriously unsuitable for those from the north: with monotonous regularity Levant Company agents succumbed to one fever or another.

'I live alone on this island, Messer Marlowe,' went on Hieronymo. 'It is a dull place.' He rearranged his capacious robes and lowered himself into a sumptuous chair. 'Company – conversation – is such a rare pleasure. I have not yet been fortunate enough to find a wife to suit me.

The Venetian governor's gaze had scarcely left Cristofano since he had entered the room. Cristofano scowled, and the corners of Thomas's mouth twitched. The room was poorly aired and over-warm, the oil-lamps in the windows multiplying the sticky heat left over from the day. Through a partially opened window, Thomas could just make out the distant dark shapes of the boats in the harbour below, but he could no longer see the *Garland*.

The governor, following Thomas's gaze, took a handful of almonds from a bowl. 'You need not fear for your ship, Messer Marlowe,' he said smoothly. 'The harbour is well guarded. Your cargo will be safe, you have my word.'

Privately, Thomas thought that Hieronymo Carcandella's word was not worth the olive-stone he had just flicked into the fireplace. Deceit shimmered in the air like the moths around the oil-lamps. The governor snapped his fingers again, and Thomas's glass was refilled.

'The Levant Company,' said Thomas, carefully, 'wishes to remain on good terms with Venice. Our only desire is to trade freely.'

'Of course, Mr Marlowe.' Intelligence gleamed in Hieronymo's small dark eyes. 'It is all any of us desires. But consider the position of poor little Zante. The Ottoman empire to the east – the Barbary coast to the west. And those devils from Segna and Fiume infesting the Adriatic to the north. Our sailors will cut their own throats rather than fall into the hands of the Ragusan sea-robbers. You must realize that you and I have something in common, Mr Marlowe – we are both of island races. I was born in Zakynthos, you see.'

'Zante has the protection of Venice.'

'Ah, yes – the Serenissima . . .'

Their glasses were filled again. Hieronymo beckoned Cristofano to sit on the heaped cushions to his side, and Cristofano, with a shuffling lack of enthusiasm, obliged. 'Zante's problems are Venice's in miniature, Mr Marlowe. Venice has suffered the envy of the world, Christian and Turk alike, over the last few decades. As you are no doubt aware, Venice's trade with the north has declined sadly. Neither England nor the Netherlands has need of Venice now. You have the ships – and the men to sail them – yourselves.'

Several chins wobbled in the general direction of the harbour, now lost in darkness. A hand, each swollen finger indented with rings, gestured to the servant to close the remaining shutters, imprisoning the heat and intensifying the cloying perfumes of the East.

The malmsey wine was strong, but Thomas's head was still

clear. 'I have come to Zante to trade fairly, Messer Carcandella. My ship may not belong to me, but while it is under my command, it will commit no acts of aggression. I'll use my cannon to defend myself, but not for acts of piracy – under whatever pretext.'

Hieronymo laughed, a great shaking of sound, and leaned forward to pat Thomas on the knee. 'You must not trouble yourself, Mr Marlowe – I think we understand each other very well. I am half Venetian, but as I told you, I am a native of Zante. Ships like yours are the island's life-blood. Cargo such as yours is necessary to our survival. And sometimes you carry the *prettiest* things.'

Briefly, the ringed hand touched the scarlet silk cap that covered Cristofano's head. 'Do not trouble yourself, Mr Marlowe,' repeated Hieronymo, softly, and Thomas drained his glass, and leaned back on the cushions, his eyelids becoming heavy with wine and heat.

There was really nothing more he could do, he thought drowsily. The game progressed, temporarily out of his control, his pieces guarded as best as he was able. Just now, the *Garland*'s fate was in the hands of the ship's carpenter, a half-crazed master-gunner, and the ancient gods of the Ionian Sea.

On board the *Garland*, William Williams and Samuel, the ship's master-gunner, played cards, very quietly, in the hold. *If there's trouble*, Thomas had said, somewhere between Livorno and Zante, *it'll be over the tin*. Tin was one of the chief constituents of bronze. A lot of people were hungry for bronze. With bronze you could cast cannon.

They had positioned themselves in the orlop deck, between the gun-deck and the hold. Below the water-line, there were no portholes to betray their presence to the Venetians in the harbour, and they were only a ladder's climb from the crates of tin. The air was dank and foul, the floor cluttered with folded sails, anchor cables, spare shot and weapons. They all carried knives, and Samuel had primed a flintlock. If he'd have let him, thought William, trumping the master-gunner's ace, Samuel would have taken one of the falconets from the gun-deck.

It was pitch-dark, the only light the single candle that flickered on one of the upturned barrels. The silence was almost tangible: there was just the sucking lap of the sea against the hold and the small flick of cards being placed on the table. Even the rats and cockroaches seemed to be asleep. The hour was late: past midnight, William thought, stifling a yawn. He did not envy Thomas his evening of entertainment by the Venetian governor; given the choice, William preferred his own company to a night of pungent red wine and rigidly guarded conversation. The master-gunner took another mouthful from his bottle of aqua vitae, and passed it to William while he scrabbled in his pocket for coins.

There was no time to place another bet, however, for suddenly the silence was fractured by the sound of footsteps as the master-gunner's mate came running down the ladder to the gun-deck. As he lowered himself through the hatchway above them, the master-gunner's mate hissed, 'There's a pinnace – and half a dozen men –'

So Thomas had been right, then. Samuel, whose face was a pattern of scars from old conflicts, smiled as he unsheathed his knife. William Williams, the hairs prickling on the back of his neck, blew out the candle.

They waited on the orlop deck, guessing that two would stay aboard the pinnace to receive the stolen cargo, and the rest would lift and carry the stuff through the *Garland*. In the silence of waiting, William's palms began to sweat, so that the knife pivoted in his grasp. Three against four was quite reasonable odds, he reminded himself, especially when one of the three was Samuel.

And they had the advantage of surprise. Those other four, trespassing through the darkness, expected an easy night of it, rifling an untenanted ship. William and the master-gunner, and the master-gunner's mate, waited until two of them were on the ladder between the gun-deck and the orlop, and then Samuel, with a cry of pure pleasure, brought the butt of the flintlock down on top of an unguarded head.

The flintlock fired, and someone screamed. The brightness of the explosion shattered the silence of the ship. William, momentarily deafened and blinded, stood paralysed for a second. But almost immediately movement and anger returned, and he, too, threw himself into the fray.

The master and crew of the *Garland*, satiated with food and wine, did not return to their ship until the following morning.

'I've a splitting headache, and Cristofano's spent the entire night protecting his virtue,' said Thomas, flinging open the door of the Great Cabin. 'Thank God dear Hieronymo favours younger men.'

William Williams closed the door gently behind them, shutting out the sounds of the sea and the men calling to each other as they readied the *Garland* to sail.

'The master-gunner's mate has a broken arm, and there's a hole in the floor of the gun-deck,' he said, softly. 'Samuel would insist on taking a pistol.'

'Ah.' Thomas looked up, interest brightening his reddened eyes. 'And –?'

'And we lost some of the tin, I'm afraid. A couple of them managed to get one of the crates up to the maindeck. They dropped it overboard, though. I think,' said William, re-flectively, 'that Samuel reduced their numbers to three. It was hard to be sure. There's a couple of bodies in the hold, and Samuel shot one of them as he jumped into the pinnace.'

Thomas, frowning, pulled the cork out of a flask of wine. 'I just paid a fortune in grossly over-inflated duties to that slug back in Zakynthos. I don't understand. I thought I did, but I don't. If they wanted the bloody stuff so much, why not just impound it? There's damn all we could have done to stop them.'

William grinned, and accepted the cup of wine Thomas offered him. 'Because they weren't Venetian,' he said, taking a certain amount of satisfaction from the expression on the pilot's face. 'They were French.'

Neither the headache nor the apparently insoluble puzzle of Zakynthos allowed Thomas to sleep that night. The headache pounded through his temples, reminding him in future to avoid

Greeks bearing gifts; the attempted theft of the tin kept him on the half-deck, watching the stars and the sea, instead of anchoring overnight in some secluded inlet.

French. The men who had boarded the *Garland* at night, to steal Thomas's precious tin while the ship's crew were safely out of the way in the Venetian governor's villa in Zakynthos, had been French. Yet, Hieronymo Carcandella had, Thomas was certain, known of the attempt beforehand – had helped orchestrate it once he had confirmed that the *Garland* carried tin.

Which made no sense. Venetian governors should not be helping Frenchmen steal the cargo of an English ship. They should be charging excessive duties, boarding ships illegally, and causing trouble in any number of other ways. But not assisting clandestine operations conducted by the French.

He heard William Williams, at his side, say, 'I'll take over, if you like.'

Thomas shook his head. 'I'm not tired.' The image of the ghost ship, with that single flickering fleur-de-lys, rose in his mind, as it had for a hundred times already that day. He said slowly, 'When I was on watch one night – a week or so back – I saw a ship. Only briefly – I almost thought I was imagining her. It was as though she peered over the horizon, and looked at us, and then disappeared. She was beautiful, Will. And she was French.'

William frowned. 'You think that she could have been the owner of the pinnace?'

Thomas shrugged. The *Garland* had spent the day unlading cloth and tin, taking on barrels of currants and ballast to substitute for the weight of the metal. Hauling barrels and bales, he had had time to think.

'I don't know. There's no logic to it, but –' He stopped. Sometimes during the day he had thought himself becoming obsessed by that ship. But it was an obsession he could not shake off, because it was fuelled by a cold, rational anger.

Turning aside from William, Thomas shouted directions to the helmsman below.

William prompted, 'And we are –?'

'Looking for her. Or whoever else it was that visited us last night. We're circling Zante. On the assumption that, if there's something going on between dear Hieronymo and the French, whoever tried to steal the tin will not have gone far. Just far enough to keep a few bruised crew-members out of sight.'

William said carefully, 'Thomas –'

'I know.' Thomas's features, lit by the silvered moon and the lantern that swung from the yard-arm, were clear and cold. 'It would be much more sensible simply to sail back to Livorno, present John Keane with his currants, earn a few pats on the back from the Levant Company. But, had you thought, William' – and Thomas's eyes, drained of colour by the night, were a hard steel-grey – 'what would have happened to the *Garland* without her ballast of tin?'

'She'd have turned arse over tit and sunk,' said William grimly. 'And no doubt your friend Hieronymo would have put it down to the age of the ship, her weakened timbers, anything but the truth.'

'And we'd have been unable to prove otherwise. My first command, and I'd have lost her.'

The *Garland* continued to cut her silent path through the dark waters of the Ionian Sea.

Thomas added, 'My bet is that our night-visitors are still hiding somewhere on Zante.' He frowned, pushing his fingers through untidy dark hair. 'I'd like to know who they are, William. I'll dream about them every night of my life, otherwise.'

They found the French ship when daylight was no more than a blur of pink on the horizon.

They might have missed her had it not been for the exquisite Ionian dawns. The French ship had by that time dropped anchor in a cove to the north of Zante. The cove, accessible only by sea, was bordered on three sides by high vertical cliffs. The strip of white sand would have been seen only at low tide, marking the inner edge of the cove. Walled on three sides by rock, unlit and with her sails furled, the ship was made visible by the coral light that drew her graceful hull and spars.

Thomas recognized her instantly, though. She was rose-coloured now, but whatever colour she had been he would not have failed to know her slim, graceful lines, her four tall masts. The greys and silvers had been an illusion, conjured by the moonlight and by the gilding that seemed to limn every part of her. She was the *Garland*'s night-visitor, and though once she had only raised the blanket and looked, her second visit had been a violation.

Neither he nor William had slept that night. But, sighting the ship, all trace of weariness evaporated, and Thomas felt nothing but the familiar squeeze of anger he had experienced earlier in the night.

'If they've seen us, with any luck they'll assume we're going north to Kephalonia or Corfu.' Thomas nodded in the direction of the galleon, as they rapidly disappeared behind the curtain of rock. 'We'll keep sailing north, but only far enough to allow us to anchor out of sight. Then I intend to take a closer look at her.'

'And then —?'

Thomas scowled. 'I'd scuttle the bloody thing if I could, Will. But did you catch sight of the ordnance on her?'

'Built for war,' said William, thoughtfully.

Thomas was walking towards the tiller. 'Aye,' he called back. 'But with whom?'

They found a convenient anchorage a half-league or so along the coast. The north-west coast of Zante was pitted with indentations like the rind of an orange, so it was easy enough to find a sheltered inlet providing access to the island.

Climbing up the rocks that backed the bay, the master-gunner at his heels, Thomas was only too aware of the frustrating realities of his situation. The French ship was a larger, better-armed craft than the *Garland*. The French ship could, if she chose, blast the smaller ship out of the sea while remaining out of range of Thomas's falconets. On the open sea, her larger sails and sleeker line would allow her easily to outrun the *Garland*.

So he would simply take a long look, discover her name. Thomas's shirt clung damply to his back as they scrambled over the stones and rough grass that covered the summit of the cliff. The sun was high in the sky, and he could feel the heat of the rocks through the soles of his shoes. The last of the summer's flowers powdered the rocks: gold and pink and violet and white. He would take a long look, and wait. Wait for the *Kingfisher's* completion, wait for revenge.

They kept parallel to the coastline, but out of sight of the open sea. Thomas felt his heart begin to beat a little faster as they reached the cove where the French ship was hidden. Crouching low, moving almost on his stomach, he scrambled to the edge of the cliff. He would have liked access to a cannon, he thought, wiping the sweat from his eyes with the back of his hand. Something the size of Mons Meg to sink that damned ship –

Only, there wasn't one damned ship. There were two.

He had to clamp his hand over Samuel's mouth to stop him yelling out loud. He knew what Samuel would have shouted, and he knew how those cliffs would have magnified it. *The Turk* would have repeated in echo, over and over again, the incriminating word bouncing like a ball off those great stone walls.

He heard his own voice whisper very softly, 'Christ.'

His gaze slid slowly from the Turkish galley to the other ship. She was French and she was exquisite, and had covetousness been Thomas's besetting sin, then it would have been that ship that corrupted him. As it was, he took one sharp inward breath before noting her graceful lines, her four tall strong masts, the feast of glittering gilt-work that seemed almost to compete with the glorious Aegean sunset, while his brain compared her with the plans, the images, of his superb, half-finished *Kingfisher*. He heard Samuel whisper, 'That's the pinnace, I'm sure of it, sir,' and he saw the smaller boat that was roped alongside the galleon.

The galleon's sails were unfurled now. The galley's oars were raised in unison, her prow, painted with a wreath of blue flowers, pointed towards the mouth of the cove.

The French ship's name was emblazoned in gold along her bows. Thomas read the name *Fiametta*, and then ran back through the heat and dust to the *Garland*.

'Because Venice doesn't favour selling tin to the Turk in order to make cannon. They've enough trouble with corsairs themselves, you see, and what we saw, you may have no doubt, Will, was a corsair ship. From Algiers or Tunis, no doubt.'

Back in the Great Cabin on board the *Garland*, Thomas, charts scattered all over the table, was already plotting his course back to Tuscany. On deck, sails were being unleashed from the spars, and the helmsman had begun to pilot the ship out of the creek.

Thomas, not looking up from the table, added, 'My guess is that the *Fiametta* has a nice little deal arranged between Hieronymo and the Barbary corsairs. The means with which to make ordnance, in exchange for a guarantee that Zante and its shipping remain unmolested. With our friend the Frenchman as intermediary. No screaming maidens abducted to Algerian seraglios, no cargoes from Zakynthos finding their way into Barbary holds. Hieronymo as good as told us the other night that he was loyal to Zante, not to Venice. Venice is not involved in this arrangement, you see. The only players are Hieronymo, the *Fiametta*, and the corsair.'

Thomas unrolled another chart, placing weights on the corners to keep it flat.

William Williams said curiously, 'So what will you do?'

'Do? Nothing, of course. Yet.' Thomas ruled a line across the chart. 'It seems a nice neat system, don't you think? After all, what have we lost? We've sold our cargo, bought our currants. We've paid a little extra in duty, that's all – but no more, I suspect, than we'd have paid in Candia or Aleppo. We lost a little tin, I suppose, but only a little, because we weren't quite as easy a target as the *Fiametta* thought we would be. At the moment I can do nothing, Will.'

He had plotted his course, taken the best available line through the future hazards before him. Thomas heard the ship's carpenter say softly, 'But you won't let it rest there.'

The compasses snapped shut, and Thomas stoppered his inkwell.

'They'd have sunk us, Will. Not in open sea, not in a fair fight. Just – casually – as though we didn't matter.'

Rising, he was surprised at the strength of his own anger, at the small hard knot of vengeance that tensed every muscle in his body. It was as though all the frustrations and betrayals of the last months had focused on this one arrogant attempt on his livelihood and self-respect.

Leaving the cabin, Thomas found that his thoughts had returned to Serafina. He had begun perhaps to understand her, to follow the impulse that possessed her cold little spirit.

'And Mr Keane?' William Williams, ahead of him on the companion-way, paused. 'Will you tell him?'

'I don't think so.' Thomas shook his head. 'I don't think the *Fiametta* need interest anyone but us.'

He would not meet William William's eyes, though. He needed the Levant Company for a while, but not, this voyage had reminded him, for ever. The justice Thomas required was personal, his own, and no concern of the company's. No concern, in fact, of anyone but him.

The English Levant Company convoy sailed into Livorno one sharp autumn morning.

There were three of them: the *Legacy*, the *Sampson*, and the *Saviour of Bristol*. Fair winds and the constant exhortations of their masters had hurried them on their way, the prospect of trade had seen them through weeks of dull food and interrupted nights. The master of the *Legacy*, on docking in Livorno, wasted no time. Though dawn was no more than a sliver of cold grey light on the horizon, he re-read the address on the letter in his pocket and went in search of John Keane.

Keane's ship, the *Garland*, had become separated from its convoy in a summer storm, and had since been becalmed for refitting and repairs in Livorno. They should surely have fixed the old tub by now, thought the master of the *Legacy*, walking away from the harbour and into the cramped streets that surrounded it. Too much time had been lost already: within a week or so all four ships must be ready to sail to Aleppo and back.

The harbour had begun to wake: fishermen were raising the sails on their boats and bundling nets into hulls. Keane's house, only a couple of hundred yards from the docks, was tall and thin, silent in the early morning light. Through an unshuttered upstairs window the familiar rounded shape of a lute, ribbons strung from its neck, could be seen carefully balanced on the sill. Impatiently, the master of the *Legacy* beat on the door. His breath formed clouds in the cold air, and the simple undecorated collar of his doublet was pulled up around his neck. He was hungry and tired, and the slippery cobbles swayed under his feet like a galleon's wooden deck.

The door opened. The man standing there wore a nightshirt under his fur-trimmed robe, and his sleep-hazed eyes struggled to focus on the figure before him. Then his whole face lightened in a smile.

'Edward!' cried John Keane, gripping the master of the *Legacy*'s hands in his. 'Edward Whitlock!'

Within less than a half-hour, Edward Whitlock was sitting in John Keane's parlour, a plate of steak and eggs in front of him, a cup of hot wine to his side.

'– they're fine ships. All three of them,' mumbled Whitlock, his mouth half-full of steak. 'We should be ready to sail to Scanderoon in a couple of weeks' time.'

John Keane, fully dressed now, cradled a pewter cup in his own hands, and avoided Edward Whitlock's meaningful glance. Ned Whitlock was a good man, an intelligent man, and an efficient man, but he had a temper shorter than John's own little dwarf kitchen-boy. Not for the first time, Keane, who had some interest in natural philosophy, reflected that Whitlock's governing humour was choler. He had the dry, reddish hair of the true choleric, and even now, while eating, he was unable to be still, and his boot tapped out some incessant and compelling rhythm on the polished wooden boards.

John, putting off explaining to Whitlock about the absent *Garland*, signalled to Antonio to refill their cups.

'What cargo do you carry, Ned?'

The steak was almost finished; Whitlock wiped his mouth with his handkerchief.

'It's mostly linen and friezes. But we've some nice pewter, and some knives and scissors. And the *Saviour* has three hundred pounds of tin made up into dishes and trenchers.' Whitlock, throwing back his large leonine head, emptied his second glass of wine. 'The *Garland* carried tin, didn't she, Jack?'

Keane, still avoiding those protuberant green eyes, threw some more wood on the fire. 'Aye. Only it was in ingots, not plate.' He grimaced. 'I think we'd have gone down without the tin for extra ballast. It was the devil of a tempest.'

Whitlock looked sympathetic. 'You did well, Jack – no one's saying otherwise.' Pushing his empty plate away, swallowing the last piece of steak, his eyes strayed back to the window that framed the nearby harbour. 'Is the *Garland* seaworthy now?'

'Oh, yes.' Mentally, Keane cursed the *Legacy* for being early, and the *Garland* for being late. 'The damage was largely superficial, and I found some good men to repair her. And I've bought another ship.'

He had Whitlock's interest at last: the boot paused in its tapping, the grey-green eyes widened even further.

'Well, *hired* another ship – she was only half built, and the shipwright had run out of money to finish her with. Cost of materials in return for five years' sailing – a profitable arrangement, I think. And she's a beauty, Ned – something special. You'll have to see her.'

Whitlock rose from the table, and gathered together his gloves and hat.

'Perhaps. Just now we should be making ready to leave port as soon as possible. Is the *Garland*'s tin warehoused, or have you already loaded her?'

There was nothing for it. Keane took a deep breath. 'The *Garland*'s loaded and sailed, Ned. For Zante.'

He did not avoid Whitlock's gaze, this time. 'Her cargo had been gathering dust in the warehouse for three months,' he went on patiently, resenting the fact that he was reduced to defending himself like some guilty schoolboy. 'Thomas offered to take her to Zante – it's a reasonable distance, and he's a damned good pilot. So I agreed.' Keane, too, had stood up and was making ready to leave.

'Thomas?' said Whitlock, frowning. 'Who's Thomas?'

Strangely, he had not seized upon the fact that the *Garland* had sailed alone.

'Thomas Marlowe is the owner of the *Kingfisher* – the new ship,' explained John. 'He supervised the repairs to the *Garland*. He'll be back before the weather worsens. He knows his job, Ned, I assure you. In fact, Marlowe's worked for the company before – he was pilot of the *Toby*. You remember, Ned, she went down off Morocco in 1593.'

He misread the expression on the master of the *Legacy*'s face. 'I think we all know that the pilot was not responsible for the loss of the *Toby*,' Keane added, hastily. 'I think Richard Staper accepted that he had erred in appointing George Goodlay as master. Thomas will take good care of the *Garland*, I've no doubt. He'll be back any day now, with a cargo of currants, and then someone else can pilot the old thing back to London.'

Again, he mentally cursed the absent navigator. Edward Whitlock had not moved: he had stood quite still for an entire minute. Then, 'Thomas Marlowe?' said Whitlock, softly. 'Well, well. I thought he was dead.'

Keane had flung his cloak around his shoulders, crammed his hat on his head. 'They'll be back any day,' he repeated, comfortingly. And then, choosing the worst possible change of subject, he added, 'And how's the family, Ned? How is that delightful wife of yours?'

He could not understand, then, why Edward roared like a bull and made for the door as though to wrench it from its hinges.

That autumn, the merchant Jacopo Capriani contracted an ague.

The fever died down soon enough, but all the potions and physic Serafina prepared could not rid him of the cough that was the sickness's legacy. The cough shook his entire body, tore at lungs already weakened by years of marsh fever. Serafina remembered writing in Kara Ali's notebook: *phthisis, a wasting disease of the lungs*, and remembered also that Allah had permitted Kara Ali to find no cure.

She had neither the time nor the energy to work out the consequences of that diagnosis to herself. Seventeen years old, and in the middle months of a deeply resented pregnancy, she found that the opportunity simply to think seemed to have disappeared as her station in life improved. As Jacopo's health had deteriorated, so had his demands on her multiplied. His whining voice grated against her increasingly exposed nerves, his constant emotional needs drained her own limited resources. If he no longer demanded the rights of a husband, then still he required her to lie beside him at night: a voice to hear in the darkness when his own wakefulness nightly reminded him of the frailty of human existence, a hand to clutch at when he remembered the loneliness of the grave. Often Serafina found her eyelids growing heavy as she inspected the ledgers, sometimes she was almost tempted to send Amadeo to examine the last bales of silk arriving in Livorno. But always in time she reminded herself of the accuracy of only her arithmetic, of the eye for a good-quality silk that Amadeo did not yet possess. That this was what she had married for, this was what she had struggled for.

Jacopo refused to pay for a physician. Vultures, he said, every one of them, asking ridiculous sums of money for useless remedies. So it was left to Serafina to administer the most suitable of Kara Ali's medicines, preparing caudles and tisanes with her own hands, administering them to a husband who became more querulous each day. She understood Jacopo's fears: she had fears of her own. If Jacopo died, if her child should be a girl, then she would be penniless again.

As Jacopo took more frequently to his bed, so Serafina's responsibility for the company increased. Refusing to allow the bitter possibility that the cuckoo in her belly should rob her of any gain, she continued to ride to Livorno herself, continued personally to select new purchases and show her goods, with Amadeo or the new clerk Michele, at the great palazzos. Her pregnancy did not yet show: she had let out the bodices of her gowns and had some new ones made, and if she laced the panels of buckram tight enough her stomach was as flat as ever. She had tried with all the strength of mind she was capable of, to ignore the reality of the next few months. But sometimes it crept up on her, imprisoning her, reminding her that some confinements were utterly inescapable. Sitting in a prince's house in Siena, she had felt the first flutterings of life inside her, and those faint fish-like movements had sickened her. She had had to instruct Amadeo to write the bill of purchase: her own fingers shook too much to hold a pen.

Only once or twice did she think of Thomas Marlowe. Heavily veiled, standing on the dockside of Livorno one cold November day, she had caught a glimpse of his ship, no longer in dry dock, but launched and moored at the harbourside. A figurehead had gleamed proudly from the prow, a great turquoise and golden bird that stared out over the Ligurian Sea as though impatient to break the cage of the harbour and skim over the beckoning waters. Looking at the *Kingfisher*, Serafina had experienced an unexpected stab of despair. A feeling of incompleteness, as if she had, by her own error, lost something of incalculable value.

Thomas had sailed from Livorno under clear blue skies that had been damp with heat and sonorous with the whine of mosquitoes. Now the air had grown sharp and cold, and the wind tugged at the sea, flecking the grey-green water with a thin foam of white. As soon as they had docked in Livorno's harbour and the *Garland* was secure and tidy, Thomas sent William Williams to announce their safe arrival to John Keane, while he himself paid immediate court to the *Kingfisher*.

Tired from an unexpectedly difficult voyage, Thomas nevertheless forgot his exhaustion as he gazed round his ship. The decks were still littered with the inevitable detritus of construction: paint pots and hammers and barrels of nails and heaps of wood shavings, but the structure of the hull was long finished, the caulking, necessary to protect the wood against sea-water, was complete. The masts and yards had been raised, and in the fading evening light, Thomas could picture the sails and rigging that would soon festoon them. Prow and beakhead were painted with intricate blue and gold whorls and curlicues; chevrons and diamonds of the same colours had begun to pattern the gunwales around the poop. Over the shifting surface of the sea, the figurehead stared out, proud-eyed and impatient.

Unwary for once, Thomas did not hear the footsteps ascending the gangway.

'My, my – she *is* an impressive sight,' said a voice from behind him. 'You have been busy, Mr Marlowe, haven't you?'

Thomas spun round on his heel.

'But then, you've never been idle. You've always liked to keep yourself occupied.'

The man standing on the maindeck was taller than Thomas, and broader. He had not immediately recognized the voice because that man belonged to Greenwich, and the past.

'Edward Whitlock,' said Thomas. He found that his mouth was slightly dry.

'That's right.' Whitlock, smiling, took a step forward. 'I wasn't sure whether you'd remember me. After all, it was my wife you knew better, wasn't it?'

Black shadows were spilling themselves on to the deck, and Edward Whitlock had a rather fine sword at his side. Thomas's heart hammered, and his hand moved, unobtrusively, closer to his own dagger.

'The Levant Company –' said Thomas, conjecturing wildly and accurately. 'The ships have arrived, and you're –'

'– the master of the *Legacy*, heading the convoy. You remember the *Legacy*, don't you, Mr Marlowe? A nice little craft, if a bit broad in the beam –'

'I piloted her.' Thomas's fingers, under the folds of his sleeveless doublet, had folded round the hilt of his knife. Silently, he cursed himself for not foreseeing this particularly horrible possibility. His last encounter with Edward Whitlock had been exquisitely memorable: he could still feel that damned ivy tearing in his grip, sense the heat of the bullet as it scorched his cheek. He could also remember the smoothness of Faith Whitlock's skin under his questing fingers, the soft fullness of her amenable body.

Dragging himself hastily back to present problems, Thomas added, 'I piloted the *Legacy* to Scanderoon. Twice.'

He did not really think he would engage Ned Whitlock in a nice comradely reminiscence about past voyages, but the longer he managed to keep Whitlock's hand from his sword, the greater chance there was that John Keane or William Williams might appear. And if Keane's diplomacy could not talk Whitlock out of violence, then William's huge bulk and placid temperament might at least help Thomas contain the damage.

But the harbour was deserted: all Livorno had abandoned Thomas to retribution and the last man on earth he wanted to see. Edward Whitlock had begun to stroll round the maindeck, his hands idly flicking at the coils of rope, the unfinished carpentry.

'We thought you'd gone down with the *Toby*, Mr Marlowe. I was rather pleased at the news, I have to admit.' He smiled unpleasantly. 'I told Faith about the loss of the *Toby* when we were attending a banquet given by the company. She did not shed a tear, Mr Marlowe. Not a tear.'

Thomas's temper began to burn then, as familiar and inevitable as the waves that lunged at and retreated from the *Kingfisher*'s hull. He said, coldly, 'Perhaps you should leave my ship, Mr Whitlock. I don't believe we have anything useful to discuss.'

Whitlock paused for moment in his circling of the foredeck, one foot on the stairs to the half-deck. 'Ah, but we do, sir. We have business to discuss.'

His gaze swept, slowly, along the length of the ship, from bow to stern. Thomas became aware of the small smile on the other man's face, and the cold dread that suddenly began to knot his own stomach.

'We have to discuss this ship, Mr Marlowe,' said Whitlock, softly. 'I believe that the Levant Company has advanced you money for the completion of this ship. I regret to have to inform you that the company no longer wants her. We have an excess of ships, Mr Marlowe, and your ship' – he had climbed the stairs to the half-deck – 'is no longer needed.'

'I had a contract.' Thomas's fingers had clenched around the knife, and he found that he had to struggle to keep his voice even. 'A contract with Mr Keane.'

Whitlock smiled again. 'I am John Keane's superior, Mr Marlowe. I have just declared that contract invalid. This ship is unfinished, and I fear' – the strong fingers gripped around the partially finished pin-rail that edged the half-deck, and pulled, hard – 'fit only for matchwood.'

He snapped the pin-rail in one swift clean movement. 'Matchwood,' repeated Edward Whitlock, breaking the painted rail in two, dropping the fragments to the deck below.

'You bastard –' Thomas, making for the stairs, had drawn his knife.

'Careful, Mr Marlowe. I'm calling in the loan John Keane advanced you a little early. Just business, I assure you. This hulk will be worth more to us in timber. The company is always short of good timber. And besides, bastards are more your prerogative, I would guess.'

So Whitlock would call in John Keane's loan, which he, Thomas, would be unable to repay. And in recompense for Thomas's despoiling of Whitlock's own property, Whitlock would ensure that the *Kingfisher* never sailed. He would cut down her masts, hack up her deckplanks, strip her hull to the matchwood he had likened her to.

No. He had fought too long and too hard. He had risked fire and water, he had lied and he had stolen for this ship.

Thomas knew then that he was going to say something unforgivable, but he found that he did not really care. Indeed, there was a pleasure in it, just as there was a similar pleasure in anticipating the violence it would provoke.

'No doubt my by-blows people Greenwich docks,' said Thomas, clearly, drawing level with Whitlock. 'As cuckolds people the houses that surround them.'

He heard the indrawn breath, saw the anger that matched his own flare and gleam in Edward Whitlock's eyes. Whitlock's sword scythed out of its scabbard, and the last rays of the setting sun dazzled momentarily into fire along the blade's edge. '*My* ship,' said Thomas, softly. 'Leave my ship, Whitlock, before I throw you off.'

The sword rose, arced, stabbed towards him. Thomas jumped aside, seizing a spare piece of timber as he did so. He had had Whitlock's measure since the other man first set foot on the *Kingfisher*: strong, but slow and heavy. That was why Whitlock preferred a pistol. He had a good eye, but lacked coordination and speed. The timber deflected the movement of the sword: there was a satisfying crunch, and splinters showered the *King-fisher*'s deck. *My ship*, thought Thomas, grinning.

But Whitlock had also grabbed something from the deck. A hammer: the thick strong arm swung round, striking the fragile railings over and over again until the wood shattered and turned to sawdust.

Someone had decorated that pin-rail with small golden flower-heads on a blue background. Thomas wanted to kill Edward Whitlock.

'Bastard!' he yelled again, hurling himself at the other man.

Whitlock's sword slipped, a clatter of metal on wood, to the maindeck below. The hammer struck at Thomas, numbing his arm so that his knife tore uselessly through broadcloth and linen. Wildly, Whitlock lashed out at the gunwales, the mizzen-mast, the deckplanks.

'Call this a ship?' he yelled, hurling a coil of rope into the sea below. 'You couldn't cross the Thames in this crate – she'd crack in two at the first breeze –'

His free hand seized a bundle of dowling and threw it down after the rope. The sea sucked greedily at the wood fragments. There was a red mist in front of Thomas's eyes: still gripping his dagger, he threw himself again at Whitlock.

And this time, he knew that he had found his mark. He felt the dulling of impetus as the blade of the knife encountered flesh and bone. Whitlock staggered, and gasped, and drops of crimson blood fouled the deckplanks.

But it was not enough. Whitlock's eyes were glazed, his thick red hair stuck to his scalp with sweat, as he swung his arm again. Ducking swiftly, Thomas felt the hammer blow fall on his shoulder, and knew that if it had reached the intended target of his skull it would have killed him. Blows rained on his shoulder and upper arm, robbing them of feeling, so that his knife slipped from his nerveless fingers, skittering to a far corner of the deck.

In the end, though, it wasn't Edward Whitlock that finished him, it was his own entrancing, devouring *Kingfisher*. They danced an absurd, deadly dance, he and Whitlock, arms clasping each to each, fingers clutching handfuls of hair, shirt, skin. There was an odd kind of unity: Whitlock's fury and his own, perfectly matched in a need for mutual destruction.

But eventually they circled one time too many, and Whitlock's greater weight forced Thomas against the unfinished gunwale. The railing, nailed at only one end, creaked, split, and then gave way, and it was only Edward Whitlock who had time to release his hold, to stagger backwards, falling to his knees as the gunwale shattered and tumbled to the sea below.

Thomas fell with it. One hand grabbed at timber, rope, anything, the other flailed nervelessly at his side. He fell clumsily, an uncontrolled rush of shattered carpentry, his head thudding off one of the larger planks that floated in the sea.

Then all that was left to him was a jumble of half-finished thoughts. The shock of the cold waves, the rush of water into his nostrils, his ears, his eyes. He seemed only to have one arm: what had happened to the other one? The sea picked him up, one more piece of flotsam, and threw him carelessly against the hull of the *Kingfisher*.

The sea, his obsession, his enemy. The *Kingfisher*, whom he had loved with a constancy he had devoted to no one else. Combining forces, killing him.

They reached the *Kingfisher* just as Edward Whitlock finished hacking down the mizzen-mast. From the far end of the harbour William saw the two figures lock and separate, and then lock again. And then, suddenly, there was only one figure.

They began to run, then, he and John Keane. To Keane, they were nothing more than blurred, faceless marionettes, but he could hear the sound of splintering wood, the repeated splashes as Whitlock hurled featureless objects into the churning sea.

They were halfway along the harbour when Whitlock exchanged the hammer for an axe. Running up the gangway, breathless by the time he had climbed to the half-deck, William dragged the axe from Whitlock's clutching hands just as the mizzen-mast creaked and fell, smashing the poop-deck to smithereens.

There had been two figures, though. As William landed a well-aimed blow on the master of the *Legacy*'s jaw, John Keane saw the broken gunwale. Crouching at the edge of the half-deck, he squinted down to the sea.

The light had almost gone, and he did not think he had ever regretted his inadequate eyesight so much. But he could just make out that down there were bits of wood, and rope enough to entangle every rudder in the harbour, and empty barrels bobbing in dark water. And there was a body, floating face down, the black curling hair stranded like seaweed, the straying, lifeless limbs knocking repeatedly against the *Kingfisher*'s hollow wooden hull.

'*William* —' yelled Keane, but the carpenter was already beside him, had already kicked off his boots, dropped his dagger to the deck.

William leapt into the water as Keane found the necessary coil of rope. Whitlock lay motionless on the half-deck: damn him, thought Keane, tying one end of the rope to the stump of the mizzen-mast, for an ill-tempered bastard. The ship that Keane, too, had coveted, Whitlock had scarred and despoiled. The ship's owner was probably dead already.

Narrowing his eyes, kneeling alongside the broken spars of the gunwale, Keane peered down into the chaos below. William Williams had hold of the pilot's hair. The sea lurched and heaved and tried to separate them, but the carpenter's arm folded across Marlowe's breast, linking them together. Keane saw and understood William's brief upward glance, and the coil of rope uncurled and flared through the air, battering against the *Kingfisher*'s hull, as fast and as lithe as a serpent. The carpenter's hand reached out and, miraculously, the tongue of the serpent snaked inside it.

That was the easy bit. The hard bit was knotting a length of rope around a lifeless man, whilst bobbing around in twenty feet of cold, choppy water. It took long, agonizing minutes, minutes which would, Keane knew, count against Thomas's chances of survival. But the job was done at last, and Keane, glancing quickly round to make sure Whitlock was still quiescent, began to haul.

It was a dead weight, and Keane, much Thomas's size and height, had to grit his teeth and strain every muscle in his body. But his hands were not only used to tuning a lute or moving a chess piece: and just as the carpenter, who had swum round the prow and scrambled up the harbour wall to the quayside, appeared behind him, Keane raised the unconscious pilot to the edge of the gunwale.

He was a battered, bruised mess. William's powerful arms rolled Marlowe on to the deckplanks; when he was face down, Keane began to pump the water from his lungs. There was blood on his arms, his back, his face; his entire shirt seemed scarlet. The sea drained the blood from a man's veins, eventually spitting out a blanched, bloated husk to tumble back and forth on some foreign sea-strand. Pausing momentarily, Keane felt under the pilot's jaw, and was rewarded with a weak but obstinately flickering heartbeat.

When he had coughed half the sea over the *Kingfisher's* damaged decks, they wrapped Thomas in John's cloak and lifted him over the carpenter's shoulders. He had not opened his eyes, had not spoken. Only Keane said, as they glanced back a last time at the ruined ship, the man still lying on the half-deck, 'And what the hell was all that about?'

Because he had only just completed a voyage of many weeks, and because the sea had tried yet again to smother him with her cold embrace, Thomas still felt the motion of the waves.

At first, there was only blackness, and confusion, a continuation of the churning water, the multiple blows that had battered him into unconsciousness. The blackness was not unpleasant: it allowed no room for thought. Then, gradually, he understood that he was drowning. He was enduring the death that all sailors dreaded: the sea would fill his lungs, replace the air in his body, turn him into a white swollen horror hardly recognizable as a man. He was on the *Toby* again, and she had capsized off Morocco: her broken spars and waterlogged sails buffeted him as he tried to swim. His limbs would not obey him, his arms were trapped, immovable. Then he saw that he had reached the sea-strand, and just ahead of him golden ducats were scattered like gilt sea-shells on the sand. Behind him, though, on the horizon, another ship hovered, a spider-web of silvered, ghostly strands. Thomas reached out to touch the coins embedded in the sand. He could feel them smooth and hard between his outstretched fingers, but they slipped from his grasp, and he felt himself sucked inexorably backwards into the sea, while the water choked him.

He became aware, eventually, that the waves had stilled, and someone was sitting beside him. Sometimes he thought it was the Tuareg woman, Jamila, glittering with silk and golden scarves. Then abruptly, he knew that it was Serafina. He had something important to tell her, but his mouth, filled with sea-water, could not form the words. She was very beautiful to him, with her smooth dark hair and her clear slanting eyes, but when she turned he saw that she bore a scar the length of her jaw.

As suddenly as Serafina had appeared, so she was gone. Thomas almost smiled to himself, because that had been the pattern of her coming to his life. But then someone began to hurt him very badly, pulling and tearing at his limbs. He wanted to scream, but the only sound he could make was the water bubbling in his lungs. Thomas found that he was glad when, finally, the waves crashed once more over his head, and he was returned to the blackness.

They had taken Thomas Marlowe back to John Keane's house and sent Antonio for a physician. The physician, clumsily poking and prodding an unconscious body, told them what they had already suspected – broken ribs, a broken collar-bone, a severe blow to the head. If, said the physician, the gentleman's skull was fractured (he could not be certain), then the gentleman would develop a fever and die. The patient had swallowed a good deal of sea-water, which always weakened the system. The physician then muttered something hopefully about leeches, and Keane showed him the door.

Thomas did not wake up until the still hours after midnight. By that time both Keane and William Williams were asleep: one in front of the embers of the parlour fire, the other in his civilized four-poster. Antonio sat in the spare bedchamber, with instructions to wake his master if there was any change in the patient. Antonio's eyelids were beginning to droop; Thomas's face was as still as a carved figurehead.

The entire household, and most of the street, woke, however, when Edward Whitlock knocked at the front door. 'Keane!' he bawled, hammering with two clenched fists. 'Keane! I know the bastard's in there!'

It was then that the pilot's eyelids flickered, opened, closed again, and then managed to remain apart. Antonio, hearing footsteps running down the stairs, pushed the bedchamber door to.

'– if you will behave as a gentleman.' John Keane's voice, cold and hard as iron, eventually floated up the stairs towards the spare bedchamber. 'I will not have a free-for-all inside my house.'

There was a silence, and Antonio felt for the stiletto dagger he always carried hidden under his doublet. But he heard Whitlock's voice reply, 'Very well then. I swear I will not lay a finger on him while he remains under your roof.'

The footsteps had grown closer, there was the sound of the parlour door being opened. 'William,' said John Keane's voice, 'this is Edward Whitlock, master of the *Legacy*. Whom you last saw on the deck of the *Kingfisher*.'

Antonio, rising silently, pushed open the bedchamber door a crack. He recognized Whitlock from his earlier visit, but now the broad forehead was ornamented with a large crimson bruise, and there was something that looked suspiciously like a bandage beneath his linen shirt.

'I have come here to tell you, Mr Keane, that I will not have that man working for the company. I do not know what arrangements you have made with him, but I will not ratify them. I'm sure that my colleagues in London will back me up on this.'

There was a pause. Antonio fingered the sharp pointed blade of his dagger. Then he heard Messer Keane say, 'Very well, Ned. He may not recover anyway, in which case your protestations will be immaterial.'

Another silence.

Then Keane added, 'And the ship? Whatever your quarrel with the man, Ned, is it really worth the loss of that ship?'

'The ship can go to the bottom for all I care!' Antonio could hear Whitlock's indrawn breath, and the pounding of his footsteps as he paced the room. 'Marlowe will pay back every penny you lent him, or I'll have that damned crate for firewood!'

'You are unjust, Edward.' Keane's voice was cold. 'I gave him my word. Whatever he has done, you are unjust.'

'No. I am generous. He may have until I return from Aleppo. And then I will have back every penny you lent him, John. Every penny.'

There was the sound of footsteps again, and doors closing. For the first time, Antonio glanced back down at his patient.

The eyes were open, a deep dark blue in the dim candlelight.

'What did you do?' whispered Antonio.

He had guessed the answer already, of course. 'I slept with his wife,' said Thomas Marlowe, and smiled at the memory, and then did not smile again.

PART VIII

1595-6

STRANGE ALTERATIONS

This is a strange alteration and very apt to deceive the sailor, unless he know the unconstancy and variation of his compass.

Letter by Gerardus Mercator touching the intended discovery of the North-East Passage:
Richard Hakluyt

As the century neared its close, those greater than Thomas Marlowe also found themselves subject to the frailties of the flesh. In Spain, Philip II, for forty years ruler of the great Hapsburg empire, fought feebly against fever and disillusionment. He had lost much of the Netherlands to Protestantism, his great armada had failed to return England to the true religion. Confined to a wheelchair for his few remaining days, the humiliating anarchy of sickness was like a scourge to Philip's proud, orderly soul.

In France, Henri of Navarre, having changed faith yet again and acceded to the French crown, struggled to pacify the last rebellious corners of his warring kingdom. Philip II's troops still meddled – France and Spain had been at war since the beginning of the year – emphasizing the increasingly inextricable mingling of politics and religion.

In England, the new favourite, the Earl of Essex, permitted Queen Elizabeth to prevaricate with the twin demons of illness and decay. England was growing cockier: Essex's army despoiled Cadiz, England's ships pillaged Spain's in the Atlantic, pillaged anyone's in the Mediterranean.

Pushy upstart England sent its spider-webs of trade across seas previously thought unnavigable, to lands once thought uninhabitable. Tuscany jostled shoulders with her rivals as the once enslaved Serafina Capriani struggled to free herself from the imprisoning cocoon of her history and her sex.

The Mediterranean was, as John Keane had said, a crowded pond. The influence of the stars tossed them at random, tempests blowing on some, sunlight warming others. Until the next inevitable shifting of position, until they faced each other, gunports open, across the blue sea.

★

'A girl,' said Galeazzo Merli, disgustedly, as he struggled with the fastenings of his doublet. 'And she looks just like her mother.'

All the candles were lit: Costanza blew out the taper. 'You have four sons already, Galeazzo.'

There was no reproof in her voice, but Galeazzo Merli looked up and smiled. 'Of course, my love, you are similarly blessed. Though you keep your treasure well hidden.'

'One daughter, my dear Galeazzo,' Costanza said, her heart drifting momentarily, longingly, to sixteen-year-old Maria, safe in her convent in Naples. 'I have no sons,' she added. And would not want them, she thought, sitting on the edge of the bed. A courtesan's name was not meant to live on through the generations.

Galeazzo Merli had arrived in Costanza's Pisan apartment over an hour before. She had given him wine, had played the lute and had sung for him, and had then, dressed in a white undershift and a robe of terracotta velvet, taken him into her bed-chamber.

'You should bring Maria to Pisa,' said Galeazzo, dropping his doublet on to the floor. 'If she's as lovely as her mother, I'm sure she'd be a great success.'

Costanza did not reply. Squatting behind her on the bed, Galeazzo had begun to remove the pins that held her heavy plait of hair in place. If she shared her bedroom with those who could afford it, yet she had never shared her heart with anyone but her daughter and a few friends. She was far too wise to let such things mix.

'What will you call her?' she asked, referring to Galeazzo's own new daughter.

'Oh . . . Caterina . . . Beatrice . . . I've really no idea. Does it matter? I doubt if the creature will see the New Year. It looks like a rat. A hairless little rat.'

He tugged clumsily at a recalcitrant pin, and she, stopping his hand, said gently, 'Let me.' In a few movements of her long graceful hands she freed her hair so that it cascaded in rich waterfalls all down her back.

Galeazzo groaned pleasurably.

'And your wife?' said Costanza. 'Madonna Merli is well?'

'Well enough.' Galeazzo had buried his face in her hair, was kissing the back of her neck, her bare shoulders. Suddenly he stopped and said, 'Have you seen the little Capriani recently?'

Costanza shook her head. Her grey, untroubled eyes were fixed on some distant point unseen to Galeazzo.

'You remember, my dear. Married the ageing Jacopo. Got into a fight at my banquet – with the Englishman . . . what was his name?'

'Marlowe,' said Costanza, 'Thomas Marlowe.' And prompted, 'Madonna Capriani. What of her?'

Galeazzo's arms had encircled her; he began to unlace the ties at the front of her robe.

'The old merchant may have a little more life in him than we had supposed. It is rumoured that the enticing Madonna Capriani is carrying his child. Well' – Galeazzo shivered as he parted Costanza's robe and felt the warm skin beneath the thin muslin – 'one assumes it is *his* child.'

She still said the right words, made the right movements, but Costanza's memory had darted back over the months, to the sound of an open palm striking a man's face, to the wet cobbles outside, and a figure huddled in a doorway.

'It's only a rumour,' Galeazzo added, 'the lady herself says nothing. But it would be interesting to know, don't you think?'

Costanza stifled a yawn. 'Then ask her, my dear.'

He shook his head. 'Madonna Capriani meddles in men's affairs,' said Galeazzo, as he laid Costanza on the bed. 'Apparently she is intending to employ artisans to weave cloth from spun silk. They say that she controls the business now, not Jacopo Capriani. A brat would soon put a stop to that. It would be a salutary experience for Madonna Capriani, to find herself subject to the usual feminine frailties. No, I will not ask her. But there are other ways of finding these things out.'

She had known him for many years now; she found that she recognized the tone of his voice. 'Galeazzo,' she said, hesitantly.

He kissed her. 'I'm curious, that's all. There's a wager . . .'

Grinning, Galeazzo heaved himself on top of her. Costanza remembered Serafina Capriani from the banquet: a small dark girl dressed in bronze silk, her high cheekbones and slanting eyes giving an exotic cast to her appearance. She remembered, too, what the Englishman Thomas Marlowe had said later, after he had explained about that wager. *She seduced me. Jesus! A virgin, and she seduced me so that she would know how to seduce the old man.* Costanza also remembered how greatly Thomas had regretted unburdening himself to her. He need not have feared; she would tell no one. Touching the scar that marred her jawline, Costanza thought she knew the fruits of gossip better than most.

Galeazzo had finished.

When he had recovered his breath, she said, 'And the Englishman?'

'What Englishman?' Galeazzo Merli rolled on to his back. His face was a dark red, his sparse hair stuck to his scalp with sweat. 'The fellow from the Levant Company, you mean, my dear? Oh, he's dead, I think. I heard there was some sort of quarrel over a ship.'

Thomas had been building a ship. It had amused Costanza at the time to hear him speak of the ship in the same way that he had spoken of Serafina Capriani. A curious mixture of love and resentment, as though he was aware of, but had not yet accepted, the way the two of them had taken over his life.

Dead, though. She was aware of a feeling, not exactly of sorrow – more, perhaps, of disappointment. It was difficult to think of the English pilot as dead: he had had a restless energy that it was almost impossible to imagine quenched for ever. Picking up the tawny velvet robe, Costanza slipped it over her shoulders.

'Dead or dying, I'm not sure which,' added Galeazzo, drowsily. Lying naked on the bed, he watched Costanza through half-shut eyes as she twisted her hair back into a knot on top of her head. 'It was a week or two ago, I believe. In Livorno.'

There were questions Costanza would have liked to ask, but she knew that she never would. Such as the expected birthday of that rather unexpected child, and whether anyone had troubled to tell Serafina Capriani of the death – or near death – of her former lover.

Galeazzo had fallen asleep. Costanza decided to visit Livorno.

★

She had no idea where Messer Marlowe lived, but it was easy enough to find out the address of the Levant Company factor, John Keane. Costanza rode from Pisa to Livorno with only her black page Hélion for an escort, telling no one where she had gone. It amused her to think that this secrecy was probably the motive for her journey: she had sold so much of herself that there was always a pleasure to be found in doing something both irrational and private.

Mr Keane's house was not far from the docks. Standing at the doorstep she could see the criss-cross pattern of the masts and spars through the pale morning light. Costanza herself had never left Italy: there had been that single journey from Venice to Pisa, long ago; there were the sadly infrequent visits to Naples and Maria. She would have liked to travel, though, to see whether the rest of the world managed things better.

Hélion knocked at the door, and it was opened, warily, not by Mr Keane himself, but by a servant.

'I would like to speak to your master, Mr Keane.'

She spoke gently, because he looked frightened, but by the time she had finished her request the servant's eyes had completed their journey from her high-soled pattens to her veiled face. She knew that he recognized her then, knew her for what she was, because his expression altered from a scowl to a smirk.

'Mr Keane's away,' said the servant, cockily. 'He sailed for Scanderoon three days ago.' He was gawping now, trying to peer beneath the black muslin veil.

Costanza's voice remained perfectly calm. 'Mr Marlowe, then. Or has he, too, sailed to Scanderoon?'

Some of the fear returned, then. The servant blinked, shook his head. 'Mr Marlowe's sick,' he said.

So at least he was not dead. 'Then show me to him, please?' Costanza moved a step forward.

'Oh, no, he's not here –' The servant, spreading his arms out to bar her way, almost tripped backwards over the step.

Costanza said patiently, 'What is your name, my dear?'

And when he had answered, stammering, she pinned back her veil, spread out her hands, and said, 'Well, then, Antonio. I am, as you see, unarmed. I have Hélion here, it is true, but he is scarcely twelve years old and as yet of little use in a fight. I do not wish Mr Marlowe any harm. I would simply like to see him, to know whether he is well.'

'He's not. He's very sick.' Antonio's eyes rested on her face, on the scar that disfigured her jaw. 'But he's not here.'

'He's in Livorno, though?'

The servant nodded, eyes darting nervously to the street and the docks.

'Then be so good as to take me to him, Antonio.'

'It's not a nice place, madonna,' he said, hastily. 'Not suitable for a lady.' And then, as his words echoed in the doorway, he reddened. 'I'm sorry. I mean –'

She touched his arm. 'No matter, Antonio. Now, shall we go and find Mr Marlowe?'

The servant had spoken the truth, though: it was not a nice place. Following Antonio through the maze of streets and cramped courtyards that lay behind the docks, Costanza had to pick her way through heaps of vegetable peelings and other more noxious refuse, her perfumed handkerchief firmly folded over her nose, her high-soled shoes slipping in the dirt.

The house Antonio took her to faced on to a small courtyard crowded with ragged children and an entire family of pigs. Someone sang in an upstairs room; washing festooned the lines slung between the windows. Picking up her skirts, Costanza followed Antonio up the stairs.

At first, when Antonio pushed open the door, she could see no one. The shutters were still closed, no candle was lit. Then, as her eyes accustomed themselves to the darkness, she saw the tangled sheets on the bed, heard the laboured breathing.

She moved to the bedside and, ignoring Antonio's protests about evil humours, flung open the shutters. Kneeling down by the bed, she thought she would hardly have recognized him as the contentious drunkard who had insulted her so neatly in Lucca. The blue eyes were closed, but the lids flickered as though they hid uncomfortable dreams. Thomas Marlowe's face was pale, seamed with sweat, his fingers pulled and scrabbled at the dirty pillow. She knew before she touched his forehead that his skin would be burning hot.

Costanza turned, and said sharply to Antonio, 'What happened?'

Antonio shrugged. 'Messer Marlowe made love to Messer Whitlock's wife. So Messer Whitlock tried to kill him.'

It looked, thought Costanza, glancing down to the bed, as though the jealous Messer Whitlock had just about succeeded.

'Messer Whitlock has sailed with Messer Keane to Scanderoon,' added Antonio. 'If Messer Marlowe is still alive when he returns, then he will kill him and destroy his ship.'

Costanza felt then, not unusually, a brief flicker of irritation at the follies of men. Then, a practical woman, she set about repairing the situation.

She sent Hélion for clean water from the well, and Antonio for linen for bandages. Then, as she unlaced sticky clothing and unpeeled layers of bloodied bandages, Costanza planned their journey back to Pisa.

In the New Year, Serafina Capriani and her clerk Amadeo rode north from Pisa, along the Ligurian coast.

The day had dawned well: the sky was clear as dawn rose coral-coloured from the horizon. Jacopo had seemed a little better recently and, carefully persuaded, had agreed to let his little Serafina out of his sight for an entire day.

Outside, riding along crisp, frosted tracks, Serafina breathed in the cold, sharp air, enjoying the wind on her face. For over a month now, Jacopo had not left the house. He would lie in the four-poster upstairs by night, on the couch in the withdrawing-room in the daytime. His cough had eased a little, but Serafina suspected that the respite would be only temporary. Jacopo's querulous voice seemed to call for her a hundred times a day: whether she was in the counting-house or the kitchens, whether she discussed cloth with a customer, or breadmaking with the cook. She could escape from the house while he slept, but only if she paid the price of hours spent cajoling and caressing him when she returned. Sometimes she found herself thinking that she had enjoyed greater freedom in Kara Ali's house, where no one had demanded any more of her than a well-scrubbed floor, or a neatly written hand.

In the saddle, the cold wind flicking at her hair, Serafina reminded herself of her achievements of the past six months. Lengths and bales of silk piled in a warehouse in Livorno. Ribbons and laces and similar gew-gaws, stored in Pisa. A small, but valuable, group of contracted customers. A list of clients from Naples to Marseilles, whom she would visit later in the year, when she was delivered of this wretched child. A house, with a dozen servants and clerks, and all the food and clothes she desired. A home, a future.

And half a dozen artisans, using the raw silk that she supplied, to make cloth to her requirements. The artisans were paid by her, and worked only for her. One day she intended to own silk-workshops like those she had seen in Florence. Even the Guardi had never woven their own silk, but had bought and sold only the finished fabric.

Serafina found that she was almost smiling, that she had forgotten the difficulties in Pisa, and the intransigent lump hidden beneath her billowing skirts. At night now, the creature wriggled and darted, inside her yet separate from her, uncontrollable by her. By day, however, she could still disregard it. Just now, the thought that she would bear a child seemed unreal, an impossibility. *This* was real — the distant black skeletons of trees against a frosted landscape, the flat plane of the sea, silvered to mirror-image by a bleached sky. Her horse's breath clouding the chill air, the chink of harness and bit. The boats cluttered in the harbours, or threading their way to nothingness over the horizon. She and Amadeo travelled to inspect a boat now, in a fishing village not far from Viareggio.

As they drew within sight of the village, Serafina could see the small gathering of stone-built houses, the poorer huts and shacks that straggled round the outskirts of the settlement. She needed a ship: she was determined to find one before the spring. She had not returned to Livorno since the autumn. Something had stopped her: the thought of the unobtainable *Kingfisher*, perhaps. She refused to believe that it was those other memories that troubled her, those of Thomas Marlowe and the beautiful, fragile Palazzo Sacchetti. That had been a simple matter of trade. Just as today's outing was concerned with trade.

She knew, however, as soon as she saw the boat that it would not do. The fisherman, one of the many Greeks who had come to Italy in response to the native shortage of mariners, led them down to the harbour and began to talk effusively about the boat that was moored against the harbour wall. Some of Serafina's good spirits evaporated as soon as she saw the ship, and noted the cracked, peeling paint, the barnacles clustered around the timbers. It was too small, too old, and in poor repair.

'– a beautiful craft, madonna. I've taken her from Tuscany to Marseilles in less than four weeks. I'll be sorry to lose her, but –'

'No.' The wind flung the single word back in the fisherman's face. With a twitch of velvet skirts, Serafina began to walk back up the harbour towards the horses.

The fisherman, hurrying to keep up with her, recovered his breath. 'Madonna, she only needs a coat of paint. Come aboard her, and then –'

'No.' Again, the recollection of Thomas Marlowe's *Kingfisher* darted through Serafina's mind. Angrily, she pushed the memory away.

It had been a wasted journey, a day lost that she could not afford to lose. Though it was only midday, she was beginning to feel tired already, a familiar lassitude that she had to struggle against more and more as her pregnancy progressed. Stopping, turning back to the fisherman, Serafina added, 'That boat needs more than a coat of paint. She's foul-bottomed and her timbers need recaulking. I dare say half the spars are broken, and the sails have rotted as well. That boat will not last another winter, sir, let alone take me to Provence in the spring.'

She heard the fisherman mutter something under his breath as she tramped back up through the pebbles and reached her horse. She knew that Amadeo had glanced sharply at her, but she did not let her fingers pause at all in unknotting her reins, even though the fisherman's words had floated to her, as clearly as if they had been fixed in amber, on the breeze.

I doubt if you'll be going anywhere but the midwife's in spring.

Amadeo was still staring. Serafina heaved herself into the saddle without waiting for his help, suddenly conscious of the expression on the fisherman's face, of the boy's shocked realization. She felt clumsy, ugly and grotesque. Kicking her horse's flanks, she rode away without so much as another glance at the village, the harbour, and the boats bobbing in the grey, sullen water.

The icy rain began as they rode back to Pisa. She did not let up her pace, however: it was as though, by riding fast, she could rid herself of the lumpen, ridiculous thing she had become, and be Serafina again, sharp-witted and desirable. The cold rain solidified, turning to sleet, stinging against her exposed cheeks and forehead. She knew Amadeo was just behind her, because she could hear the sound of his horse's hooves on the track, but otherwise the countryside was deserted, the few trees vague shadows by the roadside.

I doubt if you'll be going anywhere but the midwife's in spring. And the fisherman was right. Her life was slithering out of control again, the destiny she had so nearly regained was ebbing relentlessly away, as blurred and unobtainable as the distant Umbrian hills. If a stranger could detect her pregnancy, then for how much longer could she hope to hide her condition from the merchants of Pisa? It was probably too late already; doubtless they were sharing out the profits of their wager in the taverns and in the card-houses. And if she was known to be with child, then her chances of improving Jacopo's business sufficiently to be able to compete with Angelo ceased completely. To trade with a woman was improbable enough; to trade with a pregnant woman was out of the question.

She was aware that Amadeo was shouting something, but she took no notice. Serafina spurred her horse again, so that the sleet battered against her face, and the accumulated miseries of past, present and future hurtled past her, each one like tiny ice-cold snowflakes. Marseilles, Algiers, Tuscany – she had gathered up the past in her two strong hands, forcing it into some sort of shape, some sort of meaning. Then *this* had happened: a lightning bolt from the god that Serafina had ceased to believe in in the bagnios of Algiers. *Damn* this baby, she did not want this baby. There was no room for a baby in the life she was struggling to create.

Amadeo yelled again, closer and more urgent. 'Mind the ditch!'

she heard him call, through wind and sleet, and a thousand bitter, haunted thoughts. Serafina felt her horse stumble, its neck jerking forward as the reins slithered through her fingers. Her feet were torn out of the stirrups, and the saddle slid beneath her velvet skirts. The trees, the snow, and the horse circled as though someone had tossed them like a pack of cards into the air. Earth and sky changed places.

The breath was knocked out of her body as she hit the ground. There were damp brown leaves beneath her face, and a grey sky, tinged with yellow, overhead. Her lungs were an aching, unfillable void.

It took Amadeo's anxious 'Madonna?' to make Serafina draw in one great shuddering gulp of air, and Amadeo's outstretched hand to sit her up from the uneven hollow in which she lay curled.

She fought a humiliating desire to cry. But there was no mockery in Amadeo's face, only concern, as he knelt down beside her and offered her a drink from his flask.

The aqua vitae was like fire, steadying the shaking of her limbs, the feeble questioning of her brain. She said, weakly, 'My horse −' and waited until Amadeo had gone to attend to the animal before raising herself to her feet with the help of a nearby tree.

She felt so cold. The cold seemed to have entered her veins: she took another mouthful of aqua vitae to chase it away, to quieten her juddering muscles. She watched Amadeo as he attempted to lead the horse out of the ditch and as, the animal not responding, he leapt into the bed of dead leaves, and examined the broken foreleg. She did not watch as Amadeo slit her horse's throat, she could not watch. Her eyelids jammed tightly shut, and she heard only his voice, murmuring endearments to the stricken creature, and then silence. She let herself be led to Amadeo's own horse, and helped into the saddle. The countryside had become very silent, very open. The cold, the sleet, the wind that flicked up the old dead leaves and tossed them over the scarlet stains beside the ditch were not her enemies, they were only part of a naturally hostile universe. God formed man out of clay: but man moulded his own destiny out of the offcuts that fell to the floor from the potter's wheel. If you rode too fast on a poor road in bad conditions, then your horse was liable to fall and break its leg.

There were other ways of paying for folly, however. The pain began when they had almost reached Pisa, slow and barely noticeable at first. But it was a new sort of pain, a dull ache in the small of the back, an inescapable reminder that her body was no longer her own. She had chosen to make love to Thomas Marlowe and Jacopo Capriani; last summer she had thought them both necessary to her future. If the gods had formed the baby in her womb out of one small ball of clay, then by her own actions, her own choice, she had permitted that making.

As she rode into Pisa, perched on the saddle-bow in front of Amadeo, Serafina, for the first time since she had stood at the steps of that golden house in Marseilles, began to feel frightened.

She could hear the tambour and pipes quite clearly: they seemed to come from almost immediately below her. Scrubbing at the misted window, the courtesan Costanza peered down into the street.

An enormous band of women were gathered outside her door. They were oddly dressed: ragged, lace-edged skirts flung over improbably large farthingales, their headgear a miscellaneous selection of beads, feathers, bonnets and curls. Some carried lanterns, others were responsible for the piping and drumming. One woman was heaving at her front door with a surprisingly meaty shoulder. She heard Thomas Marlowe from behind her say, 'Shall I empty the slop-bucket over them?' and she turned, and, smiling, shook her head.

It was four weeks since, half amused at her own irrationality, Costanza had brought the Englishman back to Pisa. In those four weeks she had nursed him, fed him, let him sleep and scream and endure nightmares in her spare bedchamber. She had wondered, occasionally, at her own motives. Not desire: she did not think she would ever desire a man again. All that part of her had died a long time ago. She had killed it herself, carefully and conscientiously, in order that she might survive.

She had thought at first that Thomas would not survive: that what the sea and his lover's jealous husband had begun, fever and exhaustion would complete. But he was strong, and he had begun to fight back, almost unwillingly at first, and then with a tenacity born, she had thought, of habit rather than will. He still limped a little and tired easily, but the unnatural brightness had left his eyes, and he rarely cried out at night.

Sometimes, though, she wished he would shout, yell, weep about what had happened to him. Thomas had lost the woman he loved, had seen the project that had possessed him for years deliberately destroyed. He should have cried, should have beat his fists at the implacable demons of the past. But recently there had been nothing in those deep, pure blue eyes, neither pain nor anger. Just an emptiness that Costanza thought totally unnatural to him, a lack of response to anything but the most superficial conversation.

He also drank too much. In the beginning, he had drunk aqua vitae to deaden the pain of cuts and broken bones; now, Costanza thought, he drank to silence a different kind of pain. Soon, Thomas would drink because he could get through the day no other way, and that, she thought, would be a useless waste of a man. Tonight, silent and with a glass of wine constantly in hand, his manner hovered at the edges of boorishness, and Costanza found herself struggling to remain patient with him. She thought she guessed the cause of today's incivility, but something in his eyes, in the hard set of his mouth, had stopped her broaching the subject. She found that she was glad of the interruption from the streets below.

The pilot stood at her side, staring down at the noisy visitors. Something hit the window: an explosion of rosewater and eggshell, followed by raucous jeers and clapping from the street. Another eggshell, and then several more, hammering like small scented cannon-shot off the frame. Costanza spoke to her black page.

'Hélion, open the front door, my dear.' And then, to the Englishman's questioning glance, she added, 'It's Galeazzo. He must have ridden down from Lucca for the carnival.'

Downstairs, in the hall, the sound of singing and music from the street was even louder. Hélion slipped the bolt, and the absurd chaotic heap of women, headdresses askew, skirts hoisted up to their thighs, tumbled on to the tiled floor. The pipe and tambour rolled jangling into a corner.

Only they weren't women. They were Galeazzo Merli and half a dozen friends, all of them masked and robed and drunk. Costanza, standing on the stairs, clamped her hands over her mouth and began to laugh.

'Make me some of your tisane, my dear. You make it so much better than Lucia.'

There were three sets of stairs between the withdrawing-room and the kitchens. Sixty steps up and down, calculated Serafina as she stood in the cold, cavernous kitchen, straining calendula and comfrey.

They had returned from Viareggio the previous day, she and Amadeo. She had had to explain to Jacopo about the boat and about the horse, and he had whined about the expense involved in replacing the animal. Serafina, closing her eyes, had seen only the dark blood splashed on the leaves, heard only the silence of death.

She had taken to her bed early that evening, pleading a headache. She had not sent a servant for the midwife: she had been sure that if she could lie still and alone for long enough then the warning pains would retreat, returning to the dark cave from which they had emerged. And retreat they had; that morning, after a night of sleep aided by one of Kara Ali's more soporific brews, there had been only the smallest of twinges.

But now, after a day's work, her back had begun to ache again, an intermittent, dragging pain. Returning to the withdrawing-room, Serafina placed the cup of tisane by the day-bed, and walked to the window. It was snowing lightly, too little to settle. In the chill, dark evening, only the light of flares and sconces pulled the outline of roads and houses from the darkness. Someone was singing, and if she listened hard, Serafina could hear distant music. It was carnival time: unexpectedly, annoyingly, she felt tears prickle at the corners of her eyes.

'Shut the curtains, my dear. The draught goes to my throat.'

Jacopo's voice bit into her dreams. He had lost weight in the past months: his illness ate at him, reducing a sparse frame to an emaciated one. He sat hunched on the day-bed, a tangle of shawls and quilting around his shoulders.

'I think I could eat a little soup. If you would fetch it for me. Not too hot, mind.'

Sixty more steps; a hundred and twenty altogether. She had to pause at each landing now, catching her breath and rubbing her back before climbing the stairs again. Back in the withdrawing-room, Jacopo spilt soup on to his robe and his coverlet. More stairs: to the bedchamber, this time, for replacements. Serafina made herself think of Angelo. At Messer Merli's banquet, the Frenchman Philippe Moreau had hinted that Angelo was already suffering from some financial difficulties. She knew that was her opportunity: to rub at the open sore of debt until it would not heal. She had already sown seeds of rumour, attacking the secure reputation so essential to successful trading. And she had stolen three of Angelo's clients. They were not his most profitable customers, their loss alone would not ruin him, but she had felt an immense triumph in their acquisition, as though she had raided his treasure-chest and stolen an ear-drop, or a gold chain. She would gnaw at his empire slowly, silently, she told herself, until the whole rotten edifice tumbled to the floor. Then she would be waiting, both hands outstretched, to catch the fragments and build them into what they once had been.

But somehow, she could not feel the pleasure, the sense of approaching triumph, that she had once experienced. Today she felt beleaguered, daunted by the limitations of her sex, by the impossible fragility of life. Jacopo's eyes had closed; carefully, Serafina removed the bowl and spoon from his grasp. The pain in her back was growing worse: a fitful sickening tugging at her spine. She was afraid, and Serafina knew that hers was not only a fear of pain, but a fear of ridicule, of exile, of loneliness.

She was too tired to climb the stairs to her bedchamber. Pulling her shawl round her shoulders, Serafina closed her eyes and slept where she sat.

There were only a few streets between Costanza's house and the piazza, but it took Galeazzo Merli, his friends, and the courtesan almost an hour to make the short journey. Squares, streets, and bridges were thick with people, small boats jostled each other on the dark ochre waters of the Arno. Stalls had been set up selling roast pig, mutton and pancakes; the heady scent of spiced wine drifted into the air from numerous cauldrons. Masked figures flitted by, half seen in the darkness: masks of gold, of silver, parti-coloured half red and half black, horned, and tasselled and long-nosed. On carts hauled through the streets by horses, devils pranced, goddesses glittered, and giants almost as tall as the eaves bawled threats at the crowds. At a street corner near the Ponte Mezzo, a blind boy, dressed all in gold, stood and sang, his cupped hands crammed with coins. The night was dark and cold; a few stars struggled to be seen through a sky washed with orange by furnaces and lanterns.

In the centre of the crowded piazza a huge wooden castle creaked and swayed. Men dressed as soldiers guarded the battlements and turrets of the castle; others stormed it, scrabbling at the wooden walls, hauling at the rickety drawbridge. Revellers crowded round the castle, their faces masked, their bodies elaborately clothed. Galeazzo offered Costanza a cup of mulled wine, and she accepted it, enjoying the warmth of the pewter against her cold fingers.

As she raised the cup and swallowed, someone lit the edge of a wine-soaked cloth, and hurled it towards the wooden castle. There was a yell from the soldiers inside as the cloth landed on a turret and the thin wood caught light. Galeazzo Merli, his embroidered gown gaping at the seams, roared indiscriminate encouragement. One of Galeazzo's friends, a young notary called Niccolo, grabbed a flare from a nearby wall and tossed that, too, into the castle. A soldier emptied a bucket of water over the fire, which hissed and spat, but it was too late: the flames were already dancing along the crenellations, and besides, others were hurling fiery cloths, sticks, and lanterns into the unstable edifice. Men leapt from turret and drawbridge; tall orange flames painted themselves against the sky. The castle creaked and shivered, and then collapsed inwards in a shower of crimson sparks.

Someone clapped, others roared their approval. The heat from the bonfire turned midwinter into summer, lighting masks and faces with gold and russet and scarlet. Galeazzo's arm curled round Costanza's shoulder, someone else called out her name, and she looked up and smiled. She recognized many of the people in the square: merchants, bankers, princes and servants alike had taken to the streets, their stations in life obliterated by mask and costume. Costanza had always liked carnival; there was a pleasing disorder about it, an anarchy that appealed to some secret part of her guarded soul.

The ridiculous gown was slipping from Galeazzo's shoulders, exposing the braided edges of a doublet beneath. Some musicians had struck up a tune, and couples began to dance in the clearing around the smouldering remains of the castle. Kicking off both gown and farthingale, Galeazzo dragged Costanza into the dance.

Faces flickered by her as they circled in the darkness. Faces that were fat and thin, young and old. Faces of men she had once slept with, of wives who ignored her in the street. A brown-haired girl who reminded her of Maria, her daughter in Naples; a handsome youth who reminded her of the man who had taken a knife in his hand and left his signature on her face for ever. An unmasked man whose blue eyes fleetingly reminded Costanza of the English pilot.

When the music stopped they collapsed exhausted on the steps of the church. The snow was thickening, and bright crystals clung to the folds of Costanza's black velvet gown, brief jewel-shapes, fired with the colours of carnival; melting almost as soon as they settled. Galeazzo's friends gathered sprawled on the steps, a few still wearing ladies' gowns, others men again, in doublet and hose. Costanza ate roasted apples and drank hot wine. Snow had begun to flurry in the shadows of the steps, in the crevices between the paving-stones. Soon it would extinguish the embers of the wooden castle, and lay a blanket of silence over the music and the singing, the clatter of wooden-soled shoes on stone, the shouting and the laughter.

Galeazzo hauled Costanza to her feet, and led her across the square. She would stay a while and watch the boat-races on the Arno, she thought, and then she would return home and write a long letter to Maria. Perhaps in a few weeks Thomas might be well enough to take letters to Naples. Not only would that offer a temporary solution to the constant problem of communicating with her daughter, but it would also give Thomas something to do other than prowling round her house and drinking too much wine.

Galeazzo stopped only once on his way to the river-bank: to speak to one of the musicians, and to press a few coins into his hand.

The riverside was crowded: a red-tailed devil jostled Costanza to one side, a serpent shimmered in the darkness to the other. One of Galeazzo's friends, his buckram bodice open and unlaced, found Costanza a space beside the parapet of the bridge. Below, at the water's edge, Galeazzo was stepping into a small rowing-boat. Boats bobbed like apples on the water, each one bearing the colours and insignia of its owner. People cheered as the tiny craft dipped and wallowed in the river, as men pushed at the boats and at each other alike with oars. The Arno was lit with lanterns, each one of them guttering in the chill breeze, muffled by the falling snow.

Galeazzo, hopelessly drunk, held the rudder, and the rowing-boat circled twice, bobbing and swaying on the ripples, its small wooden hull jarring frequently against the other craft. Someone lifted a handkerchief and fired a spluttering arquebus, and the boats began to sail up the water, towards the bridge.

Galeazzo lost half his crew somewhere between the starting-point and the bridge; he pushed them out of the boat himself, grabbing the oars from them. As the boats disappeared into the archway, the crowd began to move like a many-limbed single entity towards the other side of the bridge. Strangers jostled Costanza, forcing her against the stone parapet, an unknown face leered towards her, begging for a kiss. Someone cursed as she stumbled against them, and a hand fumbled at her waist, searching for her purse. On the corner where the blind boy had stood, three youths had caught a stray dog and were tossing it in a blanket, baying with pleasure as they hurled the creature higher and higher into the air. Galeazzo's friends were nowhere to be seen. Pulling her cloak around her, Costanza began to push her way home through the crowds.

She could see no familiar face, but, struggling through the sea of men and women, she heard a voice say, 'We'll meet him in the Via S. Domenico.' The voice belonged to the young notary, Niccolo, who had arrived with Galeazzo at Costanza's own house earlier that evening. But when she turned to look there were only the masks, multicoloured and many-shaped, stealing familiarity and expression from the faces they disguised. Turning back to the river, Costanza saw that Galeazzo's rowing-boat was empty, its painter dangling in the water, its oars shipped.

She was halfway home when she suddenly changed direction. She had recalled who lived in the Via S. Domenico: the girl Serafina, cause of at least half of Thomas Marlowe's misery. Serafina Capriani lived in the Via S. Domenico with the old merchant who was her husband. *There are other ways of finding these things out*, Galeazzo Merli had said, referring to Serafina Capriani's possible pregnancy. No one would take a knife to Madonna Capriani's face, but there were subtler methods of showing disapproval, of inflicting humiliation, of returning upstarts to their rightful place. Pulling her hood over her head against the thickening snow, Costanza began to walk in the direction of the Via S. Domenico.

It was late when Serafina was woken by the knock at the door. She had slept fitfully in the chair by the window, woken frequently by the pain in her back and her belly. Rising from the seat, steadying herself against the window sill, Serafina peered down to the street below.

The Via S. Domenico seemed empty. She still could hear the distant sounds of carnival, see the fat snowflakes floating through the sky. The knocking began again; Jacopo stirred and grumbled in his sleep.

Serafina blew out the single candle as she hurried out of the withdrawing-room. The servants must all be in their beds or at the carnival: carefully, her skirts gathered in her hands, Serafina made her way downstairs. The ache in her back had become a gnawing pain, and small fists hammered inside her, clamouring for precedence.

When, at first, she opened the front door, she thought that

the street was empty. Then, as her eyes accustomed themselves to the dim light she saw the figures silhouetted against the flares.

They were all masked, their features distorted and frozen into caricature. One of them, dressed as a clerk in the Capriani colours, played a drum and recited a poem. Another, a grotesque phallus protruding from his merchant's robes, was bowed and bent like an old man. The third, white-skinned and crimson-lipped, wore a gown, loosely laced to show the swollen belly beneath.

Her heart paused, and then restarted. She did not need to listen to the words of the poem to understand, but the chanting and the drumming forced their way through the snow and the silence. A young woman had married an old man: worse, she was to bear his child. *They are laying bets, you know, on whether your senile husband will impregnate you before the year is out.* She had broken the rules, and this pasquinade was her punishment.

I am Serafina . . . I am Serafina . . . She found that her back was against the wall, which was fortunate, because the pain had begun again. A real pain, this time, an all-encompassing pain, that made everything else, even that obscene charade, irrelevant. Sliding slowly down the wall, she thought, I have sinned, but the sin was not in marrying Jacopo.

They ran from the street as Costanza rounded the corner, so that she saw only the prurient black shadows against the pale lamplit snow. It was enough, though: she did not need to see their faces to know who those men were.

But there was still one other shadow, curled up like a bundle of old clothing against the wall, illuminated by the open door-way. Costanza began to run, and did not stop until she reached the Capriani house.

She remembered Serafina Capriani from the Merlis' banquet, for her vivid, imperious face, for her manifest intelligence and ruthlessness. Costanza could understand, and even pity, Thomas's obsession. Not an easy object of affection, she had thought, not the sort of woman who would be content with a few rooms, an absentee mariner husband, and a cradleful of screaming babies.

Now, though, her pity had a different object. Serafina Capriani's skin was as pale as the snow crystals that drifted over her

hair, and she did not move so much as an eyelash. She wore no
cloak, and under the loosely laced bodice, Costanza could see
the swollen shape of her belly.

Spreading her own cloak over the unconscious girl, Costanza
went inside the house and called for the servants.

Thomas was in the kitchen when Costanza returned to her
house an hour later.

Because he was unable to be idle, he was repairing the broken
window-latch. Because he was unable to face the past, the present,
or the future, a bottle of aqua vitae stood beside him on the sill.

Costanza was alone, having found the company of men intolerable. Thomas turned, but did not notice the anger in her eyes.

'You have feasted enough?'

'Oh, yes. Enough.' She flicked the cloak off her back in one
clean movement, crushed the silk and lace mask between fingers
and palm. 'I think I am done with feasting, Thomas.'

Something in her voice made him put down the hammer and
nail. 'Where is Messer Merli?' he said.

'When I last saw Messer Merli, he was rowing down the
Arno. Messer Merli has, I hope, drowned himself.'

Thomas slid off the window-sill, and crossed the room
towards her. His arm and shoulder ached, but he had drunk
enough to deaden the pain. 'This house,' he said carefully, when
he was level with Costanza, 'belongs to Messer Merli.'

'Then I shall become a nun!' she said, fisting her hands and
beating them once, impotently, through the air.

He thought for a moment that she was going to hit him. But
that was not Costanza's way; instead, the tension relaxed
suddenly from her body, and she sat heavily in a chair by the
table, head in hands. Her hair was damp, the hem of her gown
glittered with snow crystals.

'He hurt you,' said Thomas, softly.

She did not look up from the table. 'Not *me*,' she said, scornfully. 'He could not hurt me. He hurt – someone else.'

He did not understand. He picked up the mask from where
she had dropped it on the floor, and stood silently, his fingers
smoothing the crumpled silk.

'Madonna Capriani.' Costanza's voice was small and hard.
'He hurt your Serafina.'

He could hardly bear even to hear her name. Thomas's ribs
were mended now, but he could still recall the choking sensation
he had endured for weeks after the fight, when every breath had
been a struggle. He struggled now.

'Not *my* Serafina,' said Thomas at last, coldly. 'Jacopo Capriani's Serafina.'

'Jacopo Capriani is dying.' Costanza looked back up at him,
her grey eyes disdainful. 'Of course, it is possible his wife may
predecease him.'

He did not speak, could not speak, but he watched her, waiting.

'Madonna Capriani is not well liked in Pisa.' Costanza had
recovered her composure; her hands were neatly folded in front
of her, her eyes were unforgiving. 'Madonna Capriani married
an old man for his money and his trade, and has proceeded to
try and improve that trade. A heinous offence, don't you agree?'

Her eyes judged him. Aching in mind and body, Thomas
went back to the window, and the aqua vitae. 'She married for
money – and for other reasons,' he said. 'None of them particularly creditable.'

'What else would you have her do? Would you have her
whore on the streets like me?'

Thomas's hand, which had been engaged in pouring aqua
vitae into a cup, shook and then stilled. His back to Costanza,
he said carefully, 'No. But that was not her only choice.'

'Wasn't it?' Her voice was almost a whisper. 'Are you sure?'

He succeeded in pouring out the rest of the aqua vitae without
spilling it. 'I offered her marriage,' he said, defensively.

'*When*, my good Thomas? When she was alone and penniless?
Or when she had just begun to earn something, to take charge
once more of her own life?'

Turning, he stared at her. His hands shook again, and he
knew that if he raised the cup to his lips, the rim would clatter
uncontrollably against his teeth.

Costanza said, 'You went back to her today, didn't you?'

He knew that the 'her' she referred to now was not Serafina,

but that other beloved 'her', violated and despoiled on the dockside at Livorno. Thomas nodded and, two-handed, managed to
drink at last.

It had been the first time he had seen the *Kingfisher* since the
day she had almost succeeded in drowning him. He had only a
confused memory of the weeks that had followed the fight with
Edward Whitlock. There had been John Keane, there had been
Antonio, and then Costanza. There had been a dark, hot room
in Livorno, and then cool hands and scented sheets in Pisa. It had
been weeks before he had stood and walked, much longer before
he had ridden. And today he had forced himself to confront his
worst dreams and imaginings and had found them all, unbearably, true.

'He hacked down the mizzen-mast,' said Thomas. 'Smashed
the gunwales, the stairs, the entire poop-deck.'

'It could be repaired.'

Thomas shook his head. 'It couldn't. Not without money.
And I have no money. Whitlock will be back from Aleppo
within a month or so, and then, God knows, he will sink her.'

He took another mouthful of aqua vitae to dull the images
that crowded his brain. He heard Costanza say, 'So what will
you do?'

What indeed? He knew that he could not impose on her
generosity much longer, but without the *Kingfisher* Thomas
could see no clear path for himself, no motive to his existence.
He had been given one chance; nothing more would be offered
to him. And besides, he could still remember how much the sea
had wanted him.

'The Americas,' Costanza reminded him, softly. 'The Indies. I
thought they were what you wanted, Thomas Marlowe?'

The cup paused halfway to his lips again. He had been given
one chance to find everything he had longed for, and somehow
he had wasted that chance. He had entangled himself in other
people's lives, and in doing so had destroyed his own.

'There's other ports than Livorno,' he said, raising the cup.
'Other boats. There's always work for a pilot.'

'*No!*' In one swift moment, Costanza rose to her feet and
knocked the cup out of his hand. The pottery shattered, the

colourless liquid gleamed on the terracotta tiles. Costanza's eyes were dark with fury.

'Listen to me, Thomas. Tonight, my lover Galeazzo Merli arranged a little performance for your lover, Serafina Capriani. Do you know what a charivari is? Do they have them in England? Let me remind you. If a person does something that society disapproves of – marries a richer, older man, for instance – then at carnival time the bravos dress up in imitation of the wrong-doers, while one of their band recites a poem mocking the happy couple. They did that to Serafina Capriani tonight, my beloved Galeazzo and his friends. One of the actors was old and bent, and surprisingly well endowed. The other was *pregnant*.'

He stared at her then, eyes wide, thoughts tumbling and confused.

'Madonna Capriani is about six months pregnant, I would guess,' whispered Costanza. 'Though she may have lost the child by now. Galeazzo's performance was something of a shock for her. I took her indoors, and sent for the midwife.'

It was Thomas's turn to sit down, his muscles shaking un-controllably. Men died in battle or at sea. Women died in childbirth. He managed to say, 'Will she live?'

'I don't know.' Costanza was silent for a moment, and then, crossing the room to stand beside him, she added in a gentler voice, 'She is young and strong. And she will fight. But I think that if she lives, you should go to her.'

His face was covered with his hands, but she saw the black curls shake once.

'She didn't want me.'

'Ah.' Costanza's hand moved to his shoulder, stroking it, easing the physical pain. 'Her refusal is perhaps what you will have to learn to live with, my dear Thomas. Serafina's burden is a little different. Only you can help ease it.'

He did not move, did not speak.

So she said softly, 'Because you love her. And because you are her friend. And because she has no other.'

He went to her a week later, having learned from the Capriani servants that she, like him, had cheated death.

Serafina received him in an upstairs withdrawing-room looking out to the Arno. The house was on the opposite side of the river to Costanza's house: Thomas walked through the bitterly cold weather, snow crunching beneath his boots, unaware of the ache in his newly mended bones.

He ached when he saw her, though. She lay on a couch beside one of the windows, wrapped in blankets, propped up by cushions. Her hair and eyes were black against her white skin. If he looked carefully, Thomas could see the small scar the gunwale of the tartane had made in their flight from Algiers. She looked as young now as she had then: a child, white-faced and battered by the elements.

He let the door close behind him. His boots made puddles of melted snow on the floorboards; snow crystals still encrusted the shoulders of his cloak, the brim of his hat. He bowed.

She did not speak. He would, Thomas thought, have this time welcomed sarcasm or derision. She did not say, as she once had said, *Mr Marlowe. How pleasant.* He made himself look into her dark, haunted eyes, and he knew that she, too, had known fear, and loss of hope.

He found himself kneeling beside the day-bed, placing his small gift beside her on one of the cushions. 'William Williams would have made it better,' he said. 'But he's in Aleppo.'

It was a ship, carved out of wood, matchstick-masted and silken-sailed. Serafina touched its tiny figurehead, and Thomas saw that her fingers were pale, almost transparent.

'The *Kingfisher*,' she said.

He nodded. And added, 'She's yours if you want her.'

It was surprisingly easy to get the words out, to offer something he loved almost beyond anything to the one he knew might misuse it. But he had discovered that there was an inevitability about it all, as though something or someone – Kara Ali's beloved stars, or the feckless machinations of the Mediterranean gods – had bound their destinies together. Himself, Serafina, and the *Kingfisher*.

He watched her cradle the tiny model in her hands, studying the masts and yards, the spacious hold, the elegant hull made for speed.

Eventually, she said, 'I am with child, Thomas. I nearly lost it, but they say if I rest I might carry it to full term.'

Her body was hidden beneath the folds of the blankets. 'I know,' he said, 'Costanza told me.'

She looked up at him then, frowning.

'The courtesan, Costanza. Galeazzo Merli's lover,' said Thomas. 'She found you the other night, after the pasquinade. I have been living in her house for more than a month.'

The dark eyes lidded suddenly, the thin fingers stilled in their exploration of the model ship.

Thomas said, patiently, '*Living* in her house, that's all. There was – an accident – in Livorno. The *Kingfisher* was damaged, I was hurt. Costanza looked after me – God knows why.'

He took the ship from her, placed it on the table beside the day-bed. He wanted to take her in his arms, to stroke her long dark hair, to guard her against the troubles God and man had found for her, and against those she had inflicted on herself. Instead, knowing he must resist the temptation, he rose and went to the window, looking down to the frozen Arno below.

'With money, the *Kingfisher* could be repaired,' he said. 'You wanted her once. If you still want her, you may have her, Serafina.'

It had stopped snowing now, and the sky was heavy and pale, a yellow-white almost the colour of primroses. Snow lined the roofs and the gutters, the window-ledges and sills, and made clean and white the dirty riverbanks and alleyways.

He heard Serafina whisper, 'And you, Thomas?'

He understood her immediately. He had already made his choice, but he was silent for a while, looking down to the river where people had made models of snow on the ice. Horses, and dragons and galleons in full sail. The light from the glimmering disc of the sun was translucent, like crystal.

'I go with her,' he said, eventually. 'Wherever you choose to send me.'

It did not feel, as once he had feared it might, like a defeat. Once Costanza had forced him to see that he had no chance of happiness without both Serafina and the *Kingfisher*, then his efforts at self-protection had all seemed futile. There was no

point guarding yourself against something that, however ir-
rationally, you did not wish to live without. He no longer
attempted to dictate the terms: he knew that he needed both on
whatever terms he was permitted them.

He could not see the sea: it was lost in the bleached horizon.
But he knew that it was there, free and unfrozen, waiting for
him.

'My involvement with the Levant Company is finished, Serafina. The *Kingfisher* is damaged, but repairable. You would need
to spend some money on her completion, and to lend me some
more in order to repay what I have borrowed from the Levant
Company. I would work for you as master of the ship. The
Kingfisher would fly your colours, sail to whichever port you
chose. Costanza told me that your husband is ill, that you have
been managing the business alone. Well, then – let me help
you. I can sail to Naples and Marseilles in a fraction of the time
it takes Messer Capriani to travel there by mule.'

The silence and stillness of the snow-muffled streets seemed to
have entered the room.

Serafina said only one word. '*Why?*'

He had had almost a week to find the answer to that question.
'Because I cannot bear to watch you destroy yourself.'

Turning from the window, he watched her struggling to sit
up, propping herself on cushions, a remnant of the old fire
lighting her eyes.

'I will have my property back from Angelo, though, Thomas.
I could not live without that.'

He had already accepted that possibility. Serafina's feelings
towards Angelo Guardi – whether of hatred or love – were a
part of her now. Briefly, he wondered whether she could any
longer live without them.

'I know. I won't try to stop you.'

'And the child?'

Thomas crossed the room then, leaving the window, sitting
carefully on the edge of the bed. He took her hand in his, not
allowing her any argument, sensing the fragile bones beneath
her skin.

'I've watched a lot of people die, one way or another,' he

said, gently. 'My own family died of the plague – I've a brother left in London, that's all. I've seen men die of scurvy, of cannon-shot, of drowning. I've survived a shipwreck, I've twice almost been drowned myself. It seems to me that life is worth holding on to. So you'll choose the name of your child, but perhaps you won't be the only one who cares whether it lives or dies.'

She looked at him then, at last, and he knew that they understood each other. There were some things you could never be sure of, but if Serafina's baby was born in mid-spring, as Costanza had guessed it would be, then it did not take any great mathematical ability to work out that the child could be his, and not Jacopo Capriani's.

'It doesn't matter,' he added, softly. 'I claim nothing. I told you – I have an interest in your survival, that's all. Look upon it as a trading agreement, if you prefer. *I* need money to complete my ship – *you* need someone to help you through the next few months. *Trade*, Serafina, as you said once before. I'm asking for nothing else.'

He saw some of the suspicion fade from her eyes, and for a moment her hand relaxed and almost seemed to welcome his. Her nod of agreement was almost unnoticeable, and she did not reach for a pen and paper to ratify the contract as she once might have done.

It would no longer seem appropriate, he thought, even to her.

PART IX

1596

IMPOSSIBILITIES MADE POSSIBLE

So it was impossible that the walls of Jericho should fall down. Such impossibilities can our God make possible.

266 Christians delivered out of Turkish captivity: Richard Hakluyt

Jacopo Capriani died in the middle of April, but his wife did not attend the funeral because she had been delivered of her first child three days earlier.

The birth was exhausting, undignified, and painful. When, after they had washed her and dressed her in a clean nightgown, the midwife placed the baby in Serafina's arms, she did not at first glance at it. A boy, they had said when the worst of the pain was over. And, silently, she thanked any god that might be listening, because a boy secured her what Jacopo's death had two days previously taken away; the inheritance of the Capriani property and business.

A girl, and she would have been penniless. Everything she had worked for would have gone to whatever distant male relative the Capriani lawyers were able to dredge up. She had not even a dowry to reclaim. The small squirming weight in her arms was her guarantee of a future, her just reward for the years of work and planning. Serafina felt herself smile, almost involuntarily, with triumph, with relief.

'Yes, he's a poppet, isn't he?' said the midwife, approvingly. 'A beautiful little boy. Such a pity his father didn't live to see him.'

She had not yet looked at the child. All babies were ugly, though. Slowly, Serafina turned towards the white bundle. It was an effort to move her head, an effort to raise her hand and adjust the shawl that had fallen over the small creature's face. The infant writhed and, aimlessly waving a tiny fist, opened his eyes.

They were dark, so dark that their shade was almost indistinguishable, but she thought that their colour was blue. That did not matter. She had known long ago that her child could be Thomas Marlowe's, and she had had time to make plans. Most babies were blue-eyed at first, and she would send her child to be nursed in the countryside long before any tongues could begin to wag. He would be safer there, anyway: she could not afford to let this baby, like so many others, die in infancy. Her future, her security, depended on the feeble thread of life this ugly little scrap possessed.

But he was not so ugly. Glancing at the child a second time, Serafina thought that though his nose was squashed and his head was bald, he was really surprisingly presentable. Through a haze of exhaustion, Serafina heard the nurse ask, 'What will you call him, madonna?'

The blue eyes had closed now, the creased and pursed mouth had begun to mewl. The eyes were Thomas's, but she remembered that mouth: it was her father's, and sometimes it still figured in her dreams.

'Francesco,' said Serafina, finding, as she handed the child back to the nurse, that she was smiling again. 'I will call him Francesco.'

At the beginning of February, Thomas Marlowe had begun work on the damaged *Kingfisher*. By himself, at first, working steadily, learning to ignore the ache in his shoulder and to overcome, not for the first time, a newly awoken fear of the sea.

In March, the Levant Company convoy had reappeared from Aleppo, Edward Whitlock captaining the *Garland*, John Keane the *Legacy*. Thomas had handed Whitlock the money he had borrowed from Serafina, John Keane watching all the while to make sure neither of them put a knife to each other's throat. A fortnight later the convoy had set sail for London.

The return of the convoy had brought William Williams back to Livorno, along with William's apprentice Cristofano. William would not return to England while the old Queen lived. Over hot wine in a dockside tavern, Thomas told the carpenter about Madonna Capriani, now the owner of the *Kingfisher*. He did not lie, he only made omissions, and William, who understood the conflicting forces of conscience and compromise, did not comment on the sin of omission, but agreed to the suggestion that Madonna Capriani needed a good ship's carpenter.

The *Kingfisher* would be ready to sail in a few weeks, the timbers of her shattered poop-deck replaced and repainted, a new mast rising proud above her decks. Her first journey, already planned with Serafina, would be to Naples to buy the silk goods that Jacopo Capriani had made his speciality.

But now Jacopo was dead of the fever that had attacked him intermittently throughout his adult life. The news was brought to Thomas as he began the final preparations to sail the *Kingfisher* from Livorno to the docks at Pisa. He wanted Serafina to see the *Kingfisher*: she was heavily with child, but he would carry her down to the docks in a closed litter if need be. He wanted to see her smile again, to recapture some of the certainty that Galeazzo Merli's masquerade had stolen from her. He wanted to show her all that was possible, to free her from the self-imposed restraints she had gathered from the past. He sometimes thought that though her body no longer bore the shackles of the bagnio, her mind had never succeeded in throwing off its chains.

The *Kingfisher* sailed into Pisa four days later. Thomas had spent three days supervising the final touches to the ship's completion, another day carefully nursing the galleon along the Tuscan coast. He made the voyage slowly, easily, taking his time to make countless small adjustments, taking longer to get to know the masterpiece that he had created.

It was like, he thought, finally making his acquaintance with an exotic, expensive mistress whom he had admired and lusted after for an age. He had felt oddly clumsy at first, and the sight of the thick grey water churning along her bows as they made their way out of the safety of Livorno's harbour disturbed him. He had not sailed since his return from Zante, had not given himself to the sea since William Williams had plucked him from it.

Away from the harbour, out towards the open water, the *Kingfisher* strained at the limitations Thomas set her, seizing the wind until her sails cracked and belched and bustled them along the coast. The spring weather was good, the sky clear and almost cloudless, the wind whisking white foam to the tops of the waves. The *Kingfisher*'s crew was limited to William Williams, Cristofano, and a handful of men Thomas had selected from the dockside population of Livorno. Thomas found himself master and pilot, sometimes standing on the bridge, at other times up in the rigging with a knife clamped between his teeth, unknotting a tangled piece of rope. Any fear that he had felt on consigning himself to the sea once again dissipated, quickly replaced by a more familiar respect for the waters that surged beneath the *Kingfisher*'s wooden bows.

He became aware of an almost uncontainable exhilaration. The ship was everything he had intended her to be, and more. At last all the trials of the past years seemed worthwhile: the wreck of the *Toby*, the long slow journey from Morocco to Livorno, his own near-death at the hands of Edward Whitlock and the Mediterranean Sea. Standing on the bridge of the *Kingfisher*, Thomas found that those events had become unimportant, mere steps on a road he had set himself a long time ago. He was bound to the Mediterranean now but, Thomas told himself, that would not last for ever. He would repay his debt to Serafina within a year and by then, surely, she too would see the future as he saw it, rich with possibility, untrammelled by the past. The Atlantic waited for him, to find a gateway to the East.

Inside the Villa Capriani, Thomas passed his cloak and hat to the maidservant, and kicked the worst of the mud from his boots. The house was clean, warm, and silent.

Unusually silent. There were no footsteps, no voices calling, no clerks running about, pens behind their ears, papers in their hands. No Serafina, making herself everywhere at once, a scourge and an encouragement to those who worked for her. There was only the silence and, somewhere upstairs, a kitten mewing.

It would be quiet, of course, Thomas told himself, to counteract his sudden unease. Jacopo Capriani had died almost a fortnight ago, would have been buried by now. The merchant had seemed to fade away over the last few months, a living ghost in his own house, an echo of a previous time, long done with. It had been Serafina who had kept the place alive and bustling. But now there was no sign of her: the only sounds were the maidservant's feet on the rushes, and that damned cat.

Only it wasn't a cat. Thomas felt as though someone had thumped him very hard in the stomach. He was glad that the maidservant's back was to him, because he could not have formed the words to ask the necessary question. He could not even pray coherently. He only ran, the soles of his boots breaking the silence with shocking sound, across the hall and up the stairs towards Serafina's bedchamber.

The nurse glared at him with intense disapproval as he burst open the door, and the maidservant dropped a pile of tiny white garments on to the floor. But Serafina, propped up in the bed, another white bundle at her breast, said only, 'Mr Marlowe. How pleasant.'

The beating of Thomas's heart stilled, and he found himself grinning ridiculously. Crossing the room, ignoring the scowls of the nurse, Thomas sat on the edge of the bed. The baby finished suckling, and Serafina said, calmly, 'It's a boy. His name is Francesco,' and handed the bundle to Thomas.

He was not, like some men of his age, unused to handling babies. Not because, as he had once told Edward Whitlock, his bastards crowded the docks at Greenwich, but because his elder brother Robert, of the sensible tavern and easy-going temperament, also possessed a wife and five children.

Thomas's own clothes smelt of the sea, of salt spray and pitch. Serafina's son smelt of sour milk and soap and rosewater. He had a sucking blister on his upper lip, and he was almost as bald as Galeazzo Merli.

He also had blue eyes. Silently, to himself, Thomas promised his son the sea, a ship, and all the treasures the world had to offer. To Serafina, he said, 'He has a prizefighter's fists. You must be careful, or he'll earn his living at the fairs instead of buying silk.' Then, without so much as a kiss, he handed the child, all waving arms and small searching mouth, back to his mother.

He could see that she was tired, so he told her, simply and quietly, about the *Kingfisher*. He saw the soft gleam in her eyes, the smile that touched her lips when he said that she could draw up a list of her contacts and requirements in Naples. But when her eyes finally closed, he did not move, but stayed there looking at the pair of them: at the child in the cradle, and at Serafina, her dark hair strayed carelessly over the pillow.

A week later, in the parlour where Serafina had once told Thomas of her marriage, the notary read Jacopo Capriani's will. Dressed in black, secretly delighted with the way her figure had snapped back into shape after the birth, Serafina sat, eyes lowered, hands folded, listening.

She did not move as the notary told her that she now possessed, as sole parent and guardian of Francesco Capriani, houses in Pisa, Marseilles, and Naples. She remained quite still, too, as the droning voice listed what else Jacopo Capriani had left to his wife and son. But when she finally realized just how much money was cached in various banks, chests, and purses, her heart began to hammer.

She understood then that Jacopo had worked hard all his life and had spent money on nothing. He had kept a dirty house and had worn threadbare robes and yet he had possessed assets of more than fifty thousand florins. He had refused to pay for the physician who might have saved his life, and yet he could have afforded a dozen physicians. Serafina had not wept for her husband, and she did not weep now. He had hastened his own death – for what? For a list of figures in a ledger-book, a bundle of deeds in a chest.

For the first time in months, Serafina felt some of her old excitement and energy return. Sometimes, in the dark days following the pasquinade and threatened miscarriage, she had thought herself enslaved for the rest of her life, trapped as much by the frailty of her own body as by Angelo. The sense of futility had returned, black and suffocating. Now, it was as though the road ahead had suddenly cleared, and past, present and future had begun to make sense again.

The notary, nodding a bow, had finished speaking. Lining the walls of the parlour, the clerks and servants shuffled and coughed. Serafina rose and left the room.

One pair of eyes she could not avoid, however. Thomas Marlowe lolled in one corner of the room, black-hatted, arms folded. He smiled as she passed him on her way out of the room, but the smile was ironic. Taking his sleeve, Serafina bid him follow her into the hall.

When the clerks and the servants and the notary had been dispatched, Serafina said, 'The list I gave you for Naples, Thomas. Buy double of every item.'

He nodded, unsurprised. 'You're rich, now, Serafina.'

She shook her head, took his two hands in hers. 'Not *rich*. Not yet. But I will be.'

In the morning recreation hour at her convent in Naples, Maria Garzoni tried to clean the bodice of her gown with a pan of rainwater and a hairbrush.

The bodice, a faded dark grey, was flecked with black blobs, which gave it a mottled appearance, like marble. The nuns had not yet noticed her dirty gown, because Sister Teresa, who had earlier scolded her for yesterday's misdemeanour, was hideously short-sighted. Sister Teresa had also, rather conveniently, made Maria pin a paper to her bosom which had covered the worst of the blobs. The paper said, 'For talking in needlework', written in Maria's own straggly hand. The sort of fortuitous circumstance that allowed Maria to hide today's error with yesterday's, reinforced her blithe belief in an understanding deity.

Tonight, though, at evening recreation, the paper would be removed (by Sister Bonaventura, whom even Maria stood in awe of) and her crime revealed. Sister Bonaventura had an unhappy knack of getting to the bottom of things, and Maria, who could not lie, pictured all too easily Sister Bonaventura's face when she discovered the nature of the black blobs. They were not paint, but kahveh. She had sneaked out to the docks earlier in the week, having persuaded dear Sister Teresa that she needed new gloves, and at the docks an awfully nice man had given her the kahveh beans. She had not asked for them: she had simply smiled at him because he had had pictures of snakes and trees drawn in blue all over his naked torso, and he had delved into a nearby sack and given her the kahveh. People often gave her things. Maria could guess what Sister Bonaventura would say if she knew, but Maria herself knew that there was no harm in it. People, women as well as men, liked her because she smiled and talked to them and made them feel better. That was all people really wanted.

The kahveh was quite the most curious present she had ever been given. The sailor had pointed to the handful of small dark beans, and said *kahveh*, and made gestures of drinking and lip-licking. So, in the early hours of the morning, before the rising-bell, Maria had tried to make the kahveh beans into a drink.

The experiment had not been a success, however. She had pounded the beans with a stone, as though she were grinding corn, but they had frequently escaped from her water-cup, jumping all over the floor. Then, when she had finally achieved some sort of a powder, she had mixed it with cold water to make a paste and tried to drink it. It had tasted so foul that the cup had seemed to slither out of her hand, strewing its contents over the bodice of her dress and the floor of her chamber. Things often did seem to jump out of her hand, which was partially why she was always in so much trouble. Her needlework, Sister Bonaventura frequently said, looked as though it had been stitched by a crow. Sister Bonaventura would then remind Maria of the beautiful altar-piece her mother had made for the convent. Maria, who knew that Mama had employed a seamstress to make the wretched thing, would hang her head and think happily of the pretty convent garden, or of the ships at the docks.

Now, though, even Maria could not be distracted by the budding roses and lilies around her, the blue skies, and the sunshine glittering on the newly restored face of the nearby church of S. Chiaro. The thought of Sister Bonaventura at her most forbidding set Maria's lips fluttering in prayer as she scrubbed hopelessly at the black marks.

God, whom Maria knew to be entirely benevolent, answered her prayer almost immediately. There was a clatter of footsteps and Maria hastily repinned the paper over her bodice, shoving the hairbrush into her pocket. But it was only Sister Esmeralda, Maria's dear, dear friend, pink and out of breath as usual.

'You have a visitor, my dear. Sister Bonaventura sent me for you.' Sister Esmeralda paused to mop her broad, shining face with a minute lace handkerchief, and Maria gave her a hug and tried to help her adjust her slipping veil. Sister Esmeralda had an air of permanently bewildered harassment, but she was a darling, and it had been she who had accompanied Maria on the visit to the docks.

'You'll have to hurry,' Sister Esmeralda gasped. 'You'll be late.'

Maria, who never worried about being late, picked up her skirts to oblige her friend and ran through the garden and into the cloister. A nun's voice called, 'Walk, my dear!' and she slowed her pace infinitesimally.

In the little room near the entrance to the convent, Maria saw, first, Sister Bonaventura, looking cross, and, secondly, an unknown young man standing, hat politely in hand, by the doorway. Then, filtered through the familiar convent smells of soap and incense, she recognized the scent of rosewater. Turning, hearing the rustle of silk, Maria knew immediately the identity of the fourth person in the small dark room.

'Mama!' cried Maria, and ran to hug her mother.

Costanza efficiently despatched Sister Bonaventura, almost coaxing a smile from the severe face with a promise of new candlesticks for the sacristy. Then she was alone with Thomas, who had escorted her from Pisa to Naples, and the daughter she had not seen for eighteen months.

When she had breath again, and she had blinked away the tears, she introduced Thomas. Then, standing back a little, her daughter's hands still enfolded in hers, Costanza studied her child's face in detail, learning it for the lonely months ahead.

But Maria, she thought, as she focused on the brown curls, the hazel eyes, the features that were neither Costanza's nor anyone else's that she remembered, was a child no longer. She was sixteen now, not fourteen, almost Costanza's height and possessed of a neat figure that even the hideous convent dress could not disguise.

Her figure, though, was the only aspect of Maria that could

have been described as neat. With an ache in her heart and a smile twisting her lips, Costanza thought that in some ways Maria had not changed a bit. Despite a profusion of pins, Maria's hair was in no particular style; and the fingers that Costanza still clutched in her own well-manicured hands were smudged and blackened. And, rather peculiarly, there was a piece of paper pinned to the bosom of her gown. The writing on the piece of paper was illegible.

'For talking in needlework,' said Maria, helpfully, following her mother's stare. 'We had to do French knots, and mine just wouldn't seem to go right.'

Her smile, which was her chief beauty, took in both Costanza and Thomas, and the blue skies and gardens beyond, and the high forbidding walls of the convent. Costanza knew that if she took her daughter back to her own world, with a smile like that she would be lost within a week. The vultures would be waiting for her, to pick the young flesh from her bones, to grind lines of sorrow and experience into that unmarked face.

'It is no longer needlework,' said Costanza firmly, 'so I think that Sister Bonaventura will not object if we remove this now.'

Carefully, Costanza unpinned the flapping paper, placing the pins on the nearby court cupboard. Beneath the paper, though, her daughter's gown was smeared with black as though someone had tried to rub out blots of black ink, failing utterly.

'It's kahveh, Mama,' said Maria. Her eyes, flecked with brown and green in equal quantity, were untroubled. 'I tried to make it into a drink, and spilled it. It was horrible anyway,' she added inconsequentially.

Costanza's bemusement must have showed in her face, because she heard Thomas explain, 'Kahveh is made from roasted beans. The Turks drink it. Where on earth did you buy kahveh, Madonna Garzoni?'

Maria turned her all-encompassing smile in Thomas's direction. 'I didn't *buy* it, Messer Marlowe. A man gave it to me. At the docks.'

'The *docks?*'

Maria squeezed her mother's arm comfortingly. 'It's all right, Mama, Sister Esmeralda went with me. She's a novice and she misses her mother, so we go and look at the ships. Sister Esmeralda is from Venice, you see,' Maria said to Thomas, happy, apparently, that that explained everything. 'If she sees a Venetian ship it makes her feel less homesick.'

There was the sound of footsteps in the passageway outside. 'Sister Bonaventura!' whispered Maria. For the first time, she began to look anxious.

Costanza was already removing her own black lace shawl. 'You'll wear this now,' she said, draping it around her daughter's shoulders to hide the ruined bodice, 'and I'll tell Sister Bonaventura that I'm taking you to the dressmaker's to be measured for some new gowns. And,' she added sternly, 'you'll explain to me *properly* about Sister Esmeralda. And the docks. And the kahveh.'

They ended up, of course, back at the *Kingfisher*, which was docked in Naples's harbour. Thomas had left both mother and daughter at the dressmaker's, for he had things to do other than discuss falling bands and ruffs, partlets and undersleeves. Between measurements and fittings, Costanza managed to extract a reasonably coherent account of her daughter's life at the convent, and was reassured that Maria's excursions represented nothing more than an occasional escape from the boredom of over-familiar faces and over-familiar scenery.

She made Maria promise, however, never to go out alone, and never to go to the docks again. At that, the hazel eyes had clouded and the smile vanished, until Costanza had explained that Sister Bonaventura would certainly view the docks as somewhere equally as wicked as a tavern, or worse, and that both she and Sister Esmeralda would be expelled from the convent if found out. Relenting a little, Costanza then offered to take Maria to see the *Kingfisher* that afternoon.

The sea, spread about them all shades of blue and green and violet, was calm now. It had been Costanza's first sea voyage and, had their destination not been Naples and Maria, she would have been happy never to repeat the experience. She liked the floors under her feet to be steady, and to be able to shut herself away from wind and foul weather. But she would have circumnavigated the globe for her daughter, and if Thomas had had anything to repay to her, she already considered the debt settled a hundredfold.

Thomas was still absent when mother and daughter, threading their way through the crowded docks, reached the galleon's gangway. But the youth Cristofano, apprentice to the ship's carpenter, ran down to meet them and to escort them up to the mizzen-deck.

Costanza had expected Maria to be the object of Cristofano's attentions, had resigned herself to losing her daughter for a precious half-hour so that she could be shown round the ship. What she had not expected was that William Williams, glancing up from sawing a piece of wood on the foredeck, should return his apprentice to his work and offer to escort the young lady himself. But then, thought Costanza, finding a comfortable seat on the *Kingfisher*'s bridge, there was nothing as unpredictable as love.

Nor was there any sense in the pairings it enforced. If Thomas could love Serafina Capriani, then why should not William Williams, the placid, quiet Welsh ship's carpenter, be attracted to Costanza's own disorganized daughter? And Maria was nothing if not lovable. That thought sometimes kept Costanza awake at night.

Thomas returned to the galleon when William and Maria were still below decks, examining all the complicated apparatus of a well-defended merchant ship. Costanza knew from Thomas's face that he had had a successful day, calling on the Neapolitan merchants to make his purchases, taking advantage of all the connections that old Jacopo had built up over the years.

He held his hat in one hand and two small nosegays of lily-of-the-valley in the other.

'For mother and daughter,' he said, greeting Costanza after he had quickly checked the decks of his ship.

Costanza, accepting both bunches of flowers, said, 'Maria is being shown the gun-deck and the captain's cabin. Messer Williams has taken her.' She lowered her voice. 'Poor Cristofano is sulking.'

Thomas glanced up to the foredeck and grinned. 'It will do him no harm. No doubt he's spent most of the day admiring the Neapolitan ladies.'

William Williams appeared on the mizzen-deck, a careful hand extended to help Maria, following up from the gun-deck after him. Maria's gown boasted a smart blue bodice, hastily run up by the dressmaker that morning. It was still, to Costanza's surprise, clean.

'Thomas –'

The carpenter was smiling, but there was an urgency in his voice that made Costanza glance up at him.

William Williams said, 'Madonna Garzoni has seen the *Fiametta*. She was docked here, in Naples, earlier in the week.'

Costanza saw Thomas rise and walk to her daughter's side.

'The *Fiametta*. Are you sure, madonna?' His voice was almost sharp, his expression no longer one of careless content.

But Maria, unruffled, said, 'Yes, I'm sure. She was a galleon, like this one' – she gestured to the *Kingfisher* – 'but with a lot more gilding. I particularly noticed because although she had an Italian name, she flew a French flag.'

Costanza heard the swift inward breath, saw Thomas and the carpenter glance at each other.

'It was a few days ago,' added Maria, sitting down beside her mother. 'When the sailor gave me the kahveh. The *Fiametta* was loading up in order to set sail.'

Thomas's eyes were a hard blue, like sapphires.

'Do you know in which direction she was sailing, madonna? North or south?'

Maria did not even consider. 'North,' she said. 'Yes, I'm sure of it.'

There was a silence, in which Costanza wondered about the significance of the French ship *Fiametta*.

Then Thomas, reading her thoughts, said vaguely, 'I have business with her. Nothing important, but it's long overdue.'

Delving in his pocket he passed the carpenter a list and a purse. 'I'll be away for a few days. Will, I have made most of the purchases on that list, but perhaps you could complete the final few. Costanza –'

He turned to her. She had not believed him when he had said that his business with the *Fiametta* was unimportant. She knew him too well for that.

'I'll ride north, see if I can pick up the *Fiametta* in one of the ports. You won't mind staying in Naples slightly longer than expected, will you? And both William and Rufus will be happy to escort you wherever you wish.'

Costanza smiled, and gave Thomas her hand. She said only as he bent and kissed her fingertips, 'Be careful, my dear Thomas, and be cunning. Remember that you are in Italy now, and not in England.'

Francesco had wisps of dark curling hair, and dark blue eyes the colour of lapis lazuli.

His eyes did not, as his nurse might have expected, darken to match the eye colour of his parents. Neither Jacopo's fading brown nor Serafina's near-black diminished the pure colour of Francesco's irises. Serafina, sitting by the window with her six-week-old son cradled in her lap, knew that his eyes would lighten as the summer progressed, until they all but matched the blue of the Tuscan skies.

She had fed him for the last time: a little milk still glistened transparently around his lips as she relaced her bodice. They were alone in the room, and outside the street was quiet. Only a couple of horses stood on the cobbles, their riders gentling them as they checked bridles and tightened girths. Beyond, the sun glittered on the Arno and in the distance turned the masts and spars of the ships in the harbour to silver. The ships were beginning to bring in silk again: bales of it were unloaded on to the dockside each day.

Those betraying blue eyes were closing now, and the small fists, tight and furiously waving just a half-hour ago, had relaxed into open five-petalled flowers. A last trickle of milk ran from Francesco's lips into the crevices of chin and mouth. Serafina gently dabbed him dry with her own lace handkerchief, and was rewarded with an open-mouthed, toothless smile.

She knew that what she now had to do was necessary both to herself and to the well-being of her child, yet it was hard, so impossibly hard. Harder than crossing the Mediterranean with a stranger, harder than sending that stranger from Marseilles so that she was, not for the first time in her life, utterly alone. She had not wanted this baby at all, at first, and later, she had wanted him only as a guarantee of her own security. And yet, though he had survived the first six, most precarious weeks of his life, he still seemed a part of her, as though the cord that had bound them for nine months had never truly been cut.

Francesco slept deeply now: carefully, Serafina rose and wrapped him in his shawl. Silk, she reminded herself as she tucked the fine wool round the child's face. On the dockside at Livorno, waiting for her. And Angelo, somewhere, not too far away, already surely – beginning to feel the gnawing fear of economic insecurity. Thomas, now in Naples to buy the silk goods that were still the staple of the Capriani business. The artisans, only a handful as yet, but there would soon be more, waiting for the raw silk that the *Kingfisher* would purchase. She had assembled all the pieces: she need only put aside this one small burden in order to take up the game once more. And it would be for his own good, after all.

And yet, and yet. A small wagon had been hitched to the horses outside, and Serafina could hear footsteps on the stairs. With infinite care she lifted her child and let her own cheek touch that small, velvet face. Her eyes were as tearless as a newborn baby's, yet her heart had never been so heavy.

After they had taken him away, she went to the accounting-house and made her clerks' life hell.

Thomas found the *Fiametta* in Civitavecchia, the main port of the Papal States. In four days of hard riding from Naples, Thomas had investigated every likely looking port en route and, continuing north, had resolved to ride as far as Genoa, if necessary. He would allow himself a fortnight's searching: Serafina, for once, could wait.

Yet, on a single glance at the harbour at Civitavecchia, Thomas had known that his search was over. The *Fiametta* was nestled under the huge bulk of the Forte Michelangelo, half hidden by the shadows of the castle's massive projecting bastions.

The gilding that Maria Garzoni had noticed marked her out, drawing her from the jostling of lesser craft that cluttered the dockside around her.

Dismounting from his horse and leading it by the reins, Thomas continued through the harbourside on foot. It was evening, and the sun was just beginning to set in a flurry of pink and gold. The anger that Thomas had experienced in Zante had cooled now, but it still burned, a chill dark flame that the passing months had not extinguished. Nearing the French ship, Thomas saw clearly the shape that had once appeared to him from out of the night. The name *Fiametta* was scrawled in gold-leaf along her bows, her pennants trailed damply in the evening air. A few men were swabbing the *Fiametta*'s decks, repairing sails and checking ropes, carrying out all the small tasks necessary to the maintenance of a merchant ship. But Thomas could see no master strutting on the tidy decks, no clever feather-capped owner with the sort of charm and ingenuity capable of arranging bargains between the governor of Zante and an Algerian corsair.

The *Fiametta* was larger than the *Kingfisher*, and she had as much gold-leaf on her as the Duke of Tuscany's galleys: she gleamed in the fading day, just as she had once gleamed in the moonlight. Festooned with pennants like a city on its saint's day, she surpassed in magnificence even the great galleasses that were docked at the far end of Civitavecchia's harbour.

But though she might look magnificent, walking round her hull, Thomas began to wonder whether the *Fiametta*'s magnificence was much more than skin deep. An untrained eye would have seen nothing more than the flamboyant beauty of the vessel; Thomas, looking carefully, could see minute gaps in the caulking, gaps that the sea might seep through, inevitably weakening the timbers. Thomas would have had a caulker flogged for workmanship like that.

The timbers themselves were not of the highest quality. Running a speculative eye along the *Fiametta*'s hull, Thomas found himself glad that he had lied, stolen, begged, and borrowed for decent wood. The master of the *Fiametta* had not done so: Thomas, squinting, could see the small but definite twist and warp of poor-quality timber.

A voice called down in French, 'Can I help you sir?' A sailor was leaning over the *Fiametta*'s gunwale.

Thomas, smiling and waving his hat in a salute, called back, 'I'm thinking of chartering a vessel to Toulon. Do you sail to Toulon?'

'Sometimes. On the way to Marseilles.' The sailor, wringing out the cloth he held in his hands, glared suspiciously down at Thomas. 'But the master doesn't hire the ship out for charter.'

He was unsurprised that the owner of the *Fiametta* reserved his treasure for himself. Almost casually, Thomas asked his next question.

'What's your master's name?'

'Guardi,' said the sailor before turning away. 'Monsieur Guardi owns the *Fiametta*.'

He thought at first that there was some mistake. Guardi was Serafina's name, and of no connection with the *Fiametta*, which was the object of Thomas's own private vendetta. He had ridden alone to find the *Fiametta* because she was, as he had once told William Williams, his concern and no one else's. Some affairs he would keep separate from his employment in the Capriani company. He had misheard, he told himself, the seaman was mistaken.

But – *Marseilles* –

Thomas was up the gangway within a few seconds, striding across the *Fiametta*'s newly scrubbed mizzen-deck.

'*Guardi?*' said Thomas to the sailor, who looked up again, crossly. 'Messer Angelo Guardi? Of Marseilles?'

He had scrabbled in his pocket for some coins: as they trickled into the outstretched palm he took in the sailor's nod of agreement, but no more. The gulls circling overhead, the stevedores calling to each other below, all the sounds of the crowded harbour faded into insignificance.

He imagined himself in Marseilles again, outside a house that was as bright with gold as the decks of this ship. Beside him was Serafina, dressed in shirt and breeches. Shortly afterwards, she had stolen a loaf of bread from a baker's shop.

And that golden house had belonged, like this ship, to Angelo Guardi. Angelo Guardi, Serafina's illegitimate cousin, had been for almost nine years now the owner of the Guardi cloth-carrying company. Angelo Guardi had murdered Serafina's father, had been responsible for Serafina's own slavery and dis-inheritance. Angelo Guardi was the object of Serafina's love and loathing. It was not a relationship that Thomas understood, nor one that he was capable of. But he had recognized it, long ago in the room of a tavern in Pisa, when he had first kissed Serafina in anger and jealousy and misery.

And now he knew that six months ago, it had been Angelo Guardi who had attempted to steal the *Garland*'s tin in order to sell it to a Turkish corsair. After all – and Thomas swore aloud – Angelo had traded with the Turk before. Only that time it had been human cargo that he had sold.

He realized that the sailor was staring at him, his sunburnt skin creased with suspicion. Thomas made himself replace the smile that had slipped so disastrously.

'May I speak to Messer Guardi?'

The sailor shook his head and spat into the sea. 'Monsieur Guardi's gone to Florence,' he said.

Angelo Guardi had not yet, in fact, reached Florence. First, he had had business in Livorno, where he and his entourage had left the *Fiametta*. Then, the ride inland had been a leisurely one, appropriate to the impression he needed to create.

In his late twenties now, Angelo's hair was a thick dark gold that touched his collar, his eyes the dark brown, almost black, of all the Desmoines. His face was fuller than his cousin Serafina's, the cheekbones prominent, the nose, with its high-boned bridge, well moulded. His clothes were of rich fabric and well cut: he wore a doublet of the best Persian silk, black with scarlet passe-menterie, the shoulder-wings high and padded. From one shoulder trailed a short scarlet cloak that touched the black rump of his horse.

The pace of the journey, the pleasant, warm countryside, suited Angelo, allowing him plenty of opportunity to think. Although he was more than capable of acting quickly if the situation demanded it, he preferred to have time to consider every possible avenue, to guard against every conceivable error.

Recently, events seemed to have tumbled together, allowing little time for tranquil thought. Here, riding through sun-dappled, leafy valleys, he could breathe, drop his guard a little. In France the troubled situation of the city of Marseilles seemed to be altering daily. In February, Charles de Casaulx, self-styled governor of Marseilles for four years, had been assassinated. Shortly afterwards, traitors had opened the city gates during the night to the Duc de Guise's army. Then, in March, the ambitious, shallow Duc d'Epernon had made peace with Henri of Navarre. No – King Henri IV of France, now. For although Spain still gnawed, almost out of habit, at the kingdom, it was inevitable that France would soon be firmly under Bourbon control.

But all this, Angelo thought without bitterness, had happened too late for him. Had King Henri been able to consolidate his kingdom more quickly, then Angelo might simply have been able to continue uninterrupted with his work of improving the steady, unspectacular business that Franco Guardi had nurtured. As it was, he had lived through uncommon times, and he had had to resort to uncommon measures to survive them.

The years of Charles de Casaulx's dictatorship had been particularly difficult. The common people had grown envious of the wealth of the merchants and, instead of punishing them, as he ought to have done, de Casaulx had encouraged their envy. Angelo, who had harvested his own riches from a hopelessly inauspicious start, had found himself threatened, abused, struggling to hold on to what he had fought so hard for. Marseilles's insecurity had reverberated around the Mediterranean Sea, and the rumours of insurrection had harmed his merchant's reputation. Angelo had lost customers, even some of those he had had for years. Customers who had stood beside the Guardi company through the tragic loss of Franco and Serafina had begun to shake their heads, murmuring about bankruptcy and unsecured loans. A lesser man than Angelo might have panicked, sold up, started again.

As his horse stepped delicately through the clear, shivering waters of a stream, as he breathed deeply the soft, untroubled air, Angelo congratulated himself on not making the mistakes of lesser men. If he had sold up, he would not be here now, riding through the sunlit countryside to pay court to one of the great merchant families of Florence, the Nadis. No, instead of selling, he had bought. He had borrowed and begged and bargained, and with the money he had earned he had built himself the *Fiametta*, that glittering emblem of his success. The *Fiametta* had been necessary to him for three reasons: as a visible symbol of his security, as a faster, more capable method of transporting cloth than Franco's galleys, and, most important, as homage to the girl he intended to marry.

He had not yet met Fiametta Nadi – his dealings so far had been only with her father – but he knew that she was nineteen, fair-haired, and not yet betrothed. He knew that her mother, Giulia, was a noted beauty, and that she had one sister, thirteen-year-old Nencia. Most importantly of all, Fiametta Nadi had no brothers. Her father had told Angelo that his daughter was a beauty, but Angelo doubted that. Beauties tended to marry before they were nineteen. But had she the face of a donkey Angelo Guardi would still have named his ship for her, because Fiametta Nadi would one day be very, very rich. Angelo planned to marry Fiametta Nadi just as he had once planned to acquire the Guardi company. Both, simply, were necessary to his survival.

Planning, too, was essential for survival. Since he had been a small child, Angelo had planned, taking each changeable situation, moulding it to his best advantage. As an orphaned and penniless bastard, he had been quick and charming, making himself an asset rather than a burden to the House of Guardi. He had taken the place of the son Franco Guardi had never had, acting as agent and factor, sailing at Franco's side through storm and tempest. He had worked all hours of the day and night, feast-days too, sometimes, for Franco. And at the end, Franco Guardi had entrusted Angelo with the running of the Marseilles house and business, while Franco himself sailed for Tuscany. Angelo had never doubted that the Guardi cloth-trade was morally, if not legally, his.

Ahead of him, as they continued up through the wooded sides of the valley, Angelo watched as the notary Jehan de Coniques ducked low overhanging branches, and cursed.

Sobriety was for the notary reserved increasingly only for the morning: a shorter morning each day, for there was only one cure for the headache and nausea and shaking that greeted Jehan de Coniques each dawn. It was not yet midday, but Angelo's notary lurched in the saddle, sang snatches of bawdy songs, muttered under his breath.

Sometimes, over the years, Angelo had thought that he and Jehan were just different sides of the same coin: both dispossessed, both relying on their wit and intelligence to free them from the past, yet each seeing the past in such a different light. The past seemed to eat at Jehan, so that now, with the sunlight showering through the tightly furled leaves, his face was patterned dark and light, pitted as though with disease. Angelo felt no guilt, no regret about the past. On his death, Franco Guardi would have consigned his business to bankruptcy at the hands of a young girl and an amateurish old man.

They left the forest at last, riding along the open ridge, and there below them, cradled in the purple hills, lay the city of Florence. Angelo took one deep pleasurable breath as he gazed down on the rounded terracotta roof of the duomo, the slim high tower of the campanile. Sunlight glittered on the tiled roofs, and broke the brown expanse of the Arno into mosaic fragments. Through the deaths of Franco and Serafina Guardi, Angelo had lost useful links with the Florentine silk industry. When he married Fiametta Nadi, he would reforge those links. Selling the odd crate of tin to greedy corsairs was a useful sideline, but would not bring in the sort of money that Angelo needed.

As they rode down the hillside, Jehan's horse stumbled, and the notary slipped in his saddle, losing his reins, his cap plummeting into the mud. One of the servants helped him upright, a crackling of voluminous black robes and a muttering of curses.

Angelo, watching, began to consider the past again, the years' accumulation of credit and debt.

Without Francesco, the house seemed empty.

When her breasts ceased to feel sore and to weep milk for her absent son, Serafina rejoiced in the total ownership of her body again, glad that it had been returned to her scarcely marked by the events of the past year. The weeks passed in a flurry of activity: she bought silk from Livorno, she engaged more silk-weavers, she schemed and planned. She was an inspiration and a scourge to staff and servants alike: she was everywhere at once, her sharp black hawk's eyes missing no moment of idleness, no carelessly placed stitch. She worked so hard that she did not have time to eat; she rose early and went to bed late. She did not want to sleep, because when she was asleep she dreamed: cruel, vividly coloured dreams, that she struggled to wake from, screaming for air. Always the same dream, always waiting for the moment she closed her eyes. It was better to stay awake, better to be busy. When she was busy she had no time to notice the emptiness of the house, the absence of the cradle.

When Thomas returned from Naples, Serafina was bent over a desk in the accounting-house, her head supported by one hand, a quill pen slipping from her other, loosening fingers. Her eyes had begun to close, the figures to blur until they were meaningless. The maidservant's voice jerked her awake, breaking through the restless images of the past, announcing that Messer Marlowe had called.

She had time to push a few stray locks of hair into place, to shake out the folds of her gown, before Thomas entered the room.

He bowed, flung his battered black hat on to a vacant chair. 'A successful voyage, madonna. She sails like a dream.'

Thomas's dream, she thought, her mind still hazed with sleep. Her dreams had a different, colder nature.

She heard herself mouthing conventional greetings, saw herself take wine from the bureau, pour herself and Thomas a glass. Her dreams, Serafina reminded herself brusquely, were dependent on Thomas's success, on the success of the *Kingfisher*. She made herself look up at Thomas, and smile, and notice that he had not paused to change his clothes, to tidy his hair. His shirt and doublet were stained with salt, his face tanned to bronze by the sun and the sea.

He did not yet, though, draw her list of purchases from his pocket and discuss ribbons and laces, prices and profits. His smile had disappeared, his eyes momentarily evaded hers. He repeated, 'A successful voyage.' He rubbed at the stubble on his chin, threaded his fingers through his tangled hair. 'And an interesting voyage. I found out some things that I think you should know about, Serafina.'

She noticed how quickly he emptied his second glass of wine. Rising from the table, Thomas went to stand by the window.

The house was quiet, servants and clerks having retired, exhausted, to bed. There was only the insistent gentle battering of a moth, beating itself to death around a flickering candle-flame. It was late evening; outside, the sky displayed only pinpoints of light in an inky blackness. There could be nothing of interest in the houses beyond, their windows shuttered or candlelit, or in the darkened street lit with the occasional rushlight or fire. Serafina knew suddenly that Thomas was hiding something from her. That he had something to say to her he could not yet find words to express. She dug her fingers into her palms, irritable with exhaustion and tension.

He swung round, the empty wine-glass still cradled between his short, square fingers, his expression unusually bleak. The evasion had gone from his eyes, as though he had come, alone, to some decision.

'You remember that I sailed for the Levant Company, as master of the *Garland*?'

She nodded, waiting.

'We carried cargo for Zante. Some cloth, but mostly tin.'

Tin, mined in Cornwall, was one of the English Levant Company's most valuable cargoes.

'In Zante, with the connivance of the Venetian governor, someone tried to steal our tin. I managed to trace the ship responsible. She was hidden in a cove to the north of Zante – not that she could easily be hidden. She was exquisite, Serafina, a new craft, bigger than the *Kingfisher*. I eventually discovered that she was a French ship, that her name was the *Fiametta*, and that she had intended to sell the tin to an Algerian corsair. They were together, you see, the Turkish galley and the French ship.'

They were together, you see, the Turkish galley and the French ship. Serafina drank her wine at last. She tried to think of Zante, a small island off the coast of Greece, crushed between the two mighty powers of Venice and Islam. But all she could picture was a corsair ship, the lion of St Mark's unreeling to show a blood-red crescent beneath. It was as though the past had begun to creep from the dark corner where she had hidden it, taking her from the small, drab dining-chamber, spreading out the terrible images of childhood before her.

Thomas had not moved from the window. 'When I was in Naples, I learned that the *Fiametta* had also recently berthed there. So I decided to ride north, hoping that she'd stopped at one of the Italian ports to trade as she travelled. I needed to know the name of her master, you understand. If she had succeeded in taking the tin from our hold, then the *Garland* would have sunk.'

Her hands were threaded together in her lap, pale and still against her black silk mourning gown. Serafina looked up, her dark eyes meeting Thomas's cornflower blue. She understood what the loss of the *Garland* would have meant to him, and why he had needed to know the name of the man who had planned it. None knew better than she the bitterness of that sort of theft.

But there was still a chill in her stomach, a persistent cold clutching of memory and dread.

Thomas said, 'I found the *Fiametta* in Civitavecchia, Serafina. Her master's name is Angelo Guardi. It seems your cousin Angelo has been keeping up with his old acquaintances.'

The chill flowered and spread, a hand opened and infected her veins with ice. She whispered, 'Angelo.'

When her mind, frozen by shock, worked again, she thought: Angelo sold tin to the corsairs, enabling them to cast the ordnance needed to rob Christian ships. French ships, Marseillais ships. Cogs and merchantmen and galleys. The *Gabrielle*, the *Mignon* and the *Petit Coeur*. *Angelo has been keeping up with his old acquaintances.* Acquaintances he must have made a long time ago. Acquaintances who had helped him, perhaps, in earlier years . . .

'There's always a shortage of tin, you see. But to collude with the Turk is dangerous, Serafina. Not a course to take lightly.

Angelo's trying to make up for a shortfall in more conventional sorts of trade, I would guess.'

She stared at him, not at first understanding. Then she realized just what he was telling her, just what he was offering her. Of course. Hope rose, almost unbearably tantalizing, swamping her previous dread. The French wars of religion, Charles de Casaulx's isolationism, the Marseillais's hatred of the wealthy merchant classes – all these must have threatened Angelo. *History had not been kind to Angelo.* Thomas was right. Angelo would not commit acts of piracy, would not collaborate with the enemy, if he were not already uneasy about his future.

If he were not already, perhaps, desperate.

Her hands had begun to flutter, to shake. Pinioning them against her sides, she struggled to think clearly.

Financially, Angelo was no longer secure. And she had already increased that insecurity, perhaps, by taking his customers, by spreading rumours about his solvency. Yet, incongruously, there had been the golden house in Marseilles, taunting in its extravagance. And now there was the *Fiametta*. *She was exquisite*, Thomas had said . . .

She did not realize she had spoken aloud, until she saw Thomas staring at her, his eyes bleak with a mixture of concern and disquiet.

He said, evenly, 'The *Fiametta*'s breathtaking to look at, yes. Bigger than the *Kingfisher*, and with a hell of a lot more gold-leaf. But I had a close look at her in Civitavecchia, Serafina, and found out that she isn't quite what she seems. The good Messer Guardi has spent too much on gold paint, and not enough on timber and caulking.'

She listened, her whole body taut, as he explained briefly the importance of waterproofing a hull correctly. Of buying the best-quality timbers that would not warp or gape, of paying the most skilful caulkers to seam the planks watertight with pitch. Of careening the ship in dry dock, instead of, as was too frequently the custom in Mediterranean countries, carrying out a botched job while she was still afloat.

Her mind locked everything quickly into place, reaching a dazzling, triumphant conclusion. 'So Angelo has economized – cut corners?'

Thomas shrugged. He looked tired. 'Possibly. Or maybe he's
taken bad advice. Or maybe he's ignorant.'

'Ignorant! Angelo was never ignorant,' said Serafina, scornfully. Her fingers were clenched, her eyes dark and intense, her
voice muted, as though she had forgotten Thomas's presence.
'He always relied on his own judgement. He'd ask other people's
advice, but he always made his own decisions. No.' She shook
her head, hugging her arms around herself. 'Angelo is short of
money,' Serafina said, jubilantly. 'He's keeping up appearances.'

'I came to the same conclusion.' Thomas's voice, dry and
devoid of expression, echoed her wildly darting thoughts. 'Appearance is important to any merchant. If it began to look as though
the Guardi business was failing, then investors – customers –
would withdraw their money and custom immediately. Thus
the house – thus the ship.'

She had begun to smile at last: a small, secretive smile that
closed her off from Thomas, locking her in the bitter old conflicts
of the past, the new conflicts she intended to create. She knew
now what she must do. She must return to Marseilles, the web
she had spun must take her back to that city of betrayal.

Rising, taking the wine-flask, Serafina crossed the room and
refilled both their glasses. Raising her own glass in salute, she
said, 'To the confusion of mutual enemies, Thomas.'

They stood side by side. The glasses chinked in the silence, the
red wine drew swirls of light from the candles.

She had wanted everything returned to her, and she knew
that she was still unable to accept anything less than total restoration. She might be a rich woman, a successful woman, the
mother of a fine son, the owner of three houses and part-owner
of a ship. But it was not enough. She needed to repossess everything she had lost. Her home, her company, her name. She
closed her eyes and she saw Angelo, as clearly as she had seen
him in her dreams. Only now he was kneeling before her, his
head bent in the position of the supplicant, or the suitor.

She wanted Thomas to leave. She needed to be alone, to
think, to plan.

She must travel to France, to Marseilles, back to the beautiful,
deceitful city of her birth. Since she had been ten years old her

life had had only one direction, one impetus, an impetus that tonight had gathered force until it was ready to hurl itself into the unknown abyss of the future.

She heard herself say, 'You need not unload the *Kingfisher*, Thomas. You can load up the cloth from the warehouse, and we'll set sail for France within the next fortnight.'

She left Thomas's side, and walked slowly round the table. Jacopo's table, scratched and old. She had intended to replace it: now, perhaps, she need not bother. Soon, she would live in her own house in Marseilles, amongst her own people. The rooms, the furniture, the name that had been hers in childhood, would belong to her again. In Marseilles she would see Angelo again, but this time she would choose the time, the place, the tenor of their meeting.

Her heart was beating fast, but she was thinking clearly now, her mind racing ahead of her tongue.

'We'll sail to Genoa first. We should reach Marseilles by August.'

She looked up at Thomas at last, expecting to see her own excitement reflected on his face. But there was no joy in his blue eyes, no shared expectation, only suspicion, and judgement.

He said just one word. '*We?*'

'I shall sail with you.'

He was staring at her as though she had said something preposterous, or indecent.

Unable to control herself, Serafina snapped at him, 'Are you like the rest of them, Thomas? Do you think that I should keep to the kitchens or the nursery? Of course I will sail with you.'

He said coldly, 'And Francesco?'

'Oh.' She had picked up her skirts, and was making ready to leave the room. 'I have sent Francesco away.'

Thomas moved quickly, reaching the doorway, one arm across the jamb to prevent her leaving.

'What do you mean, you've sent him away? Where? When?'

His face was only a few inches from hers. For a moment she had forgotten that Francesco was Thomas's son, too. But now she saw the heat of possession in his eyes, and she found that she resented that possessiveness, resented the physical strength that kept her imprisoned in her own house.

Her voice was small and tight, frosted with ice, her eyes dark with anger. 'It is none of your business, but since you ask, Francesco has gone to the countryside. I sent him a fortnight ago.'

'So that you can go to Marseilles? So that you can pay court to your cousin again? Is that what your son is to you, Serafina – a burden to be put aside when it's inconvenient?'

She found that she was shivering, that she wanted to strike him again, as she had struck him at Galeazzo Merli's banquet. His eyes still judged her, finding her wanting. She hated him for that.

With a fierce effort of will, Serafina controlled the trembling, made her fists unclench. The glorious optimism had evaporated as quickly as it had been born, destroyed by the look in his eyes, by the sudden painful memory of her own small son. She hated him because he could do this to her: because he could take away the hope she so desperately needed, because he could make her feel worthless again. Once, she had promised to herself that no man would ever again be able to hurt her like this. Without even touching her: by the expression on his face, by his words. She had erred: she had let Thomas Marlowe come too close to her.

She said, intending to wound him in return, 'Did you think that I would let him stay here? That would have kept me to the kitchens and nursery more certainly than anything else. I am going to Marseilles to trade, Thomas. I cannot do that with a newborn baby in my arms.'

Thomas's hand had slipped from the doorway. He said, his voice bitter, 'My God, you are a selfish bitch. I realized that years ago, of course, but I didn't realize just how selfish.'

Serafina felt the shock of his words, saw the scorn in his eyes. They were like a physical assault, a breathtaking, sickening series of blows to the stomach. She heard herself gasp, felt the strength dissolve from her limbs. She did not want this; she could not bear this. Somehow, she had allowed him to believe that he had some claim on her, on what was hers. But no one had any claim on her now: she had cast off the last shackles of ownership with Jacopo's death.

'We have a job to do, Mr Marlowe,' she said, summoning up her last vestiges of strength. 'Both of us have contracts to keep. Do we not?'

He did not move, did not speak. She saw the pain in his eyes, and for a moment she exulted. She said, 'Luisa has made up a bedchamber for you,' and she left him, and almost ran for the solitude of her own room.

There were more bottles of wine in the cellars, and the *Kingfisher* was waiting at the docks. Thomas chose to go to neither, knowing that each would offer him only a temporary escape. Instead, he remained standing in Jacopo Capriani's ugly accounting-room, with the half moon outlining the street beyond, and the moth still hopelessly attracted to the candlelight.

In Civitavecchia, once the initial shock of discovery had subsided, Thomas had found that he had half dreaded, half longed to tell Serafina about Angelo and the *Fiametta*. He had wanted her to see clearly that Angelo perpetuated the same evils he had begun years ago. Yet he had also known that he was offering her hope; hope that would let her pursue again her own unalterable path to revenge and repossession.

He had witnessed the fascination in her eyes: he had known immediately, of course, why she intended to sail to Marseilles with him. To see Angelo again, to renew her acquaintance with the black prince, the fallen angel, of her childhood. For that, she would abandon everything else, even her own small son.

Thomas remained in the accounting-room for a long time, letting his temper cool down, resisting the twin temptations of the wine-bottle and of turning on his heel and leaving the house. He had made his choice six months ago, at Costanza's prompting, and he had no reason to alter that choice. He had always known what Serafina was: the folly was his, in loving her. He had needed to see her: to see that familiar, beloved, infuriating face, to watch her walk, to hear her speak. To be with her, to share the same room as her. He was not capable of refusing her. They would sail to France, they would dock in Marseilles. Both he and Serafina.

Thomas found himself, for the first time in years, thinking of

England again. He had committed both himself and his ship to Serafina and the Mediterranean, but that commitment would one day be over. Staring through the unshuttered window-pane, Thomas imagined grey skies, rain-washed streets, the sound of his own language in the market-places and taverns. He knew now that for him the Mediterranean would always be associated with Serafina: that he would see her in the high, clacking heels of the Tuscan girls, hear her in the song and chatter of the piazza. To be free of her, he must leave Italy and go home. It had been a long time since he had thought of England as home.

But not yet. Turning from the window, Thomas knew that England and all the ambitions he had once associated with her were years away, and perhaps for ever unobtainable. He had work to do here, the *Kingfisher* to prove, Serafina's need for retribution, now inextricably entangled with his own, to fulfil. And besides, Edward Whitlock lived in England, and he had not yet the courage to face the man who had so nearly destroyed him. He must fight a different enemy: he, too, as Serafina had pointed out, had an account to settle with Angelo Guardi. At last, wearily, Thomas left the window and went out of the room, climbing the stairs to find his allotted bedchamber.

He heard the sound as he reached the first-floor landing. Not a child's cry this time, but an adult's, raw with incoherent pain.

He went to her without thought. Just as he would have comforted one of his own small nephews and nieces, Thomas forgot his own anger and, finding the source of the cries, pushed open the bedchamber door. He said her name, but there was no response, only that dreadful tortured moaning, increasing in pitch until it was almost a scream.

As he drew the bed-curtains aside, the light of Thomas's candle illuminated Serafina's face. Her fists were balled and tight, pushing against her closed eyes as if to rub out the visions hidden there. She was repeating something over and over again, but Thomas could not understand what she said. The words she spoke were not of any language he had heard before. Placing the candle on the table, Thomas's own hands enfolded her clenched fingers and he said her name again, louder this time.

Her eyes opened, black with fear, but did not see him. Her

hair was tangled and matted, her nightgown soaked with sweat. He put his arms round her and made her sit up, saying 'Serafina, it's me – Thomas,' over and over again until the shaking slowly lessened, and her breathing no longer came in short, shallow gasps.

She clutched at the unlaced halves of his doublet, hiding her head in the hollow of his shoulder. He rocked her in his arms like a baby, his hand stroking her head. The house was silent, and the candle on the table outlined her narrow, trembling shoulders, the fall of dark hair against his breast.

When she was able to listen, he said, 'You had a bad dream, that's all. Tell me about it.'

She did not speak at first. Her fingers still clawed at his shirt, and he could feel her rapid breath against his skin. At last he heard her whisper, 'It's always been the same dream. Until tonight. I can see my father –' She stopped, took a deep, shuddering breath.

'There's a janissary beating him. The janissary has Angelo's face. I call out to stop him, but I can only speak the lingua franca of the slaves. He doesn't hear, he just keeps on. And he's laughing.'

She stopped again, sitting up and relaxing her grip on him a little. 'Only tonight it was different.' Her eyes were wide, the pupils indistinguishable from the iris. 'It wasn't my father that they were beating. It was Francesco.'

Shadowed by the candlelight, Thomas could see the marks of exhaustion on her face. He thought, You push yourself too hard, but he said nothing. She looked up at him, seeming to see him clearly for the first time.

'I had to send him away, Thomas. Babies die in the city. I didn't want to. I miss him.'

'I know,' he said. He could feel the warmth of her skin through her thin nightgown. 'I know.'

She was shivering again, but at least her eyes were clear, her speech intelligible. Picking up a blanket, he wrapped it round her shoulders. As he bent over her, he heard her whisper, 'Don't go, Thomas. Please don't leave me alone.'

He could see in her large dark eyes the twin images of the

candle-flame, and his own face, diminished in reflection. There was never any choice for him, of course. He simply nodded and, raising her face between his two palms, kissed her forehead. And when she did not demur, and her breathing quickened again, but with a different cause this time, he kissed her mouth, her breasts.

It was not like the first time: it was as though he had discovered a different country, one shadowed with sadness and knowledge, but still exquisite. He knew that whether they fought or made love, murmured endearments or hurled insults, he would still love her. She had become a part of him. He could not return to the person he had been before he had known her.

Serafina slept almost immediately afterwards, but Thomas lay awake for a long time that night. It was not only the physical closeness of her body, of her perfumed skin, that kept him sleepless.

He knew that the truce they had made was only temporary, that they were stranded together in the eye of a storm, waiting for the wind to begin to howl again, the rain to beat against the window. They had forgiven each other, the harsh words both had spoken had been forgotten. But one day, Thomas thought, stroking the soft dark hair that trailed across his chest, one day forgiveness might no longer be possible.

PART X

1596

OPEN TO THE WAVES

A Crased ship might be safe in a calme
Sea, but lyes open to the waves upon any
storme.

Itinerary: Fynes Moryson

In London, dinner was served at the Whitlock house for Edward and Faith Whitlock, for John Keane and his second cousin Dorothy, and for half a dozen other members of the Levant Company and their wives and sweethearts.

The meal had gone reasonably well, thought Faith, signalling to the servants to bring in the coloured tarts, the almond creams, and the jellies. Better than her married life, which threatened to founder on familiar rocks since Edward's return, a few weeks ago, from the Levant.

Edward, glowering again, was involved in some sort of argument with Richard Staper, now governor of the company. Faith sighed inwardly, and began to arrange bowls of crystalline fruit and sugared flowers in the centre of the table. Edward's temper had been particularly uncertain following his latest voyage. John Keane had explained to Faith the cause of Edward's megrims. Privately, one evening when Edward had been away on business, he had called on her and told her what Edward had kept to himself: that Thomas Marlowe, one-time employee of the Levant Company, was alive and well and had built a ship in Livorno.

The news had not sent Faith into ecstasies of bliss, because she had never loved Thomas Marlowe. She had liked him tremendously, had enjoyed his company a great deal, and his love-making even more, but she had not loved him. She loved Ned, who was now six, and her little Alice, who was almost two. Men were good, thought Faith as she counted spoons, for keeping you warm at night, but not for a great deal else. She had taken Thomas to her bed three years ago because she had liked his face and his body, and because he had made her laugh.

Still, Faith was glad to hear that he was alive. Somehow, the unconfirmed reports of his drowning on board the *Toby* had never quite convinced her; her final morning with Thomas had demonstrated to Faith his notable talent for survival. So she had thanked John Keane, who was a kind and good man and who would one day perhaps make his second cousin Dorothy a quite acceptable husband, and, silently, she had wished Thomas well.

Edward's fist thumped on the table, and the spoons that Faith had just set out bounced on the polished wood. Directing a bowl of damson cheese, Edward's favourite, towards her husband's end of the table, Faith sat down next to John Keane.

'When will you sail again, John?' she asked, as she cut the tarts, red, green, and white, into slices. 'Edward is weary already of dry land.'

'Then Edward has poor taste,' said John Keane, courteously. 'He comes home to a warm house, a beautiful wife, and two lovely children. I envy him.'

'Then find yourself a wife.' Faith levered a slice of green tart on to John Keane's plate. 'I'm sure you can think of a suitable candidate.'

Her copper-coloured eyelashes flickered once in the direction of Dorothy Jenkinson across the table. Dorothy was perfectly suited to become John's wife – she was averagely pretty, but possessed an unaverage intellect and a considerable musical ability. Faith could picture them together, she singing airs, he accompanying her on the lute, for the rest of their lives.

'Or hasn't Doll's wretched old father died yet?'

John Keane's mouth twitched. 'Regretfully, no. You are quite delightfully outspoken sometimes, Faith. He is not well, though. But to return to your previous question, I expect we shall set sail again in the autumn. It's safest to go round Spain late in the year, you see – Spanish sailors grow sea-sick in winter gales.'

Despite the damson cheese, Edward's fists hammered the table a second time. Faith sighed again.

'Guns, my dear Mistress Whitlock,' explained John, helping himself to almond cream and crystallized fruit. 'Your Edward wants better ordnance on board the *Legacy* and the *Saviour of Bristol*. I had the cannon on the *Garland* upgraded when we were in Livorno, so she'll do for a while. Richard Staper, of course, is reluctant to spend the money.'

Faith studied her husband for a moment, red-faced, his fists clenched. Really, the house was so much quieter when he was away in Scanderoon or suchlike. *And* she was able to continue with her own interests . . .

'And do you agree with my husband, John?'

Keane nodded. 'I do. The Inland Sea is awash with our enemies now, Faith. The Spanish, the Venetians, the French, Islam, and, of course, all the dammed corsairs. And though Tuscany may ostensibly be on our side for the time being, they won't be for much longer. We're too successful, you see, and nobody likes that.' He grinned, and pushed away his empty plate.

Faith thought again what a nice sensible man John was, and how happy Dolly would be when her rich old father finally died and the two of them could marry. 'You're smiling,' said Faith, gently. 'Why are you smiling, John?'

He turned back to her. She was glad that she had worn the dark green velvet, trimmed with a silver shot silk that Edward had brought back from one of his voyages.

'I had much the same conversation with Thomas Marlowe once,' said John. 'At midnight, in Livorno. And he, too, was lecturing me on the importance of not economizing on guns.'

Faith turned away, directing the servant to unstopper the malmsey wine. Her eyes were still bright, but she was conscious of a small pain in her heart.

'Thomas was right,' added John, with a frown. 'And so is Ned. We'll go on squabbling for a while, but matters will come to a head some day. That's why Staper will give Ned the cannon he asks for. And that's why we'll use them. And that's why, one day, we'll have to sail a little bit further for our cinnamon and silk.'

At the banquet in Florence, Fiametta Nadi wore a gown of white satin embroidered with silver and trimmed with fresh-water pearls. Her sandy hair, a pale echo of her mother's bright red-gold locks, bristled from the coils and ribbons and braids that bound her head.

The whole of Florence came that night to the Palazzo Nadi. The Donati, the Frescobaldi, the Lamberti, and the Malespini – all the prominent members of the most important guilds, their high-soled shoes tapping on the marbled floors, and their silks and satins brushing along the box-edged paths in the garden. The same musicians who played for the Medici plucked airs and dances from lutes and citarrons, and sang the exquisite sad songs of Josquin des Prez. They danced in the withdrawing-room, they danced in the banqueting-hall; they danced in the garden among cascades and parterres, grottos and statuary. Wine-bottles cooled in the water that ran through the centre of a stone table; mock guns, fireworks, and water-bombs burst in the perfumed air like many-petalled, noisy flowers. Someone cut open a pie filled with live frogs, which leapt beneath the ladies' farthingaled skirts. To avenge themselves, the ladies threw candied peel and jellies at the gentlemen. Towards the end of the feast, the servants carried in a sugar mountain covered with sugar animals. Scented fire issued from the mountain's rocks and crevasses.

Lorenzo Nadi, Fiametta's father, calculated the combined assets of the guests present, and estimated them worth all the gold the illusory El Dorado had to offer. He watched Angelo Guardi, whom he had begun to consider as a prospective son-in-law, and noted that his appearance and manners were impeccable. Appearance was so important in matters of business: a man's worth was judged by the cut of his cloak, the confident show he made to the world. Lorenzo had given Messer Guardi an easy introduction to Florence – meeting with the family yesterday, attending the banquet today – but tomorrow would not be so easy. Tomorrow, they would talk trade, alone and undistracted by the entire nonsense of courtship and love.

The Guardi notary, a rather unpleasant Frenchman, became very drunk and Angelo Guardi had to take him away into a back room. The notary did not reappear the entire evening, but he was not missed. Angelo Guardi was an intelligent, charming young man, who could handle a drunken employee just as capably as he could steer a ship, or take a few dozen horses and five thousand ducats' worth of cloth to the fair at Lyons.

Giulia Nadi, Fiametta's mother, danced with a Medici prince and a Donati lord, and then retired, prettily exhausted, to the garden on the arm of the younger Frescobaldi. She would dance with dear Angelo later, when both her daughters had retired to bed, and Lorenzo had found some tedious old bore to play backgammon with. On their first introduction Giulia had seen and noted the flutter of interest in Angelo Guardi's dark eyes, and had been amused by the fact that he had quashed that interest almost instantly. She had known then that Angelo, as well as being handsome, was intelligent. Sitting on a marble bench inside a grotto, with nice young Niccolo Frescobaldi crawling among the shells to kiss her insteps, Giulia anticipated an enjoyable week ahead.

Nencia, Fiametta's younger sister, watching the banquet from the top of a staircase, scowled and chewed her fingernails to the bone in envy. Fiametta herself saw her, peering furiously through the banisters, so Fiametta made herself smile even brighter, dance even more gaily so that Nencia should see what a wonderful time she was having. Mama had almost given in to Nencia's entreaties and given the wretched child permission to attend the banquet, but Fiametta had put her foot down for once, refusing to speak to anyone or dance with anyone if Nencia came. Nencia had her mother's hair and large dark blue eyes. She was small and neat, and she *flirted*. Even when, like now, she was sulking, Nencia still looked pretty. She had not, like Fiametta, spent each summer bleaching her hair in the sun, whitening her skin with milk and raw veal.

Once, Fiametta had intended to marry a prince, to live in a house in Florence with three dozen servants, to wear a different gown every day of the year. But no prince had offered: every available prince, thought Fiametta, her smile twisting bitterly, had already fallen in love with her mother. Soon they would fall in love with her sister. So instead she might marry Angelo Guardi. Messer Guardi was rich and good-looking and well-mannered, and of mixed French and Italian origin, but he was not a prince. He had a large cloth-carrying company in Marseilles, and a ship that he had named after Fiametta. Apart from that ship, Angelo had courted her father as much as he had courted

Fiametta herself, admiring papa's extensive silk-workshops, his highly skilled weavers and dyers. His attentions to Lorenzo Nadi were necessary: if his suit was accepted, Angelo Guardi would marry the Nadi business empire just as much as he would marry Fiametta herself. And it was not she who would decide his acceptance.

Taking Angelo's hand in the complicated steps of a galliard, Fiametta wondered momentarily what it would be like to share a bed with him. She knew what would be expected of her, of course. If Mama had not yet found time to explain, then still she had seen dogs copulating in the street, a kitchen-maid and her lover on an attic landing. Coldly considering, she knew that she would not like such intimacy: she knew also that she would endure it, because it was expected of her. The only alternative was the convent, and the sort of power and privacy that a mother superior might possess. But Papa would never allow that.

The following morning, Lorenzo Nadi sent for Angelo.

He made his bow to the older man in Lorenzo's study, an impressive book-lined room, with panelled walls of polished beech. There was a carved, gilt ceiling and a marble doorway and fireplace. He had had only four hours' sleep, but Lorenzo, who had still been playing backgammon when Angelo had finally retired to bed, must have had less.

'Angelo. Sit down.'

Lorenzo gestured to a nearby armchair. Lorenzo himself sat behind his desk, which was piled with papers, festooned with quill pens. He had already, estimated Angelo from the length of the letter in front of him, put in at least an hour's work that day.

'You enjoyed the banquet last night?'

It was hardly a question, more a sort of demand, but Angelo smiled, and said, 'Immensely, sir. It was an impressive occasion.'

'Quite.' Lorenzo shook back the sleeves of his fur-trimmed robe. 'And so useful, too, don't you agree? I'm sure that half the business of Florence is carried out at such affairs.'

Lorenzo was of more than average height, bull-necked and bald-headed, his power reflected in his heavy build. Lorenzo

Nadi had two hundred silk-weavers and dyers and carders working for him. But he was a banker as well as a silk-merchant, with a banker's head and a banker's heart. Not for him the excitement of finding himself part of a huge chain extending from Cathay to the northern cities, an excitement that had infected Angelo long ago, standing in Franco Guardi's warehouses. Lorenzo was fired by ducats. And by écus, and florins, and silver reals, and by nothing else.

Angelo murmured his agreement. Lorenzo's tragedy was that he had two daughters, nineteen-year-old Fiametta and thirteen-year-old Nencia, and no sons. Daughters were nothing but an expense: even the Duke of Tuscany would claim seven crowns in every hundred of Fiametta's dowry. Without sons – without grandsons – the houses in Florence and in Umbria, the silk-workshops and the bank, were all futile. Lorenzo Nadi's accumulated wealth would be inherited by an obscure and disliked second cousin in Naples.

'But still. To other matters.' Lorenzo sprinkled sand on the letter in front of him, tipping the excess neatly into the palm of one hand. 'My business has grown a great deal in the past few years, as you know, Angelo; indeed, I am almost outgrowing Florence! I intend to look for other markets – reliable markets.'

Angelo took a deep breath, knowing that his opportunity had arrived. 'The Guardi,' he said smoothly, 'have traded with the cities of the north for fifty years now. In their heyday, we used the cloth fairs at Lyons – now I send my mule trains further north. We went as far as Paris last year. In Paris, you can buy cloth from London, Antwerp, Amsterdam. In time, they say, we will be able to purchase furs from Muscovy there.'

Angelo found that his mouth was rather dry, his tongue seemed to stick to the roof of his mouth. Unusually for him, he longed for a glass of wine.

But Lorenzo Nadi only nodded in agreement. 'Furs, linen, broadcloth – I have not yet traded in such items. But one must diversify, don't you think? If not, one atrophies.'

Or dies, thought Angelo. He, too, had diversified over these last, difficult years. He had found outlets for trade that even Lorenzo would never have considered. His dealings in tin, for instance, had proved gratifyingly profitable. Until his last voyage, the *Fiametta*'s maiden voyage, when things had gone wrong. It had all seemed so simple. He had had information from an acquaintance of his, Tommaso di Credi, a Pisan merchant, that an English ship, the *Garland*, was carrying tin from Livorno to the Levant. The information had proved correct, but even so Angelo had lost three men, and had almost quarrelled with the Turk.

Still, he might not need Hamid for much longer, and there was time enough to repay the *Garland* for her impudence. The English Levant Company's ships were becoming more and more of an irritation in the Mediterranean. It was time that someone clipped their wings a little.

'Diversification,' said Angelo, 'contacts – are invaluable. But so is transport, Messer Nadi. With my ship, the *Fiametta*' – he smiled – 'I can buy raw silk in the Levant as well as the best Persian cloth. At the most reasonable prices, of course. With the *Fiametta* I can trade, ultimately, between Muscovy and Scanderoon.'

The idea of those webs of trade, stretching their spider skeins across most of the known world, appealed to Angelo. And to Lorenzo Nadi, too, he thought, watching the older man. The lashless lids had hooded, the firm lips had tightened, twisted.

'You have the ship, you have the business contacts,' said Lorenzo, looking up. 'What more do you need, Messer Guardi?'

What he meant, but did not say, was *why do you wish to marry my daughter?*

The back of Angelo's neck had begun to perspire, but his expression was unchanged. He said, 'I need an alliance with someone who owns silk-workshops. The Guardi used to know a family here, but the connection was lost.'

The Corsini had owned silk-workshops. The head of the family had been Michele Corsini, little Serafina's intended betrothed, whom even Angelo had not had the gall to court after the deaths of Franco and his daughter.

'I need that sort of family connection – that sort of goodwill – again. That would improve my profits considerably. And . . .' He paused and swallowed. His dark eyes were wide and disarming. 'The last few years have not been easy for the merchants of Marseilles, as I am sure you know, Messer Nadi. Things have changed now, it is true, we have a King again, but . . . there is still the legacy of those lean years.'

Lorenzo Nadi said drily, 'You have debts, sir?'

Angelo swallowed again. Old devil, he thought. He was roasting over a hot spit, and that spit was being turned, quite deliberately, by Lorenzo Nadi. 'Yes,' said Angelo, simply. 'I have debts.'

Which was why he was here, of course, courting a tall, freckled girl, and enduring this interview. Lorenzo asked the inevitable question, and Angelo gave him a reasonably honest answer: the sum of his debts. And while Lorenzo sniffed and calculated and asked impertinent questions, Angelo considered Fiametta, his prospective betrothed.

Fiametta had missed utterly the unarguable beauty of her mother, Giulia. Now *there* was a woman – a neat, curving figure, hair like the metal threads in cloth of gold, eyes of unmistakable invitation, and an air of indolent fragility that her elder daughter utterly lacked. It had been Nencia, thirteen-year-old Nencia, who had inherited her mother's hair and eyes and manner. In Fiametta, the red-gold hair had become sandy, the eyes had lightened until their colour was indistinguishable. She was tall, almost Angelo's height, and because she knew that she was tall, she carried herself badly. She also lacked the easy flirtatiousness of her mother and younger sister; her conversation was as gawky as her body. She had scarcely allowed Angelo to touch her, dancing last night.

Angelo supplied Lorenzo Nadi with another figure and, stifling a yawn, considered the prospect of taking Fiametta to his bed. It would be like making love, he thought, to the ice-blocks they dragged down the mountains to provide coolness in the summer: forbidding at first, and then a pleasurable melting. If he could have chosen, then Angelo would have had Giulia, or little Nencia, instead. But he could not choose, and because of that, he had not openly responded to Giulia's invitation. Even Giulia's charms were insufficient for Angelo to risk Lorenzo Nadi's wrath, so he had confined himself to indulging in the occasional

enjoyable fantasy. Nor had he flirted: he had known, in-
stinctively, how much Fiametta would have loathed him flirting
with her mother.

Lorenzo's pen was still scratching numbers on the paper. He
was surprised, thought Angelo wryly, that Lorenzo had not sent
for his clerks and an abacus. All the struggles and vagaries of
Angelo's past four years were inscribed there, with no regard
whatsoever for Angelo's feelings. But Angelo found that he
respected Lorenzo for his method, his hard-headedness, his lack
of emotion.

Eventually Lorenzo straightened, putting down his pen. 'It's a
tidy sum, Messer Angelo.'

Angelo noted the continued use of his forename with relief.
He kept his voice calm, his attitude unharassed.

'That's true. But with a single successful voyage I could repay
the bulk of it. That's the value of the *Fiametta*, you see, sir.
That's why I borrowed in order to build her.'

'You would need,' said Lorenzo, folding his hands in front of
him, 'to borrow more money in order to finance such a
voyage.'

Angelo did not let his gaze drop. 'Yes, sir.'

'If your voyage was successful, then you could, as you say,
pay back most of what you owe. If, however, it was unsuccessful,
then' – and Lorenzo raised his cold eyes, Fiametta's eyes, from
the paper – 'then you would be bankrupt.'

Lorenzo smiled. Angelo inclined his head, acknowledging the
truth of the older man's words. He watched as Lorenzo Nadi
rose from the desk, and went to stand by the small-paned
window that looked out over the Nadis' garden.

Eventually, after a pause that seemed to Angelo to last for an
hour, Lorenzo said, 'Very well, then. I shall consider lending
you the money for your next voyage – at a suitable rate of
interest, of course. As for Fiametta – I shall also consider your
betrothal. I will write to you, Messer Guardi. Be assured that I
shall look upon your suit favourably. Quite favourably.'

Lorenzo said just one more thing as Angelo rose and walked
towards the door.

'Oh, and by the way. Your notary, Messer de Coniques. A

good and faithful servant, no doubt, but perhaps you should consider whether he has not worked for you long enough. His behaviour last night did you no credit at all.'

Old devil, Angelo thought as he left the room, closing the door behind him. He found that he could almost feel the heat of hell scorching the soles of his feet.

It was two hundred and fifty miles from Pisa to Marseilles, two hundred and fifty miles of threading their way round the Gulf of Genoa, past the Côte d'Azur and the Iles d'Hyères, and into the Gulf of Lions.

Before the *Kingfisher* set sail, however, its owner and its master went on another journey. Into the green Umbrian countryside, this time, to visit the youngest Capriani, safely hidden where the only seas were those of ripening corn, fringed with poppies and cornflowers.

Francesco was well, his wet-nurse content, Serafina having paid over the odds to guarantee that contentment. She did not stay long, there was not time to stay long. She rode away within the hour, Thomas her only escort, back through the heavy heat-hazed countryside. Stopping for a drink of water in the shelter of an orchard, they found themselves making love again. Around the orchard was a fringe of flax: the gentle violet-blue echoed the colour of the sky. The air was sticky with heat, and when, afterwards, she dressed herself, Serafina discovered bruised petals glued to her gown, dotting the black silk with sapphire. The physical comfort that Thomas Marlowe had offered and she had accepted helped to blot out the misery of leaving her baby.

They set sail two days later. The *Kingfisher* was loaded with silk goods, velvets and taffetas, cloth-of-gold and silver. The weather was still very warm, and the mariners had to search for a breeze, adjusting sails and rigging to make the most of what little wind there was. Images fluttered through Serafina's mind as the galleon made her way out of the harbour at Pisa. Herself, ten years old, encased in black velvet, standing on the poop-deck of a galley, her hands clutching the gunwale. It had been hot then, too, and the sunlight had hurt her eyes. Now she shaded her eyes with her hand, watching the spires and towers and rooftops of Pisa fade into irrelevant distance, watching the life she had created for herself slip away as she gave herself up once again to the uncertain sanctuary of a ship. If she felt fear, it showed only in the whiteness of her knuckles, in the sharpness of her voice as she spoke to her maid, Luisa, who, like the long-lost Mathilde, was sea-sick.

She found that she envied Thomas his busyness. He had his charts and his instruments, his instructions to call to his helmsman, his bosun to supervise. She had only to make sure that she was neither a distraction nor an impediment. At night, if he was lonely, then Thomas had the stars to read, companions to talk to. She had only the four wooden walls of her cabin, shared with the miserable Luisa.

She began to understand the workings of the ship, and the men who sailed her. The masts were no longer just masts, but a mizzen-mast, a foremast, a mainmast, and a bowsprit. The sails ordered themselves into mainsails and topsails, topgallants and spritsails. Even the stars at night, when Thomas found time to teach her, became comprehensible patterns. Sometimes, when they sailed out of sight of the coast, the sky was a limitless blue bowl, the sea its reflection, the horizon lost in the meeting of water and air.

After three days' sailing, the Lanterna, Genoa's great lighthouse, appeared from the darkness like just another star, low-slung on the horizon. The air, the sea, and sky were almost motionless; the dreamy peacefulness of the midsummer evening had pervaded the decks of the *Kingfisher*. Serafina was still on deck, having put off the moment of confinement in the oppressive heat of her cabin with the nauseous Luisa until the last minute. Standing at the gunwale, she saw the star, not where a star should be, and exclaimed.

'It's the Lanterna, Madonna Capriani. The lighthouse. We've reached Genoa.'

William Williams, the *Kingfisher*'s carpenter, stood beside her. He was a head taller than Serafina, and a quiet, gentle man – quieter, Thomas had explained with a grin, since his voyage to Naples, and his encounter with the courtesan's daughter, Maria.

With the sighting of the lighthouse, the tranquillity of the scene shattered. Thomas's voice split the heavy air, calling instructions to the helmsman and bosun, judging the *Kingfisher's* entrance into the harbour with all the skill of twelve years' experience.

It was late evening, and the port of Genoa was lit by the great glow of the lighthouse, by the sconces on the walls and the open doors and windows of the taverns. Serafina could see the boats that crammed the harbourside: the fishing boats, the barques, the great galleasses and, of course, the galleys. Genoan galleys were seventy-five paces long, and each chained four hundred slaves to the benches.

As the *Kingfisher* neared the dockside, she could see also the expressions on the torchlit faces of those who watched. Envy, pleasure, and admiration mingled as the *Kingfisher* slid smoothly into port.

The next day Serafina left the ship to call on the merchants of Genoa. The cobbled streets seemed unsteady under her feet, the beautiful Via Aurea confining after the freedom of the open sea. But here she was no longer workless or useless. In Genoa, a Spanish possession, Serafina, armed with Thomas as her factor and the respectable alibi of widowhood, introduced herself to Jacopo's customers and acquaintances, charming them, bargaining with them, trading with them. She bought luxury fabrics, sold ribbons and cockades and semi precious stones. Once she sold bezoar, at a considerable profit, and did not look at the English pilot's face as she smiled at the customer and said, *Antelope's tears. To cure snakebites.*

In the evening, she found herself invited to banquets, dinners, masques. She went to every one of them, complaining about the heat with the ladies, striking bargains to do with grosgrain, or bombazine, or panne velvet with the men. She met the great families of Genoa: the Fregosi, the Adorni, the Doria. She walked in exquisite, dusty Genoese gardens, talking of ducats and écus, interest rates and transport problems. She had become that rare, desirable creature: a beautiful and rich young widow. Men brought her wine, sweetmeats, sent her posies of flowers and perfumed handkerchiefs. If she had been plain, still they would have courted her, but she knew from the light in their eyes that she was not plain. She accepted their gifts graciously, on moonlit terraces, in marbled halls. And when she turned, Thomas was always there, with an arm for her to lean on when finally she tottered home at night. They never shared a bed, were rarely alone in each other's company. Serafina had learned the lesson of the charivari too well to court that sort of humiliation again. But sometimes she found herself watching him: seeing the tanned, muscular forearms as he rolled up his shirtsleeves and spread out his charts on a table, noting the line of his shoulders beneath the silk doublet.

They left Genoa after a fortnight, having sold many of the silk goods bought in Naples, and filled the gap in the hold with the finest Genoese luxury fabrics. The cloth was all colours, jewel colours, rainbow colours, trailing through her fingers like striped and shaded river-water. One day, thought Serafina, as she climbed up from the stifling darkness of the *Kingfisher*'s hold to the sunlit deck, she would manufacture fabrics like that. Capriani cloth would be prized as greatly as Venetian, or Genoese.

By midday, the city of Genoa was long out of sight and they were following the line of the Ligurian coast. The narrow maritime seaboard of the Kingdom of Savoy was lost in a haze of lavender and indigo. The *Kingfisher*'s sails bellied in the breeze, the sailors, stripped to their waists in the July heat, adjusted sails and rigging to make the most of the wind. The coastline was dotted with ships like autumn leaves on a pond. Caiques and barques, fishing boats and rowing-boats, galleys and galleasses. The smaller boats put in frequently at the tiniest fishing ports to trade: a barrel of fish in exchange for a cheese, a basket of oranges for a length of sailcloth. Even the ocean-going round-ships like the *Kingfisher* put into port most nights, dropping anchor in some moonlit bay, and sending a loaded rowing-boat into harbour to trade if prospects looked worthwhile.

The following day, climbing up the stairs on to the foredeck, Serafina's light silk gown felt heavy in the intense midday sun. Thomas was standing on the bridge, the familiar battered black hat crowning his head, his wide shirtsleeves flapping a little in the wind. He was staring out to sea, beyond the bowsprit, beyond where the figurehead, gleaming blue and gold in the sunlight, struggled to take wing.

Reaching his side, Serafina followed Thomas's gaze out to sea, to where a single ship gleamed far away on the horizon.

She guessed the name of that ship before Thomas spoke a word. The specious calm of the past few weeks snapped; the pleasures of Genoa, the tranquillity of the open sea, all faded, like the mirage she knew them for. Peace was only an illusion: the djinn were still out there, shaking at the walls of her home.

The ship was a threading of gold against a turquoise sky: a demon ship, with masts of gold and a crew of ghosts. In spite of the heat, Serafina shivered.

'It's the *Fiametta*. I'm sure of it,' said Thomas, evenly. Turning, reckoning in his blue eyes, he called for his bosun.

He had no fear of the *Fiametta*. She might still figure in his dreams, but she had long ceased to be the nightmare phantasm that he had once mistaken her for.

But he saw the expression, an impossible mingling of terror and hope, hatred and loss, on Serafina's face. When he had finished calling instructions to his crew, Thomas drew Serafina aside, and said, 'We could go and take a look at her. Would you like that?'

She nodded. She said simply, '*Can* you?'

'Yes.' Thomas, leaning on the gunwale over the bowsprit, stared out again to sea. The golden ship on the horizon drew infinitesimally closer, shape-shifting from shimmering insubstantiality into a thing of timber, rope and sailcloth.

Serafina's dark eyes were fixed on the *Fiametta* as though even at such a distance she could find that one, well-remembered face, and study it, and become intimate with all her enemy's weaknesses. Thomas, touching her arm, felt that he was trying to pull her back to the present, to reality.

'She won't know me, of course,' he said, nodding in the direction of the *Fiametta*. 'I'm sailing a different ship now, flying a different flag. Of no possible connection with the English Levant Company's *Garland*. The *Kingfisher* – the Capriani company – is of no significance to Angelo Guardi.'

He might have added *yet,* because he did not intend it to remain that way. But Thomas saw Serafina's eyes narrow for a moment, and then a rare smile – a true smile of happiness and pleasure – brightened her small severe face. Above them the flags of Tuscany and the pennants of the Capriani company, blue and gold, curled in the wind. He saw her take a deep breath.

'Then – let me see how fast she can sail.'

He felt his own smile answer Serafina's. For a moment, Thomas let his hand fold over hers, small and white and clenched on the gunwale. Then, leaving her, he returned to the business of letting his ship fly untrammelled for the first time, unleashing her so that she could stretch her wings as she soared across the Ligurian Sea.

It became a race. The two ships would have sighted each other at much the same time, and were, Thomas guessed, bound for the same port. How could any master, navigating his pride and joy across the wide blue seamless expanse of sea, resist such a challenge? In spite of the oppressive heat, each ship strained to gather the wind and reach Marseilles first. Standing on the bridge of the *Kingfisher,* Thomas knew that Angelo, too, used every inch of sailcloth, every available man, to put an extra yard between the two galleons.

By mid-afternoon, there was still half a league of water between the two ships, but they were close enough for those on board the *Kingfisher* to read the name that gleamed on the *Fiametta*'s hull, to distinguish the tiny figures on her decks.

William Williams, coming to stand beside Thomas on the bridge said, nodding to the distant ship, 'And when you catch her – what will you do?'

He had asked the same question nine months before, in Zante. And still the answer was unchanged.

'Nothing,' said Thomas, studying the *Fiametta.* 'Yet.' He added, 'The one thing Messer Guardi hasn't economized on is cannon. He's enough ordnance on that ship to start a small war. And besides –'

He stopped. William finished the sentence for him.

'And besides, a pitched battle between a French and a Tuscan ship might not be such a good idea?'

Thomas grinned. 'Not here, anyway. In the Levant, perhaps, where no one would notice.'

But he had not, he thought, as his gaze slid for the hundredth time that day to Serafina, now sitting alone on the quarter-deck, any real intention of rolling out the *Kingfisher*'s demi-culverin. Serafina wanted to destroy Angelo Guardi, but not by drowning him. And whatever his own right to vengeance, Thomas knew that it was insignificant compared with hers. Almost ten years ago, in these same seas, Angelo had taken by treachery almost everything that Serafina had valued. Whatever she was now, it was Angelo who had made her. Sometimes Thomas feared that she would remain for the rest of her days a puppet of Angelo's creation.

She was sitting by the gunwale on the quarter-deck, quite still, her features pale against her dark hair and black gown. Her face was turned towards the *Fiametta*, and Thomas knew too well who she was looking for.

That night they weighed anchor in a small cove off the southern coast of France. Half a mile further up the coast the *Fiametta* did the same. The following morning, the *Kingfisher* set sail early. But as they rounded the headland, they saw that the *Fiametta* was already out on the open sea, her sails the only white in a cloudless sky, a long V-shaped wake dividing the water behind her. Angelo Guardi, thought Thomas, intended to use this apparently casual encounter to prove both his ship and his seamanship.

By mid-afternoon they had lost sight of the *Fiametta*. Avoiding the treacherous passages around the Iles d'Hyères, Thomas had taken the *Kingfisher* well out to sea, away from the sharp rocks and treacherous sandbanks. Angelo, who had sailed the route from childhood, still clung to the coast for speed.

Soon, however, rocks and shallows were no longer Thomas's only preoccupation. The sky was no longer clear, a great band of cloud thickened the sky to the south. The heaviness of the air had become almost tangible, and the wind fidgeted irritably around the *Kingfisher*'s sails and rigging. There would soon, Thomas knew, be an almighty thunderstorm.

Quickly checking the decks, he saw Serafina and her maid still sitting on the quarter-deck. She had scarcely moved from there since he had first sighted the *Fiametta*. Glancing at her every now and then he had recognized her tension in the set of her narrow shoulders, heard it in her ill-temper as she snapped at her maid.

His concern was a different one now, though. She was his responsibility, her safety was dependent on his skill in navigating the galleon through a storm. Crossing the decks to her, nodding a perfunctory bow, Thomas said, 'I'd like you both to go to your cabin. Now.'

He knew as soon as he spoke that he had, as so often, chosen his words unwisely. The maid, Luisa, rose obligingly, her embroidery gathered in her hand, the corners of her mouth already trembling. But Serafina's cold dark eyes studied him and she did not yet rise.

'Because there's going to be a storm, Mr Marlowe? I think I would prefer to stay on deck.'

And of course, she, too, had noticed the freshening wind and ominous grey-green clouds massing on the horizon. And, of course, she had inevitably turned a reasonable request into a challenge. He almost said, *You'll go to your damned cabin now if I have to carry you there myself*, but he became aware that some of his crew were listening, hoping for entertainment. Cristofano, in particular, had put down his mallet and nails, and was openly grinning.

Thomas felt the familiar exasperation rise, and he struggled to keep his temper.

'Madonna, we are in for one hell of a thunderstorm. And though *you* might prefer to stay on deck, *I* would prefer you both to go to your cabin. You'll be safer there.'

'Mr Marlowe.' Serafina had risen now, her voice was soft, her smile sweet. 'Perhaps you may recall that I have sailed through storms before now.'

The scar from the gunwale of the tartane was still visible, high on her brow. If she had been one of his crew, thought Thomas angrily, then he could have punished her for insubordination, but she was not one of his crew, she was a part-owner of his ship. And he was not going to provide his men with the enjoyable spectacle of a quarrel between ship's master and ship's owner.

Thomas said, equally softly, 'Whatever you wish, madonna. No doubt my men will appreciate the sight of you with wet hair and soaking clothes. I certainly will. But for God's sake, send your maid below decks, before she drives us all insane with her snivelling.'

He was rewarded by a scowl almost as black as the thunder-clouds, and the sight of Serafina turning on her heel and stalking off below decks, with the dismal Luisa scuttling behind her. Thomas heard a poorly disguised snigger from Cristofano, who had been close enough to hear every word of that small encounter, so he gave the youth the unpleasant job of checking the safety of the goods in the hold, and went to his cabin to consult his charts.

He wondered, as he studied the pattern of sandbanks and coastlines, what the *Fiametta* would do. He himself was too far out to sea to make seeking any shelter other than Marseilles worthwhile, but if he had been Angelo Guardi, he thought, he would have put in at the nearest available cove in the Iles d'Hyères. But somehow, he had begun to doubt whether Angelo would do that. He was beginning to build up a picture of the master of the *Fiametta*, from what Serafina had told him, from what he himself had seen in Zante, in Civitavecchia, in Marseilles. The master of the *Fiametta* was a clever man, undoubtedly: it would have taken both cleverness and cunning to arrange matters in Zante. And to organize the original abduction of Serafina and her father from these waters. He must also be diplomatic, and charming. He had made an ally of Hieronymo Carcandella in Zante and, far more difficult, had bargained with an Algerian corsair. Long ago, he had gained the trust of Franco Guardi and corrupted the lawyer Jehan de Coniques. And he had enchanted the child Serafina. Some of that enchantment still lingered.

But he was not faultless, because no one, Thomas had long ago realized, was faultless. Angelo's mistakes were beginning to form a pattern, a fascinating, coherent pattern. There had been the house in Marseilles, gaudy with gold-leaf. And there was the

Fiametta, her gilt beakhead and stern battered by the churning surf. Both beautiful, both flawed, both, in their way, follies. That ostentatious, taunting house was surely a folly in a city as febrile as Marseilles; the ship was a folly because Angelo had spent too much money on decoration, and insufficient on building a sound structure. He was keeping up appearances, as Serafina had said, spending his money on outward show: a typical mistake of the nameless and base-born.

So, though it might be sensible of Angelo Guardi to turn tail and take the nearest shelter, it occurred to Thomas, as he rolled up his charts and secured his astrolabe and backstaff, sand-glass and log line, that he would not do so. The *Kingfisher* might be a stranger, their race a mere bagatelle to brighten an otherwise dull voyage, but to Angelo it might be a little more than that. Angelo Guardi would, guessed Thomas, want to win. Angelo Guardi would *expect* to win, because his entire adult life had been spent in winning.

Thomas did not welcome the tempest, but he knew that, however well a ship might sail in fine weather, a storm was the only true test of its seaworthiness.

And besides, he, too, wanted to win. For himself. And for Serafina.

In Marseilles, the following day, the fisherman Jules Crau watched the two galleons sail into port.

Although he was a fisherman by trade, he no longer owned a boat of his own. He had owned a boat once, his father's boat, but age and bad weather had done for her, and eventually, no matter how much he had patched her, he had known her to be no longer seaworthy.

So he had sawn up his boat, and used her for firewood one particularly bad winter. That had been four years ago, the winter his wife had died – of a miscarriage, ostensibly, but in reality of too little food and too much work.

Jules had one child, a girl of seven, called Isabelle. Since the loss of the boat he had earned a living by providing an extra pair of hands on other people's boats. That living had always been poor, and had lately become almost non-existent. Work had been difficult to obtain for years. Things had improved when Marseilles had fallen under Charles de Casaulx's government, but Casaulx had been assassinated in February. Jules had admired Monsieur de Casaulx, had stood in the street and cheered with the rest of them when he rode past. There had been hope then. Now, Jules looked around him at the grand houses of the rich merchants, and knew there was no place for him in the scheme of things.

Had it not been for Isabelle he sometimes thought that he would have disposed of himself as he had once disposed of his boat. But Isabelle was the light of his life: without her, there was, simply, darkness. So he continued to search for work, because of Isabelle. Isabelle would have been pretty if she had had more to eat: she had inherited her mother's curling brown hair and smooth dusky skin. Last winter, though, she had developed sores round her mouth, and her eyes, great dark eyes, had become sad and resigned. She was silent for hours, sometimes, sitting in the corner of the room they shared, her hands loose in her lap, staring at the wall.

She was at home now, sleeping soundly, because that morning Jules had taken her out to the countryside, to the fields of poppies and marguerites that surrounded Marseilles. The sun had shone and the sky had been a clear purplish-blue, the grass fresh with rain from the previous night's storm. Jules had carried his daughter out into the fields and woods, a heartbreakingly weightless burden balanced on his own square shoulders. He had picked daisies for Isabelle, and had sung songs, and once she had even laughed.

But halfway through the morning her eyes had dulled, and she had put her hand to her belly and told him that it hurt. She so rarely complained that he had been frightened. She had not even been able to walk back to the path: her pathetically thin little legs had collapsed like spent matchsticks, and he had had to scoop her up in his arms again. He had known the cause of it, of course. She was, quite simply, hungry. She was permanently hungry, had been hungry all her short life. He had also known, with terrible certainty, that she would not live through another bad winter.

She had been so tired when they had got home that he had wrapped her in a blanket and laid her sleeping on her pile of straw in the corner of the room. Asking a neighbour to keep an eye on her, Jules had then gone out to the docks to search, as usual, for work.

And again, as usual, there had been nothing. He had tramped around the rows of small fishing boats moored against the harbour wall. The fishermen, who were his friends, had shaken their heads and spoken of hard times, and he had seen his own pity and hopelessness reflected in their eyes. One of them had pressed a package of mussel shells into his hands, and Jules had accepted their charity, for Isabelle's sake.

He could not offer himself as a deckhand aboard the larger merchant ships because of Isabelle. He had no one that he could trust to look after the child while he was away at sea, and he knew that the thin thread of her life would break without his constant care and attention. He knew also that his own fragile sanity would not survive such a loss.

Jules watched the two great galleons dock as he sat on a barrel, the package of mussels beside him. He could not read, but he knew from the flags that one ship was Tuscan, the other French. Some of the French ship's sails flapped, uselessly ragged, on the yard-arms, and one of the foremast stays trailed in the water. Casualties of last night's tempest, thought Jules Crau. The Tuscan ship, which had arrived at Marseilles a half-hour before the French, was still in good repair, however, and its crew were already beginning to furl the sails to the yards.

But it was the French ship that held Jules Crau's hungry eyes, because of the feast of gold on her superstructure. The occupants of the golden galleon had begun to file down the gangway. Servants carrying bags and boxes, sailors checking the ropes that bound the ship to the quayside. And a man, surely the master of the ship.

The master was dressed in red, with a short red and silver cloak. He was rich, young, handsome, and Jules found himself walking across to him, intending to do something his pride had never permitted him before.

He heard his own voice, rough and clumsy, mumbling something about the hard times and his starving daughter. He saw the ship-owner flinch as his own dirty hand touched the smooth velvet sleeve, and then, miraculously, the rich man fumbled in his pocket and dropped something into Jules's outstretched palm.

Opening his hand, Jules looked down.

A button, made of horn.

To Angelo Guardi, Marseilles looked dirtier and more crowded for his weeks of absence in Italy. The docksides and streets stank; Marseilles was rough, coarse, lacking the elegant sophistication of Florence. And the beggars seemed to breed like the rats they increasingly resembled, milling in every alleyway, every courtyard, ugly and foul-smelling.

Angelo despised beggars. Like many self-made men he found the beggar's lack of pride and lack of industry contemptible. He, who had created himself from nothing, rejected those who still wallowed in the gutter they had been born to.

It was all his, though, he thought, inside the spacious old house that had once belonged to Franco Guardi. Yet sometimes, even after ten years, it still felt strange to him to walk inside this house unannounced, to sit at this table and drink wine brought to him by a maidservant, and ask no one's permission. There were ghosts here, sometimes: Franco's laughter echoing against the painted walls, the whisper of Marguerite's silk skirts in the passageways, and the child's footsteps, light on the tiled floors. Still, sometimes, he found his hand bunching to knock at a door, his footsteps hesitating at the entrance to Franco's study. Still, all that he had struggled for occasionally seemed insubstantial as though, closing his eyes, he would wake to find everything turned to dust.

Methodically, Angelo attempted to shake off the low spirits that seemed to have accompanied his return to his birthplace. His factor had traded well in Naples and Civitavecchia, he himself had selected profitable luxury cloths in Florence. He told himself that any lingering anxiety was foolish: that he should account the visit to Florence a success, that he could not have hoped for more from a man such as Lorenzo Nadi. But he found that he was not used to worrying about the future; he was used to controlling it. He told himself that Lorenzo would write soon giving his consent to the betrothal.

Cradling his wine-glass in one hand, rubbing his closely shaven chin in the other, Angelo thought that if Fiametta Nadi was no beauty, then there were surely some advantages in marrying a plainer woman. Unlike Lorenzo Nadi, he would not have cause constantly to doubt his wife's faithfulness. Knowing himself to be good-looking, attractive to women, Angelo could expect both devotion and constancy from Fiametta.

Raising his eyes, Angelo could see through the window the harbour, crowded with ships. At last, gazing at the masts with their furled sails, black spillikins against the turquoise sky, he identified the cause of his low spirits. Two days previously he had sighted a Tuscan ship off the Ligurian coast, a galleon that had borne, peculiarly, the English name of *Kingfisher*. She had been a fine ship, the *Kingfisher*, but he had known the *Fiametta* to be her equal, and had allowed himself to be drawn into a race with her. He had hardly slept last night, nursing the *Fiametta*, somewhat battered by the sudden tempest, round the treacherous Iles d'Hyères. Then, to his chagrin, he had discovered on reaching harbour that he had lost. The Tuscan ship was already in port: she had swung round from the open sea into the Gulf of Lions, reaching Marseilles before him.

Angelo almost laughed at himself, that he should mind losing a casual, unannounced challenge from a stranger. He knew then that his melancholy was only a natural consequence of the exhaustion following a sleepless night and he wondered, idly, whether the master of the *Kingfisher*, too, longed for his bed.

The master of the *Kingfisher* had, in fact, just fallen into a deep, dreamless sleep, when the joint-owner of the *Kingfisher*, knocking at the door of his cabin, woke him.

She had to go over to his hammock and shake him. Serafina found some pleasure in doing so, some small repayment for the boredom of a night encased with a weeping, vomiting Luisa in a cabin the size of a dog kennel.

Eventually, cursing her, Thomas groaned and swung himself out of the hammock.

'I'm going to open Jacopo's house,' said Serafina, eyeing Thomas critically as he ran his fingers through his tousled black curls. '*My* house, that is.'

He frowned, looked blearily up at her. 'You woke me up from the first sleep I've had in thirty-six hours to tell me *that*?'

She said impatiently, 'I've woken you to tell you, Thomas, that though *I* will live in the Marseilles house for the duration of our stay here, *you* will remain on board the *Kingfisher*.'

His eyes were blank for a moment, and then he scowled and looked at her suspiciously. 'Why?'

'Because it will be more suitable. People will gossip if we share the same house. I am a widow, after all.'

He was silent for a moment. Serafina found that she avoided his gaze.

'Don't,' said Thomas eventually. 'It's too dangerous and you'd only hurt yourself. Wait. You'll get your chance.'

She felt her face grow heated, but she made herself speak calmly. 'What do you mean, Thomas? Don't what?'

He smiled nastily. 'Don't call on cousin Angelo. Don't invite him to a nice cosy dinner à deux. Don't arrange yourself on the altar like some damned sacrificial lamb.'

But this time, instead of berating him for his intolerable interference in her life, Serafina laughed and said, 'I have no intention of doing anything of the sort. I will live alone in the Capriani house because it will be more respectable to do so, that's all.'

And Thomas, rolling back into his hammock, said only, 'Then at least I'll get my bloody cabin back,' and, closing his eyes, fell asleep.

In Pisa, the courtesan Costanza entertained the banker, Galeazzo Merli.

They had eaten together in the company of several of Galeazzo's friends and associates; they had sung together, Costanza's warm low voice drowned by Galeazzo's tuneless bawl. And then the friends and associates, at Galeazzo's bidding, had left, and there was only a table full of dirty wine-cups, and a rug scattered with breadcrumbs and grape-pips, and Galeazzo, seated in an armchair, watching Costanza.

He was still eating: grapes travelled steadily from hand to mouth, pips were spat purposefully to the floor. But his eyes studied Costanza as though she were a particularly interesting set of account-books: interesting, but not necessarily likeable. Galeazzo was always eating or drinking, thought Costanza, rising and taking her lute from where someone had placed it carelessly in a pool of wine. Eating, or drinking, or making love. She did not offer him love, because she never offered him love. It was up to him to ask for what he was owed.

Tonight, though, he did not grab her as she walked by, nor pull her up the stairs to the bedchamber. Instead, he just sat there, surrounded by the squalor that his friends had made, watching her. Eventually, he said, 'You had a house-guest, recently. An Englishman.'

Gently wiping her lute clean, Costanza almost smiled to herself. So that was it, she thought. Messer Merli feared the loss of one of his possessions.

'That's right. He stayed with me earlier in the year – Thomas Marlowe. You remember him, surely, Galeazzo.'

Her voice was calm, because she had, after all, nothing to hide concerning her relationship with Thomas. Besides, she had made no vows of fidelity to Galeazzo. Theirs was a business arrangement, an exchange of money for services received.

'Oh, I remember,' said Galeazzo, taking a peach from a nearby bowl. 'He was at my banquet last autumn. He arrived with the Levant Company representative – what was his name? – Keane.'

He split the peach in two with his thumbs: pink juice spilled over his doublet as he prised out the stone. 'I hear,' said Galeazzo slowly, 'that you sailed with Messer Marlowe recently. To Naples.'

She replaced the lute on the corner-table. She had unthreaded the ribbons that hung from its neck; they had been ruined by the wine. Turning to Galeazzo, Costanza said, 'Messer Marlowe was kind enough to offer me a passage to Naples on board his ship. He viewed it as an attempt to repay me for the weeks I let him stay here. There was never anything more than friendship between us, Galeazzo, I assure you.'

He had placed one half of the peach in his mouth: the juice dribbled stickily on to his chin. His small dark eyes still watched her, so she went to his side and placed her hand on his shoulder and said, firmly, 'Nothing more than friendship.'

He had finished eating the peach. One of his hands circled her wrist, tightly and stickily.

'Messer Marlowe is also a friend of the widow Capriani,' said Galeazzo. 'Or so they say.'

Costanza said nothing. Galeazzo had begun to lick the sticky circle that surrounded her wrist: she could feel the rasp of his chin against the back of her hand. She knew that he wanted to pull her into his lap and take her here, amongst the orange peel and the dregs of the wine. But she was not a common whore, so she freed herself, and started up the stairs, letting him follow behind.

When he had finished, and slept, she heard the knock at the door. She had risen, tidying her hair and putting on a robe, before she heard the scuttling of feet as Hélion ran to the door and opened it. Galeazzo still slept, sprawled naked on top of the sheets, sweat glistening on his face and scalp. The small ineradicable fear that always accompanied unexpected visits, or footsteps behind her in alleyways, resurfaced, so she took the stiletto knife from her bureau and a candlestick and walked noiselessly down the stairs, shutting the bedchamber door behind her.

She heard Hélion's unbroken voice first. And then the second voice: high-pitched, too, but this time a girl's voice.

She recognized that voice immediately. Dropping the stiletto on the stairway and placing the candlestick on a table, Costanza had her only daughter Maria in her arms in less than a minute.

When she had reassured herself that Maria was safe and well, she stood back, looking at her wayward child. Maria wore the new gown that Costanza had had made for her in May, and her brown hair, poorly contained by a rather ugly hat, sprang in unruly curls and ringlets around her forehead. The gown was torn at the hem, and some of the lace was already coming away from the collar. Her eyes, meeting Costanza's with no attempt at evasion, were untroubled.

'Talking in needlework?' said Costanza, sternly. Her voice was not quite steady. 'Visiting the docks?'

Maria shook her head. 'Sister Esmeralda had to leave,' she said. 'And it was my fault.'

Gradually, amid the chaos of Costanza's dining-chamber, the whole dreadful story came out. Maria had found a kitten: no – a man had given a kitten to Maria. It was a Persian kitten, with blue fur and yellow eyes, and it was absolutely adorable. It also had an injured front paw. Maria had stolen ointments from the convent infirmary and hidden scraps of food in her pocket, and slowly the creature, cradled in a chest in her bedchamber, had begun to recover.

Unfortunately, whenever Sister Bonaventura had walked past Maria's room, she had begun to sneeze. Maria, fearing discovery as Sister Bonaventura's suspicions grew, had been forced to transfer the kitten to Sister Esmeralda's care. Even more unfortunately, Sister Teresa, who normally would not have noticed an elephant hidden in the cloisters, saw Sister Esmeralda, the kitten buried beneath the folds of her habit, on her way back to her cell. Fearing the worst – demons and suchlike – on spotting the writhing beneath the starched folds of linen, Sister Teresa had called for Sister Bonaventura.

'She drowned the kitten,' said Maria, mournfully. 'And when I tried to explain to her, Mama, that it was nothing to do with poor Esmeralda, that it was all my fault, she wouldn't listen. She said that Sister Esmeralda had accepted a gift from a man, and so she was not a suitable person to become a nun. I was to scrub the kitchen floors for a week during morning recreation, that's all.'

She added, 'It's because you promised her candlesticks, and Sister Esmeralda's family have nothing, isn't it?' and Costanza, who had been about to fulfil her weary maternal duty, and scold, was silenced.

She said instead, 'How did you travel, my dear?'

'Oh, I found a ship. Not a galleon, like Messer Marlowe's, but a little barque. It was wonderful. And – and I left a note for Sister Bonaventura.'

'Good,' said Costanza, faintly.

She saw that there was no point in reasoning, in writing placating letters to the convent of S. Chiaro, in promising more candlesticks, more altar-pieces. She saw also, looking at Maria's calm hazel eyes, that her daughter had made her decision, logical amidst a morass of hypocrisy, and that any attempt to alter that decision on her own part would be equally hypocritical. There was nothing for it: for a while, at least, Maria must live in Pisa.

She had, for a moment, forgotten Galeazzo. But a heavy footstep on the stairs, and the opening of the dining-chamber door reminded her abruptly of why she had sent Maria to Naples in the first place.

He was fully dressed now, a powerful, imposing figure. Costanza saw his eyes light upon Maria instantly, and she rose and went to her daughter's side, one arm protectively around Maria's shoulders.

Galeazzo smiled. 'Perhaps you should introduce me, Costanza.'

She said, stiffly, 'Maria – this is Messer Galeazzo Merli, a friend. Galeazzo – this is Maria, my daughter.'

Maria smiled. Costanza heard the tautness, the anxiety in her own voice as she added, 'Go to bed now, my dear. It's late.'

She saw Galeazzo Merli's eyes following her daughter's trim figure as Maria left the room. Had the stiletto knife been in her hand, she knew that she would have used it, there and then.

She heard Galeazzo say, softly, 'Sometimes one remembers the infinite charms of youth,' and then she felt his hands gripping her shoulders, turning her and forcing her to look in the silver mirror opposite.

The light of the single candle emphasized the channels of age in her face, dug from nose to chin, and the shadows around the deep-set eye-sockets. The scar that pleated the curve of her jaw seemed just as much a violation now as the day she had received it.

'Do you think,' whispered Galeazzo, his fingers digging into the soft, slightly sagging skin of her neck, 'that you will be able to earn your own living much longer? Look in the glass, Costanza, and think again. You may have to get others to earn it for you.'

Never, she thought, fighting for breath through anger and fear as he released her and turned and walked out of the house. *Never.*

PART XI

1596

RIDING AGAINST DUST

Handkerchiefs with silk of several colours wrought. Glazen eyes to ride with against dust.

Things to be carried, from the Notes for the Discovery of the North-East Passage:
Richard Hakluyt

If she had feared that she would have, in Marseilles, too much time to think, then Serafina found that at least that torment was denied to her. The days, crowded with small irritations and small triumphs, were too busy for coherent thought.

She opened up Jacopo's house on the outskirts of Marseilles, flinging sheets off furniture, choking at the dust she raised, transfixed momentarily by the way the sunlight turned the motes to gold. She had lived in this house before, two years previously, when Jacopo had hired her as a serving-maid from the fair. A great deal had happened in two years.

The house was ugly and poorly furnished, but she did not care. She turned a downstairs room into an office for herself and her clerks, engaged a reasonable cook and a few servants. She hardly noticed the heat, the flies that worked their way through shutters and curtains, the noise from the nearby alleyways and courtyards. She worked long into the night, and rose early in the morning. Because there was work to do, and because here, in Marseilles, she could not sleep.

She told herself that it was the heat that stopped her sleeping, but she knew that it was not. When she closed her eyes the past returned: vivid, varied dreams that allowed her no rest. Sometimes she would dream of nothing more than the harbourside, only a short distance away, and would wake, dazed with illusory happiness, because she had stood looking at the ships, her father's hand in hers. At other times, there was the janissary, with the branding-iron, and an acre of hot, empty time to be endured before dawn.

She avoided Thomas as much as possible. Foolishly, she had let him know her too well, so that he had come to understand the fears and ambitions her soul was made of. She did not need his understanding: she needed only his intelligence and energy. She confined conversation between them to the subject of business – the transfer of cloth from ship to warehouse, the capacity of the *Kingfisher's* hold, the length of time it might take to sail from Pisa to the Levant. She kept her other discoveries to herself, to occupy the silent hours of darkness. That Angelo Guardi was rumoured to have borrowed too much money, that he was struggling to pay for the goods with which to fill the greedy hold of the *Fiametta*. If her dreams had not kept her awake, then those tantalizing, half-expected snippets of information would still have denied her sleep. She knew that Thomas would see the hope in her eyes, so she kept her distance from him, dining with him occasionally, perhaps, her expression bright and uncommunicative, her touch rare and deceitful.

Business was successful, Marseilles's new freedom from isolation allowing an easier transfer of goods to the north. She had Jacopo's long list of customers and contacts as well as her own, culled from the bankers and merchants of Pisa, Livorno and Genoa. She had the respectability and freedom of widowhood, as well as the attractions of youth. She had something they all could respond to, whatever their natures: charm or beauty, or common sense. A head for figures, a figure to turn heads. The columns in the order-book grew satisfyingly; the cloth and silk oddments she had bought in Naples or manufactured in Pisa were sold for a good price. In the evenings, when the rest of the house was sleeping, she sat in the accounting-room studying figures.

Eventually, she walked by herself to the golden house. She went in the daytime: at night-time, she knew, a drawling voice would say, *I'd as soon sleep with my mare, Pietro. At least she only stinks of horse-shit.* Standing at the street corner within sight of the house that had once been her home, Serafina wore an embroidered black silk gown, and a veil of Brussels lace. Her skin was perfumed with patchouli, softened with rosewater and oil of hypericum. Men glanced at her as they walked past, and smiled, and nodded their heads in a bow. She was no longer poor, or plain, or dirty.

Shading her eyes from the sunlight, Serafina saw that the gilt on the Guardi house had begun to fade a little, the gaudy paint to peel from the walls. Beneath the gold-leaf was the pale brick-work she remembered from childhood. It was as though the house itself had begun to slough off the glittering new skin that Angelo had impressed on it, shaking away the scales to show the true form beneath.

She was smiling as she walked back through the busy streets. When she reached the Capriani house she went into the office and began to write the letter.

The notary Jehan de Coniques brought two letters for his employer, Angelo Guardi.

The first Angelo opened immediately, his face almost betraying his concern as he broke the seal in half. His eyes were hooded, hidden from Jehan as he scanned the paper. He read quickly. The letter was from Lorenzo Nadi, setting out the details of their proposed agreement. More of a contract than a letter, in fact, thought Angelo wryly, smiling at last.

Jehan, watching him as he studied the letter, sniggered and said, 'I'm sure she'll keep herself virgin for you, Angelo. They're shut away like nuns, these Italian girls.'

It wasn't so much the coarseness of the notary's speech that provoked Angelo to an untypical anger – born, he later realized, of tension – but the casual use of his own forename. They had once been equals, he and Jehan de Coniques, with a history of disinheritance in common, but time and the patient manipulation of people and events had drawn their stations apart. But the notary had never acknowledged that distancing: the name Angelo slid as easily from his tongue as it had in former days when, to safeguard his own position, Angelo had courted him.

He did not yet let his anger show, however. 'You'll draw up the necessary papers, Jehan,' he said, coldly. 'I expect to become betrothed to Madonna Nadi in the spring.'

The notary slopped more wine into his glass, and giggled. 'Mon ami, I'm good at drawing up papers,' he said. His voice was slurred, his skin grey and slack. 'To your bride,' added Jehan de Coniques, raising his glass. 'To the beautiful – and rich

– Fiametta Nadi. To transgression's reward – fifty thousand ducats and a nineteen-year-old's maidenhead –'

The notary's hand trembled so that wine spilled over the carved table, eating into the polished wood. Angelo moved behind him, one hand gripping the bony wrist, the other spanning the thin neck.

The wine – *his* wine, the best Candian wine – sprayed over the rugs and furniture. The glass, a cut Venetian goblet, shattered into fragments on the table-top.

'Transgression,' said Angelo, softly, his mouth close to Jehan's ear, 'in which you took as great a part as I. Does your conscience trouble you now, my compliant lawyer? Does one nubile young girl remind you of another, sent to a different marriage-bed? A marriage-bed we both arranged?'

He still gripped Jehan's hand so that it faced down towards the table. Slowly, Angelo pushed the notary's open palm towards the shards of glass that glittered on the wood. He heard Jehan's indrawn breath as his skin was pierced, and glass ground its way through flesh and tendon.

He let go, suddenly disgusted by the ragged greasy hair that swung in his face, the sensation of bone and loose skin beneath his fingers. The notary had not cried out: only his eyes had reddened, as though with tears. Though, years ago, Angelo had mocked Jehan de Coniques for his old name and his tattered inheritance, he had once respected the notary's competence with the labyrinthine ways of the law. Now, Jehan seemed to have drowned that respect in a sea of alcohol and envy.

Walking to the window, away from the marbled crimson and scarlet that pooled the table-top, Angelo threw wide the shutters. Behind him, he heard the notary rise and shuffle to the door, his breath coming in painful gulps. There was dust from the shutters on Angelo's hands, and the stench from the ordure in the street below assaulted him. He found that he was shaking, that the events of the past few months had tired him: he, whose greatest asset had been his unlimited strength.

He reminded himself that the worst was over, that now he need fear no longer the loss of all that he had fought for. With the sudden overwhelming onset of relief, his heartbeat slowed and Angelo drew the other letter from his pocket. First, he split the seal, which he did not recognize. Then he read the inscription at the foot of the page, *Capriani*, and his eyes, amused now, were drawn back to the harbour, to the forest of ships, great and small, that crowded the water. He could not see the galleon *Kingfisher*, but he knew the name of its owner. Thorough as always, he had discovered that the galleon was owned by the merchant Capriani, and, much more interesting, that the merchant Capriani was a woman.

He found that he was smiling. He found also that he was curious. He reminded himself that he deserved to celebrate, after all. The widow Capriani might be an ugly old hag with a hook nose and double chin, but Angelo thought not. He had – and he smiled again – heard reports to the contrary.

Calling his secretary, he began to dictate replies to the two letters. The first, to Lorenzo Nadi, was easy enough. The second, to the mysterious Madonna Capriani, took a little more thought, but he was, eventually, pleased with the result. In deference to the addressee's nationality, the letter was written in Angelo's own perfect Tuscan Italian. Madonna Capriani, owner of the *Kingfisher*, was requested to dine with Messer Guardi, owner of the *Fiametta*.

In London, in Greenwich, Faith Whitlock helped her husband pack for his forthcoming voyage.

'Shirts,' she said, pointing to the pile on the linen-room table. 'One dozen linen, a half-dozen silk. Falling bands and ruffs. I've starched them all, Ned, but they may wilt if it's hot.'

Edward Whitlock, who was always fidgety before a long voyage, fiddled with the baskets of pegs, the jars of starch and pot pourri on the window-sill. Outside, the rain disguised the season, flicking spitefully against the panes, churning Faith's herb garden to mud.

Faith said, with an eye to the weather, 'When will you sail, Ned? How is the wind?'

Edward, crumbling pot pourri between his fingers, grimaced. 'Turning, I think. We should be gone by the end of the week. I intend to sail round the Cape in October. The Spaniards should be sleeping then.'

She never allowed herself to worry for him or for any of them, never dwelt on shipwrecks or storms, greedy corsairs or vengeful Spaniards. She would not have kept her sanity had she done that. She had learned long ago that the only way to survive on your own was to make a life of your own, a life that was as enjoyable and absorbing as possible. Calmly, Faith counted the bundle of laces in front of her, while Betty, the maidservant, folded the shirts and placed them in the open chest, scenting the linen with sprigs of dried lavender.

'– forty-nine, fifty,' finished Faith, taking a spare lace and tying it round the bundle. 'Did you get your ordnance, Ned?'

'Oh, yes. Richard Staper always sees sense eventually.' He turned, knocking over a box of brazil-wood set aside for dyeing. Stooping, Edward scrabbled around the floor, clumsily picking up fragments of wood. 'The *Legacy* and the *Saviour of Bristol* have each a half-dozen more cannon. And the *Garland* was refitted last year in Livorno.'

There was a short silence.

Then Faith said lightly, 'Help Master Whitlock with the brazil-wood, Betty. Does John Keane sail with you, my dear?'

Edward stood up, wiping his hands on his breeches.

'John's taking the *Legacy*. He's to marry Dorothy Jenkinson on his return. Did you know that, Faith? Her father died last week. Old devil – even poor Doll is relieved, they say, though she wouldn't admit to it.' He grinned briefly, and added, 'I'll sail as master of the *Garland* – she's a cranky little ship. Needs someone who knows her. She'll make it to Alexandretta and back, though, Faith. I've never lost a ship yet.'

Turning, he began to scrub his hands, dusted red-brown by the brazil-wood, in a bucket of water. The rain was slowing, and the small band of watery sunlight on the top of his head showed where his red hair had begun to thin, and the scalp to show through. 'What's this stuff for, anyway?' he said, gesturing to the box of brazil-wood that Betty had replaced beside the sink.

'It's to dye the bed-curtains,' said Faith, folding doublets. 'They're looking a mite faded.'

Edward said nothing. His back was to her, his head bowed as

he bent over the bucket. Faith, putting aside the doublets, went to him, placing her arm round him, leaning her head against his shoulder, embracing him as tenderly as she would embrace her own small son or daughter.

'Dear Edward,' she said. 'Little Ned would like a janissary's curved sword, but you're not to bring him one. Some chessmen will do – he's lost most of the last set you bought him. And Alice will have beads, or some such fripperies. And you're to buy me a length of silk if you can, for the christening gown. The lining is a little torn.'

He turned, his hands dripping water. He looked puzzled, confused, thought Faith, which he never looked when planning an eight-thousand-mile round trip to the Levant. Kissing him, she insisted that he smile.

'Having a baby is a simple thing, after all,' she said, gently. 'And it will keep me busy, won't it, my dear?'

Serafina went to the golden house alone.

It was over a month since the *Kingfisher* had berthed in Marseilles: a month of buying and selling, planning and searching for information. And she had known, long before she had sailed from Pisa, that this meeting was the only true end of her voyage.

And yet, somehow it seemed to have come too quickly. She was not ready: she should have had more time. Standing at the foot of the steps that led up to the house, Serafina told herself that that was nonsense. She had intended this meeting for months – no, years. For two and a half years, in fact, since she had last stood here; since she had begun to learn that, along with fear and loss, there existed also betrayal. Since then she had manipulated people, coaxed events, all to this end. She had planned with care, she reminded herself, and now her plans were about to come to fruition. Thomas was in Avignon and could not possibly return until tomorrow; her business in Marseilles was almost done, the *Kingfisher*'s hold was loaded with valuable cloth. Only this one most important business remained.

The door was opened by a maidservant who took her gloves and light shawl. She could see her reflection in the silver mirror over the fireplace in the hall: an exquisite gown, black, beaded with dusky pearls, trimmed with cuffs and a half-ruff of stiffened blonde lace. Dark hair, coiled smoothly into the nape of the neck. Great dark eyes and a smooth, pale skin. She had thought of brightening her cheeks with the red lead, but, remembering Thomas's criticisms, had angrily replaced the jar, unused, in her bureau.

Mine, she thought, looking round the house. My home, occupied by someone who has stolen my name. Yet, unexpectedly, looking round, she found that the familiarity of the house was only partial, as though she had previously seen it in a picture, or glimpsed it in a dream. The rooms that followed off the hall seemed smaller, less mysterious, their furniture bland, lacking the colour of her memories. She recognized the layout of the house, and some of the furnishings, but only by referring to the catalogue her mind had made of the past. Kitchens, scullery, and linen-room, leading from a passageway to the right. Hall and offices on the ground floor. Upstairs – following the maidservant's clacking heels on the oak treads – the dining-chamber and parlour. A twisting brass candelabra on a table: once, she had enjoyed replacing that candelabra's finished candlesticks. A tapestry, motionless in the airless evening: once, she had counted the horses on that tapestry, and given them names. Destrier and Bayard and Dancer and –

'Master,' said the maidservant, when they had reached the top of the stairs. 'This is Madonna Capriani.'

And her eyes, which had flicked through the familiar yet unfamiliar house, unable to rest on anything, looked to the doorway. A man, standing framed by the architrave, the candlelight burnishing his dark gold hair.

Angelo.

If the house, by some strange alchemy of stone and mortar, had changed, then Angelo had not. He was just the same: those features matched exactly the ones printed in love and hatred on her memory. Eyes, mouth, nose, hair, a living representation of the face that had haunted her dreams for years. She did not need to study that face: she knew it. It was in her heart.

Because she had spent most of her life hiding her feelings, she was able to hide the emotions that swamped her now. She was able to give him her hand so that he might kiss her fingers, and smile, and murmur inanities about the weather, the unbearable heat.

It was only when she had preceded him through the doorway that her eyes closed for a moment, the lids squeezing tightly shut. She recovered herself quickly, though. She saw that the table was set for two. She had hoped for that, because what she intended to say to Angelo Guardi was better said in private. She knew also that Angelo did not recognize her, that the years that had transformed her from child to adult had changed her beyond recognition. Angelo saw neither the scrawny child who had sailed into the corsair's embrace, nor the filthy boy who had once slept at the foot of his own well-scrubbed steps. And after all, he thought she was dead. He would not expect the hot September night to have conjured up a ghost.

'It was impertinent of me to write to you, Messer Guardi,' she said. The name, her own name, was hard to use. 'I was curious, you see, to meet the owner of the *Fiametta*.'

Angelo smiled, as the servant poured them both wine. 'Madonna, if it was impertinence, then I could only wish to encounter impertinence more often.'

She took the glass, and sat down at the table. This room had always been the dining-chamber; here, a long time ago, her father had told her of her betrothal to Michele Corsini. If she closed her eyes again, what spirits might she not summon up?

But her eyes remained open. She knew that she must keep herself to the present, that she must make use of every ounce of wit and intelligence she possessed.

Angelo seated himself opposite her as the manservant began to bring in the food. 'You have a fine ship, madonna. The *Kingfisher* is an English name, I believe?'

She nodded. 'The galleon was built by an Englishman.'

She had a suitable lie ready, if necessary. A false name, a shipwright who had since returned to the country of his birth. She knew that Angelo might recognize Thomas's name, his nationality. That was one reason why she had kept the English pilot on board ship, or sent him riding up the Rhône valley to trade, instead of allowing him to remain in Marseilles. But not the most important reason.

But no lies were necessary. Angelo merely raised his glass, and said, 'Let us drink to the winner of the race, then, madonna. I congratulate you. I'm not often bested, and the *Fiametta* too is a fine ship. But I find myself content to lose to such a delightful adversary.'

The glasses touched, a small sound like the chime of a bell in the drowsy silence of the room.

'Not *adversary*,' said Serafina, softly. 'I would not have you an adversary, Messer Guardi.'

'Then what would you have me, madonna?'

She did not reply, but she saw his dark eyes widen a little, and a smile curl the corners of his mouth.

He added, lazily, 'You are a widow, I understand, Madonna Capriani?'

She was eating, but she did not know what she was eating. It might have been oysters and strawberries, or earth and dust.

Angelo's dark eyes studied her with unmistakable interest. Serafina's hand trembled as she lifted her glass. Somewhere in the back of her mind Thomas's voice echoed, *You were in love with him. My God, you still are.* But, she told herself, Thomas was mistaken. The emotion she felt for Angelo Guardi, the emotion that burned, she knew, in her own eyes, was nothing other than hatred.

She drained her glass, seeking, unusually, equanimity in the wine. 'Yes, I am a widow, Messer Guardi. My husband, who was a merchant from Pisa, died earlier this year. I had the temerity to think that I might attempt to continue his trade. For my child's sake, you understand.'

'You have a child, madonna?'

She inclined her head. Did Angelo ever think of that other child, the one he had sent to her death almost ten years previously? If she said the name, *Serafina*, would his face whiten, his jaw drop?

'I have a son. Francesco is only a baby. But he'll inherit the Capriani business when he comes of age. I merely – inadequately, I'm afraid – try and preserve his inheritance for him.'

'Inadequately?' Amused, Angelo dismissed the waiting man-servant with a wave of his hand. 'You don't do yourself justice, madonna. I've made enquiries. I hear that merchants of twenty years' standing are in awe of you, that you strike such hard bargains they tremble at your footstep.'

He had put down his glass. He wore a silk shirt, lace-collared, covered by a sleeveless scarlet doublet, paned with bands of black taffeta. His eyes studied her intently, and Serafina felt a film of sweat gather on her upper lip, the back of her neck, between her breasts.

'For myself,' he said, gently, 'I might tremble for a different reason. I hear that you are a powerful woman, madonna. And I see that you are a very beautiful one.'

There was no breeze in the room. Her eyes were held by his as though he were a candle-flame, and she a fumbling, light-starved moth.

Eventually, she said, 'Beauty is a two-faced card, Messer Guardi. Some of your fellow-merchants regard a beautiful woman as a precious glass, too fragile for the rough world of trade. Others think that she must be hollow – stupid – that she can have nothing else but beauty. And others think, simply, that she must be a whore.'

She had put down her knife, unable to eat any more. She could hear the whine of a mosquito, and servants' voices calling from below. But they did not seem part of this house, this moment.

Angelo, too, had finished eating. He rose from his seat, giving Serafina his hand to help her to her feet. He did not let go of her hand, but enfolded it in his fingers, holding it close to the black and scarlet panes of his doublet.

'A fragile woman would not race a galleon through a tempest. A stupid woman would not have earned herself a respected reputation during a month's trading in Marseilles. And a wanton woman –'

He paused. Serafina could feel his heartbeat through the thin covering of silk. She knew that her heartbeat, like his, pounded faster and harder than normal. She felt as though the intense late summer heat was melting her, stripping her of covering until she was bare to the bone.

'A wanton woman,' Angelo said at last, releasing her hand, 'would not have written me a business letter. She would have made sure to encounter me – by accident, of course – at the harbourside, or in the market-place, or in another merchant's house. It would have been easy enough, wouldn't it? She would have hidden her face behind her fan, or laughed, and shown me a glimpse of ankle beneath a ruffled hemline. Then she would have walked away. And I, eventually, would have followed.'

There was a silence. Once, Serafina thought, he had rejected her, laughed at her. Now he wanted her. She could see it in his eyes.

And that frightened her. That he might still possess the power that had captivated her infant soul, so long ago. She could not think of such a thing.

'Trade.' Her voice was raw, uneven. 'You trade in cloth, I believe, Messer Guardi.'

He bowed, and held open the double doors of the dining-chamber, so that she could walk into the ante-room beyond.

'As you do, Madonna Capriani. I buy broadcloth and linen and fustian from the north, silks and brocades and taffetas from Italy and the Levant. I built the *Fiametta* to make the transporting of cloth as economical as possible.'

It was no cooler in the ante-room. The windows were open and unshuttered, but there was no breeze. The air was thick and heavy, as it had been in Algiers.

Serafina said dreamily, 'We silk-merchants try to barricade ourselves against all possibilities, don't we, Messer Guardi? You with the *Fiametta*, I with the *Kingfisher*. But there are always variables, aren't there? Always the unexpected, that we cannot guard ourselves against.'

Angelo leaned back in the chair, stretching his elegantly hosed legs out in front of him. The room was small: he had shut the doors so that she felt enclosed with him in the tiny space. 'I disagree, madame,' he said softly. 'I seek to have everything under my control. I plan for every misadventure. That's the secret of my success. That's why I have this house, this ship, this business. I was not born to it, madonna.'

She felt an appalling desire to laugh, to cry, to claw at his smooth, unblemished skin. But words were her only weapon here, so she controlled herself and said, 'Neither was I born to the situation in life in which you see me, Messer Guardi. We have both fought for what we want, then. And yes – you have a house, a ship, a business. But I have made enquiries, and I have looked with my own eyes. The paint is peeling from your house, sir, and your ship was built with borrowed money. The Marseillais have endured hard times, everyone knows that, and the merchants of Marseilles have suffered more than most. You can plan, Messer Guardi, but you cannot plan against the tides of history. They are invincible.'

She thought that she saw a flicker of anger in the opaque dark eyes. But it passed in an instant, replaced by a smile, a gesture of acknowledgement.

'Madonna Capriani, you are superb! And you are correct, of course. The years of dictatorship, of isolation, were not easy for me – or for many of my associates. And yes, I've borrowed for my precious *Fiametta*. But I've survived, as many older names have not. But still, I say, we must plan. We must plan for every contingency God sends.'

'We cannot read the mind of God.'

There was a bitterness in her voice that she had not intended to show. Serafina saw Angelo rise from the chair and walk to her side and, kneeling, take her hand in his.

'You speak of your husband, of course, madame. You are very young to have experienced such a loss.'

He had knelt beside her: she could have reached out and touched the familiar dark gold hair, have let the back of her hand brush against his cheek, his mouth. She could have kissed him; she could have closed her eyes and recalled in every detail the kiss he had once given her, standing on the hillside beyond this city. Yet she had since learned that kiss to have been nothing more than a mark of betrayal, just as every smile, every kind word, every touch of his, had also been a betrayal. Angelo's pretended affection for her childhood self had been nothing more than coinage with which to buy Franco Guardi's trust.

She felt her self-control slipping through her hands like sea-water, filling up a vast and uncontainable ocean of desolation.

She knew she must keep hold of herself; that she had struggled for years to gather the means to wound him, to destroy him, to possess him. But ghosts haunted this room, making the house suddenly familiar. Flickering traces of the past and its inhabitants assaulted her, distracting her.

She dug her fingernails into her palms, so that four red crescents formed on the white skin, like the scarlet symbols of Islam that had marked the corsair's bleached sails. The ghosts dissolved, she could think clearly again.

'I love my son, but I never loved my husband, Messer Guardi. My husband was an old man. I married him because he was an old man. Women, too, plan. I still plan, for my son's sake. Shall I tell you why I wrote to you, why I wanted to see you? I have made enquiries, you see. I know that you are deeply in debt, and I come to offer you a solution. A merchant needs capital, or he dies. Can you afford to finance another voyage, Messer Guardi? Can you afford to repay your debts?'

She was insolent, she knew. Yet Angelo's face did not betray resentment, only interest. He was looking at her, his hands gripping the ends of the arms of her chair so that she was encircled by him. His eyes were bright, steady. Almost loving. She had learned to distrust that affection, had learned to fear the fascination he exerted.

'A solution?' said Angelo slowly. 'Tell me, Madonna Capriani – what solution do you offer?'

She made her eyes meet his, made herself say the words she had planned for so long.

'I am offering to buy your company, monsieur. So that I may combine it with my own. In Pisa I have money to spare but insufficient room for expansion. Let us solve our mutual problems. Let me spare you the ignominy of bankruptcy.'

She wanted to see the fear in his eyes at the word, *bankruptcy*. Yet there was nothing: the dark almond-shaped eyes, the mirror of her own, were expressionless.

'I would keep the name of Guardi, of course.' Her voice shook slightly. 'It is, after all, so much better known than Capriani.'

Suddenly Angelo rose to his feet in one neat movement, and

she found herself expecting the casual violence of her dreams, the planned, unregretted violence she knew him capable of. She had to steel herself to remain motionless, not to draw back from his physical presence.

But he did not strike her, did not lift his hand. Instead, Angelo threw back his head in a great peal of laughter, and said, 'Again, you are superb, Madonna Capriani! I could almost offer you my ship, my business, myself. But no –'

Shaking his head, he took her hands and drew her to her feet. He smiled. 'It will not do, you know,' he said, gently. 'I cannot sell myself to you. I cannot even – as I might almost be tempted to do – offer you a different sort of partnership, my dear. Because I do not need you. I have already found a solution to my problems, large though they undoubtedly are.'

His dark eyes were amused, confident, and utterly fearless.

'I am to be married, you see,' he said.

Angelo, and his beautiful, rich young bride. Serafina had not known, could not have known, how that news would touch a dagger to her heart, pressing the blade inwards, slowly. A part of her, it seemed, was still in the hills behind Marseilles, rosemary and columbine threaded through her hair. She had wanted restitution, she had wanted what was due to her. She had wanted a restoration of all that she had lost. She had wanted the future to atone for the past.

But Angelo, in a perverted mirror-image of her own long-distant hopes, was to marry a well-born Florentine girl. He would sail to Tuscany, his galleys gilded and pennanted, his rich clothes and bride gifts stored in treasure-chests in the hold. And no corsairs would waylay him, cutting his life in two. He would marry, and he would father children. Legitimate children.

She had remained in the golden house for another quarter of an hour or so, mechanically saying the right words, making the right gestures. As soon as she had felt strong enough to do so, she had risen and taken her leave, and made her way into the street. Yet she did not return to the Capriani house. Instead, she wandered round the silent streets, through alleyways and courtyards where no woman should have walked alone. She thought, later, that the expression on her face had protected her, that even a thief would not rob a ghost. For in Marseilles, Serafina now knew, she was nothing more than a ghost, a forgotten remnant of the past, a shadow that should no longer have existed.

There were beggars sleeping against the doorsteps in the alleyways, and huddled in barrels and crates in the courtyards. Surely there had not been so many beggars before. Great throngs of the dispossessed, hungry and diseased, workless and nameless. A hand touched her skirt, and she cut the purse from her waist and let the coins, gold and silver, shower on to the cobbles. As she walked on, Serafina took the wedding ring from her finger – Jacopo's ring – the pearl drops from her ears, and the pendant from her neck and threw them to the dark, writhing figures.

Later, at the harbour, she stood at the edge of the quay. It would have been easy enough to take a step forward, to let herself slip from the safety of the stone into the sticky lapping black water below. Yet she no longer had the will to make that choice. She was a slave again, existing, functioning, but not living, denied the fundamental human right of choosing between life and death. She was nothing: she saw the truth clearly now, reflected in the still opaque water. She was homeless and nameless, she was the powerless product of another person's whim, just as if she had never left the bagnios of Algiers.

Eventually the sun rose, streaking the sea with orange and pink. A signal to return, for the revenant to go back to its half existence. Walking through familiar streets and squares, Serafina knew only that she must leave Marseilles, and never come back.

She did not arrive at the Capriani house alone, however. As she reached the doorway, another figure was riding down the street. Black hair, blue eyes: she did not recognize him at first, because he belonged to a different life. But she allowed him to lead her out of the street and into the house.

Her hair had become unpinned and trailed about her pale face; she wore no jewellery, and her gown was hemmed with mud. Serafina's appearance shocked Thomas: he thought that if he touched her, her brittle soul would fragment into a thousand pieces. He said, with utter certainty, 'You went to him.' It was a statement, not a question.

She nodded, her eyes dead.

Then, supposing another, appalling, reason for her condition, Thomas said, 'He hurt you.'

She looked up at him slowly, and shook her head. Then she said, 'No. Not in the way you mean. Angelo didn't touch me. He didn't know me. I've been walking, that's all.'

One fear receded, immediately replaced by another. Walking all night, she meant. Wandering round this tense city on her own, from midnight to dawn. Her skin was almost translucent, her eyes darkly shadowed. In spite of the heat, she shivered.

Thomas found her a comfortable seat in her own accounting-house, wrapped a warm shawl round her shoulders, and forced a glass of wine into her knotted fingers. He thought of sending for her maid, but decided against it. Servants gossiped. He had returned from Avignon early, distrusting Serafina's motives in sending him there. Now he knew his distrust to have been merited.

When, at his insistence, she had drunk some of the wine, Thomas said, 'Serafina. Tell me. What happened?'

The glass was cradled in her lap. Eventually she looked up, her dark gaze not finding him, focusing on nothing.

'I went to his house to offer to buy the company.'

'The Guardi company?' Leaning against the window-ledge, Thomas stared at her. 'But how could you? It is not –'

'Angelo is near bankruptcy, Thomas. I made enquiries. I've helped him travel a little further down that road myself. By taking his customers, spreading rumours.'

Her voice was flat, toneless. The wine in her glass swayed and bobbed as though she were on board ship. He realized that even he had not fully understood her ruthlessness, the meticulous detail of her planning.

'And –?' said Thomas, gently. 'Were you mistaken?'

She shook her head. 'No. I was not mistaken.' Her mouth twisted in a travesty of a smile. 'I discovered that Angelo has already found someone to sell himself to. He's to be married.'

Thomas let out his breath. He wanted to go to her, to cross the gulf that lay between them and put his arms round her, holding her in the tender embrace she had so rarely permitted him. But he knew that to do so would be folly, that though she might have grown to respect his ambition, his competence, she had never loved him, and never would until she freed herself from the entanglements of the past.

'She is Florentine,' said Serafina. She stared ahead, her eyes flicking aimlessly over Thomas, the accounting-house, the distant sunlit Mediterranean. 'She comes from a wealthy family. Her father is a banker and silk manufacturer. Angelo has the ship, the contacts, the knowledge of the trade routes. Messer Nadi has the capital and the weaving-shops. They will benefit each other.'

There was something in Serafina's voice now, even if it was only bitterness. A little colour had returned to her cheeks, and her hands had steadied. Meeting Thomas's eyes for the first time, she said, 'Angelo's bride is nineteen and her father's only heir. She has no brothers. Her name is Fiametta Nadi.'

Fiametta. Of course. That great gilt ship.

'He named his ship for her. What woman, he said, could resist a man who builds her such a beautiful galleon?'

He could hear the pain in her voice, and something else, too: envy, he thought.

'I should have guessed,' added Serafina, to herself. 'Of course he would marry. Of course she would be rich, beautiful, and wellborn. Women always liked Angelo.'

He noticed that her eyes were red with exhaustion, not with tears. He thought how rarely he had seen her cry. Thomas knew that there was nothing to say, no words of comfort he could offer. She had regained some of her usual possession, but there was still that dreadful emptiness in her eyes, replacing the anger or deceit that now, strangely, he had almost begun to miss.

Serafina said, 'Angelo intends to sail to the Levant. If the voyage is successful, he and Fiametta Nadi will become betrothed on his return. The marriage, I should imagine, will follow soon afterwards. He will not want to wait.'

Thomas had thought once that she might forget Angelo, that, absorbed both by her son and by her work she might allow the injustices of the past to remain in the past, unrevenged, if not forgotten. Now he saw that that was not so, that she would destroy herself if she could not destroy Angelo. And still, he could not bear to watch that.

She had risen, putting her wine-glass aside. She began to pile books and papers into a chest, kneeling down on the floor, her muddied silk gown falling in wide folds around her. She added, 'Angelo will travel to Florence first to collect the gold with which to finance the voyage. Monsieur de Coniques sails with him to witness the drawing up of the marriage settlement. Monsieur de Coniques – '

She stopped suddenly, and sat back on her heels. '*Monsieur de Coniques,*' she repeated slowly.

Thomas heard in her voice the unmistakable rediscovery of hope.

Monsieur de Coniques, she thought. *Jehan.*

She had not seen the notary the previous evening, but he had been there, somewhere, excluded by Angelo from the evening's entertainment. She had not wanted to see him: she had been afraid that those sharp familiar eyes would know her secret.

Now she thought, *Jehan.*

She wished that Thomas had not been there, because then she would have been able to think through this impossible, tantalizing idea alone. But Thomas had not moved, he still leant against the window, frowning, eyes narrowed, because her hands would no longer fold cloth round the pens, or tie ribbons round the bundles of letters. Mistakenly, she had let Thomas come to know her too well.

'Monsieur de Coniques,' repeated Thomas, evenly. 'Come on, Serafina – did you see him?'

She could answer that, at least, honestly. Movement returned: she shook her head.

'He wasn't there. Rumour is that he drinks too much.'

'He drank too much two years ago when I met him in Livorno.'

She hardly heard him. Jehan, she thought. Jehan and Angelo. Ten years ago, Jehan and Angelo had arranged the capture of the Guardi ships by Barbary corsairs. No – *Angelo* had arranged the capture of the ships, and Jehan had drawn up the will that allowed Angelo to inherit the company. Jehan knew *everything.*

Somehow, Jehan must be persuaded to tell everything. To

write it down on a piece of paper, signed and sealed, just as a good notary should. How?

Her thoughts darted feverishly. There was blackmail, and there was bribery. Impossible, she thought, dismissing both ideas quickly. Without evidence, she had nothing with which to blackmail Jehan de Coniques. As for bribery, Jehan had not wanted money, but position and respect. Would he risk for a second time his reputation, his life, for money?

Serafina thought not. Which left only threat. She found that she enjoyed the thought of Jehan de Coniques with a knife against his throat, Jehan de Coniques frightened, pleading for his life. Just as once she too had been frightened, just as once a corsair had held his curved sword to the jewelled bodice of her own dress.

She had forgotten Thomas, but she felt a hand touch her elbow, raising her to her feet, turning her round to face him. He had a sword at his side, a knife in his belt. She could not track Jehan de Coniques down some lonely alleyway and make him confess all past injustices. She had not the strength, nor the competence with weapons. Even a man like Jehan, more used to the pen than the sword, and overfond of the bottle besides, would merely laugh at her and push her aside. She had worked alone to secure herself both riches and reputation, but now she needed another's help.

'Tell me,' said Thomas, softly. He was still staring at her, and his hands lightly grasped her wrists. 'Go on, Serafina, tell me. Jehan de Coniques. What are you thinking of?'

She paused only momentarily. She thought of Thomas locked in a Florentine gaol instead of standing on the bridge of his ship; Thomas hanged at the gallows in the Piazza della Signoria instead of breaking through the ice to discover the North-West Passage. She saw herself reflected in his blue eyes, small and dark and finite, and then she put aside sentiment, and said, 'There is another way, but I cannot do it alone. It concerns Jehan.'

He understood immediately. His eyelids flickered, the pressure on her wrists increased.

'Ah,' he said, lightly. 'Persuade the servant to betray his master?'

'He used not to be Angelo's servant.' Serafina recalled the past, Jehan and Angelo and their mutual despite. 'They were equals within the company. Angelo was of my mother's family, of course, but Jehan was the better born. Things have changed now.'

'You think that the notary may resent that?' Thomas smiled briefly. 'You *hope* that he resents that?'

'I hope' – and Serafina found that her voice was almost choked with the realization of this, her last and most desperate hope – 'that Jehan resents it enough to betray Angelo.' She added, her mouth dry, 'He may need a little prompting, though.'

Thomas laughed, dropped her hands. 'What an interesting career I shall have had. Ship's pilot for the English Levant Company, master of a Tuscan cloth-trading vessel, and assassin. I really must write my memoirs. If I live that long.'

'Not assassin,' she said. Her whole body was tense, waiting. 'You will not need to kill him.'

'Only,' said Thomas, thoughtfully, studying her, 'to scratch him a little?'

She imagined a knife nicking at that forbidding figure of her childhood. Red drops of blood trailing thinly down Jehan's skin: she closed her eyes tightly for a moment, and then opened them again.

'I cannot force you, Thomas.' Her voice shook slightly. 'If you do not wish to help me, then you will be good enough to forget that this conversation ever took place.'

Thomas's smile broadened a little. 'And meanwhile you'll scour the back alleys of Marseilles in search of any ruffian who's good with a knife?'

He knew her too well. The house had begun to stir: Serafina walked to the door and slipped the bolt, to keep the clerks from their desks.

'Yes,' she said, simply. 'I'll find someone. It's my last hope, you see.'

'And it still matters – that much?'

She nodded. It mattered more than anything else in the world. More than the Capriani money gathered in banks and chests, more than the houses in Pisa, Naples and Marseilles, more than the fine ship that sailed at her bidding. More, even, than Francesco.

'Angelo and Jehan will sail to Italy,' she said. Her hands were twisted in front of her, her fingers rigid. 'As soon as the *Fiametta* is loaded, they'll go to Florence to collect the finance for the voyage from Messer Nadi. And to make arrangements for the betrothal, of course.'

Another picture had formed in her mind: of Fiametta Nadi, Angelo's intended betrothed. Fiametta would be beautiful, graceful, possessed of the sort of confidence that only a lifetime's comfort and money could give. Serafina hated Fiametta Nadi.

'Angelo and Jehan won't live in each other's pockets,' she added, harshly. 'Jehan must be alone sometimes. He was alone when you met him in Livorno.'

'Alone and talkative,' said Thomas. 'Embittered, envious. And careless with his words.'

He paused. She could see that he was thinking, seriously considering her proposal for the first time. Outside, the streets had begun to bustle and grow busy; in the kitchens, she could hear the cook shouting at the maidservants. Serafina found it hard not to hold her breath, hard not to resent the fact that, yet again, someone else held her destiny curled in the palm of his hand.

At last he said, 'Yes. I'll do it.'

She heard her own rapid exhalation of breath.

Thomas added, 'On one condition.'

She would have agreed with anything: whatever he wanted he could have. She would throw her jar of red lead into the sea, hide in her cabin the entire voyage home. '*Anything.*'

'I'm going to write a letter,' he said. 'To my brother in England.'

He sat down at one of the clerks' desks, and found a clean sheet of paper. Serafina did not yet understand what Thomas's single condition of service might be: she did not care. She felt exhilarated and alive, after a night in which she had glimpsed death. Her mind raced ahead to Florence, to Jehan, cowering in some dark corner, his hand trembling as he confessed to all the iniquities of the past.

Thomas's dark head was bent over the desk, his pen fast covering the paper. When he had finished, he sprinkled sand over the paper, folded it, and sealed it with blobs of wax. Turning back to Serafina, he said, 'I have a house in England. Nothing grand – it belonged to my parents. They left it to Robert, my elder brother, but he had the tavern, so he let me have the house. Thought it would steady me, I suppose, keep me on dry land.'

He stood up, the letter held in one hand.

'To go to Florence – to persuade Jehan de Coniques to talk about a crime that was committed years ago – will be dangerous, Serafina. Very dangerous. Not only for me, but for you also. If I should make some error, if I should fail, and Angelo should discover my name, and make the connection with you, then he might well begin to reconsider the past. He might remember little Serafina Guardi, he might wonder whether the corsair failed to carry out his instructions. And then you would be in danger, and so would Francesco. And I will not have that.

'If Angelo discovered your identity, Serafina, then Italy would no longer be safe for you. Nor would France, of course. But England would, I believe. It's sufficiently far away. This letter tells my brother who you are, who Francesco is. The truth. It asks Robert to give you the keys to my house. If I do not return from Florence, then you must promise me that both you and Francesco will go to England. You have the *Kingfisher* – William Williams will find you a pilot capable of taking you round the Cape. But you must promise me, Serafina, or I will not go. You must promise me this on whatever you still hold dear.'

She would have promised him all the stars in the sky, all the fishes in the sea. This letter, this promise, would not be necessary: she felt with all the unreal clarity of a sleepless night, of half a lifetime's obsession, that the end was near, that her battle would soon be over.

But she took Thomas's letter and read the inscription on the paper. Then she laid it safely in the chest, and promised, silently, on her father's name. As she went to unbolt the door, she heard Thomas say, 'And if I fail? How will you live then, Serafina?'

But though she understood him, she did not reply.

After the episode with the galleon, Jules Crau knew that he was no longer a fisherman, but a beggar.

He abandoned all hope of finding work. Isabelle had contracted a stomach complaint and he dared not leave her for more than an hour or so. And besides, there was no work. When the child slept, he would leave the single room that was their home, and walk out into the city. He would wander through the streets of Marseilles, past the beautiful houses of the rich, along the stinking alleyways of the poor, his hand always outstretched, his eyes always alert for a loaf that had fallen from a baker's barrow, a maidservant's unattended shopping-basket. He became a creature of the night, the darkness. Isabelle slept better at night, her fever easing with the coolness of evening.

The streets were still crowded at night, though. It seemed to Jules as though the dispossessed of the world had come to Marseilles, populating its winding alleyways and enclosed courtyards with their misery and hunger. He saw gypsies, cripples, wounded soldiers, useless remnants of the years of civil war, and peasants who, crushed by years of bad harvests, had abandoned their smallholdings in a vain attempt to seek a better life in the city. God had abandoned them, thought Jules, shuffling, like the rest of them, down a cobbled alleyway. God had cursed them with the wind and the rain and the paralysingly cold winters. It had not, he thought, trying to remember his childhood, always been like this. Once the rain had not flattened the growing wheat, once the Gulf of Lions had not frozen in the icy January weather. They were tumbling towards the end of the century, to the black abyss which, had it not been for Isabelle, Jules would have long ago given himself up to. A travelling friar in the market-place had told them all that the world would end with the dying century. At night Jules Crau believed him.

One night he found himself in the beggars' place of assembly, the Court of Miracles. The Court of Miracles was a squalid courtyard at the end of a fouled cul-de-sac. The houses of the poor crowded round, tumbledown tenement buildings, storey after unstable storey, leaning over each other until the roofs almost seemed to touch. Someone grasped Jules's ragged sleeve and said, 'Look! The King of the Beggars!' and Jules stared through the milling, muttering throng of people. The King was dressed in layer upon layer of ragged clothes. Clothes that had once been rich men's clothes – taffetas and silks and velvets. Under the light of the torches held by the King of the Beggars' attendants, the garments looked splendid again, scarlet and turquoise and emerald, fold upon fold of rich and luxurious colour. He looked, thought Jules, truly a King.

The King's voice was deep and mellow, his gestures wide and graceful. He spoke, gently at first, about the Brotherhood, of which all those in the courtyard were members. Then, his voice gradually rising in intensity, he spoke about the rich merchants with their painted wives, their extravagant houses, their lavish feasts. The merchants' greed forced the price of food to rise, compelling the poor to beg and steal. Yet the merchants still persecuted the beggars, and hanged the petty thieves. The King's eyes were red in the torchlight: Jules had stared, hypnotized, at those crimson pupils. By the time the King had finished speaking, the rest of the crowd were roaring, stamping their feet, waving their fists in agreement. Jules, hearing nothing but the King's words, forgot, for a moment, even Isabelle.

The following day there were fights in the streets, a few stalls overturned in the markets, a merchant's stables set on fire. The city authorities had put the feeble flickerings of insurrection down to the heat, which was intense. Jules, spending the day indoors with Isabelle cradled in his lap, saw nothing. But that night, a curious thing happened.

He found himself in the Court of Miracles again, hoping for the King with the wild eyes, the glorious rags. But the King had not come: only a handful of beggars, like him, had slept and squabbled on the cobbles. Jules, too, had wanted to sleep: he had even closed his eyes for a moment and, waking, had seen a ghost.

He recognized her immediately for the spirit of his dead wife, Marianne. She was dressed in black, and he knew the long dark hair, the smooth olive skin, that once he had loved. She walked through the rabble – lightly, almost floating – and as she walked she had cast from her purse coins and jewels. He had caught one of the coins – a gold florin. He had tried to touch her, but she was insubstantial, fleeting, melting away before he could stumble to his feet.

The gold florin fed Jules and Isabelle for a month.

PART XII

1596

BEGINNING TO BE DARK

They who have license to Cary swordes in
the Cittyes, yet must not wear them when
the evening begins to be darke.

Itinerary: Fynes Moryson

Florence was rose-coloured, umber, terracotta, and ochre. Florence's palaces and piazzas glistened in the fine autumn rain that tracked Angelo Guardi's ride along the valley of the Arno. Florence had hope, promise, even an auspicious rainbow shimmering feebly in the distant hills.

Inside the Nadi palazzo, Angelo was welcomed, if not yet as a son-in-law, then at least as a family friend. In the evening, in an elegant room hung with dark tapestries and curtains of brocade, he and Jehan dined with the Nadi family. A lutenist played in one corner of the room, and the braided ribbons hanging from the neck of his instrument shone in the candlelight. In the grate, a fire burned scented wood, although the evenings had not yet grown cold.

Lorenzo Nadi talked of cloth and money, Giulia of parties. Nencia simpered whenever Angelo addressed her; Fiametta was monosyllabic, speaking only when spoken to. She looked, he thought, studying the pale, lowered eyes, sullen. Later he would coax a smile, a kiss, from the downturned mouth. He needed the insurance of Fiametta Nadi's desire for him. There was never anything wrong with a bit of insurance.

Lorenzo was inquiring about Angelo's stay in Marseilles.

'I have broadcloth and fustian – and some good quality gros-grain as well. But there's plenty of space left in the hold of the *Fiametta* for your silks, Messer Nadi.'

He did not yet dare address Lorenzo Nadi by his forename. Later, thought Angelo, accepting a portion of pheasant stuffed with quail from the manservant. When he was married.

His smile took in the whole of the Nadi family. Nencia giggled again and tossed back her red-gold curls; Giulia, looking particularly elegant and fragile in turquoise silk, said, 'What an honour, is it not, Fiametta, for Messer Angelo to have named his ship for you!'

Fiametta mumbled something and stared at her plate.

Giulia added, 'When I was young and pretty a prince named four of his galleys for me. Giulia in the spring, the summer, etcetera. Quite charming.'

Fiametta scowled.

Angelo said, courteously, 'When I discover a new sea, Madonna Giulia, I shall name it for you. And the honour is mine, surely, to be able to sit and dine with three such beautiful ladies.'

Raising his glass in salute, Angelo thought, with the smallest pinch of regret, that not one of the three Nadi women possessed looks, wealth, and availability. He found himself recalling that evening in Marseilles, those hot summer hours he had spent with the widowed Madonna Capriani. Madonna Capriani had wealth and beauty. And intelligence, and courage, and an impertinence he was forced to admit he had found seductive. And there had been something else besides: knowledge, or experience, he could not precisely define it.

'You'll sail to Scanderoon, then?'

Lorenzo Nadi interrupted the flood of compliments. He had a dozen bales of luxury silk invested in the *Fiametta*'s forthcoming voyage; and a chestful of gold besides.

Turning, waving aside a plateful of truffles, Angelo said, 'To Scanderoon eventually, yes, sir. Though I haven't yet decided whether to call at Zante first.'

He heard a snort of amusement from Jehan's end of the table.

Ignoring the notary, refusing to let his displeasure show in his face, Angelo added, 'I've done business in Zante before. The governor of the island, Messer Carcandella, is an old acquaintance.'

'Angelo,' said Jehan, draining his wine-glass, 'has many acquaintances. They come from all four corners of the Mediterranean. France – Venice – the Ionian Sea –'

'And soon,' interrupted Angelo smoothly, 'Scanderoon. As you know, the Guardi have not previously been able to buy raw silk from Scanderoon. But now, with the *Fiametta*, and with your backing, Messer Nadi, the entire Mediterranean is open to us. Eventually – who knows? – we may travel beyond the Mediterranean. To the northern countries, for instance, or the Indies.'

'In the Indies,' said little Nencia, threading her fingers beneath her chin, and peering over them at Angelo, 'the women wear only a scarf tied round their waists and beads round their necks. Imagine!' She smiled, showing small white even teeth.

Fiametta said crossly, '*Nencia*,' but Angelo smiled back, and said, 'And in Morocco the women swathe themselves from head to toe in black so that only their eyes can be seen beneath their veils. I am glad,' and he touched Fiametta's hand, 'that there are not such fashions here.'

She withdrew her hand immediately, as though his touch had stung her. Her pale skin was blotched with pink, her eyes, fringed by lashes that were almost white, stared fiercely ahead. She was like a rabbit, thought Angelo, amused, a great clumsy white rabbit, quivering with sulky nervousness.

The lutenist, having returned his instrument, had begun to play again. 'Bianco fiore', thought Angelo, recognizing the tune. White flower. He hoped that Fiametta Nadi was a white flower: pale and cool and passionate, but he suspected that she was not. But she must be a virgin, and there was always an especially sweet pleasure in deflowering a virgin. He enjoyed experienced, knowledgeable women, too, but he looked forward to that particular frisson of being the first. Later, he would coax what passion he could from that gauche body, but, sexually, he knew that she would not satisfy him. It did not matter: Fiametta would be content and therefore faithful, and faithfulness in marriage was, after all, so much more important in a woman than in a man. He knew too well the importance of parentage. He must know that his children were his own. And in Florence – elegant, sophisticated Florence – there would always be plenty of opportunity to relieve the boredom of monogamy.

Giulia signalled the servant to bring in the desserts. Pies, and tarts, and syllabubs and jellies; extravagances made of sugar, of ice, of crystallized flowers. 'When,' said Giulia, peeling a fig, 'do you expect to return from the Levant, my dear Angelo?'

'In the spring, I hope.' Angelo's words were addressed to Giulia, but out of the corner of his eye he still watched the notary, who was pouring himself yet another glass of wine. He had realized that he no longer trusted Jehan de Coniques – could, perhaps, no longer rely on his silence. Since the incident in Marseilles, things had changed subtly between them: the notary's envy had become more blatant, his words barbed, threatening. Drink was making him careless. In Marseilles, Jehan had set fire to his bed-curtains, had toppled a candle and lain there, snoring like a drunken sow while the figured damask scorched and then flared into flame. The alertness of Angelo's servants had fortunately saved the house and, less fortunately, the notary himself.

He could not throttle him here, though, in Lorenzo Nadi's splendid dining-chamber. Taking an orange from the fruit-bowl, Angelo stripped off the peel, and added, 'I can't be certain, though. It's a long voyage, madonna – the variations in weather mean that the journey could take a couple of months, or almost a year. But I hope' – and Angelo smiled at Fiametta – 'that it will not take that long. After all, I have good reason for wishing to be back on dry land.'

'Fifty thousand ducats worth,' said Jehan. 'Good reason indeed.'

There was a silence, broken only by the notary's laughter at his own tasteless remark. Even the lutenist had stopped playing, even the flames in the fire seemed to ebb. Angelo felt the blood drain from his face, and his hand clenched round the stem of his wine-glass.

'Perhaps,' said Lorenzo Nadi, slowly, 'you should leave the table, Messer de Coniques. You are not fit for present company.'

The notary did not move. Angelo, rising in one clean movement to his feet, crossed to the other side of the table. Taking two handfuls of musty black robes in his hands, he hauled Jehan de Coniques out of his chair.

The notary was almost weightless: there seemed to be nothing solid beneath the crackling layers of material. He was a remnant of another time, other loyalties. If Angelo gripped the skin and bone beneath the robes they would crumble at his touch, and then there would be nothing but dust. Angelo had to manhandle Jehan out of the dining-chamber, half kicking, half pushing him up the stairs to his bedchamber. He found that he enjoyed the kicking.

He left the notary sprawled on the floor beside the bed. Their eyes met only once as Jehan rolled over, his mouth gaping, his eyelids red and weeping. I hope he chokes on his own vomit, thought Angelo as he left the room, slamming the door shut. I hope he trips on the stairs and falls and breaks his neck.

Out in the passageway, the stairs swam beneath him for a moment, and then were steady. He knew what he had to do, though, just as he had once known what to do about Franco Guardi. He knew that there was, as then, no choice.

He thought of waiting until they were back on board the *Fiametta*, and consigning the notary to the welcoming arms of the sea. But he had not planned to take Jehan to the Levant: he had intended him to sail back to Marseilles alone. He knew now that he could not allow the notary to return to Marseilles. Nevertheless, a change of plan might look suspicious. And besides, it was so difficult to be alone on board ship.

Neither would he use poison. He was not Italian enough for poison: the Frenchman in him cried out that it was too dangerous, that the procurement and application of the dose was fraught with difficulties. No, there were far simpler solutions. Angelo had always liked simple solutions.

Fiametta had not found the notary's words offensive; he had only, after all, told the truth.

Later, when the glossy, irritating dinner was over, she allowed Angelo Guardi to take her, alone, to the gallery. There, multi-stranded candelabra dipped from painted ceilings, and pictures of lustful gods chased fat-buttocked nymphs on the walls. Pausing halfway down the gallery Angelo, as Fiametta had known he would, took her in his arms.

He was half a head taller than Fiametta: she could see the pulse in his throat, the fine, closely shaved golden down of his beard. His smell disgusted her, a mixture of red wine and sandalwood. She knew he was going to kiss her, so she screwed her eyelids tightly shut, and held her breath.

It was worse than she had expected. His tongue forced its way between her lips and into her mouth; his fingers dug into the back of her head, pulling at her fine sandy hair. She supposed that this was passion. She let her own palms rest on his back, because that was expected of her, and felt his muscles move beneath the thin silks of his doublet and shirt. He was strong and confident and he reminded her of her father, and she had always, though she hid it well, been afraid of her father. She despised her mother and Nencia, but she feared Lorenzo for his power and strength.

Angelo left off kissing her mouth at last. He did not let her go, though: opening her eyes, Fiametta stared stonily at a portrait of Zeus and Leda while Angelo's lips nuzzled her cheek, her neck, her shoulder. Great swan's wings beat in the air as Angelo's fingers kneaded the front of her gown, bruising her large, flat breasts. Coldly glancing down, she saw that his skin was flushed, his forehead beaded with sweat. She thought what fools men were, to lose their senses so easily, so that the merest touch of the plainest woman changed them into birds, or beasts.

And if I fail? How will you live then, Serafina?

She had not answered and he, of course, had not expected her to. But Thomas's own question had haunted him throughout the long journey from Marseilles to Tuscany, throughout his methodical search of the city of Florence. The memory of the emptiness in her eyes disturbed him.

It had not taken him long to find the Nadi palazzo: the youngest apprentice, the dimmest serving-maid could have directed him to it. The palace was large and impressive, fronting on to a street not far from the church of Santa Maria Novella. The high plaster walls were patterned with painted circles and lozenges, some of the circles infilled with portraits of heraldic symbols. The windows were arched and shuttered, the roof low-pitched and tiled. The building represented wealth, security, pride. All around him, the great houses of the rich and successful towered into the misty air, their shutters closed, their doors bolted, impenetrable fortresses in a city of secrets.

It was raining, a fine, cool rain that hazed the impressive panelled front doors of the Nadi palace. Half hidden in an open doorway, Thomas thought of Angelo Guardi and his âme damnée, Jehan de Coniques. They would not stay in Florence long: Angelo, like Thomas, would be impatient to set sail for the Levant. Jehan de Coniques might, Thomas knew, remain inside those four walls day and night, until the time came for the Guardi retinue to leave Florence. He might have given up drink, and become a sober, taciturn, conscientious lawyer.

But Thomas thought not. The man he had met in the tavern in Livorno had been destroying himself, slowly but inevitably. He had been weighed down with guilt and bitterness. Sooner or later, Jehan de Coniques would leave those confining walls and walk out into Florence's alleys and taverns.

Thomas, leaning back against the wall, fingered his knife and promised to be patient.

It was dark when the notary finally left the Palazzo Nadi. The pitch-black night was relieved only by the glimmer of candles through closed shutters, and the lanterns carried in the streets. Short, richly coloured cloaks swirled in the changing light from the sconces; shadows were carved in the faces of the passers-by. Thomas's knife was hidden inside his doublet: it was not permitted to carry weapons in Florence by night.

When Jehan de Coniques shuffled out of the Palazzo Nadi, Thomas's heart beat loudly once, then returned to its normal steady pace. He recognized the lawyer immediately, remembering the loose, stained robes, the hunched shoulders, the beaked nose jutting out of a hollow face. Thomas began to follow the Frenchman along the street and into the square.

The church of Santa Maria Novella, its patterned geometric shapes pale in the moonlight, towered over them. The notary's pace was steady and direct. He glanced behind him several times, but Thomas kept to the shadows, the brim of his hat shadowing his face, his feet silent on the cobbles. They passed the great prominences of the duomo and the baptistery, green and white and ghostly in the lack of light, and headed down the Via del Proconsolo towards the river.

He could have had him now, in the sheltering darkness of the tall buildings on either side of the street, but still Thomas waited. He wanted Jehan de Coniques talkative, so he wanted him drunk. He watched from an alleyway as the notary made his way into a small tavern not far from the Arno. He would have welcomed a drink himself, but he resisted the temptation. He needed a clear head, and besides, the Frenchman might recognize him.

It was, estimated Thomas, about an hour later when Jehan de Coniques left the tavern. Thomas saw him stumble over the step as he walked out of the doorway, grabbing the lintel to keep himself upright. There was a bottle hidden beneath the folds of his cloak, and every so often the notary would raise it to his mouth and drink deeply.

He passed within a few feet of Thomas, hidden in the shadows. The notary was whispering something under his breath: the whisper rose first to a mutter, and then to a shout.

> Sur les march' du palais
> Sur les march' du palais
> Il y a un' tant belle fille.

Jehan de Coniques laughed, and took another mouthful of red wine. Thomas, emerging from the alleyway, followed him silently along the cobbles.

> Elle a tant d'amoureux
> Elle a tant d'amoureux
> Qu'elle ne sait lequel prendre –

The pattern of the notary's walking was uneven, a wavelike swaying from one side of the street to the other. From one of the houses that towered above them, a shutter opened, and Thomas had to hide from the sudden flare of light that painted the street. A voice yelled something insulting in Italian: Jehan de Coniques shook a clenched fist and continued his unsteady progress.

He was heading for the river, realized Thomas. 'La bell' si tu voulais', bawled Jehan, and then his voice sank to a whisper again. 'Nous dormirons ensemble' echoed in a whisper off the gilded plaster, the secretive doors and shuttered windows.

Thomas found that he was shivering, that his palm, curled round
the hilt of his knife, was damp.

> Dans un grand lit carré . . .
> Dans un grand lit carré . . .
> Aux belles taies blanches . . .

The cracked mocking voice had sunk until it was scarcely
audible. The notary paused, leaning against the corner of the
house, the wine-bottle held to his lips. Thomas, flattened against
a wall, could see the Arno beyond, its black water flecked by
reflections from the Ponte Vecchio downstream. The road
branched here into a darkened alley and a wider street. Thomas
waited, every muscle taut.

Jehan began to stumble down the alleyway. The smallest
shadow of a smile touched Thomas's lips, and his eyes were dark
and bright in the moonlight. The notary began to sing again.

> Dans le mitan du lit . . .
> Dans le mitan du lit . . .

He never finished his verse. A hand grasped Jehan de Coniques's
shoulder, forcing him round. Another hand held a knife against
the notary's stained doublet.

'Dans le mitan du lit,' said Thomas Marlowe, softly, 'La
rivière est profonde.'

The notary blinked, his mouth opened and closed like a fish.
Now that he was close enough, Thomas could see the effects of
time and alcohol on the Frenchman's face. The greying skin was
slack, puffy round the eyes, grainy in the poor light.

'La rivière est profonde,' repeated Thomas, smiling. 'Très, très
profonde. Shall we walk to the river, Monsieur de Coniques?'

There had been, Thomas had noticed, in the notary's first
reaction, a satisfying flicker of fear. Fear had gone now, though.

Jehan de Coniques's voice was surprisingly lucid, though. 'If
you like,' he said. 'Monsieur –?'

'Marlowe,' said Thomas. 'Thomas Marlowe. Yes, we have
met before, Monsieur de Coniques. In a tavern in Livorno.'

The notary screwed up his small bloodshot eyes as he studied
Thomas. 'You're English,' he said, at last.

'That's right. But I haven't been to all this trouble, Monsieur de Coniques, so that we might discuss geography. Come, let's walk to the river.'

One hand was threaded through Jehan's arm, but the other hand, hidden under the folds of Thomas's cloak, still held the dagger to the notary's side. They began to walk down the alleyway in the direction of the river: a shuffling, awkward gait, with the Frenchman frequently stumbling on the cobbles. Jehan de Coniques smelt sour, an unpleasant mixture of old wine and unwashed clothing.

'You were asking questions,' said the notary, suddenly. 'In Livorno. About Angelo.'

They had reached a narrow passageway only a few yards from the Arno. The sounds of the city at night were silenced: there was only the gentle lapping of the river, and the rustling of black robes on wet cobbles. Thomas could see a glimmering of intelligence in Jehan de Coniques's bleary eyes, and an ironic sort of interest.

'That's right.' The notary's back was pressed against the wall. Thomas let go of the man's arm, but kept the knife balanced against his ribs. 'I asked you about Angelo. And about Franco and Serafina Guardi. And you told me that Angelo was a clever bastard.'

Jehan sniggered, but his expression was bitter. 'So he is. A damnably clever bastard.'

'And getting cleverer by the day. He's doing well for himself, don't you agree, Monsieur de Coniques? The ownership of the Guardi company, the master of a handsome galleon, and he's about to marry a rich and well-born young woman. La bell' si tu voulais. What do you think of that, Jehan?'

The notary's lower lip stuck out like a small child's. 'It doesn't matter what I think of it.'

'Ah, but it does.' Thomas's voice was soft and clear in the darkness. The rain had begun again, blackening the creased folds of the notary's robes, mingling with the sweat that iced the back of Thomas's neck. 'I'd like to know what you think of it, Jehan. After all, you were very helpful to me once before.'

The notary's lids, which had half closed, jerked open. 'I told you nothing!' he hissed.

'Come, come, Monsieur de Coniques. Don't you remember? Have you forgotten our little conversation? Oh, dear – then let me remind you. You told me that Angelo Guardi was a clever bastard. And you told me that Angelo had arranged his employer's death in order that he might inherit the Guardi company.'

'I never –'

'You said' – and the smile on Thomas's face had metamorphosed into a broad grin – 'you said that the corsair ship took Franco Guardi and his daughter before the girl could be betrothed.'

The notary shook his head, and raised the bottle to his mouth. 'Happy chance,' he said, lightly. 'For Angelo, at least.'

He was sniggering again as he drank, the wine trailing in a red line down his chin, mingling with the rain on his doublet. Thomas wanted to use the knife, or to strike that clever, stupid face.

Not yet. Not yet. *Patience.* 'It took me a long time to work out what was wrong,' said Thomas, dreamily. 'Then I realized. She should have been ransomed. The girl, Serafina, I mean. A wealthy merchant and his only daughter should have been ransomed.'

Jehan de Coniques wiped his mouth with the back of his hand. 'They were dead,' he said. The red-rimmed eyes were scornful. 'They were both dead. You can't ransom a dead man. Franco died of a fever in the –'

'– bagnios of Algiers,' finished Thomas, bored. 'Not quite accurate, Monsieur de Coniques, wouldn't you agree? Franco Guardi did not die in the bagnio, he died of the bastinado, and therefore, it is true, could not have been ransomed. His daughter, however, could have been ransomed. Yet she was not.'

The notary's eyes were fixed on him now, black and glistening. 'The devil – what are you saying?' he whispered.

'I am saying, my honest notary, that Serafina Guardi survived her cousin Angelo's little scheme. That she is alive, and that I met her in Algiers.'

The wine-bottle slid out of the notary's fingers, and shattered on the cobbles. Red wine trickled between the stones, mixing with the rainwater, thickened by the litter of the streets.

'I need you to do something for me, Monsieur de Coniques.'
Thomas's voice was cold, unemotional. 'I need you to write a
statement explaining how it was done. How Angelo met the
corsair, how you altered the will – I am right, aren't I, you
altered Franco Guardi's will? I want you to put down everything.
From the day Angelo dreamed up the idea, to the day he took
over the ownership of the company. In writing, with the appropriate witnesses and seals. You know the sort of thing. You're
a notary.'

The Frenchman was laughing again, but he squeezed out one
cracked, faltering word. 'Why?'

'Why?' Thomas paused, studying Jehan de Coniques as though
he were some strange, repulsive creature collected from an unknown continent. 'Because I wish the Guardi property and
company to be returned to its rightful owner. And because if you
don't, I'll kill you.'

The broken laughter echoed off the walls again, and beyond
to the black, shivering plain of the river. 'And if I do, *he'll* kill
me! I've seen it in his eyes!'

And *he*, of course, was Angelo Guardi. Because Jehan was
afraid of Angelo Guardi.

'But I'll do it,' said the notary, suddenly.

Jehan was grinning now, his spaced, uneven teeth cutting his
long face in two. 'La bell' si tu voulais,' he hissed, 'nous dormirons ensemble. Only she won't sleep in *my* bed, will she? No
– she'll sleep in Angelo's bed. Not that,' he added, jerking his head
aside, 'I'd want the arrogant bitch.'

The phrase *arrogant bitch* made Thomas feel suddenly chilled
to the bone, as though the fine warm rain had frozen and turned
to sleet. Did the notary refer to Fiametta Nadi or to Serafina
Guardi?

'But I'd have liked the money,' added Jehan. His voice had
shrilled to a whine, a single raindrop trickled from the end of his
nose. 'And the position. He's nothing but a bastard, after all. He
never gave me my due. He used to laugh at me – I come from
one of the oldest families in Provence: did you know that,
Englishman? – and he used to laugh at me. But he'll lose everything without this marriage, and I shall enjoy watching him

tumble back to the gutter. He overspent himself hopelessly building that damned ship.'

The *Fiametta*. 'Messer Guardi trades in merchandise other than cloth, doesn't he?' said Thomas. 'Tin, for instance.'

He saw the notary frown, his eyes suddenly glazed with suspicion. 'What do you know about that?'

Thomas shook his head. 'No matter.'

Jehan seemed to have forgotten him. 'Can't make silk in Marseilles,' he mumbled. 'No water. Angelo lost his contacts, you see. Old Franco bought silk cloth from the Corsini, of course. But even Angelo' – and the notary giggled again – 'did not dare keep up that connection.'

So in murdering Franco Guardi, Angelo himself had begun the slow destruction of the business he loved. The stench of failure, of corruption, seemed to catch in Thomas's throat. It disturbed him: it was almost as though it was infectious, like the plague, to be avoided by sucking sweetened lozenges, or burning phials of sulphur.

'I kept the will,' said Jehan, suddenly. 'The first will, the original. Insurance, you see.'

Thomas, staring at him, could not speak at first. Then he took a deep breath, and drew a hand across his face to wipe the rain from his lashes and the tips of his hair.

'Bring it to me. I can take you as far away from Angelo as you like. I, too, have a ship.'

He was no longer capable of feeling happiness, but Jehan de Coniques felt something reminiscent, perhaps, of triumph, as he shuffled back alone through the silent streets.

Serafina Guardi was alive: that knowledge made him want to laugh. It was as though the gods that had always seemed to work at Angelo's bidding had acted freely at last, providing a twist of fate that even Angelo had not foreseen. Serafina's survival offered Jehan the opportunity to grind Angelo into the ground, just as, in Marseilles, Angelo had ground Jehan's hand into the fragments of broken glass. Jehan wished that he had not dropped the bottle of wine: giggling to himself, he knew that such a rare bubbling of the spirits would only have been improved by a drink or two.

Because he was laughing, he did not at first notice the footsteps behind him. He was within a few streets of the Nadi palazzo, had already passed the duomo and the church of Santa Maria Novella. When, finally, he heard the faint pattering on the cobbles, he thought that it was the rain. Then, as the pattering magnified into footsteps, almost an echo of his own, he believed that it was the Englishman.

He knew that he was wrong, though, when he heard the whisper of silk and velvet. Thomas Marlowe had worn linen and broadcloth. Jehan turned, tried to run, but it was too late. He was alone in the silence and the darkness with the only man he had ever feared.

The thin cord bit into his throat. He could not even try to pull it away: his hands were nerveless, clumsy. As he opened his eyes for the last time, his face contorted by death, Jehan de Coniques saw looking down at him the dark eyes of Angelo Guardi.

Thomas heard the news two days later. A man had been washed up on the shores of the Arno, on the left bank, where the exquisite mosaic façade of the church of San Miniato looked down over the city. The man had not drowned, the potboy had added, delightedly. He had been strangled and robbed, and when they had carried him up from the shore, the string had still been knotted round his neck.

Thomas had spent an edgy couple of days, waiting for a visitor who had not come. The notary might have changed his mind, might have confided in Angelo Guardi, or might simply, confused by alcohol, have forgotten the arrangements that Thomas had made. But when the potboy told him the news, he guessed with chill certainty that he had been too late. One day earlier, that would have been enough. Just one day earlier. *He'll kill me, I've seen it in his eyes*, Jehan had said. And he had been right.

He knew that day the bitter taste of failure. As Thomas rode out through the city gates, he found that he was whispering the final verse of Jehan's song.

Nous y pourrions dormir
Nous y pourrions dormir
Jusqu'à la fin du monde.
Lon la
Jusqu'à la fin du monde.

The discovery of Jehan's death allowed Angelo to leave Florence. He had been afraid that the slack yellow waters would carry the body out towards the sea or, worse, that the swollen corpse would bob about in the river for weeks. But at last a courting couple found it, washed up amidst a litter of vegetable peelings and river-weed, sprawled on the clammy sand.

Angelo had identified the corpse, had displayed appropriate grief and regret, and had offered a suitably large reward for the discovery of the murderer. He had then ordered the immediate packing of his bags. The Nadi servants were efficient: his retinue would be ready to leave after they had dined at midday.

He found, though, that he could not eat. He had seen dead bodies before, but not after two days' immersion in river-water. The iced marchpane that the Nadi servants put before him reminded him of the smooth shininess of Jehan's naked limbs. The slices of veal were too reminiscent of the single bloodless gash on the notary's forehead, inflicted long after death by some sharp stone or shell. Angelo had felt the same nausea two and a half days earlier, carrying the corpse to the Arno. He still broke out in a sweat when he thought of that journey, but it had been necessary: the notary had died too near the Palazzo Nadi to leave the body in the street. He had had to force himself to empty Jehan's pockets, to make it look like a robbery.

His revulsion had surprised him: it was not something that he had previously experienced. It was Florence, Angelo told himself, the over-rich food, the strain of appearing the perfect prospective son-in-law for Lorenzo Nadi.

He did not regret what he had done, though. Earlier, he had inspected the contents of Jehan's room. Hidden carefully in one of the drawers of the desk, he had found what could have destroyed him: Franco Guardi's original will. He had known then that part of Jehan had for a long time intended treachery, and he had found, to his surprise, a certain respect for the notary's unexpected prudence.

Costanza had come to dread the sound of men's boots outside, the hammering at the door of her house.

But this time she knew that it could not be Galeazzo because, although it was still afternoon, Galeazzo was asleep upstairs. He had arrived at midday for food and wine and lovemaking and, satiated, he slept.

She found the courage to open the door, and saw Thomas Marlowe, whom she had once, on an impulse, nursed in this house. His boots were rimmed with mud, his clothes dusty with travel. Holding up a forefinger to her mouth to bid him be quiet, she beckoned him inside.

'Galeazzo is upstairs,' she said softly. 'It would be better not to wake him.'

She saw Thomas's eyes darken, his mouth set in a thin line at the mention of Galeazzo Merli. Thomas loathed Galeazzo Merli because Galeazzo had publicly ridiculed Madonna Capriani. Thomas loved Madonna Capriani. In a different world, with a different past, Costanza might have loved Thomas.

She led him into the parlour, where the weak autumn sunshine streamed through the slats of the shutters. On the table was a pile of mending: a petticoat with a torn frill, a hat with a ribbon trailing limply from the crown. She poured Thomas a cup of wine. She could not decide whether he had been drinking already: his eyes were an intense, angry blue, not solely, she thought, due to Galeazzo.

'I'm sorry,' said Thomas, smiling apologetically at her. 'I've washed myself up on your doorstep again, Costanza. On your generosity, I should say. But only for a half-hour this time. It was thoughtless of me to appear when you might have a visitor.'

There was no sarcasm in his voice as he said the word, visitor. Others, thought Costanza, sitting opposite him, might have used a different term. Like customer.

She said, quite truthfully, 'No matter – Galeazzo always sleeps for at least an hour. And I am glad to see you, Thomas.' She picked up the hat, and began to repin the ribbon to the brim 'But you look tired.'

He grimaced. 'I've just ridden from Florence. Without stopping. It seemed important to make the journey as quickly as possible. But now' – he shook his head – 'I find that I can't quite face the end of the journey. Ridiculous, isn't it?'

She guessed what he meant by end of the journey. At the end of all Thomas Marlowe's journeys was Serafina Capriani, once the young wife of an ageing and miserly merchant, now a rich and successful woman in her own right. She sensed disaster there: at another time she might have questioned, comforted. Now, however, Costanza found that her mind was too preoccupied with impending disasters of her own.

She heard Thomas say, 'But so do you look tired, Costanza. Are you unwell?'

She shook her head and managed to smile. Each morning she looked in the glass and saw the seeds of age sowing their myriad tiny furrows into the skin that had once been smooth. But that was no illness, it was natural. It should not have mattered.

'I'm quite well,' she said. 'It's just – Maria has come home.'

She had not meant to tell him. But she had not realized how much she needed to share her dread with another human being.

Thomas frowned. The pale sunlight from the shuttered windows deepened the shadows and contours of his face so that he, too, for a moment, looked old. He said, gently, 'I thought that would have given you joy.'

'Yes. It would.' Her voice was brittle; for the first time in years Costanza found herself wanting to cry. 'It does. But – there's Galeazzo, you see.'

She saw that still he did not understand, that still he did not know exactly what it meant to be owned by someone else. So she said, stitching the ribbon on to Maria's hat-brim with great, savage stabs of the needle, 'He has seen her, Thomas.'

At first there was silence, and then she heard him curse. Standing up, he walked to the window, flinging open the shutters as though to breathe in the clean autumnal air beyond.

'He wants her,' he said baldly.

'Of course he wants her.' Costanza's eyes were as hard as

homas's. 'Wouldn't any man want her? And Galeazzo has a penchant for young girls. He has a habit of marrying sixteen-year-old virgins who later die in childbirth. He was quite dismayed when his third wife survived the birth of their daughter.'

The anger retreated from her eyes as suddenly as it had appeared. She added softly, 'He shall not have her, Thomas. I'll kill him while he sleeps rather than let him have her. Only where would that leave Maria, when they hang her mother in the market-place?'

She bent her head again. She had not meant to say so much; she found the unburdening of her soul frightening, as though, once more, she was offering up another piece of herself. Blinking to clear her eyes, she began to sew again.

She felt the comforting pressure of Thomas's hand on her shoulder. 'Where's Maria now?' he said.

'With Messer Williams.' She looked up, smiled apologetically. 'I'm sorry, Thomas, to take him away from his work. I sent a messenger to him – to the *Kingfisher*. I trust him, you see. Messer Williams takes Maria out of the house for a few hours. It's better that way.'

She had finished the hat; picking up the length of petticoat, she began to snip off the torn lace.

'The *Kingfisher* sails soon,' said Thomas. 'William goes with her as ship's carpenter.'

Looking up, her eyes met his. 'I know,' said Costanza, bleakly. 'Maria has told me. And you'll not repeat any of this conversation, Thomas – not to Messer Williams, not to anyone. Maria's safety is my problem, no one else's.'

He was about to interrupt, to contradict her, but there was the sound of footsteps upstairs. She knew that Galeazzo had woken up, was shuffling about the bedchamber to retrieve his clothes from where he had flung them to the floor.

Thomas whispered, 'I'll go. But don't despair, Costanza. I'll think of something.'

He was gone, shutting the door silently behind him. She knew that he could not help, that no one could help, that she was, as always, on her own. But she found, as she tidied her hair and put the mending aside, and made ready to greet Galeazzo, that it had, in the end, helped to lay her misery before another human being. There had been the comfort of human touch, and the knowledge that someone cared, just a little.

He had the beginnings of an idea in his head as, climbing back on to his weary horse, he rode away in the direction of the Via S. Domenico. Thomas was glad to have something with which to occupy his mind; it distracted him from the thought of the forthcoming interview with Serafina.

It was only a short journey, through a Pisa that was grey with autumn, chill with the knowledge of forthcoming winter. Bundles of dead leaves, shuffled by a sharp dry wind, already gathered in the gutters, at street corners. Docked a few miles away was the *Kingfisher*, presumably by now readied for her forthcoming voyage to the Levant.

And on different roads Angelo Guardi also travelled: to Livorno, where the *Fiametta* lay docked. He had not yet seen Angelo Guardi, but increasingly Thomas felt that their lives, his and Angelo's, seemed to have acquired a consanguinity, as though something drew them together, like lines of magnetism on an unknown globe, echoing and rebuffing each other's actions.

Serafina knew that she had lost before Thomas finished speaking, before he so much as opened his mouth. She knew from the expression on his face, his refusal to sit when she offered him a chair.

He was untidy and travel-stained, his face seamed with dust and exhaustion. He threw his hat on to a nearby table, and said, bluntly, 'I saw Monsieur de Coniques. With a little persuasion, he was reasonably cooperative. But shortly after I spoke to the good gentleman, his neck became entangled with a piece of rope, and he fell into the Arno.'

She had had several weeks to get used to the possibility of defeat. Since Thomas had said, *And if I fail? How will you live then, Serafina?*, she had forced herself to look into the darkness and find what answer she could. I'll run my business, and bring up my son, and continue to exist, she had thought. Exist, mark you, not live.

Still, his words shocked her. She sat down suddenly, as her legs no longer supported her. *Todo mangiado*, she thought, peering into the abyss, and then realized, eventually noticing Thomas's expression, that she had spoken aloud.

'It was something they said in the bagnio at Algiers.' Her voice was cracked and uneven. '*Todo mangiado.* Lost beyond recall. Nothing left. *Nothing at all . . .*'

Now she could not see his face because her vision had blurred. One image was insistent: wet, white skin, a livid purple line about the throat. But she closed her eyes only for a moment, and took a deep breath to steady herself. 'Angelo?' Serafina said, at last.

Thomas's eyes were bleak. 'I'm sure of it. The notary was in mortal fear of him. He made it look like a robbery, of course, but I have no doubt that Angelo killed Jehan de Coniques. My only surprise, I find, is that he didn't do it years ago. Old times' sake, perhaps.'

There was a ridiculous desire to laugh at the thought of Angelo and Jehan entwined in a comradely, but deadly, affection. 'No,' she said, her voice still a little unsteady. 'I expect that it was not convenient.'

She saw Thomas glance sharply at her. They were in the upstairs front parlour, where Jacopo had once coughed and whined on the day-bed, and where, long ago, Serafina had bound scarlet and crimson ribbons in her hair. And all for nothing, she thought. *Todo mangiado.* Lost beyond recall.

Through the fear that welled up in her heart, Serafina heard Thomas say, 'I'll kill him, if you like.'

He had her attention then, dragging her sharply back to the present.

Thomas added, 'Angelo, of course. I'd be happy to. He's vermin. Worse than Galeazzo Merli – I realized that on the way back from Florence. If you wish it, I'll kill him.'

She saw something in his eyes, something she had never seen before. The look of defeat.

Serafina shook her head. 'No,' she said, simply.

He did not let the subject drop. He had sat down at last, in Jacopo's favourite chair, the one with the wide curving arms. He ran his fingers through his dusty black hair, and said, watching her, 'Not just for you, Serafina. For myself also.'

She found that she had regained the use of her muscles. Rising, she went and rang the bell for the maidservant. Reassume the mask, continue with the ordinary, humdrum daily tasks. The taverns from Florence to Pisa were of variable quality: Thomas might not have eaten for hours. Her back was to him; Serafina chose her words carefully.

'No, Thomas. You have the right, it is true, but I ask you – I beg you – not to. Promise me you'll not kill him, Thomas. It would gain me nothing, you see.'

She was exhausted and confused; she no longer even understood herself. If the thought of Jehan, garrotted and flung into the Arno, had momentarily sickened her, then still the image of Angelo dead, Thomas's sword in his belly, unnerved her.

'You're not to – promise me you will not kill him.' Her voice was harsh, hovering on the edge of hysteria.

And Thomas nodded, once, his face expressionless.

The maidservant came, and she ordered food and wine. Serafina forced herself to recover the appearance of normality.

When they were alone in the room again, Thomas said, 'He'd kept the original will. Jehan was going to bring me your father's will, Serafina. The one he and Angelo suppressed.'

She would not drink with him, she thought. The wine would taste of gall.

'I don't think,' said Thomas, taking bread and wine from the tray as the maidservant returned, 'that Angelo can have learnt anything from Jehan. The body had been in the water some time before it was found. I spoke to one of the Nadi servants, who enjoyed telling me all the delightful details. I've seen drowned men, Serafina, and I suspect that Jehan was killed shortly after he met me. And surely Angelo would have searched me out if Jehan had given him my name.'

He broke off a piece of bread, dipped it in the wine. 'So you're safe,' he said. 'Thank God.'

Francesco is safe, he meant. Thomas had once made the error
of staking his claim to the child, and Serafina knew that he did
not intend to make that mistake again. But that did not mean he
did not care for the boy. She found, unexpectedly, that she
wanted to comfort him.

'Francesco is here,' she said. 'He's upstairs.'

Thomas stared at her, confusion on his face. On her return to
Italy, Serafina had paid a surprise visit to the wet-nurse. Francesco's clothes and bedding had been soaked with urine, his
skin red and chafed and covered with an angry rash. She had
lost her temper, had slapped the highly recommended wet-nurse
and taken her baby back to Pisa immediately, and had then
tramped the back streets of the city until she had found a woman
capable of nursing him.

'The place was not suitable,' she said. 'The wet-nurse was an
incompetent idiot. Francesco can stay here until he is weaned.'

He had put aside the remainder of the food, and risen from
the chair, a new expression in his eyes.

She said, crossly, 'I cannot afford to lose him,' and then could
have bitten her tongue. She might just as well have struck him, as
she had struck that fool of a nurse.

'Insurance,' Thomas said, and smiled unpleasantly. 'Francesco
is your insurance, isn't he, Serafina? Just as the will was Jehan's.'

She knew that they teetered, yet again, on the edge of a
precipice. Part of her wanted to let the quarrel run its course, to
shout and rage at him, to reinforce his judgement of her. But a
greater part knew that today she would find no redemption in
that sort of scene, that she no longer had either the energy or the
passion. That Thomas had, after all, tried his best for her, and
that the world had narrowed, almost unbearably, to Francesco,
asleep in his cradle upstairs, and Thomas, just a few feet from
her, his eyes a dark angry blue. There was, simply, nothing else.
The emptiness of her soul would never be filled.

So she bit her lip, and said, 'He's all I have, Thomas. Of my
blood, there is Francesco, and there is Angelo. That's all.'

The moment of danger retreated. Serafina found herself going
to Thomas, inviting him to put his arms round her, to rest his
face against the crown of her head, to caress the unbound silky

dark hair. She heard him say, 'I've a favour to ask of you, Serafina.'

It was no favour at all, really. Yes, she would be happy to give a home to Maria Garzoni, Costanza's daughter, for as long as necessary. Maria could play with the baby, could keep an eye on the new nurse. She was happy to do it, because she, too, had debts to pay. To Costanza, who had helped her, pregnant and ailing, from the street. And to Galeazzo Merli, who had made her a laughing-stock when she had been at her most vulnerable.

It hurt her though, as Thomas slipped the bolt in the door and she allowed herself to seek distraction in the only way she knew, it hurt her to consider the irony of it all. Because the greatest debt, the one that had been owing to her for years, would never now be repaid. And when, finally, she closed her eyes and gave herself up to the pleasure of his body, she found that it was Angelo's mouth she imagined, pressed against her own skin, Angelo's body she felt welcoming hers.

PART XIII

1597

GOOD COMPANY IN ALEPPO

In the year of our Lord 1583, I, Ralph Fitch of London merchant being desirous to see the countries of East India, being chiefly set forth by the right worshipful Sir Edward Osborne knight and Mr Richard Staper citizens and merchants of London, did ship myself in a ship of London called the *Tiger*, wherein we went for Tripoli in Syria: and from thence took the way for Aleppo. Being in Aleppo, and finding good company, we went from thence to Birra.

Voyage of Ralph Fitch from Goa to Siam:
Richard Hakluyt

For the representatives of the Levant Company – John Keane, master of the *Legacy*, Edward Whitlock, master of the *Garland*, and Izaak Taylor, master of the *Saviour of Bristol* – the Inn of the Customs at Aleppo was the culmination of an exhausting five-month-long voyage.

They had made good speed, though, thought John Keane, as the manservant showed them their allotted rooms in the European merchants' khan. They had rounded the coast of Spain in late October – and, thank God, no over-zealous Spaniards had been lurking in the choppy waters of the Cape to avenge their royal master's ignominious defeat of 1588. The convoy had reached Livorno in December, using the port that had been John Keane's home for most of 1595 to make any necessary small repairs to the ships, and to replenish stores. They had then sailed from Livorno to Aleppo, docking in Scanderoon, Aleppo's port, only a fortnight previously, and making the uncomfortable camel trek from Scanderoon to Aleppo in a bone-bruising three days.

Now, thought John, stripping off his dusty shirt and rinsing his face and chest with great handfuls of cold water, now the fun really started. The bit that he enjoyed most. The trading, the bargaining, the gaining of a few extra ducats for a bale of broadcloth, a few more for a barrel of tin. He was not, when it came to it, a true man of the sea, enjoying the discovery of new routes, new countries, above the absorbing game of trade. He was not an Anthony Jenkinson or a Ralph Fitch, carving out a name for himself in distant wastes, on unseen waters. He endured the months at sea merely as a means to an end, as a passage to the limitless rewards of trade.

John Keane began to dress himself in crimson doublet and hose, to attach a modest ruff and cuffs to his clean shirt, to run his damp hands through his sparse hair, coaxing it into some sort of order. From outside the shuttered windows of the khan floated the sights and scents of Aleppo. The song of the muezzin, calling the faithful to prayer, the 'Destur!' of the street-porters as they ran through the crowded suks and mahalles, laden with baskets and baggage, the scents of camel dung and horse dung and spices and coffee drifting through the balmy Levantine air. John, squinting into a scrap of mirror, trimmed his beard and moustache with his razor, and smiled to himself.

The English vice-consul's house was pleasantly situated in one of the nicer parts of Aleppo. The acting vice-consul, George Dorrington, welcomed the masters of the English ships with enthusiasm, and showed them into a large cool room furnished in a mish-mash of Turkish and European styles. Three ornate, charcoal-burning braziers heated the room; there was, as with most Turkish houses, no glass in the windows.

'A good journey?' inquired George, waving vaguely in the direction of chairs, cushions and sofas.

'Good enough.' Edward Whitlock perched on the edge of a stool, and John Keane and Izaak Taylor lowered themselves awkwardly on to the cushioned sofas. 'A spot of bad weather round the Cape, but then, that can be to our benefit.'

'Aye.' Dorrington, a large, placid man, chuckled. 'Keeps the bloody Spaniards in port, eh, Ned?'

A manservant appeared, handing round trays of wine and nuts and sugary Turkish sweets. Dorrington squeezed his bulk into the room's only armchair.

'Can't live Turkish-style,' he complained, gesturing again at the banks of cushioned sofas. 'Takes half an hour and a couple of men to get me up from one of those damned things. Same with the food.'

He took a glass of wine from the tray and scooped up a large sugary pastry in one plump paw. 'I'm quite partial to the odd bit of *this*, but what use is it without a nice glass of wine to wash it down? Fortunately, the fellows from the last convoy brought me an excellent crate from Candia.'

Two vague blue eyes focused hopefully on Edward Whitlock. John Keane said hastily, 'I'm sure we can spare a few bottles, George. You can ride back with us to Scanderoon and choose what you want.'

The vice-consul's pleasant broad face looked relieved. 'Life's a bit short on pleasures here, you see,' he said, mournfully. 'You can get a glass of wine in the Jewish or Armenian taverns, but its in damned short supply elsewhere. And I can't bear their bloody kahveh, and the only time I tried opium it gave me a headache that lasted for a week. And as for *women*' – Dorrington's eyebrows threatened to disappear beneath his dun-coloured curling hair – 'well, who wants to pay for his pleasures by having his head chopped off?'

'The taverns,' said John Keane, delicately, 'the bath-houses –?'

'The bath-houses are full of ringleted little boys,' said Dorrington, through a mouthful of pastry and honey. 'And the whores in the taverns are all Greeks and suchlike. I like blondes,' he added, his voice plaintive. 'Besides, it's unhealthy enough here without giving yourself a dose of the pox as well.'

Keane, half smothered by cushions, let the manservant refill his wine-glass. 'Are you keeping well, then, George?'

'Averagely so,' George Dorrington pulled at his collar, further flattening the limp folds of his ruff. 'My damned knee's playing me up again, and I was sick with an ague for almost three weeks last autumn. But then' – he took another pastry from the servant's tray – 'no European lasts long here.'

'A year or so, at the most,' said Ned Whitlock, fidgeting on the edge of his stool. 'Michael Lock did well to stay two years in Aleppo. The climate doesn't suit us.'

'Scanderoon's worse.' Izaak Taylor, a tall, thin, lugubrious man, sprawled awkwardly on George Dorrington's silk-swathed sofa. 'The fever breeds off the marshes.'

'Yes, well.' Whitlock shook his head impatiently at a bowl of sugared almonds. 'We can't expect it to be easy. And the rewards of the Levant are great, aren't they, gentlemen?'

George Dorrington, smiling, nodded. The rewards were silk, spices, cottons, pearls, porcelain – all the rich treasures of the Orient. Aleppo, positioned at the junction of the Silk Road and the Incense Road, acted as a market-place for the vast caravans from the East.

'Besides,' added Whitlock, taking a letter from the inside of his doublet, 'I've good news for you, George.'

Dorrington's soft blue eyes gleamed as he slit the seal on the letter and began to read. 'It's from Ralph Fitch,' he said, joyfully, after he had scanned half a page. 'He'll be here in a couple of months to take up the post of consul. I'm going *home!*'

Finishing the letter, he stuffed it into his pocket. His wide baby face was infused with excitement; the corners of his mouth quivered.

John said kindly, 'You should be in England for the summer, George. Think of it – no more veiled ladies or uncomfortable cushions.'

'Fitch should do the job well.' Whitlock, who had sat still too long, rose from his stool and began to pace around the room. 'No one expected to see him back from his last voyage.'

John Keane, who had consumed too much sugary pastry and sweet wine, silently agreed. Ralph Fitch's great voyage had taken him from Tripoli to Ormuz, and from there to Goa, and on to the kingdom of the Great Moghul, and to Siam. He had returned to London eight years after he had sailed from it, to find that his colleagues had given him up for dead.

'There's talk,' said Ned Whitlock, pausing to warm his hands over a charcoal-filled brazier, 'of starting up a new company soon. Serious talk, George.'

Dorrington's blue eyes gleamed with interest. Wiping his sugary fingers on a damp cloth provided by his servant, he said, 'To trade with the Indies?'

John grinned. Even Ned's face had lightened a little.

'The Levant Company's monopoly was extended to the Indies in 1592,' said George. 'It would be a logical step eventually to set up a separate company.' He paused. 'There would be – difficulties, though.'

In this part of the world, there were always difficulties. In spite of the three struggling braziers, the room had begun to chill with the darkening of the sky. John wished he had not abandoned his cloak to the servant.

'Who would make those difficulties, George?' he said, rubbing his palms together for warmth.

All traces of vagueness and self-indulgence had left George Dorrington's face. He shrugged. 'Even the Sultan himself cannot guarantee the safety of the inland routes. They can bribe and threaten all they like, but cities like Basra, Baghdad – even Aleppo itself – will rebel if they feel so inclined. And there's the desert robbers, of course, who'll have the clothes off your back and leave you walking naked home. If you're lucky. The big caravans can protect themselves, but any small party of Europeans are easy prey.'

'Ralph Fitch found himself thrown into prison in Goa,' said Ned Whitlock, meditatively. 'And they're a strange people in the Indies, by God. They think it a sin to kill a fly, but the women are expected to burn themselves to death on their husbands' funeral pyres.'

There was a silence.

Then: 'Pepper, ginger, nutmeg, camphor,' said George Dorrington, slowly. 'Musk, amber, rubies, sapphires, spinels. And diamonds. Fitch saw them all, Ned.'

The expression on all four men's faces was an identical mixture of hope and fear and fascination.

Then John Keane, seeing that the light was fading and that they soon must return to the merchants' khan, said, 'But now we must consider the present. Have the silk caravans come in yet, George?'

Throughout Europe, there was hunger. The rain had fallen three-fold for years, it seemed, battering the young corn in spring, cursing the growing grain with moulds and fungi. A cold winter followed the poor harvest, and sour winds whipped and tossed the ships on the sea, driving their way through the patched walls of every poor man's dwelling.

In France, in Marseilles, the beggar Jules Crau, who had thought he had seen everything that misery had to offer, found that there was more, much more. The predictions of the wandering friar he had listened to in the market-place were fulfilling themselves before his very eyes. They were hurtling towards the close of the century with relentless speed, forced to watch the world destroying itself. Jules had not yet seen sea-monsters rising from the deep, nor the Wild Hunt yelping their way across the skies, but he had witnessed enough to prove to him the truth of the preacher's words. In the towns, vagrants huddled at every street corner, the children's swollen bellies protruding through their ragged clothes, the skin of the adults falling in slack, wasted folds from gaunt limbs. In the country, the hungry pulled plants from the ground and stuffed them into their mouths as though they were exotic dishes from a rich man's table. Sometimes they died like that, their stomachs unable to accept what should have been the fodder of animals. Then they lay still in the fields, their eyes closed at last, fronds of green grass bristling from their frozen lips.

They became eaters of carrion, feasting on the flesh of dead horses, asses, and cattle. The roads swarmed with people, all of them hungry, all of them workless. Finally, they became cannibals.

Jules himself had eked out his dead wife's gold for as long as he was able. Isabelle's health had improved during those good weeks: the sores had disappeared from her mouth, and there had even been a little pink in her cheeks. She had begun to talk again, to take an interest in what was around her. Jules had felt as though he had drawn back from the brink of some nameless gulf, that his feet had found once again the comfort of steady land.

Now, sitting in their tenement room, the gulf yawned again. Isabelle was curled in a corner, scraps of ragged blankets heaped on her in an attempt to keep warm. Stroking her matted dark hair, Jules saw that her fingers were white with cold, her lips cracked and blistered. She slept most of the day, and Jules thought that one day she would simply sleep and never wake up. Then he would tumble into the darkness with uncontrollable speed, and be consumed.

The King of the Beggars had told him the causes of his suffering. The rich men in their palaces: the merchants and lordlings in their glittering houses, their dinner-tables heaped with extravagant food. They did not fulfil the duty that God had laid on them: to set the poor to work. Their lives were unchanged by bad harvests or unseasonable weather. Sometimes, standing outside one of those gilded palaces, Jules wanted to seize the bars on the window frames, and rattle them until the whole gleaming façade tumbled to the ground.

Lost in the clamour and darkness of the port of Scanderoon, Thomas waited at the harbourside.

He had tracked the *Fiametta* from Livorno to the Levant. Round the toe of Italy, across both the Ionian and Aegean Seas, beyond the islands of Rhodes and Cyprus. A few days – even a week – behind sometimes, always keeping out of sight. There had been no profitable stops at Zante, this time. The *Fiametta* sailed straight to Scanderoon, otherwise known as Alexandretta, the port of Aleppo.

The *Kingfisher* docked the following day, well out of sight of the French ship. If Angelo Guardi did not know Thomas Marlowe's face, then he did know Madonna Capriani's ship.

He knew that there was no sense to this final, secret pursuit. He knew also that when he had said to Serafina, *I'll kill him* he had meant it: he, who had never before killed in cold blood. He could have murdered Angelo Guardi with his bare hands, and taken pleasure in the act. But he would not, because other memories were more implacable. Serafina crying, *Todo mangiado.* Lost beyond recall. Serafina, forbidding him to kill Angelo Guardi.

He was within sight of the *Fiametta* now. He could see her gilded spars, bright against the fading light, see the name of Angelo Guardi's bride etched ornately along the bows.

Beyond the docks, the port of Scanderoon seethed with cosmopolitan activity. Tucked into the Gulf of Iskenderun, Scanderoon was a fever trap, surrounded by swamps, backed by the Amanus Mountains. The harbour was crowded with cumbersome single-masted merchantmen from the Black Sea, northern European galleons, and fast, frail caiques. And corsair galleys from the North African states, bobbing on the water. Thomas's eyes, narrowed, lingered on the corsair galleys. Some of the galleys were festooned with silk, ridged with banks of half-naked oarsmen. Many of the vessels carried a wreath of blue beads on the prow to keep away the Evil Eye. And one of them – just one – had a wreath of blue flowers painted round its prow.

But Thomas's gaze never left the *Fiametta* for long. He wanted to see the man who had damaged Serafina beyond repair, to see the man she still, despite everything, protected. The man who, unreachable, made happiness *lost beyond recall*. The man whose place Thomas knew now he had never begun to fill. He might have fathered her child, have given her the finest ship in the Inland Sea, have helped her build up her business until it had the possibility of greatness. But still, compared with her obsession for Angelo Guardi, he was insignificant, and their child was insignificant. Both he and Francesco were nothing more than pawns in a game Serafina and Angelo Guardi had played since childhood. A fatal, destructive game, but all-absorbing nevertheless.

It was because of Serafina that he waited here: Serafina of the dark eyes and dark hair and cold, closed heart. Throughout the three years they had known each other, Serafina had used him over and over again, in order to further her own ends. He had not understood her, at first; and then, when he had finally seen her for what she was, he had thought himself able to live with the knowledge of her indifference to him. Now, since Florence, since he had been forced to witness the expression of loss on her face, the anguish in her voice, he was not so sure. Once, it had been enough simply to see her, to share a room with her, to be invited to her bed, on her terms, when she needed him. Now, he recognized that her lack of need for him might destroy him. He had had other hopes and ambitions once: he thought sometimes that if he stayed in Italy much longer he would lose even them. And then he would be nothing, dust ground under a high-heeled jewelled slipper.

Although Scanderoon was a Moslem town, there were places where, if you knew where to go, you could find agreeable company.

Angelo, leaving the *Fiametta* that evening, needed respite from the strains of the past year. Surely he was due some sort of reward for having kept afloat, some sort of release from the restrictions he had enforced upon himself? It had not been an easy year; Angelo felt as though he had been continually forced to duck and weave to avoid disaster. For the first time in his life he felt tired, drained by the continuous effort required for survival.

He was walking through the darkened fish-market. The paved square was empty, but his feet slipped and slithered on the scaly stones. The stench of gutted fish still thickened the air, even though the fishmongers had long since quitted their baskets. Angelo did not press a perfumed handkerchief to his nose, however: he was not a gentleman, to pretend horror at the smells of the city. He was a bastard, an upstart, an opportunist. Because of that, he respected Islam, and had no qualms in dealing with its less orthodox representatives. The Moslem states, unlike their Christian counterparts, allowed bastard upstarts to fulfil their worth. Here, slaves could become rulers of men, if they worked hard enough. Angelo had always worked hard. It was only lately, since he had had to kill Jehan, that his industry had begun to leave a mark on him.

He passed the bath-house, closed now, the coffee-maker no longer squatting outside, head bent over glowing charcoal. He was heading for the Armenian tavern, following instructions relayed to him by the comitre of the corsair galley in the harbour. Angelo had the true traveller's gift of finding his way through unknown streets almost by instinct.

He thought, as he reached the Christian mahalle, that he heard a footstep behind him. But when he turned, studying the darkness of the unknown city, there was nothing.

Inside the tavern, the room was low-ceilinged and poorly lit, lined with wooden benches. Clouds of smoke from pipes and bubbling crystal-bowled nargilehs scented the air with the heavy, sweet smells of bhang and opium. The tavern's clientele were a mixture of sailors from the port, and the Armenians and Jews who largely populated the Christian quarters of Scanderoon. But there was also a group of janissaries in one corner of the room, their high sugar-loaf turbans almost touching the ceiling.

The noise was shocking after the quiet of the streets: the plangent notes of the dulcimer, played in the centre of the room, were drowned by the quarrelling of the janissaries, the shrieks of laughter from the women, the calls for wine and tobacco. Only the opium smokers were silent, isolated in the timeless world of their dreams.

Angelo stood in the doorway, a confident figure dressed in red velvet lined with black silk, letting his gaze slowly wander the width of the room. A woman, wearing the bright multi-layered costumes the Armenians favoured, stepped forward out of the smoky darkness and touched his arm, but he smiled and shook his head. That could wait. Eventually, looking around, Angelo saw, through all the seething, noisy figures, a single familiar face, so he pushed his way through the crowds.

The man, seated on one of the cushioned benches that lined three sides of the room, was dressed in Moslem fashion, and was about ten or fifteen years older than Angelo.

'Brother,' said the corsair, smiling, and bowed.

His name was Hamid, and his acquaintance with Angelo had originally been one of chance and mutual convenience. But over the ten years since their first meeting, if they could not have called each other *friend*, then at least an affinity based on mutual respect and recognition of the other's worth had developed between them.

'Wine?' said Hamid, indicating the carafe on the table between them. 'Tobacco? Hashish?'

The corsair smoked a nargileh, a mouthpiece attached to a long flexible tube and a bowl which could contain tobacco, hashish, or opium. Angelo drew up a stool and sat down opposite the corsair. 'Wine,' he said. 'For now.'

He took the carafe and poured some red wine into a tumbler. With the first mouthful some of the strain of the past few months began to ebb away, and the image of Jehan's drowned corpse, which had haunted his sleep since Florence, began to seem unimportant, distant. Here, he could believe again that fate would rise if he clicked his fingers, and dance to a tune of his own making.

'And how, brother,' said the corsair, watching Angelo, 'is your fine ship?'

There was only the merest trace of irony in Hamid's voice. They had not met since Zante, and that meeting had, for Angelo, been a humiliation. Angelo glanced across the table, almost expecting mockery. But the corsair's dark eyes were interested, almost affectionate, and his mouth, showing blackened, broken teeth, was still smiling.

'The *Fiametta* is in good repair,' said Angelo. He found that his brow and the back of his neck were damp with sweat, even though the unglazed windows of the tavern sucked the heat and smoke from the room. 'She's heavy with gold, Hamid, to spend in the great cities of the Levant.'

The corsair's eyes flickered, and he touched the greying tips of his beard. 'Then shall I waylay you, brother? Shall I point my cannon at your so fine ship and rob you of your gold?'

In the far corner of the room the group of janissaries had begun to sing tunelessly. The dulcimer player still crouched over his instrument, but only he could hear his melody. Someone had sat down on the bench next to Angelo and the corsair and, always careful, Angelo checked that the stranger's face was unknown to him, his tattered European jacket and hat unremarkable. One of the many European sailors from the port, thought Angelo, in need of a drink and Christian company.

'Brother,' said Angelo, gently, to the corsair, 'your feeble bâtards would not breach the *Fiametta*'s hull, your lean oarsmen could not outrun her sail.'

Hamid's grin split his lean, weatherbeaten face in two. 'I would not wish to sink the *Fiametta*, my friend,' he said. 'Merely to take her back to Barbary with me, so that I could study her piece by piece and see how she is made.'

The stranger sitting next to Angelo had applied himself with enthusiasm to a bottle of red wine.

Angelo said, his own smile matching the corsair's, 'Would you abandon your galleys, then, Hamid?'

Hamid was not drinking: the pipe he smoked gave off mingled scents of tobacco and hashish. Angelo breathed in the heady perfume and thought, yet again, that the ways of the East were really so much more sensible than those of Christianity. With hashish or opium you could find yourself a glorious peace, a peace that for Angelo had always been unobtainable through alcohol. He had never understood Jehan's obsession with a drug that simply made its adherents boorish and uncouth. Wine did not offer opium's delicious rush of pleasure, that sinking of the senses into something altogether unexpectedly delightful.

Later, though. There were some pleasures that opium interfered with, and Angelo intended to have his fill of those as soon as possible. After all, on his return to Italy there would be Fiametta, and a necessary pretence of adoration until their marriage, at least. An unexciting prospect: that brief encounter in the gallery of the Nadis' house had shown Angelo that, for him, the only gain to be found in the marriage must be financial.

The corsair, momentarily putting aside his pipe, said, 'The days of the galley are numbered, my friend. The new European ships can put to sea in all weathers, at all times of year. They are fast and strong and they do not need a hundred Infidels to row them. Soon, they will outrun and outfight us. We, too, must change with the times, or we die.'

The janissaries had begun to squabble, drawing their great, curved swords. There was the sound of breaking pottery, metal clashing against metal. The innkeeper hastily cleared the centre of the floor, making a space for the dancing-girls. The black-hatted European next to Angelo had folded his arms and closed his eyes, and was snoring slightly.

Angelo said, his voice pleasant and detached, 'There's a European ship in Scanderoon at the moment. An English vessel, from the Levant Company. Her name is the *Garland*.'

The girls ran into the centre of the room, a shiver of scarlet and emerald and gold, beribboned tambourines in their hands. A drummer sat cross-legged on the floor to the side of the dancing-girls, a fiddle-player squatting beside him.

The corsair's eyes moved slowly back to Angelo. 'Our friend from Zante,' he said, slowly. 'The Englishman who cheated us of our tin?'

'Yes. I've made enquiries.' Angelo pushed his fingers through his damp hair, loosened the laces at the neck of his doublet. 'There are three English ships, but their masters are in Aleppo at present. They will return here soon, though.'

The girls had begun to dance, their movements rhythmic and swaying. There were half a dozen of them, four grown women and two younger girls of fourteen or so, twins, identical in appearance and dress. All were Armenians, dark-haired with smooth, ivory skins, their dress a gaudy layering of skirts and jackets, trimmed with jangling beads and bangles, edged with ribbons and braid.

Angelo, his eyes resting on the two young girls at the front of the group, added, 'The *Garland* is a small ship, somewhat patched and old. But the other two vessels – the *Legacy* and the *Saviour of Bristol* – are galleons. Well built and seaworthy the pair of them. Take just one back to the Barbary coast, Hamid, and dismantle it piece by piece, and you have your pattern for the future. With the assistance of a suitably talented shipbuilder, of course.'

'Oh . . . ' With a smile, Hamid leaned back against the cushioned wall. 'We pluck shipbuilders from the sea like carp. Our fleets are built and crewed by such fine Christian fish.'

The youngest dancing-girls had moved back from the centre of the floor, and a woman a few years older had taken their place. Kneeling on the floor, she swayed her body steadily backwards, so that the light caught on her hollowed throat, her small waist and round, full breasts.

'The janissaries call her Leilah,' whispered Hamid to Angelo, 'which means, black as the night.'

Angelo saw that the woman's thick black hair now brushed against the dusty ground, a great blue-black waterfall, rippling and glinting in the candlelight. Gold and silver chains circled her forehead, wrists and ankles, so that if he narrowed his eyes all he could see in the darkness were those swaying golden lights, that hypnotic, night-black hair.

A silence had blanketed the room, until there was only the hoarse repeated notes of the two-stringed fiddle, and the incessant drumbeats. The drumbeats quickened, echoed Leilah's movements as she sank further and further downwards until the back of her head touched the floor and her body arched like a snake before it pauses to strike.

Angelo found himself rising, like several others, to spit on a gold coin and press it to her damp exposed forehead. Soon, Leilah's forehead and shoulders were covered with small coins sticking to her hot skin. She was like a Byzantine mosaic, faceted with gold. Angelo, bending over her, saw that her black hair had fanned out around her, her lips and eyes were half closed, her skin translucently white. She looked – drowned, thought Angelo, shuddering. The music had stopped: he was seized by a feeling of dreadful emptiness.

Angelo found that he was perspiring as he turned back to the corsair. The sweat was cold, trickling down his back like ice.

'Drink, brother,' said the corsair, gently, pushing the carafe across the table. 'You look as though you have seen an afreet.'

Merely a memory, Angelo wanted to say as his trembling hands accepted the carafe. Of a fool and a drunkard. He could not think why the thought of Jehan, of all people, should haunt him. Or was it the child that he had seen in that drowned face? Little Serafina, taken so long ago from the bagnio or harem, bundled into a sack and thrown, still living, into the sea?

No. Angelo took a deep breath, and reminded himself that that had not, in the end, been Serafina's fate. Serafina had died, like so many others in her situation, of a fever whilst enslaved in a house near Oran. God had taken her before Angelo had been able to carry out his own arrangements. Hamid himself had told Angelo that, ten years ago.

He swallowed a long draught of wine. The corsair said slowly, as a troupe of dancing-boys took the place of the girls, 'Concerning the *Garland*. I would not set two ships against a convoy of three English vessels. The odds would be too poor, brother, much too poor.'

Angelo did not reply, at first. He had almost forgotten the *Garland*; he found himself gazing at the dancing-boys as though he, like the janissaries, appreciated their sort of beauty. Dressed like girls, with long, curling hair, the boys snapped their fingers and turned and twisted in time to the music. The janissaries shouted their appreciation, and banged their fists on the table. Nearby, the black-hatted sailor had sprawled forward on to his folded arms, and was sleeping, dead drunk.

Angelo knew that the corsair was right, that to set the *Fiametta* and the corsair galley against the three English galleons would be folly. And yet he was surprised at how much he resented that admission. He knew that the key to his success had always been his cool-headedness – his intelligence, charm and appearance had been invaluable, of course, but it had been his ability to separate his emotions from his intentions that had served him so well. He had thought it a good omen when he had found the *Garland* in Scanderoon: recompense for the difficulties that Charles de Casaulx, Jehan de Coniques, Lorenzo Nadi, had given him. Not forgetting the English master of the *Garland*.

Eventually, Angelo said, 'Of course. Such a venture would be suicidal. Though they'll be laden with silks and spices, which should slow them up. And the *Fiametta* would be a match for them, I warrant you. But we'll see. I'll wait a while. One of the ships may break off from the convoy. Winds may separate them – who knows? After all, they might carry tin' – and he smiled again – 'for Cyprus or Candia.'

The boys had finished their dance. Crooking his finger, the corsair beckoned to one. The boy was olive-skinned, neat-boned, about ten years old, perhaps.

'And you, brother?' Hamid asked Angelo, folding his hand over the child's jewelled fingers.

Angelo understood him immediately. The dancing-boys stood, always smiling, their faces beaded with perspiration. The girls had not left the room: they sat on the floor, their heavy colourful skirts flowering out around them. He saw the woman to whom he had given the gold coin, black-haired Leilah, who had momentarily reminded him of what Serafina might have become. But his eyes did not linger on her; instead they travelled to the twins sitting beside her. The two girls were small and dark and self-composed. Serafina, he thought, as she once had been, before both he and God had interfered. Perhaps it was time to exorcise a ghost.

Angelo shook his head, and nodded in the direction of the Armenian twins.

'Which one?' asked the corsair, grinning.

'Both,' said Angelo, and rose from his seat.

*

It was only when Angelo and the corsair had gone, accompanied, to the curtained rooms behind the tavern, that the black-hatted European, who was not drunk at all, sat up.

He had blue eyes and black curling hair, and he was out of his seat and threading his way back through Scanderoon's silent streets before Angelo Guardi had stripped the two giggling Armenian girls of their layers of complicated clothing.

The following morning, Thomas Marlowe set out for Aleppo.

Serafina had been glad to say her farewells to Thomas. Alone, she could lick her wounds, and sort out the complicated tangle of feelings that on his return from Florence had threatened to overwhelm her.

In the beginning, she had thought of nothing but Angelo. The Angelo of her childhood, who had crowned her with rosemary and bindweed before he had betrayed her. The Angelo of her recent voyage to Marseilles, whose touch had mesmerized her, and who had said, *I have already found a way out of my difficulties.* The Angelo of Florence, drawing a line of red across Jehan de Coniques's throat.

That image had haunted Serafina, adding to her familiar nightmares. When, at night, she had woken, shaking and screaming silently into the darkness, the loneliness had been unbearable. *Thomas,* she had found herself saying, as her empty arms clutched the pillow for comfort. Eventually she had risen and, wrapping a shawl round her shoulders, had gone to the nursery. She had not taken Francesco from his cradle, but had simply looked at him, a candle clutched in one hand, the other hand gently stroking the small curved cheek, the warm fragile head in its lace bonnet.

She began to let Amadeo and Michele take over more of the day-to-day running of the company. Amadeo had proved himself during her absence in France; Michele was honest and hardworking. Other matters needed her attention, now. One of them was Francesco, of course, but the other was the courtesan's daughter, Maria.

She had agreed to take Maria into her house as payment to

Costanza, and to avenge herself against Galeazzo Merli. Maria arrived as Thomas left for Aleppo, a whirlwind that swept through the house, changing it beyond recognition. The order that Serafina had imposed on the Capriani house dissolved, so that books and pens went missing, to be found three weeks later in some totally ridiculous place, and strange clutter covered the chairs, the tables, the passageways. Once, Serafina almost tripped over a sleeping kitten curled on the top of the stairs; once she discovered a bird's nest, complete with fledglings, in Jacopo's favourite chair. Oddities from the market-place and harbour jostled on the window-sills and bookshelves: an ivory elephant, a collection of silver bells, a jointed wooden clown for Francesco.

But Serafina found, unexpectedly, that she enjoyed the girl's company, that the house altered with Maria in it, finally sloughing off the drab skin of Jacopo's making. With the baby's babble and Maria's chatter and laughter, the Via S. Domenico seemed a happier, brighter place. And Maria, only a few years younger than Serafina, was not the empty-headed scatterbrain that she appeared to be. She was patient and affectionate with Francesco, and a source of conversation in the evenings for Serafina herself. *Female* conversation: a luxury hitherto denied Serafina, lacking both sisters and friends.

Once, sitting in the parlour with Maria, Serafina became aware of an unfamiliar feeling. The cold afternoon light streamed through the window: outside, apprentice-boys made castles of ice on the Arno, just as they always did at carnival-time. Francesco, crawling already, was trying to heave himself to his feet with the help of a chair. His nurse often scolded and tried to keep him in his cradle, but Serafina took a guilty pleasure in watching him stumble about the room like an ungainly puppy. In the counting-house below, Amadeo and Michele were writing up the ledgers for the day: in artisans' homes throughout Pisa, silk was being woven for the Capriani company.

And, somewhere, hundreds of miles away, Thomas Marlowe sailed the *Kingfisher*. To buy raw silk and precious fabrics, to sell the broadcloth and linen they had bought in Marseilles and Avignon, and the ribbons and trims from Naples. Thomas would

not return to Pisa for months, until midsummer, estimated Serafina. Suddenly, she found herself missing him, wishing that he
was here now, watching his blue-eyed son drag the tasselled
table-cloth to the floor, listening to one of Maria's complicated
stories about the convent. It would have felt complete, then.

She shook herself, and told herself not to be foolish. When
she and Thomas were together, they only quarrelled. Thomas
was needed in the Levant, and she was more than capable of
managing on her own in Pisa. She did not need him. You
should not miss a business partner.

Still, Serafina found herself scooping Francesco up from the
floor and lavishing kisses on his round, bare head.

John Keane, returning to his room in the Inn of the Customs in
Aleppo, discovered that he had an unexpected visitor.

Having drunk too much of George Dorrington's precious
Candian wine, having mapped unimaginably glorious futures
for both the Levant and the new East India companies, John
knew that both his head and his stomach were far too unsettled
for sleep. The khan was silent; outside, the streets of Aleppo
were drained of both people and light. Closing the door behind
him and placing his candle on the table, John yawned, loosened
the laces of his doublet, and prepared for the tedium of a sleepless
night.

It was then that he heard a small noise in the darkness, and spun
round, his hand reaching for his dagger. But another hand folded
over his, stopping him drawing his weapon from the sheath, and
a voice said softly, 'Neither a thief nor a djinn breaking through
the walls of your chamber. You won't need your knife, John.'

He recognized the voice instantly. 'Thomas Marlowe, by God,'
said Keane, and released his grip on his dagger. He squinted; his
eyesight, poor at the best of times, was particularly inadequate
in the darkness.

'I apologize for the dramatic entrance,' said Thomas, cheer-
fully. 'I told the servants I was an itinerant Spanish camel-trader.
It's amazing what some people will believe.'

'There is,' said John Keane, recovering his breath and indicating Thomas to sit down, 'a door.'

Thomas grinned. 'I know. I picked the lock. But I wasn't sure whether this room was yours or Whitlock's. Thus the lurking behind the curtains.'

'Ah.' John, seated now, studied his visitor. It had been only a year since he had seen Thomas Marlowe for the last time; when Marlowe, more or less recovered from his near-fatal fight with Ned Whitlock, had repaid Whitlock the money he had earlier borrowed from Keane to complete the *Kingfisher*. With John watching, of course, to ensure neither drew a sword from his scabbard.

And yet, squinting again, Keane thought that Thomas had aged more than a year in that time. He must be about thirty now, John estimated, but he looked older. The single candle on the table fought feebly against the darkness, but Keane thought that there was a bruised look about Thomas Marlowe's eyes and mouth, as though the struggle with Ned Whitlock had not been his last. John, remembering the gossip he had heard during his latest visit to Livorno, frowned.

'What brings you to Aleppo, Thomas?'

'Much the same as brings you, my friend. Trade.' Thomas leaned back in the chair, one booted foot resting on his knee. 'Silks and taffetas and kerseys and linens and serge. In lesser quantities than the Levant Company, of course. I haven't the contacts – yet.'

'I meant,' said John Keane, with a smile, 'what brings you to my room in the Inn of the Customs? Disguised as a Spanish camel-trader – if there are such things. *Trade?*'

He kept his voice low: both Ned Whitlock and Izaak Taylor had nearby rooms.

'Not quite,' said Marlowe. 'Though I wouldn't mind being pointed in the direction of a good dragoman. Mine has the most appalling stutter. But – no. Let us say that I am hoping for conversation, John. To hear gossip about London, the company. To hear my own tongue again.'

There was, thought John Keane, watching him, some truth in what the navigator said. Not the entire truth: he would have, he thought, to wait a while for that.

'I can find you wine, if you wish,' he offered. 'We've a bottle or so somewhere. I've had enough of the stuff at George Dorrington's house.'

Thomas shook his head. 'Is Dorrington consul now?'

'Acting vice-consul. A temporary stopgap. We go through consuls in Aleppo at a shocking rate. The damned climate. George is a good man,' said John Keane, 'but so bloody lonely stuck out here you get smothered with hospitality whenever you visit. I' – he patted his stomach ruefully – 'have just gorged myself on Turkish sweetmeats and Madeira wine.'

A little of the tension had relaxed from Thomas's face. He said, 'Is the company doing well, then, John?'

Thomas Marlowe, noted John with interest, might have lived away from the country of his birth for the last three years, and might now sail for a young, pushy Italian widow, but to him, the English Levant Company was still, 'the company'.

John nodded. 'Extremely well. In fact' – a moment's thought, and he took a calculated risk – 'we're considering setting up a sister company.'

He saw the blue eyes widen briefly. 'The Indies?' asked Thomas.

'Of course. After Fitch's expedition it's the obvious next step. The Levant Company has profited well enough to finance such a venture.'

John was silent for a while, recalling that evening's conversation in George Dorrington's house. Then he added, 'We would need men, of course. And ships.'

Marlowe's brows twitched, but he said nothing.

Keane said, gently, 'Come home, Thomas. You've been away long enough. Four years now, isn't it?'

Marlowe frowned. 'Almost. The *Toby* sank in the autumn of 1593.'

The darkness had etched deep shadows into the pilot's face, from nose to chin, between his brows.

'Come home,' repeated John Keane. 'The company has need of you. And of your ship. She's a beauty, Thomas, I knew that the first day you showed her to me. She's made for wider seas than the Mediterranean.'

Thomas said, as John had known he must, 'And what of Ned

Whitlock? If I'd found myself in his room by mistake, I doubt if he'd be begging for my company.'

Keane, wishing he had not drunk so much wine, knew that he needed all his judgement for this conversation. He had seen the look of longing in Thomas Marlowe's eyes.

'Ned,' he said, carefully, 'is settling down a little. Faith is pregnant again – Ned's hoping for another son. I suspect that if you managed to keep out of his way for a while, he would eventually come to tolerate you. And, after all, unless you sailed in the same convoy, you would not have to see too much of each other. And besides –'

He paused, took a deep breath. 'How long will you go on hiding from Ned, Thomas? For another year – another decade? Until you die?'

The muscles in Marlowe's mouth clenched; his hand, resting on the side of the chair, whitened. Thomas did not reply immediately and, for the hundredth time, John Keane found himself wondering why the pilot had not returned to England after the shipwreck of the *Toby*. He knew, though, why Thomas Marlowe remained in Italy now.

'I have other commitments.' His voice was heavy, as though he found no delight in those other duties.

John said, 'I know. We docked in Livorno on the way here. I enquired after you there.'

Thomas glanced up sharply, anger in his eyes. 'And you discovered – what?'

'That you are working for a woman, called Capriani. A silk merchant.'

What he had heard, but had left unsaid, hovered dangerously in the air between them. Vicious Tuscan gossip said that Thomas Marlowe's relationship with Madonna Capriani was one closer than that of mistress and servant. That Madonna Capriani, once a maidservant, had bewitched a rich old man and married him for his money. That, once married, the scheming bitch had exhausted her aged husband of his strength so that he had died within the year. The most scurrilous tongues had said that Madonna Capriani had poisoned her husband. That the beautiful, elegant Madonna Capriani was a witch.

He would have a fist slammed in his face if he repeated that
sort of rumour.

Changing the subject, John said, 'I'll have influence within the
Levant Company soon, Thomas. I'm to marry Dorothy Jenkinson on my return to London – you know that we've waited
long enough – and Doll wants me to take control of the company shares she's inherited from her father. They'll give me
influence, they'll allow me to make decisions. To choose whom
I sponsor, which ships I'll back. I doubt if I'll sail much more
myself – my eyesight is worsening. But I still want the *Kingfisher*,
Thomas, and I want you to sail her.'

He saw Thomas open his mouth and make ready to refuse
him, but he interrupted the pilot, laying his final, most tempting,
cards on the table.

'Think. The inland route's a poor one, as you know. Too
many bandits and brigands – even the Turks themselves can't
guarantee its safety. We need to look for better routes. Round
Africa, or the Americas. We need navigators with experience
and imagination.'

Thomas said nothing but, looking at him, Keane knew that
the pilot was no longer in Aleppo with the scent of spice and
bhang and kahveh and camels, but on the wide empty ocean,
where there was only salt water and pitch, and the endless battle
against forces of almost unassailable strength. Some men went
mad out there; others became addicted to it, as the pipe-smoker
was addicted to his opium.

'No,' said Thomas, suddenly, and shook his head. 'I'm sorry,
John. I'm glad for you – glad to hear about Dorothy – and I
wish the East India Company every success. But, for the moment
at least, my commitment is to Tuscany.'

His voice was brisk, emphatic, but John knew that he had
forced him to think, to consider where his true loyalties lay.
Watching him, John Keane also knew that the rumours he had
heard had been correct. Thomas and the Italian woman, he
thought, wonderingly. She could be the only reason the navigator had refused his offer.

Then let Thomas waste his talents in the Mediterranean a little
longer. Let him learn to long for the freedom of the ocean, the

independence offered by an organization such as the East India Company.

Thomas stood up. 'Listen to me, John. This is not a social call, as I'm sure you've realized. I'm here to warn you. In return for having fished me out of the sea at Livorno.'

Keane glanced up sharply. His head had cleared, but his stomach still grumbled its revolt. '*Warn* me?'

'Yes. Listen – when I sailed to Zante for you last year, I had a little encounter with another ship. A French ship.'

Briefly, Thomas outlined to John Keane the episode of Hieronymo Carcandella, and the tin, and the corsair galley.

When he had finished, John Keane, frowning, said, 'There are no rules, nowadays, we all know that. Sadly, Christians attack other Christian vessels all too often, as you once reminded me yourself, Thomas. Though I must admit, I have not often heard of Christians assisting the Turk in piracy.'

'The point is,' said Thomas, softly, 'that the *Fiametta* is docked in Scanderoon. And so is the Turkish corsair.'

John Keane swore. 'And?' he said.

'And I overheard a rather fascinating conversation between Messer Guardi and his infidel friend. Messer Guardi regrets the loss of the tin. Messer Guardi still takes considerable interest in the cargo of the *Garland*.'

Keane stared at the pilot. He thought rapidly. 'And will neither know – nor care – that she now has a different master?'

Leaning against a carved wall-screen, Thomas shrugged. 'Of course not. So be careful, John, on your way home. You may not find your return voyage totally uneventful.'

He paused, seemed almost ready to go. Then he added, 'Of course, there is another way.'

'– so sweet,' said Maria Garzoni, making clucking noises with her tongue. 'Isn't he, Serafina?'

'He' was a bad-tempered balding green parrot that, bored with his perch in the corner of the market-square, was proceeding to pull out his colourful tail-feathers, one by one.

'And the gentleman says, only ten ducats!' finished Maria, triumphantly.

She glanced at Serafina anxiously. The bitter winter had softened a little at last; a weak primrose sunshine gleamed on the cobbled streets and tiled rooftops, a few spring flowers quivered in the breeze. The improved weather had propelled most of Pisa out of their houses: to talk on street corners, to bargain for overpriced vegetables in the market-place. Maria breathed in the heady chill air that was the beginning of spring, and gazed at the parrot again.

'The fledglings all died, and Leo spends most of his time hunting,' she said, mournfully.

Leo was the cat, given to Maria by William Williams before he had sailed for Aleppo. A scarlet tail-feather fluttered to the ground, and the parrot swore.

Serafina said tactfully, 'Leo wouldn't care for a parrot. It is possible that he had something to do with the fledglings. And just think what vocabulary Francesco might acquire.'

'Oh.' Maria, never downcast for long, held out a hazelnut to the parrot, who accepted it, cursing. 'I suppose so. Though Thomas would like it. Sailors like parrots.'

'Sailors,' said Serafina, firmly, 'like a degree of tranquillity after a long voyage. Not some noisy creature bawling swear-words every time they come into a room.'

Maria allowed herself to be led away from the parrot towards the ribbon stall at the side of the square. Standing back, she watched Serafina finger the strands of silk and velvet, impatiently putting each bundle aside as she searched through the piles. Staring up at the sky, cloudless for the first time in weeks, Maria's thoughts drifted to the absent *Kingfisher*. How much longer would it be until the galleon returned to Pisa? Months, surely. When the *Kingfisher* returned, Maria and William Williams would marry. They had not yet told Costanza, because Costanza would worry and say she was too young. Costanza worried all the time now, it seemed to Maria. Maria tried to cheer her mother up with frequent visits, and trinkets given to her by Serafina. A piece of braid from Naples, a square of silk from Ormuz. Once, one of Costanza's eyes had been blackened and the side of her face bruised. Maria had hugged her mother and made her a poultice for the eye, but she had not asked the source of the bruises. There were some things, Maria knew, that Costanza would never discuss.

She heard a footstep at her side, a voice then said her name. Turning, Maria did not recognize the gentleman at first, and then, looking a second time, she knew him for Mama's friend, Messer Merli.

Messer Merli bowed, swept off his plumed hat. 'Madonna Garzoni. What an unexpected pleasure.'

He was a large, bald-headed man, dressed in expensive clothes. Maria smiled, because she smiled at everyone.

'Messer Merli,' she said, and curtseyed.

'Madonna Garzoni – Maria – may I call you Maria? I thought you might have forgotten me.' Messer Merli, too, was smiling. 'You are never at your mother's when I call.'

'That's because I stay with Madonna Capriani, now,' said Maria helpfully.

'I know.' Messer Merli's voice was gentle; his small grey eyes slid to where Serafina discussed silk trimmings with the stall-keeper, pouring scorn on the quality of the goods on display. 'I didn't know that your families were friends.'

'Oh, we are!' Half of Pisa was a friend to Maria, and Serafina, in the absence of the unfortunate Sister Esmeralda, was Maria's most especial friend.

She tried to explain the relationship to Messer Merli, who was, she thought, looking puzzled.

'Messer Marlowe – who sails the *Kingfisher* for Madonna Capriani – is a friend of Mama's. Madonna Capriani has a dear little baby, called Francesco, and she wanted someone to help look after him.'

'A nursemaid's job, surely?' said Messer Merli, raising his eyebrows slightly. 'A young woman as pretty as you, Maria, should not have to work for her living.'

She had never regarded playing with Francesco as work. 'Francesco is a darling,' Maria said, firmly. 'I'm very happy to keep him company.'

Messer Merli smiled again. 'Of course,' he said. 'And is he a healthy child? He's Madonna Capriani's only son, I believe.'

Not far away, the parrot was squawking and rattling the iron chain that attached him to the perch. Maria considered Francesco who, next to William and Mama, was the joy of her existence.

'He's a very healthy baby,' she said. 'And – yes, he's Madonna Capriani's only son. Her husband died a few days before Francesco was born, you see.'

Which, when she had first heard it, had struck Maria as a very sad story. And Madonna Capriani had, it was true, been unhappy when Maria had first gone to live in the Via S. Domenico. So Maria had talked to her, and encouraged her to play with the baby, and gradually Madonna Capriani had cheered up. Sometimes she even laughed, now. And when Messer Marlowe came home, Maria thought that Serafina Capriani would be happier still. Maria liked Messer Marlowe a lot.

'And the baby – Francesco,' said Messer Merli, casually, 'does he resemble his mother?'

Maria considered for a moment. 'He has Madonna Capriani's dark hair,' she said, mentally picturing Francesco's small round face. 'And her nose and mouth. But his eyes are blue.'

'Really?' Messer Merli's gaze travelled back to Serafina, bundling ribbons into a bag. 'How interesting.'

The first cloud had covered the face of the sun, blotting out the rays of light. The colours of the market-place diminished, scarlets darkening to crimson, golds dulling to ochre. Messer Merli, taking up Maria's hand, began to stroke his thumb along the inside of her gloved palm.

'I saw your mother yesterday,' he said. His eyes studied Maria's face and figure intently. 'She did not look well.'

Maria wanted to draw her hand away, but the grip on her fingers was firm. 'Mama?' she said, anxiously. 'Ill? What do you mean, Messer Merli?'

He raised her hand towards his mouth. 'I mean,' he said, 'that you should have a concern for your mother's health, Maria. That it is your duty to consider, perhaps, that dear Costanza will not be able to continue working for much longer.'

His lips touched her fingertips, trailed down her fingers towards her palm, yet she could not move.

Then a different, more familiar voice said, 'It's time to go, Maria. The company here is not always to my taste.'

Serafina's voice was an ice-cold accompaniment to the wind that had begun to stir up the leaves and litter beneath the market-stalls. Maria felt her hand dropped suddenly as Messer Merli turned on his heel and walked from the market-square.

Serafina said sharply, 'What did that man want, Maria?'

Maria shook her head. She found that she was shaking, that although she did not understand at all what Messer Merli had wanted, she was frightened.

'He asked where I was living,' she whispered. 'He asked about Francesco. And he said Mama was ill!'

She saw Serafina's eyes narrow fiercely. She looked, thought Maria, even more angry than she had been with the artisan who had used inferior silk to weave her cloth. Maria's own eyes ached with unshed tears.

'Your mother isn't ill,' said Serafina, firmly. 'I saw her myself yesterday. She's a little tired, that's all. But you shouldn't speak to Messer Merli, Maria. He's not a good man.'

Maria's hand burned where his lips had touched it. She wanted to pull off her glove, to grind it into the dirt with her heel. Some of the tears spilled over her lids.

Serafina said gently, 'Forget him. There's no harm done.'

An arm linked comfortingly through Maria's; Maria scrubbed at her face with the back of her hand. She heard Serafina add, 'Besides, haven't we more shopping to do? A parrot to buy, for instance?'

The sea, as Angelo Guardi's ship the *Fiametta* neared the island of Cyprus, was like old glass. Smooth and translucent, an endless pitting of small rivulets and waves.

He was, Angelo reckoned, as he looked out to sea from the bridge of the *Fiametta*, almost within sight of the English Levant Company's foolish *Garland*. When he rounded the next headland, there he would sight her, small and heavy, her cannon without half the reach of the *Fiametta*'s.

He had scarcely been able to believe his luck, when he had watched the *Garland* sail alone from Scanderoon in the direction of Cyprus, while her sister ships, the *Legacy* and the *Saviour of Bristol*, travelled south towards Alexandria. A quarrel, he had been told. The master of the *Garland* had wished to trade his cargo of tin and broadcloth in Cyprus in return for honey, turpentine, and alum. The masters of the *Legacy* and *Saviour of Bristol* had favoured Alexandria, and its fine cottons. The master of the *Garland*, a fiery man, had lost his temper, had shouted and waved a pistol about until anyone with any sense had moved well out of his way. He had then set sail for Cyprus alone, whilst the *Legacy* and the *Saviour of Bristol* had set off sulkily south for Alexandria.

Angelo, quickly readying his ship, followed after the *Garland*, but at a discreet distance. The corsair ship which, with its banks of oarsmen, possessed a useful finishing speed, followed after the *Fiametta*. Under lavender-coloured, cloudless skies, Angelo tracked his victim round the tip of Cyprus's panhandle.

He felt relaxed and in good spirits after his stay in Scanderoon. He had done a little business there, had begun to arrange purchases, to place bids for the bales of silk from the next camel train. When he and the corsair caught up with the *Garland*, trapping her in a pincer movement like a scorpion's deadly embrace, then Angelo would have the ship's cargo and Hamid her crew. Tomorrow he would return to Scanderoon and sell that cargo, so that he could repay some of the debts he had not told Lorenzo Nadi about. Then, providing he did good business in Aleppo, his future would be assured.

It was late afternoon. They had sailed since dawn and the sun, a small shell-pink disc, was sinking towards the horizon. It must be today, though, thought Angelo. He would not wait, in case the *Garland* put in at some fishing village on the way to Kyrenia.

Resting his elbows on the gunwale, Angelo thought of the two Armenian girls. He had spent three enjoyable nights in their company, and had rewarded them handsomely for their efforts on bidding them farewell. He thought again how sensible the ways of Islam were. In Aleppo, had he taken the turban, he could have had a seraglio-full of jewels like those.

Rounding the headland, Angelo caught sight of the *Garland*. The little ship was almost within range now, silhouetted like some black paper cut-out against the rosy sun. Calling to the master-gunner, Angelo ordered his men to clear the gun-decks and ready the *Fiametta*'s cannon.

The gunports were opened, the cannon rolled forward. The gunners began to push powder into the barrels with the gun ladles, lifting the heavy iron shot from where it was piled on the deck. They were good cannon: bronze, their barrels highly ornamented with lettering and scrollwork. Angelo had spent a great deal of money on them.

He remained on the bridge, perfectly calm, the small breeze ruffling his hair. He was smiling: the *Garland*, heavy with tin, bobbed on the sea like an unsuspecting game-bird on a pond. The stillness of the weather was to Angelo's advantage: the *Garland* could not sail at any speed without a strong wind. The *Fiametta*'s own broad sails gathered every small scrap of wind, transforming it into speed. Behind them, Angelo could see the corsair ship, growing larger and larger by the second. Fifty long oars dipped and raised in unison, skimming towards the two galleons like a malevolent water-boatman.

The master-gunner called to Angelo that the *Fiametta* was ready for battle. Angelo nodded, and felt the vibration of the cannon-shot through the wooden decks. The ball fell wide of the mark by a hundred yards or so. Angelo was not perturbed. His intention now was to frighten the *Garland*, to demonstrate to her that to fight was futile, that if her master and crew wished to survive, then she must surrender. He did not want battle. He wanted tin, and Hamid wanted slaves.

But the *Garland*, who must have known by a single glance that she was outgunned and outclassed, did not signal her surrender. Instead, there was an answering orange flash and a cloud of white smoke, and a cannonball soared into the air and fell, considerably short of the *Fiametta*'s bows.

The *Garland* must have seen the corsair galley by now, thought Angelo. Every man on deck would know that they were fighting not only for their livelihood, but for their nationality, their religion, their freedom. Angelo's smile had widened into a broad grin. It was like a chess-game, he thought, another move in the contest he had begun more than a year ago, in Zante.

There was another crack of thunder from the *Fiametta*'s

cannon, closely followed by a thud and the sound of splintering wood from the gun-deck below. The smile disappeared from Angelo's face as he saw smoke billowing out of the gunports, clouding the sunlit image of the *Garland*.

As he ran down the steps from the bridge towards the gun-deck, the heat of the flames struck Angelo in the face. He seized the nearest sailor and shook him.

'The ropes on the cannon broke, sir!' The man's face was a patchwork of red and black with the heat and smoke. 'It crushed two of the men –'

The fire, shrinking already, thank God, was confined to a corner of the wooden deck. Angelo could see scraps of scorched clothing, tangled limbs that hardly approximated to humanity. Grabbing, like the rest of them, a bucket of water, Angelo threw it on to the flames.

At last the fire sizzled and died, and the smoke began to disperse, so that Angelo could see round the deck. He saw that the ropes that had been slung to his fine bronze cannon to dampen their recoil had snapped, so that the five-hundred-pound gun had hurled itself backwards, shattering the floor of the gun-deck, pinning two gunners to the broken boards. The fire had been begun by a stray spark catching on a bundle of sailcloth that someone had carelessly left on the deck.

If the flames had caught the barrels of gunpowder – stacked much too close to the cannon – then they would have blown the *Fiametta*'s hull in two.

Angelo, glancing round the disorderly deck, felt a cold, over-mastering anger. And beneath the anger, a frisson of fear, reminding him uncomfortably of the nausea that had overtaken him in Florence, after he had identified Jehan's naked corpse. He had used not to feel fear. This fear told him that, though he always planned, he had somehow overcommitted himself, and events were slithering out of his control.

The master-gunner pointed to the two men trapped beneath the cannon. 'What shall we do, sir?'

Had they been injured dogs, or horses, thought Angelo, then he could have slit their throats. It was all they deserved, after all, for not maintaining the cannon.

He said curtly, 'Give them a pint of brandy each, and let them lie there till we reach port. We'll not shift the cannon now.'

He knew that the two men would die of shock and loss of blood within the hour. No one survived wounds like that.

Climbing the steps to the main deck, he shouted to the master-gunner, 'Ready the cannon again. Aim for the galleon's bows the next time.'

He was glad to leave the inferno of the gun-deck for the comparative silence of the maindeck. His ears pounded with the noise of the cannon, the screams of the injured men. He was breathless, as though he had been running, but he told himself it was from the foul air below decks, the stench of blood and smoke and saltpetre. Taking a lungful of fresh air, wiping the smuts and soot from his face, Angelo stared out to sea.

He thought it was a mirage, at first. Or a trick of the fading Levantine light, or some strange reflection, called up by the slowly setting sun.

But, blinking, wiping the smoke-induced tears from his eyes with the back of his hand, Angelo knew that what he saw was reality: damnable, unbearable reality.

For the *Garland* was no longer alone. There were two more ships facing the *Fiametta* now, and their names were the *Legacy* and the *Saviour of Bristol.*

Angelo guessed straight away what had happened, and the thought was intolerable to him. They had tricked him: somehow the English ships had known his intention, and had deliberately set out to revenge themselves for his previous attempt on the *Garland* in Zante. The two larger galleons must have changed course as soon as they were out of sight of Scanderoon, circling Cyprus from the south. And the *Garland* had crawled at a deliberate snail's pace, a tempting stalking-horse for any greedy merchantman, allowing the two greater galleons to reach the northern coast of Cyprus in time. Angelo, fists clenched, teeth bared, found the thought that he had been outwitted unbearable.

Then there was no more time to think. He yelled his orders to his men; he heard the cannon readied with an unprecedented speed, saw every man on board pick up and load an arquebus.

Angelo, too, had his flintlock, and his sword, and his knife. Looking back, he saw that the corsair galley had sighted the *Legacy* and the *Saviour*. As he watched, the blue-wreathed prow swung round as the galley dipped her oars and turned against the wind, heading back towards Scanderoon. Cursing Hamid and all his brothers, Angelo heard the creaking of the *Fiametta*'s timbers and the beating of her sails overhead as a groan of despair, but he did not, like the corsair, turn tail and run.

They hurled cannon at each other like tennis balls, batting them across the open sea, fracturing the glazed green surface. One of the *Fiametta*'s shot hit the *Legacy*'s superstructure, another deprived the *Garland* of the top of her bowsprit. And then one of the *Legacy*'s cannon-balls struck off the *Fiametta*'s hull.

It should not have mattered. It was a glancing blow, hastily aimed, missing its true target. Had the *Fiametta*'s timbers been of good quality, had they been properly caulked in dry dock, then it would not have mattered. But the long strip of planking shivered and split and tumbled into the sea. Angelo, running to the gunwale, saw the sea, which had seemed so calm, so kind, reach up and throw itself against the *Fiametta*'s damaged hull. The planks on either side of the splintered timber fell away as though they were no more than poorly glued matchsticks, and the sea wormed its way through the gaps in the pitch. Weakened since the day she had been launched by the constant drenching of the sea, the *Fiametta* seemed almost to welcome her ravishing by the waters. Even as Angelo ran down through the darkness of her decks to assess the damage, he could hear the dreadful sound of the sea forcing its way into the *Fiametta*'s hull, dragging her beautiful, neglected frame downwards.

Angelo heard himself screaming as he ran back up endless stairs to the open air. He did not know what he was screaming; he thought his voice was the *Fiametta*'s, railing hopelessly against fate, that always won in the end.

That he saved himself was instinctive, the consequence of a lifetime devoted to survival. Had he taken time to think, then he would have drowned, like the rest of them.

He was in the water, and he could see a barrel a few yards

away, bobbing in the waves, one of his own seamen clutching the rim. The barrel was not buoyant enough for two, so Angelo took his knife from his belt and stabbed the sailor before the other man even looked round. The sailor's fingers loosened, the clear blue water thickened with red. Angelo held on to the barrel.

Behind him, the *Fiametta*, and all of Lorenzo Nadi's gold, sank inexorably into the sea. The corsair galley was already out of sight. The three English ships, having achieved their purpose, were rolling their cannon back into the gunports. The sea, soon, was silent, Cyprus's coast stained purple and crimson by the setting sun.

Not much of a swimmer, Angelo let the tide wash him and the barrel up on some silvery beach. There, he slept.

PART XIV

1597

FALSE AND SOPHISTICATED COMMODITIES

Take with you those things that be in perfection of goodness. For false and sophisticated commodities shall draw you and all your commodities into contempt and ill opinion.

Notes for the Discovery of the North-East Passage: Richard Hakluyt

A few small wooden boats on a crowded pond. The news of the loss of one of those boats spread ripples throughout the Mediterranean, the circles of rumour growing ever larger in the telling.

For Edward Whitlock and John Keane, sailing for the English Levant Company, the sinking of the *Fiametta* was nothing more than a day's work, a task necessary to the continuation of trade. Another story for Ned to tell to his son when he returned to London, another reason for John to give in to his failing eyesight and accept thankfully that he need not be a sailor much longer.

At the dockside in Alexandria, two months later, Thomas Marlowe heard the news whilst directing the loading of the *Kingfisher* with cloth. One of his fellow-countrymen bawled the latest gossip over the sounds of hammers and saws and clouds of black, whining flies. The Englishman was celebrating the victory with a bottle of aqua vitae: invited to share, Thomas shook his head, and waved one clenched triumphant fist in salute to the all-conquering sea. Then he hustled the ship's boats out towards the *Kingfisher*, impatient at last to return to Italy, and Serafina.

The ripples lapped only gently at the distant shores of Italy. Lorenzo Nadi, checking the calendar, frowned a little. And Serafina Guardi, cradling her one-year-old son in her arms, thought only of the present, and not at all of the past or the future.

In May, the beggar Jules Crau and his daughter Isabelle walked to the Church of the Holy Spirit in Aix-en-Provence. Rumour said that the rectors and bursars of the church were to give out bread to the poor, and Jules, seeing Isabelle's dull brown eyes and stick-like limbs, determined to walk to Aix.

The sun was shining, and the sky was a clear purplish-blue. They had survived the winter – just. Many others had not. Jules felt his daughter's fragile weight on his shoulders, her thin hands touch his head. Once, he had picked daisies for her and sung songs; today, in spite of the sunshine, he found he was no longer able to do so. Hunger and despair had gnawed at him until the effort of putting one foot in front of the other seemed all-consuming, and even Isabelle's frail body was an almost intolerable burden.

Inside the Church of the Holy Spirit, there was the smell of incense and unwashed bodies. High darkened walls, indented with statues and coloured glass windows, towered above them. All Provence, thought Jules, wonderingly, had come to beg for a crust. Isabelle stood beside her father, her small bony hand folded in his. The dead expression had left her eyes: she looked frightened.

Jules could not see the rectors and bursars. He knew when they arrived with the bread, however, because a new smell, sweet and warm, drowned the incense and sweat. Then the people began to move forward. Individually at first, but then the disparate parts cohered into a mass: the huge, uncontrollable body of the hungry of Provence.

Jules's tired mind was suddenly aware of a danger he had not predicted, and he tried to pick Isabelle up, to lift her back on to his shoulders. But he could not bend, could not free his arms, which were pinioned by the pressure of the crowd to his sides. He cried out, 'Belle! Belle!' with a choked voice, but even the sound of despair was lost, stifled by the press of the people around him, and by the echo of hunger against the high walls of the church. He felt her small fingers slip from his, and he could do nothing to staunch that inexorable lessening of touch, nothing to seize back the life that was more dear to him than his own.

Later, they reckoned that there had been twelve hundred people in Aix that day, hungry for bread. When they finally managed to clear the crowds from the church, they found that seven women and children had died there, trampled to the ground and suffocated.

Jules Crau's daughter Isabelle was one of the seven.

★

Angelo, having taken passage on a Cypriot fishing boat, a Cretan barque and, finally, a merchantman belonging to one of his countrymen, found himself in Italy by June.

In Naples, in a rented room, with the bright sun glaring through the dusty shutters, he wrote a long, blustering letter to Lorenzo Nadi. Angelo, a realist, knew that the letter would achieve nothing, but at least he had tried. Lorenzo Nadi would, in all probability, demand the repayment of his lost ducats as well as forbidding the alliance of Angelo and his daughter.

Scrawling his signature at the bottom of the paper, Angelo paused, thinking. He had also written, separately, to Fiametta: a rather more successful letter, he thought, summing up the pain of loss with a few well-chosen strands of poetry. But again he acknowledged that the effort was almost certainly futile. Had Fiametta Nadi possessed the passion of either her mother or her sister, then he might have had some kind of hold on her. But she had been a cold, gauche creature, and he expected to receive no reply to his letter. Fiametta Nadi and the dreams she had once represented were lost to him as her namesake, now no more than a clutter of waterlogged timber on a distant shore. He wrote only because he knew he must be thorough, leaving no loose endings, no profitable avenues unexplored.

Besides, he was not dependent on the Nadis' favour. Angelo had realized that in Cyprus when, after a week's illness, his capacity for survival had reasserted itself and he had begun to plan again. In Cyprus an old peasant woman, finding him beached upon the shore, had taken him into her hut. The sea had hurt him more than he had realized, and to begin with, lying on a straw-filled pallet, swallowing mouthfuls of foul-tasting soup, he had scarcely had the strength to fight back against his bruises and fever. Then, opening his eyes one silent, star-filled night, Angelo had seen the solution to his problems, and both the fever and the terrible, haunting sense of despair that had taken hold of him since the shipwreck of the *Fiametta* had left him.

He had dragged himself up from nothing before, he had reminded himself, as at last he had felt some of his old fire returning. He had been born with nothing, and once already he had almost lost everything he had held dear. Then, ten years

ago, his own will to survive had pitted him against Franco
Guardi's lack of foresight. Franco Guardi had said, *You are to
marry Michele Corsini, Serafina*, and he had seen all his hopes and
ambitions shiver and become insubstantial. He had had to take
extraordinary measures to secure his own position then, but he
had succeeded, catapulting himself to a position one of his birth
could never have hoped to achieve. And he would rise again, he
told himself, because despite the loss of the *Fiametta*, he still had
his looks and his strength and his intelligence, and nothing – no
one – could take those qualities away from him. Staring out
through unglazed windows at the black Cypriot night, Angelo
had known that he could fight back, begin again, because now,
at last, he had worked out where to begin.

His recovery had been quick, then: the following day he had
taken the old woman's small store of coins from their hiding-
place in an amphora and had left the hut while she was out
tending her flock of scraggy goats. A fishing boat had taken him
to Crete, where he had friends. There, he had borrowed clothes
and money, and had taken passage on a barque to mainland
Greece. In Greece, he had found a merchantman to take him
back to Italy.

Rising, Angelo went to the window and opened the shutters.
He could see the sea, a calm deep blue, flecked with silver. The
sky was cloudless, the horizon an almost seamless blending of
colours. Higher up, where the azure darkened to indigo, a flock
of birds whirled and soared on the currents of warm air. The
blue of their feathers was brighter and more intense than the
blue of the sky.

He found, watching the darting, swooping birds, that he was
smiling. Kingfishers, he thought, staring out of the window. How
apt. Had he believed in such things, then he would have thought
them an omen, but he left superstition to those fools who needed it.

He was smiling because there were, after all, other ships than
the *Fiametta*. One of those other ships was named – oddly, for a
Tuscan ship – the *Kingfisher*.

In Pisa, Maria fed the parrot hazelnuts and stared out of the
window in the direction of the docks.

The parrot was no longer as bald as Galeazzo Merli: green and yellow and blue feathers sprouted from his head, and his tail fanned out in glorious crimson whenever Maria stopped to speak to him. Even his language had moderated, so that he now only cursed when tormented beyond endurance by the cat, or by an increasingly mobile Francesco.

His perch was by the window because Maria had taken up almost permanent residence there. The ships were coming in daily to the docks now, laden with silks and spices and precious stones. The *Kingfisher*, too, must soon return from her voyage. Every time she glanced downwards to the street Maria expected to see Messer Marlowe, walking jauntily down the Via S. Domenico with William beside him.

'It's getting dark,' said Serafina, coming into the room and closing the door behind her. 'You'd better close the shutters.'

'Oh, just a little longer – please!' Maria, turning, looked up at Serafina. She added coaxingly, 'They said at the docks more ships were expected tonight.'

Serafina sat down at the table, a pile of ledger-books in front of her. It was a warm June night, and there was no wind to ruffle the pages as she turned them.

'Very well, then, a little longer. But when I light the candles you must close the windows, or the room will be full of insects.'

Maria rested her elbows on the sill again, her hands propped under her chin. There was silence for a while, broken only by the scratch of Serafina's pen across the paper, the occasional footstep from the street below. A feeling of peacefulness seemed to have settled over the city, making the sounds small and unobtrusive, the dying colours of the sun a celebration of summer and something else – security, that was it. A few days ago Maria had tried to explain to Serafina that she felt safe here, and Serafina had looked at her in surprise and then, unusually, hugged her. If William would come back everything would be perfect: she almost thought that if she closed her eyes and concentrated, then she could conjure him out of the darkness by the strength of her longing for him.

'They'll be back soon,' said Serafina, glancing up briefly from the ledger-book. 'The *Kingfisher* is a fine ship and Thomas an excellent navigator. The best. I don't really expect them back for a couple of weeks or so. They'll have gone to Alexandria, you see, and many of the ships arriving in port now will have only travelled as far as Scanderoon.'

Maria sighed. A sensible girl, she tried not to think of pirates, and tempests and unfriendly states. 'I know,' she said. 'Only . . .'

Her words trailed off into silence. Only it had been six months since she had bidden William goodbye on the harbourside at Pisa. Only Mama was looking tired and ill and nothing Maria said seemed to help any more. Only that awful man Galeazzo Merli had followed her to the harbour twice recently, talking to her and pawing at her. At Serafina's insistence first, and then of her own volition, she now took a Capriani manservant with her on her excursions, in case of encountering Messer Merli. She would have liked to have bought a very large and vicious dog, but Serafina had pointed out that she wished her house to remain a home, and not become a bestiary.

Sighing for a second time, Maria looked out into the street again. Out of the encroaching darkness a figure had materialized, a man, his face lost in the shadows. For a moment her heart began to beat wildly, but then, looking again, disappointment swamped her, and she turned back to Serafina and said, 'We've a visitor. I thought it was William or Messer Marlowe. But he's got yellow hair.'

Serafina rose and put down her pen and walked to the window. Looking down, Maria saw that the hair of the man in the street below was not really yellow, but a kind of dark gold, temporarily lightened by the flares in the sconces. He wore black velvet, and a black feathered cap that she had momentarily mistaken for Thomas's familiar broad-brimmed hat. Maria peered downwards. 'Do you know him, Serafina?' she said.

Serafina did not answer at first. Then she nodded and said, 'Yes, I know him. I knew him well, once.'

Angelo. Angelo had come unbidden to her house. Why?

Some instinct made Serafina, as soon as she had sent Maria off to bed, run down the steps and answer the door herself instead of waiting for the drowsy servants. The clatter of emotions in her breast was a tangled, ill-assorted mess: she only knew that she had never wanted any witnesses to their meetings. She was only capable of encountering Angelo Guardi alone, when there was no one else to draw on the reserves of strength and self-control she had built up painstakingly over the years.

She had no time to change her gown, or even to check her face in the looking-glass. He was there, on the doorstep, as she ran down the last few steps into the tiled hallway. As she opened the door Angelo bowed and made his apologies. Serafina found herself able to make the appropriate greetings, to bid Angelo inside and lead him upstairs to the withdrawing-room. One of the maidservants appeared, but she sent the girl away with a flick of her fingers.

Her life had settled to a rhythm these past six months: now, shockingly, that rhythm was broken. She could not breathe, she felt as though her heart had risen into her throat, choking her.

Angelo looked out of place here, Serafina thought, her gaze darting wildly round the small withdrawing-room. They no longer belonged to the same world: Angelo had become part of a different setting. An accident of birth had deprived him of a natural right to the backcloth he required, and she had intentionally been deprived of the life that should have been hers by right. Angelo looked incongruous here, amongst the humdrum clutter of the ledger-books, parrot feathers, and baby toys. He belonged to that decaying golden house in Marseilles, to a city which had become alien to her.

The parrot squawked and bawled insults so Serafina threw a cloth over his cage. The simple action gave her time to recover her breath and to think: to understand that now, surely, Angelo must be the petitioner.

Angelo, with a graceful movement of the hands, said, 'Madonna Capriani. I apologize a thousand times for calling on you without an invitation. And at so late an hour. But I was in Pisa – and remembering that we were friends –'

Another charming shrug of the shoulders. He added, 'You are well known in Pisa, madonna. I asked a passer-by for a merchant by the name of Capriani, and was directed here immediately.'

It was true: everyone knew her in Pisa, but Serafina had

begun to suspect that her fame bordered on notoriety. People stared at her in the street, whispering behind closed fingers as she passed them by, and once, a fortnight or so ago, a group of boys had thrown stones at her in the street. She did not care: she did not need friendship. She had Francesco and Maria, and she had her work.

Angelo refused Serafina's offer of food, but accepted a glass of wine. The pounding of her heart had lessened a little, so that she was able to say calmly, 'When we last met, Messer Guardi, you told me that you were soon to be betrothed. May I congratulate you yet?'

He smiled. The memory of that smile had once almost broken her heart, but now she found that though she could still admire the full, curved lips, the dark, almond-shaped eyes so like her own, she felt curiously distant from him, as though what she saw in front of her was only a recollection, a portrait of what had once existed.

She made herself drink a glass of wine to steady her nerves, to focus her mind. She heard Angelo say, 'I am not betrothed, madonna. I no longer intend to marry Fiametta Nadi.'

She had to clench her hands together in her lap to stop them shaking. She was seized with a wild uncontrollable joy: she had won. She knew now that her instinct had been correct, that now Angelo was a supplicant, a beggar, no longer her suzerain.

She looked up, raising her eyebrows inquiringly, enjoying the moment. 'You have disappointed the lady then, Messer Guardi?'

Angelo winced. But he answered, smoothly, 'Not quite, madonna. As you know, I had financial difficulties. These, sadly, grew rather too pressing. The arrangement was broken – with my consent – by Madonna Nadi's father.'

Her heart had started beating furiously again. Rising from her chair, forcing her stubbornly disobedient limbs to work, Serafina closed the shutters and began to light the candles. Out of utter defeat had come, somehow, triumph. Her fingers trembled as she touched the tinder to the wick.

Only a short while past, restitution had seemed impossible. Six months ago, on Thomas Marlowe's return from Florence, she had given up all hope of recovering what was due to her.

She had lived through those six months by teaching herself to be content with her work, and with Francesco, and with awaiting the arrival of the *Kingfisher*, laden with treasures from the Levant. But she had never been content. And now, suddenly, when she had abandoned all hope of restitution, she had unexpectedly been given all she desired.

What had happened to Angelo, out there in the Levant? Serafina could only guess at what might have taken Fiametta Nadi from him and sent him scuttling into a different sort of embrace. She had always been good at hiding her feelings; the years — Angelo — had taught her well. The façade she presented to him was the same façade she had shown in Marseilles: a beautiful, confident, self-composed young woman was reflected in Angelo Desmoines's black bright eyes. She knew that she had it within the palm of her hand to tighten her fingers and crush him, that the gilded youth of her childhood, the arrogant tyrant of her nightmares was dissolving before her eyes. She could have wielded the whip over him: he had set himself before her, offering himself to her, his head bowed.

But that was not what she wanted: she would not be so crude. Instead, she would allow him to hope for a while, just as once she too had hoped. Once you allowed yourself to hope, then you were vulnerable, because the death of hope was the most dreadful thing in the world.

She smiled. 'Then you are broken-hearted, Messer Guardi?'

He had settled back in the chair, one elegantly booted foot resting on his knee. Serafina noticed that Angelo had relaxed a little, that he believed the worst was over, assuming that now she had accepted his guarded admission of financial ruin, the rest would be easier. She had given him hope.

'Not at all, madonna. It was a business arrangement, that's all. My heart was quite unaffected by the breaking of an understanding with a rather plain Tuscan girl. It takes a different sort of woman to break my heart.'

'Really?' She had regained her control; the emotion she felt now was excitement, pure and bubbling like spring water. Fiametta Nadi, whom she had invested with every sort of fortune and beauty, diminished, and became an ordinary nineteen-year-old, no longer wanted by her lover. Putting the tinder back in the drawer, Serafina turned back to Angelo.

'What sort of woman would break your heart, sir?'

'Oh, she should be dark – Madonna Nadi was fair. And she should be small and neat, not tall and ungainly. And she should have a liking – no, a passion – for cloth. For silk.'

It was as though the two disparate halves of her life had finally coalesced. Serafina the child, the only daughter of a wealthy silk-merchant; Madonna Capriani the successful businesswoman. Her childhood – Marseilles, Algiers, all of it – had formed her into what she had become. Angelo wanted both now.

She said, watching him, 'That is somewhat ... perverse of you, Messer Guardi. Many of your fellow-merchants regard my interest in trade as an unfortunate blemish.'

'If such admiration is perverse, madonna,' he said, softly, 'then, yes, I am perverse. I appreciate you in your entirety, you see. I do not pick and choose.'

He rose from the chair, crossing the room to stand beside her. The candle-flames fought feebly against the twilight, casting long indigo shadows through the room. Angelo's face was shadowed too, an incised pattern of black and gold, emphasizing the strong lines of his features, the heavy thickness of his hair. She felt his hand touch hers, and as their fingertips joined a ripple of fire ran through her, igniting every nerve in her body. He means to seduce me, she thought, and she wanted to throw her head back and laugh. Such an old-fashioned form of trading. Why, she had used the same coinage herself.

Angelo drew her hand to his lips, kissing her fingers one by one. She could feel his warm, full mouth, the slight roughness of his shaven chin. Softly, he whispered, 'And you, madonna? I made enquiries – I was concerned – but I discovered that you have not yet remarried.'

She smiled. 'No one has offered, Messer Guardi. At least, no one who does not wish to pick and choose. Some would marry me for my looks, some for my money, and – one or two – would marry me for my head for business. But they are old men, and I would not marry an old man again.'

My life has been drawn by old men, she thought. By my

father, who would have married me to a stranger. By Kara Ali, who had rights of ownership over me. By Jacopo, who had an old man's impossible wish to recover his youth. Soon I will be free of them all. No man will own me.

She had not drawn back her hand. She would let him hope for a little longer, let him believe that he could buy what he wanted with his looks, his charm. Angelo's other hand touched the back of her head, tracing the twist of dark hair that curved around her crown. She felt him slip the hairpins from her head, and her hair tumbled in shining coils down her back. She looked up, studying his face, seeing the Aucassin of her childhood: thick gold-brown hair cropped around a broad, high-cheekboned face, curved red lips, and dark oblique eyes.

She said, softly, 'What do you wish to buy, Messer Guardi? And what are you selling?'

He smiled. 'I wish to buy a future. A future that, perhaps, we might share together. The future that you offered me in Marseilles, madonna, last summer. Our ships, bearing the Guardi banners. Our agents, in every port in the Levant.'

For a moment she saw it: a glorious vista of possibility. But then he took both her hands in his, raising them to his lips. 'And in return I offer you my name. And my reputation,' he added. 'And my history.'

You sell nothing that is yours, she thought, angrily. Everything that you offer is already mine. She felt the old familiar hatred stab at her, and she wanted to strike him, to claw at those bright, confident eyes, to tear at his velvets and silks.

But instead she let Angelo draw her closer to him, until she could feel the warmth of his body against her, smell the dusky scent of sandalwood that lingered on his skin, his clothes. She knew suddenly that she paused on the edge of a precipice, ready to take wing and fly into a dangerous unknown. She could possess him, as he had never succeeded in possessing her, and in doing so she could reweight the balance of the past.

Her voice shook a little as she said, 'And you, Messer Guardi? Do you also sell yourself?'

He understood her. His dark eyes flickered and widened, and she was aware that his breathing had thickened infinitesimally.

'If you wish it,' he said.

He did not stand in a slave-market in Algiers, and neither did he strip himself to tempt an old man into his bed. But he was no different: she understood him perfectly. They were so alike, she and Angelo. She wondered that he did not know her, that he did not realize that he stared into the mirror of his face and his soul. They shared the same blood, the same ambitions, the same passions. Angelo's need – her need – was for those great bales of coloured silks. Scarlet, turquoise, emerald, flame-coloured, the colours of a desire that had been implanted in infancy, a desire that only they, the Guardi, understood. They would both sell themselves for a few bright strands from the silkworm.

He bent his head, his mouth touching her forehead, her cheek, her neck. And then his lips found hers, drawing her to him, completing a circle that had been begun long ago, on a hillside near Marseilles. She returned the kiss, discovering that the excitement of triumph had not been quenched; instead, it was quickly but unmistakably transmuting into a different sort of passion.

She heard herself whisper, 'Then, this is not a room for the sealing of bargains.'

She led the way out of the withdrawing-room and up to her bedchamber, a single candlestick in her hand. The house was silent, blanketed with the peace of summer, isolated by memories. Angelo had offered himself, and she would take him, just as she had once taken a loaf of bread from a baker's shop, just as she had once stolen a blue bowl filled with almonds. She had learned a long time ago to take what was offered, not because she needed it, but because it was there. She wanted everything from him, because only that would recompense her for what she had lost.

But there was desire, too, bewitching and betraying, subtly altering what should have been the final move in a game plotted by hatred. Lying in her marriage-bed, her cousin's arms around her, Serafina thought once, briefly, of Thomas. Through a chink in the bed-curtains she could see the single candle in front of the window. Beyond the slatted shutters was the city of Pisa, bordering on the wide blue expanse of the Mediterranean. And above her she could see Angelo's face, blurred by darkness. His hands, his mouth, pressed against her body. Out of some distant time a familiar voice whispered, *You were in love with him. My God, you still are.* The thought came fleetingly to Serafina that she was in bed with a stranger, that she had grown used to the comfort of a different body.

She was reaching the end of a path drawn long ago, a path on which Angelo himself had set her, waving farewells to her from the dockside at Marseilles. She had no choice about what she did; she had never had a choice. Her bondage had been set upon her years ago, by this man. She tasted his salt skin, and felt his body, hard and demanding, move against hers. The excitement blossomed once more in her, compelling and sweet, an excitement born of both conquest and desire. She felt him enter her as she called out, for the first time in ten years, his name, and then she closed her eyes and shut out the light and gave herself up to the darkness.

Serafina did not think she would sleep, but she did. When she woke, the pure, clear light of early dawn was showing through the shutters.

She dressed quickly and silently, not disturbing the man who lay sleeping in her bed. Outside, the sun was an arc of silver on the horizon, washing the city clean. Standing by the window, Serafina's gaze rested on Angelo.

She looked at him, studying, as she had the previous night, every line and curve of his face. She felt nothing. The enchantment had gone, dispersed utterly by one short night. Looking across at the bed, she felt neither love nor hatred, desire nor loathing. Whatever spell he had woven over her had been broken, cast to the breeze like thistledown.

You were in love with him. No, not love. Infatuation, perhaps, or fascination. The allure of the handsome fairy-tale prince for the young girl. But she was a child no longer, and Angelo had never been a prince. Just a man, a deeply flawed young man.

It was time, she thought. Time for a final disclosing of secrets, time for an end to deceit. Serafina drew the bed-curtains and opened the shutters to let in the morning light.

Angelo stirred, opening his eyes. She saw, for an instant,

confusion and something else – fear? – in his dark eyes. Then the
fleeting expression was gone, and he yawned and stretched and
sat up in bed.

'Good morning, Madonna Capriani.'

She was standing in front of the window, framed by the
sunlight, balanced against the sill.

'Madonna Capriani – a little formal, don't you think, Angelo,
in the circumstances?'

She saw Angelo start briefly at the sound of his forename.
Swinging his legs over the edge of the bed, pulling on his shirt
and hose, he said, 'You are better informed than I, madame.
Perhaps you would do me the honour of telling me your name.'

'Serafina,' she said. 'My name is Serafina.'

He paused only for a fraction of a second. 'Serafina,' said
Angelo. 'It's a pretty name.'

He still did not know. His pause had been one of remem-
brance, not suspicion.

She said, calmly, 'I meant, I am Serafina.' She moved a few
steps towards him, away from the silhouetting sunlight. 'Look
at me, Angelo. Don't you know me? I am Serafina.'

The blood drained from his skin, leaving it bleached, like a
drowned man's face. His hair was still tousled, his features
blurred with sleep.

'I am Serafina Guardi,' she said. 'Franco Guardi's daughter.'

He was staring at her, his eyes wild. 'No,' he whispered. 'No.
Serafina is –'

'Dead?' She smiled. 'Then I am a spectre, an afreet. No,
Angelo. Serafina Guardi did not die. You made a little mistake.'

And his mistake, she now knew, had been in not considering
the possibility of love. It had been her one most precious wild
card: that the renegade physician Kara Ali had loved her, that
Kara Ali had loved all humanity, and therefore had not allowed
the janissary to take an eleven-year-old child away and kill her.
Love existed, but not in Angelo Guardi's world.

Angelo sat unmoving, a stocking halfway up one calf, his
shirt unlaced. He looked ridiculous.

'Franco –' he said, hoarsely.

Ah, Franco. Franco of the kind eyes and warm, generous

smile. She had never before said her farewells to him; now, at last, she must do so, consigning him to the silence of the past.

'My father died in the bagnio, as you ordered,' Serafina said. 'But I was taken from him and sold into slavery in a house near Oran.'

Angelo's voice was raw with effort. 'Hamid traced you there. He sent a janissary who discovered that you were already dead.'

He could not take his eyes from her. He watched her as though she were, truly, a spectre.

Serafina shook her head slowly. 'My master showed the janissary his own daughter's grave. I stayed with him for six years and then he helped me to leave Algiers and return to France. I went back to Marseilles and found that you controlled the company and owned the house and ships. And it was mine, Angelo, all of it. It is mine now.'

His mouth twitched until he was grinning in a parody of a smile.

'Take it,' he whispered. 'There's nothing left. I'm ruined.'

'Oh, I know.' She sat down at the small table, resting an arm along the polished wood. 'I have spent four years trying to recover what you owed me, Angelo, but in the end it was fate that chose to help me.'

Again, that terrible smile. 'No, not fate,' he said. 'The English Levant Company.'

She could not think what he meant, at first. Frowning, she heard him say, 'I tried to rob one of their ships a year or two past. A nice little cargo of tin, conveniently anchored in Zakynthos. It should have been easy . . .'

She knew which ship he referred to. The *Garland*, the English Levant Company ship that Thomas Marlowe had piloted to the island of Zante.

'They didn't take kindly to my interference, though.' Angelo's throat rattled in an attempt at laughter. 'And I have just returned from Scanderoon, where the visit was returned. Only the English were a little more successful than I —'

She did not understand him at first. Then she said, 'The *Fiametta*?'

'Is at the bottom of the Mediterranean Sea. Or scattered on the beaches of Cyprus.'

She knew, suddenly, with an instinct she could not have explained, that it had been Thomas who had been responsible for the sinking of the *Fiametta*. That great golden ship which the *Kingfisher* had raced to Marseilles was now nothing more than driftwood. Six months ago Thomas had said, *I'll kill him*. That he had not done so was due, perhaps, to the vow she had forced him to make, but his revenge had been sweet, just the same.

'Fifty thousand gold florins,' said Angelo, dreamily. 'Lorenzo Nadi's money, you see, Serafina. It was in my cabin. Fish food, now.'

Her voice cut through the stillness of dawn, a single small arc of pain, 'Why? Why did you do it, Angelo?'

He understood her straight away. They had always been close; in childhood, she had never had to explain to Angelo Desmoines, that had not been necessary.

Fastening his shirt, pulling on his doublet, Angelo said, 'Franco could not live for ever. He intended to leave the company to an ignorant Florentine lordling, and a woman. The Guardi company would not have survived in Michele Corsini's hands, Serafina. The Corsini owned silk-workshops, but they knew nothing about trade. They were old money, an old name, and that was why Franco wanted you to marry into them. He was always a fool for an old name. Remember Jehan.'

I could have done it, she thought. The tears were suddenly there, pricking behind her eyes. She knew now that if she had been allowed to run it, the Guardi company would not only have survived, it would have flourished. Yet neither Angelo nor her father, knowing her well, had considered her. An ignorant Florentine lordling and a *woman*. Once she had intended to ask him, Didn't you regret, just a little, what you did? Now she found that she no longer cared.

'I know what you did to my father,' she said. 'And to Jehan. But what of Monsieur Jacques? And Marthe?'

His hands, lacing the front of his doublet, paused at Jehan's name. One of the muscles around Angelo's eyes had begun to jerk with a small, uncontrollable rhythm.

'I hoped that I could make Jacques see sense,' he said. 'He was good at his job. He would have been useful. But then I saw that he was bound to make trouble. So I' – and the lace in Angelo's bunched fingers suddenly snapped – 'I made sure he couldn't talk.'

'You killed him.'

Her voice was flat, unemotional. She saw him nod briefly, abandoning the broken lace. 'Yes. As for Marthe – well, she was an old woman and she sickened and died. I had no hand in it.'

She believed him, and yet she found that she hated most of all what he had done to Marthe. He had let her die in the belief that her beloved charge was dead.

'What are you going to do, Serafina?' said Angelo, suddenly. 'Call the justices, make a deposition – slit my throat?'

He had regained some of his self-possession. He was smiling again, a true smile, born of a lifetime's confidence in his looks, his charm, his strength. No, she would not call the magistrate; nor would she hire assassins to kill him. It was complete. Even hatred had dissipated. A part of her life was finished with and could never return.

Serafina shook her head. Rising from the chair, turning towards the window, she saw the city of Pisa below her. Sunlight gilded its roofs and towers, and the clear blue light promised her everything. She wanted nothing more of Angelo Guardi. He had become insignificant: she was free of him. She felt the burdens of the past slide from her, tumbling to nothingness. She had everything she wanted: she had found all that was important, almost by accident.

She heard Angelo rise, and then the door opened and closed as he left the room. But she did not look back, because her eyes had fixed on the streets below, on a familiar figure striding through the early morning crowds.

A seaman's broadcloth and linen, a battered black hat over tangled dark curls, a bag slung over one shoulder. Thomas Marlowe, returning to Tuscany, having made good speed from the Levant. She had not expected his return for a week or so yet, but she knew now that Thomas was part of what she wanted, part of what she had found for herself in the years of struggle. Gathering up her skirts, Serafina ran down the stairs.

The front door was swinging open as she reached the hall.

She saw Angelo pass within a few feet of Thomas as he left the house, and Thomas, heading for the doorway, stop suddenly, staring at him. Then his eyes left Angelo, and he faced Serafina as she stood framed in the doorway. She had time to witness the shock of understanding in his blue eyes before he turned on his heel and began to walk away from the house.

Her hair still trailed loosely down her back and she wore only thin velvet slippers on her feet, but she ran after him. The streets were already crowded: apprentices going to work, maidservants hurrying to the baker's with baskets over their arms, stray dogs snuffling in the gutters for food. She pushed her way through the throng, the cobbles hard beneath her slippered feet, calling Thomas's name.

He did not stop until, catching up with him at a street corner, she grabbed his elbow. Even then he did not turn, until she cried, fighting for breath, '*Thomas.*'

He swung round. His skin was tanned, but he had a bruised look around his eyes; he had travelled, she thought, for a very long time.

He said, 'I thought he was dead.' And then, focusing on her at last, he added savagely, 'Why don't you marry him, Serafina? Angelo, of course. You could carve up the Mediterranean between you. You could have fleets of ships, houses in every damned city. You could even have slaves.'

She thought of Ibrahim, the household slave of her childhood in Marseilles, and she thought of herself in Algiers. She knew that she flinched.

'He's gone,' she said. 'Angelo won't be coming back.'

'Oh, you'll get him back.' Thomas's eyes were ice-cold: their expression unfamiliar to her, unglimpsed even in their worst quarrels. 'Of course you'll get him back. It seems to me that you get everything you want.'

Her hand had slipped from his elbow. They were crushed by the crowds into the curve of the street corner, no more than a few inches apart, yet not touching.

She said, trying to make him understand what she had fully understood herself such a short while ago, 'But I don't want him, Thomas. I realized that this morning. It's over. I'm free.

This' – and she gestured to the city of Pisa, bright and busy under the rising sun – '*this* is what I want. I am happy with this.'

'Congratulations,' he said, drily. 'I'm glad that one of us is happy.'

'I want *you*, Thomas!'

Even as she said it, she knew that it was true. She wanted Francesco, and she wanted the *Kingfisher*, and she wanted the glorious business of trade. But most of all, she wanted Thomas Marlowe.

'I love you,' she said. 'I know that now.'

Someone turned, smiling for a moment at hearing a woman declare herself in the middle of a busy street. But Thomas's face only changed infinitesimally, becoming a little sadder, perhaps.

'Don't you love me just a little?' she said, softly.

He did not move, did not answer, but just stood staring at her, his eyes bleak. Then he said, 'I loved you more than my life, once. Now – I don't know. I'm tired, Serafina. I've had enough. I'm going back to England.'

She could not take in what he said at first. She could not believe that she had lost him, just as she had finally recognized her need for him.

His eyes softened a little. He looked, as he had said, very tired.

'I'm taking the *Kingfisher* and going back to England,' he said, gently. 'I've been thinking of going home for some time now. I think I've repaid my debt to you. I've debts to pay to the Levant Company, too. They're unloading the cloth from the *Kingfisher* into the warehouses. We did good business in the Levant. You'll make a fine profit.'

She wanted to say that the time for profit and loss was past. But she could only repeat, her voice a mournful whisper, echoing off the old walls that embraced them, 'But I love you, Thomas.'

He touched her at last, his hands momentarily clasping her shoulders. 'Do you? I wonder. You've lied so often over the past years, I doubt if you'd recognize the truth if it came and knocked at your door.'

Letting go of her, he bent and picked up the bag he had dropped to the ground. 'Look after Francesco,' he said. 'Build a ship for him, one day.'

She still could not believe that he meant to go. 'But – Edward Whitlock?' she said.

Slowly, Thomas shook his head. 'I'll take my chance.'

She could not move. She understood finally that, despite everything, in the end she had lost. But, clawing at some of the pride that had sustained her for years, Serafina forced herself to smile. She whispered, 'You've done with ferrying woollen caps and ladies' stockings, then?'

Thomas had swung his pack over one shoulder. He called back as he started down the street, 'They say they're talking about starting up a new company in London, to explore the Indies. Perhaps –'

He was gone; a wave of tattered black hat, a sudden silence in all the noise and chatter around her. Serafina's eyes stung.

Perhaps, she thought. Perhaps.

In Florence, Fiametta Nadi, after enduring an interview with her father, knocked on her mother's bedchamber door.

Giulia was still in bed when Fiametta entered the room. Although it was midday, the bedchamber was dark, the curtains and shutters closed, the light filtering only slowly through the slats in the shutters. The bed and windows were hung with dark green fabric, and slippers, gowns and undershifts were flung carelessly on to the floor and furniture. Treading clumsily across the rumpled rugs and discarded clothes, Fiametta drew back the heavy velvet curtains, filling the room with the clatter of brass rings and a swarm of dust-motes.

'Darling –'

Giulia Nadi groaned and rubbed her eyes and sat up in bed. Turning, Fiametta surveyed her mother dispassionately: the crumpled silk nightgown, the disordered hair, the pale, puffy face.

'I need to talk to you, Mama. About my future.'

Giulia pulled a shawl around her shoulders. The air of the bedchamber was thick with the cloying odours of chypre and lavender. The scent, and the memory of her father's anger, made Fiametta want to retch, but she stood quite still at the end of the bed, her fists clenched in front of her.

'Your future is settled, dearest.' Giulia yawned. 'When darling Angelo returns –'

'Angelo has returned. But his ship has not.'

She had her mother's attention at last. The great blue eyes, a little faded in the bright morning light, focused on Fiametta.

'Papa received a letter this morning. Messer Guardi's ship will never return to Italy,' said Fiametta, blandly. 'It has sunk. The *Fiametta* has sunk.'

Giulia's jaw had dropped. She looked ugly, thought Fiametta, with her sagging chin and her creased brow, and the hundred small wrinkles that seamed her mouth. It would take a saucerful of paint to right that face for the world.

'With all of Papa's gold on board,' added Fiametta. 'He's very angry.'

It was the witnessing of that anger that had led her to this room, her errand only half formed in her mind. Only once or twice in her entire life had she seen Papa like that, but the threat of his fury was always there, as menacing and oppressive as a smouldering volcano. She resented his anger: she was tired of placating her father; she felt that she had spent her whole life taking Lorenzo Nadi's temper into account.

Giulia had climbed out of the bed and pulled on a robe. She, too, looked frightened.

'You'd better go to him, Mama,' said Fiametta, coldly. 'You can usually distract him.'

'Yes.' Her mother's voice was thoughtful, preoccupied. Sitting in front of a small table she began to brush out her long red-gold hair.

'Let us hope,' continued Fiametta, 'that Papa hears nothing else to annoy him. Don't you agree, Mama?'

Giulia twisted her hair into a knot on top of her head. 'Well, of course, dear. We must all be very careful. And you must not be upset, I'm sure we can find someone else for you. I always did think,' she added, her mouth full of pins, 'that Angelo Guardi was just a little . . . well, a touch of the parvenu, don't you think, darling?'

'I'll never marry.' Fiametta pulled at her plait of brittle, sandy hair.

Taking a rabbit's foot from a bowl, Giulia began to powder her face. 'Don't be silly, darling. You've had a disappointment, that's all. He was good-looking, I warrant you, but looks aren't everything. He's not worth pining over. Once they hear you are free again, Fiametta, the young men will be queueing at our door, I'm sure of it.'

'I'm not pining for Messer Guardi.' Fiametta threaded her strong freckled fingers together. 'I hated him. And I won't marry anyone else. I'd hate them all.'

Her mother, rabbit's foot in hand, turned round on the stool. 'Darling –'

'You're to let me enter a nunnery, Mama. And you're to endow it with a large amount of money so that I can be sure of becoming an abbess eventually.'

Giulia stared at Fiametta, and then she laughed. 'Don't be ridiculous, darling! Why should a daughter of mine enter a nunnery? Your dowry will guarantee you a good husband. And,' she said, frowning, 'Papa wouldn't like it. You know that. He wants you to make a good marriage.'

Fiametta's eyes were hard and cold as she studied her mother. She thought that although there were many women she despised, there had not been one she had ever feared.

'I won't do it, Mama,' she said, her voice cold and clear. 'I don't wish to marry, not anyone, not ever. And just think' – and she fixed her mother with a chill pale eye – 'how much angrier Papa would be if he was to hear about you and Niccolo Frescobaldi.'

Giulia gasped and dropped the powder jar. Powder clouded into the air, sweet and sickly.

Fiametta said, 'I'd make a good abbess, and a bad wife. It's up to you, Mama. But I think that if Papa was to find out about Messer Frescobaldi now, he might just kill you.'

Giulia's face was white with powder, white with fear. 'You are a wicked girl!' she gasped. Clumsy for once, she tried to sweep some of the spilled powder back into the bowl.

In spite of a lifetime spent nurturing an appearance of helpless prettiness, Giulia was essentially a practical woman. After a moment, she said thoughtfully, looking back at her daughter,

'So will Lorenzo kill me if I tell him that you intend to become a nun?'

'No, he won't.' Fiametta moved towards the door, a large, awkward girl clad in a gown of unflatteringly stiff pink brocade. 'He's still got Nencia, after all. She'll make a brilliant marriage for him. And you've always been able to persuade him to do anything you like, if you put your mind to it. I expect you'll still be able to do that,' she added cruelly, 'for a little while longer, at least.'

She left the room. Giulia, staring into the looking-glass, did not move at first, and then she rose and called for her maid.

He went back to Marseilles, his birthplace. Franco Guardi's home – Serafina Guardi's home – was his home, after all, the only one he had ever known.

Angelo sailed on board a Genoese carrack, buying himself a passage with the hollow tarnished coinage of his name, his reputation. Arriving in Marseilles, he went straight away to the Guardi house. His key slipped in the lock: he stood like a fool, trying to control the shaking of his hand, and in the end a servant had to open the door for him.

Inside, the house seemed strange, unfamiliar. He found it hard to recall which room was which, hard to remember the contents of each cupboard and chest. The sureness of touch that had once been his had been denied him, frozen to ice by long dark hair and a cold, remembering eye. He knew that now he saw everything through those other eyes, that Serafina Guardi's censorious gaze had entered his veins and was slowly paralysing him.

He went through the motions, however, he had sufficient pride – God in heaven, the family failing! – to continue to write letters, to enter figures in ledger-books, to calculate the extent of his ruin. He knew that he would lose the house, the servants, the smaller ships, all the trappings of his laboriously acquired status. But he continued to fulfil the role demanded by the life he had carved out for himself, because it was the only life he had ever known.

If it had been different, he thought once, waking in the middle of the night. But he knew that it could not have been different; the mould had been wrong since the day of his birth. His birth and his ambitions had always been out of step.

He knew that there was no solution to his problems: his existence was that of a rat trapped in a barrel, scurrying in ever more desperate circles through useless litter and old dead leaves. Angelo often regretted that he had not allowed himself to accept the embrace of the sea, and sleep.

Thomas, sailing the *Kingfisher* through the vast blue bowl of the Mediterranean beyond Sardinia and Majorca, made good speed.

Mostly, he thought neither about the past nor the future, but only of the present: the plotting of a course, the shortening and lengthening of sails, the search for the most useful wind. The continuing watch for other sails, the necessity of deciding, when others were sighted, whether they were friends or enemies.

He caught up with three ships a couple of days after he had left Pisa and, recognizing them, hung back, slowing the *Kingfisher*'s pace a little. The *Legacy*, the *Garland*, and the *Saviour of Bristol* were returning to England at last after having docked in Livorno for trading and repairs on the way back from Scanderoon. He would have preferred their journeys to be further apart, but the rapid departure from Pisa had given Thomas no choice. As it was, he would tread cautiously behind the three English ships, careful to offer nothing that could be interpreted as a challenge by Edward Whitlock. He would face Ned Whitlock in London: sane, sensible London, away from the feverish, fly-specked heat of the Mediterranean. He would have John Keane to speak for him there, and the *Kingfisher*, too, more eloquent than any words of defence he could conjure. A dove, for once, instead of a water-bird. A peace offering.

If Thomas thought of Serafina at all, it was to recall at sudden, unexpected moments, fragments of their life together: Serafina in Pisa, working in Jacopo Capriani's house; Serafina at the Merlis' banquet, proud and angry, already carrying his child. Most unbearably, Serafina in his arms, her face stained with tears, pliant and passionate. And Serafina on horseback, travelling at his side from Valencia to Marseilles, head bent, both of them

riding against the wind. It was all over now, but he was, thought
Thomas, looking out to sea, still riding against the wind.

Since Jules Crau had buried his daughter in an unmarked grave
on the outskirts of Marseilles, life had seemed purposeless, confusing. He felt as though he existed for some reason that he had
forgotten. He found that he could not recall one detail of how
he had spent the days since Isabelle's death, could not remember
having slept, or eaten, or spoken. Life consisted of a series of
unrelated, disjointed moments, with no rational thread linking
them together.

He found himself one evening in the market-place. On one
side of the market-place was a house made all of gold: the
sunlight picked that house from the others, lighting it like a
beacon. In the intense dying sun the reflected light from the
façade of the golden house hurt Jules's eyes, streaking his vision
with rhythmic beating flashes of purple, of silver, of red. He
could not look away from it. It seemed to Jules that the house
was evil, because he could not turn his eyes aside. The house
drew him, mocking him. He knew suddenly with utter certainty
that he was about to understand, that tonight he would be
shown the reason why he still existed.

At some point in the darkening evening he was aware of
someone beside him, saying his name. Out of the corner of his
eye Jules saw that one of his comrades from the Court of the
Beggars stood next to him. Even then he did not move or speak,
because he knew that he must not speak. The voices had told
him not to speak. He grinned instead, a terrible distorting of the
face which caused his friend to scuttle away, searching for his
fellows.

The evening was hot; sweat trickled down Jules's back beneath
his layers of clothing, but he was unaware of any discomfort.
Other beggars now crowded the square, brought by his friend.
Still Jules stared at the house, hypnotized by the many-coloured,
flashing sunlight. The house seemed to move and swell, filling
his vision, filling the sky.

At length, the front door of the golden house opened. Jules's
eyes flickered, and he swayed. A man walked down the steps,

and then turned into the narrow alleyway at the side of the house. The man was dressed in scarlet, and he had fair hair. He was evil, Jules knew that from the colour of his clothes. Scarlet was the colour of the devil. The voices told him so. Jules began to follow the man into the narrow tunnel-like darkness of the alley. Behind him, the hungry of Marseilles moved too.

When he was halfway down the alley the man turned, hearing footsteps behind him. His hair was golden in the sunlight that filtered through the roofs, and he was young and handsome. So had Lucifer, the light-bearer, been gilded and beautiful. Jules, seeing that face, gasped, and understood. This man, who had just issued from that wicked, shifting house, was known to him. The merchants were responsible for the misery of the poor: someone – Charles de Casaulx or the King of the Beggars – had told him that. And last summer, at the dockside, this merchant had given Jules a button. A button made of horn.

At last Jules understood why he had been required to remain alive when everyone that he had loved had died. It was to rid the world of the evil that had blighted Marseilles. The evil that, like this man, emanated from the golden house in the square.

Jules found his voice at last, but no words. A howl of anguish, born of loss and fear and hunger, echoed against the enclosing walls of the houses. Behind him, shambling down the street behind him, his fellow-beggars echoed his cry.

Filled with a sudden, insane strength, Jules struck the merchant before he had time to draw his sword. He had no weapon but his hands and feet, but they flailed through the air, wildly lashing out, tearing at handfuls of shirt and scarlet doublet.

The sky overhead darkened as the beggars surged down the alley. They were one person now, and that gave them strength. Their howls were the howls of the wolves that still prowled the loneliest forests of France: hungry, anguished, and hating. Dirty, calloused fingers found the merchant's fine jewelled sword, dragging it out of the scabbard.

After they had hacked him limb from limb they surged into the merchant's house, battering through the doors and the windows. Inside, they beat the pictures and furnishings to matchwood and set fire to the exotic carpets and hangings. They gorged themselves on fine food and wine from the pantries, cramming themselves with delicacies until their shrunken stomachs revolted, and they were sick. They clawed with their fingernails at the walls of the house, so that their palms were stained with gold dust.

Eventually, the militia were called out, and the beggars themselves escaped or were put to the sword. When all was quiet again, and the sun had disappeared into the clean cool depths of the Mediterranean, the moon shone on the alleyway beside the merchant's house.

Scraps of red silk dotted the flagstones and walls, blown about by the sweet warm wind. They were like the poppies that danced on the hills beyond Marseilles, opening their faces to the sun, dying before the first chill winds of winter.

In the weeks that followed Thomas's departure from Pisa, the hostility that Serafina had noticed began to harden into something more frightening.

It began with a single word daubed on her front doorstep: *whore*, smeared crudely in black paint on the stone. She sent one of the servants to scrub it off, resisting the temptation to kneel there herself, exorcizing her anger and her misery in hard work.

Two days later there was another word scrawled on the step. A different word: and for the first time Serafina felt fear rather than anger when the servant timidly pointed it out to her. *Bastard*, it said, and she thought of her blue-eyed Francesco playing peep-bo with Maria upstairs. Her hand clutched the door jamb, and she gazed wildly up and down the empty street. She thought that the walls of her house had begun to feel fragile, that, looking up, the roof appeared patched and poorly fixed as though it might blow away in the next strong wind. She began to keep a light on in the hall all night, directing one of the servants to act as night-watchman.

Things changed: they did not improve. It was midsummer now, and Pisa was overheated, cursed with flies and rank air from the nearby marshes. Someone spat at Serafina in the street, walking back from the warehouses one evening, but when she spun round there was only the sound of laughter and the patter of running feet on cobbles. At home, she pulled off her fouled gown, throwing it to the floor and kicking it, scrubbing her face and hands in water.

When she looked up Maria was there, watching her, her hazel eyes no longer carefree, but blurred with tears. 'Mama says that Messer Merli says you poisoned your husband,' she said. 'It's a lie, isn't it?'

And Serafina, pausing for a moment, the towel still covering her face, said, 'It's a lie.' She had stolen, she had deceived, but she had not killed. Only Angelo had killed: that was the difference between them.

She sent letters to Costanza, who was in Lucca, and to William Williams, who had not sailed with the *Kingfisher*, but had remained in Livorno. At night, she woke frequently, believing that she could hear voices at her door, footsteps in the passageways. She discovered that though you could spend years weaving yourself a home, a life, a family, everything could unravel at a single word. The words whispered as she walked through the streets, the market–places, the docks became louder. Whore. Bastard. *Witch*.

When unknown hands killed Maria's cat, and unknown voices pronounced the poor creature a witch's familiar, she wrote for a second time to Costanza, explaining that she could no longer guarantee her daughter's safety. At night, Francesco slept in Serafina's room, his cradle beside her bed. She did not fight back against the rumours, against the possibility that everything she had worked for would be ruined. She could not fight back: there was nothing tangible to fight against. She had worked so hard for this, she had abased herself for this, she had lost the man she loved for this, and yet she knew that she might lose it all. There was an inevitability about it that Kara Ali, she thought, would have understood. Lying awake in the middle of the night, Serafina knew that she had juggled too high and too long, that the golden rings she had thrown into the sky might soon come plummeting down, overturned by a whisper.

She collected money from banks and chests, making secret and complicated arrangements for its disposal. She sold what cloth she could, but trade was poor. Men did not want to buy goods from a witch, a murderess. The servants who had been in the house since Jacopo's days began to murmur. Some of them handed in their notice, their eyes not meeting Serafina's. She packed herself and Francesco a bag, and kept it always beside her. She found herself keeping inside Jacopo Capriani's unremarkable house, drawing the curtains and closing the shutters, imprisoned there as surely as she had been imprisoned in Algiers.

One night, falling asleep at last, she was woken in the early hours of the morning. She thought it was dawn, at first, but then, looking around her at the unnatural orange light that bathed the room, she knew that it was not. Running to the window, she pushed the shutter open a fraction.

Outside, they had built a bonfire in the street. The effigy they had thrown on top of the bonfire was made of wood and of wax, and was dressed in black. As she watched, the wood began to char, and the wax face and body to melt, distorting the crudely shaped female features into grotesque. The street was filled with people: the light from the flames underlit their faces, transforming them into unrecognizable demons. The waxen effigy began to spit and bubble, and crimson sparks darted into the air.

She dressed herself and Francesco as quickly as she could and, running to Maria's room, woke her and gave her the baby. Then, treading silently down the stairs to the accounting-room, she found the chest.

She searched desperately through the papers, throwing them all, books, letters, bills, accounts, to the floor. It was here, she knew it was here, a year ago she had put it in here herself. When she had found it, she read the inscription on the front of the letter, and then hid it inside the bodice of her dress.

She could hear fists beating at the door as she started back up the stairs. Men's hands were shaking the heavy iron bolts, rattling them until they gave way, and men's voices were chanting.

Whore. Bastard. *Witch.*

Thomas was woken in the early hours of the morning by cannon-fire.

He was asleep in the Great Cabin of the *Kingfisher*, somewhere not far from the Cape. The noise woke him instantly, dragging him from tortuous, complicated dreams. Rolling out of bed, he heard the lookout's feet on the steps outside.

He had opened the door before the sailor had time to raise his fist. 'Sir –'

'I know. I heard it.' Thomas, already dressed in shirt and breeches, headed for the bridge.

The breeze was lively, tossing up the waves and staining their peaks with white. It was not quite dawn, but the horizon, as he watched, was momentarily tinged with scarlet. Then, following almost immediately after the scarlet splashes, that low, dreadful booming. A shiver ran down the back of Thomas's neck and he screwed up his eyes, but it was too dark, too far away.

The boatswain, coming to stand beside him, said, 'Spaniards?'

Thomas frowned. 'Could be.' Still staring out to sea, he could hear the *Kingfisher* waking around him, fluttering her wings to the sound of men rolling themselves out of hammocks and running, grumbling, to the decks.

The helmsman was already heading down towards the whip-staff. The boatswain, hearing the course Thomas called out, spoke again.

'Sir, we could –'

'Put about and head back into the Mediterranean?' Thomas's eyes were a bright pure blue in the half light, and a smile touched the corners of his mouth. 'No. We're going to have a look. I'm curious, you see. Curiosity was always my failing.'

Only it wasn't curiosity that made him send the *Kingfisher* flying in the direction of the cannon-fire, but restlessness, and misery, and a terrible familiar need for action. And, sailing towards the scene of battle, he soon saw that it wasn't the Spaniards, but a different enemy entirely who had positioned themselves round the three ships that had begun to thread their way through the Cape.

The three ships were, as Thomas had already guessed, the *Legacy*, the *Saviour of Bristol*, and the *Garland*. And they were fighting a whole flotilla of Barbary corsairs.

Thomas heard Rufus, beside him, curse. He saw too the

fleeting look of fear on the faces of some of his men. He had taken on some new hands in Livorno to replace the sailors who had chosen to stay behind in Italy. Some of them were Greek, a few French, but there were several Englishmen. He had cajoled and bullied them into shape during the weeks at sea, until they were part of the single great entity that was the *Kingfisher*.

He knew that no fear showed on his own face, but just for a fraction of a second Thomas found himself pausing, considering, weighing up the odds. He could, as the boatswain had been about to recommend, turn tail and run. This was not his fight, he could have told himself, this was between the English Levant Company and the Barbary corsair. He had no part in this.

But he knew, as soon as the thought crossed his mind, that was simply not true. He had every part in it. This ship, this crew, the clothes on his back, had been financed originally by the Levant Company, by the golden gifts from the gods that he had taken from the wreckage of the *Toby*. He owed the Levant Company everything.

And besides, he had made his choice weeks ago, back in Pisa. *I am going home*, he had said to Serafina. I am going home to England. He had not planned to say that, but he had known as soon as he had spoken that he had started upon the only route left to him. To return to the country of his birth, to begin once more to realize the ambitions that, through Serafina, he had almost forgotten. The image of how she had looked that last morning was imprinted on his mind as a die stamps a coin: her dark hair, blown by the warm wind round her face. Her eyes, filled with a joy that he had, quite deliberately, quenched. Her mouth, struggling to smile. The anger he felt when he thought of Angelo Guardi kissing that mouth, caressing that body, was intolerable.

Now his anger had a different target. Triangular pennants inscribed with the red crescent of Islam flared in the wind; red crosses fluttered on the masts of the Levant Company ships. There were six corsair ships, sleek and fast, well burdened with ordnance. They surrounded the three English ships in well-planned formation, and even as Thomas watched he saw one of the corsair ships fire again, its shot glancing off the *Saviour of*

Bristol's bows. He could not hear the cries of the men aboard the stricken *Saviour*, but he could see the blackened hole that the corsair's cannon had made in the galleon's bows, see the frantic activity as men struggled to patch a repair to the damage.

He gave the order to clear the decks of the *Kingfisher* as, shading his eyes from the rising sun, he identified the corsair ship that had struck the *Saviour*. A sleek, workmanlike galley, with a wreath of blue flowers painted on the prow to ward off the evil eye. He had seen that galley less than six months before, in Scanderoon. It belonged to Angelo Guardi's friend, the man called Hamid.

So Hamid had, as Thomas had earlier warned John Keane, tracked the English ships back through the Mediterranean. Only this time his ally was not the Frenchman Angelo Guardi, but an entire fleet of Barbary corsairs, hungry for silk and spices and men to crew their ships.

On board the *Kingfisher*, Thomas's men hurried to clear the gun-decks. Hammocks, bedding, clothes and furniture were swept aside; and tools and piles of shot and barrels of powder set out by the gun crew. Tubs of water stood ready to cool the over-heated guns, and sand and salt were scattered on the decks to make them less slippery underfoot. The *Kingfisher* was a well-armed vessel, the larger cannon situated lower down in the ship, the lighter ones above. On the foredeck and half-deck light cannon – falconets – were pivoted to aim in the direction of the Barbary galleys. Thomas heard the creak and whine as the wooden gunports were opened, and then the low metallic rumbling of the cannon as they were wheeled into place. Above Thomas, sailors soared up the rigging to secure the yards.

The *Saviour of Bristol* was still afloat, her men having made some sort of hasty repair to the hole left by the corsair's cannon. But another such shot, thought Thomas grimly as he yelled his instructions to the helmsman, would surely sink her. Not that the corsair would, for preference, sink her. Hamid and his brothers would rather have the Englishman's cargo and crew than see the *Saviour*'s treasures scattered on the seabed.

They had not seen him yet, thought Thomas, as he eased the *Kingfisher* into exactly the right position. Both the corsairs and the English were too absorbed in the desperate game they played to notice another vessel, improbably throwing herself into the fray. Thomas found that he was smiling as he raised his hand to give the signal to his master-gunner. Then the *Kingfisher*'s cannon flared in deadly salute, and he was no longer a spectator, but a player.

On board the *Legacy*, John Keane heard the *Kingfisher*'s cannon fire. The noise broke through the intense concentration that had possessed him since the corsair ships had first been sighted; it was as though he had been woken, shockingly, from some hideously convoluted and oppressive dream. His muscles, his bones, his teeth seemed to vibrate in rhythm with the sound.

The corsairs had taken them unawares that morning, darting like so many deadly silver fish from out of nowhere. They had quickly succeeded in breaking the line of the convoy, threading themselves between the *Garland* and the *Saviour of Bristol*, blocking the Levant Company's exit to the Atlantic or their return to the Inland Sea. It had been the sort of possibility that John Keane always dreaded, and more than usual this time, knowing that the English ships had been weakened already by that little skirmish off Cyprus. They had repaired the *Legacy*'s superstructure at Alexandria, and made a reasonable job of it, but the *Garland*, small and ageing anyway, had limped somewhat since their encounter with Thomas Marlowe's greedy Frenchman. Six Barbary war-galleys against two heavily laden galleons and a struggling pinnace was not good odds. Since the corsair's cannon had struck the *Saviour of Bristol* the odds had become unpleasantly poor. All it needed, John Keane had thought grimly as the *Legacy*'s defences had whirred into action that morning, was for the bloody Spaniards to join in.

Standing on the bridge, Keane screwed up his eyes and willed himself to focus on the sea that surrounded them. He could not at first identify the source of the gunfire. Below him, the men were reloading the *Legacy*'s cannon; John's own shirt was already blackened by smoke, reeking of powder. The *Saviour* was still struggling to right herself after that damned ball in her side.

His pilot gripped his arm, hard. 'Look, sir —'

Keane turned, cursing his eyesight, staring desperately back towards the sunlit Mediterranean. He could just distinguish a ship, a great and beautiful ship, framed against the early morning sun. 'Her *name* —' he hissed angrily to the pilot, frustrated in his attempt to make out the letters scrawled on her bows, the colours of the oriflammes dancing from the masts.

'The *Kingfisher*, sir,' said the pilot.

Keane looked again, not believing. The galleon drew closer, silhouetted against the pinks and violets and turquoises of the rising sun. On the prow of the ship, a water-bird struggled to free itself from the beakhead. The galleon's pennants were blue and gold, but there was, gloriously, a red cross flying from her mainmast.

'Christ,' said John Keane. 'Thomas Marlowe.' He rubbed his eyes. 'What the hell is he doing here?'

But he had no time to ponder, and little time to glory in the delightful conclusion that Thomas had reconsidered the offer he had made in Aleppo, and was sailing to England. That red cross affirmed him as a part of the English Levant Company. John dragged his gaze from the *Kingfisher* as the *Legacy* repositioned herself and readied her guns. And as the *Legacy*'s cannon fired, he heard a second, echoing blast from the *Kingfisher*. It seemed to John that the whole vast bowl of sky and sea was blackened with smoke and daubed with flashes of scarlet fire.

If Ned Whitlock had, as he surely must have, recognized the *Kingfisher*, then he, like any sensible man, had also welcomed her arrival. John never knew whose shot hit the first corsair ship. By that time all four English ships were firing — chain-shot and bar-shot and firebombs as well as the heavy iron cannon-balls. The corsair ship, which had found itself encircled by the *Garland*, the *Legacy* and the *Kingfisher*, was hit first by a piece of iron shot, and then by a firebomb. The mast snapped like matchwood, and John heard the dreadful cries of the galley-slaves, pinioned by falling wood. Christians all of them, perhaps his own countrymen. The fire caught first on the covered awning at the poop, and then flared along the galley's rambades, licking the dry wooden superstructure, the sails and rigging, the clothes of the galley-slaves into hideous scarlet life. John Keane closed his eyes only momentarily. As he opened them again the galley was already sinking below the waves, its oarsmen still chained to the deck.

After that, all thoughts of pity, of home, of England, of Dorothy, vanished from his mind. Just as they always did: there was no place for pity or love out here: those emotions were irrelevant, reserved for another existence, one that just now he had utterly forgotten. All his mind was concentrated on giving orders to his crew, on helping the pilot direct the positioning of the *Legacy*, on helping defend the other ships when they needed it, reinforcing their fire-power when they found themselves in an advantageous position.

At some time in the endless morning the *Kingfisher*, aided by the *Garland* as a decoy, sank a second corsair ship. The second galley was drawn into the water with hideous but inevitable slowness, as though some great thirsty whirlpool sucked her negligently into the deep. That gave the crew of the *Garland* time to board her, to put the Turks to the sword, and release the Christian captives. The galley's crew fought furiously, killing two of Ned Whitlock's men until they themselves were released by English swords to a martyr's death of endless delight. Whitlock took the galley-slaves on board the *Garland*: two dozen exhausted men, who had had the best meal they had eaten for months given to them that morning, before they were forced to make war on those of their own religion.

In the rescue attempt the *Garland* lost her mizzen-mast, felled by a chain-shot which wrapped itself around her rigging like some deadly and clinging ivy. The mast cracked in two with a sound so like cannon-fire that John Keane almost expected to see red flames issuing from the splintered wood. Men crawled over the pinnace like ants, hacking at the tangled rigging, throwing ropes and sails to the waves. But the odds were equal now, John thought, as he reloaded one of the foredeck's falconets and aimed in the vague direction of a corsair galley. Four all, damn it, and the *Kingfisher* and the *Legacy* were surely worth two of any corsair.

He was scarcely aware of the midday sun rising high over the

Legacy's masthead and continuing its arc downwards to light the route back to England. He had no time to eat: at some time in the early afternoon he found himself taking great mouthfuls of water from the buckets on the gun-deck: at another time he took the remaining bottles of aqua vitae from his cabin and went round the entire crew, making sure that every man and boy took a mouthful. One of the ship's boys – a lad of twelve or so – took a bullet in his knee, and John held him down on the table in his cabin while the surgeon filled him full of aqua vitae and took off the lower part of the damaged leg. For a while afterwards he held the boy in his arms while the surgeon bandaged the bloody stump, and the boy spluttered and cried and called for his mother. Then, thank God, the lad fainted and John, retching as he walked, found himself back on the foredeck, amid the stench of gunpowder and scorched pitch and salt and sweat.

The *Saviour of Bristol* went down at mid-afternoon, having resisted her inevitable end for almost nine hours. The shot that felled her was the merest graze, but the hole in her bows that her men had laboured so desperately to patch gave way for a second time, and the water poured in. John saw the *Saviour*'s crew jump into the sea as the galleon keeled over in the waves, balancing momentarily at an obscene and improbable angle before the tips of her masts dipped beneath the surface of the water. Some of her men, unable to swim, drowned even as John, his throat raw with shouting, took the *Legacy* rapidly round to the scene of the shipwreck. Others he managed to pick up, but one of the corsair galleys, sprinting across the waves, hauled Christian sailors on board, as well as the bales of silk and barrels of spices that the dying *Saviour* released from her hold.

John's eyes were dry as he sighted Izaak Taylor, master of the *Saviour of Bristol*, shackled to an oar. He was only aware of a rising and almost uncontrollable hatred, and the discovery that even he, civilized John Keane of the lute and the chess-games, would, if he had the opportunity, kill every one of those bearded, turbaned men with his bare hands: aye, and enjoy it, too.

Four, three. They were all tiring now, surely: the oarsmen on the Barbary galleys, despite the comitre's whip, pulled more slowly. His own men, confused with tension and fatigue, began to make mistakes. John's temper, normally so unexcitable, became unpredictable even to him. He found himself about to strike one of his crewmen for leaving a smouldering length of tinder unguarded on the gun-deck. He managed to stop himself just in time, clenching his fist as his hand reached for his sword, and walking up to the foredeck and out into the air.

Only the *Kingfisher* seemed to remain cool, imperturbable. If the rest of them made mistakes, then the *Kingfisher*'s movements were faultless, cold and calculated, as though Thomas Marlowe's fiery temperament had been quenched in the heat of battle, and hardened to a steely inflexible purpose. Whenever John looked up from his hopeless aiming of the falconet, whenever he had finished reeling out yet another string of orders to his boatswain or carpenter, there was the *Kingfisher*, proud against the fading sky, her sails and rigging unblemished by shot, her cannon marking out the endless day with volleys of destruction. Thomas had sunk another corsair ship before John Keane, resting exhausted for a moment against the gunwale, had fully understood his purpose. The galley sank with one perfectly aimed ball to the bows, leaving scarcely a ripple on the surface of the sea to show that she had ever existed. Then John, wiping the filth and perspiration from his face with the palms of his hands, understood.

The *Kingfisher* was not hunting just any corsair ship, she was hunting a particular corsair ship. The longest, fastest, sleekest galley: the one with the wreath of blue flowers painted around the prow. The other galleys were merely distractions in this deadly game of hide-and-seek: mites biting against the skin of a ravening wolf, to be brushed aside when the irritation became too great.

He understood also, straightening himself, forcing himself to listen to his master-gunner warning him about the dwindling stocks of powder, that the corsair ship knew it was hunted. For those two, the rest of them might not have existed.

He was sufficiently tired for his mind to make the leap of intuition, and realize that that ship was, without doubt, the one Thomas had warned him about in Aleppo. It all made perfect sense: a tit-for-tat struggle that had already lasted for months –

no, years, thought John Keane, remembering what Thomas had told him about the voyage to Zante. Had it not been that his own life and livelihood, and the lives and livelihood of all his crew, were at stake, then he could almost have enjoyed watching the duel between the *Kingfisher* and the corsair galley. As it was, he had to force himself not to become preoccupied by that fascinating, deadly dance, to ensure that he focused every scrap of his ragged concentration on the task in hand.

In the end, though, it wasn't John Keane who made the final mistake, but Edward Whitlock. Ned's task had been the hardest part of all: the *Garland* was the convoy's weakest, slowest ship, but Ned had sailed her brilliantly, using the *Garland*'s size to her advantage, darting between the Barbary galleys, refusing to allow them to grapple and board.

But now John Keane, frantically engaged in unknotting a piece of the *Legacy*'s tangled rigging, saw the *Garland* make her first and only error. Swinging round, she blasted all of her cannon in the direction of one of the smaller corsair galleys, breaking the galley's rudder. But she had failed to notice that the largest galley, the one that Thomas hunted, was approaching her from her leeward side, oars beating fifty to the minute, the comitre's voice hoarse with shouting, his whip hand blistered and raw. As John watched, the galley positioned herself broadside to broadside against the *Garland*, and the grappling hook, flung up towards the galleon's superstructure, hooked itself around her gunwale.

The *Legacy*'s pilot saw and understood the situation. With dreadful slowness the ship dragged herself round, making ready to sail to the aid of the *Garland*. But, as John grabbed and loaded an arquebus, he saw that the *Kingfisher* had sailed up behind the corsair galley.

It required the most expert gunner to place a cannon-ball in the bows of the galley, and not hit the *Garland* as well. John Keane held his breath as a single shot arced through the air.

The corsair ship sank immediately, the grappling chains trailing futilely into the sea, the blue flowers disappearing last beneath the waves.

John, hurling his hat from his head, began to cheer. Then,

looking round, he saw the last remaining galley, and the howl of victory froze uncompleted in his throat.

He could not understand, at first, why Thomas Marlowe did not also see the corsair galley. Then he knew that, looking west towards the Atlantic, the master and crew of the *Kingfisher* would have seen nothing but the setting sun, nothing but that blinding flaring orange and silver globe dipping into the horizon.

He heard himself call out a warning, but his voice was lost, ripped to shreds by the wind, before it had travelled half the distance between the *Legacy* and the *Kingfisher*. He heard the final, dreadful blossoming of cannon-fire; and he saw the hole ripped in the *Kingfisher*'s hull. Then the entire frame of the great galleon quivered once, as though she, too, had been taken by surprise, and began to list towards the waves.

The sky was dimming, and the sea was dark, almost black.

He had hold of a spar of wood, but he had always been a good swimmer anyway, and it was not hard to stay afloat. He knew that two ships sailed across the indigo sea towards him: the remaining corsair galley, and John Keane's *Legacy*. He realized that the galley was travelling faster than the galleon, but he did not care. It was unimportant.

It was the noise the *Kingfisher* made that broke his heart. A whispering that gradually but unmistakably altered into whimpering as the wooden structure was pulled apart by the waves. Sometimes the ship screamed as nails were wrenched out of the timbers; at other times she moaned as the planks were driven against each other by the waves. The moaning was closely followed by shrieking as the wood splintered and shattered.

Thomas, treading water, did not let his eyes leave her for an instant. He saw the *Kingfisher*'s masts buckle and break, and heard the crack of snapping wood echoing against the sky, the sea. He saw the waves run through the body of the ship, their formation and their progress unchanged by the fragile, disintegrating structure. To the great expanse of the sea the passing of the *Kingfisher* was nothing, the eradication of a brief and ephemeral folly, the blowing out of an insignificant candle.

There was no single moment to mark the end of what he had fought for, lied for, stolen for. Just a relentless, disinterested destruction as hull, figurehead, masts and spars disappeared for ever.

He had lost everything: Francesco, Serafina, the *Kingfisher*, and perhaps soon, he thought, knowing himself to be exhausted, he would lose his life. Yet his feet kept on treading water, his hands clutched the wreckage of his dream.

He thought, as his ship became no more than a bubbling beneath the waters, *I did it for her*. To even things up, to make them right again, to return things to their proper place, their rightful owner.

But Thomas was unsure, as they leaned over the gunwale of the boat and hauled him out of the water, to which *her* he referred.

PART XV

1599

THUS BEING WEARY

And thus being weary and growing old, I am content to take my rest in my own house.

Anthony Jenkinson's voyages:
Richard Hakluyt

In the end, we are what our pasts allow us to be. Kara Ali was right, of course, there is no choice.

That last dreadful night in Pisa, we left the house by means of back doors and hidden alleyways. Maria, Francesco and I were free of the Via S. Domenico before they had finished battering the door down. We escaped to William Williams's lodgings in Livorno. I had planned it all before: if nothing else, my childhood taught me the value of planning. From Livorno we travelled to Naples, to stay in Jacopo's house. After six weeks, during which time William and Maria were married, and I made what legal arrangements were necessary, Francesco and I took passage on a ship for England. Thomas was right, you see, Italy would not have been safe. I had broken too many rules. And I will never go back to France.

The house in Naples I left to Costanza. Because she saved both my life and Thomas's. And to repay Galeazzo Merli, of course, and because no human being should own another.

We arrived in England in the winter-time, when the trees were threads of bare black lace against a yellowing sky. I had been cold, I remember, ever since I had sailed round the Cape, and I continued to be cold as I searched for lodgings in London. I found some decent rooms, though, and the innkeeper was content to take any coinage so long as it was gold. And Francesco, my beautiful blue-eyed Francesco, was passport enough. Within a day of our arrival he was ensconced in the innkeeper's wife's kitchen, taking sea-coal from the bucket and feeding it to the cat. He spoke three words of English by the end of his first day in London, and they were 'cat', 'no', and 'more'. For myself, it took me a month to frame a comprehensible sentence in the

language, for Thomas and I had always spoken in French or
Italian. I had such ease with languages when I was a child, and
yet in London I found my tongue refused to form the strange,
angular words. My first night there I wept, because my lack of
speech reduced me to a baby, or an idiot.

Two days later I rode to Southwark. The innkeeper found me
a guide, a young man who had once been in the service of the
French ambassador. Roland is with me still, only now he writes
my letters, and is training to become a notary. That day, however, I showed him the address on the letter that Thomas had
given me, long before, in Marseilles, and together we travelled
to Southwark. Francesco rode on my saddle-bow: my passport
again. No one seeing him could doubt that he was his father's
child.

We found the tavern easily. It was the biggest in Southwark,
with a sign painted with a picture of a swan swinging outside in
the breeze. I remember how cold it was: my hands and my
fingers were numb, and Francesco began to cry for the wind in
his ears, so I hid him inside the folds of my cloak. The breeze
seemed to lift itself off the grey river, taking drops of water and
turning them to ice as it travelled. I could have wept again,
alone in such a cold country. Thomas, I thought, as Roland
took Francesco from me and I climbed down from my horse,
Thomas will make me warm again.

Robert Marlowe's tavern was warm, though. There were
candles on the window-sills, and a vast log fire in the grate, and
spits loaded with roasting steers and salted bacon. It was midday,
and apprentices from the shops and sailors from the docks
crowded the rooms. They turned and stared as I walked in, and
I felt small and female and foreign, but I kept my head high, my
footsteps steady. I have been bought and sold, I have been
married, and I have given birth. I have won and lost everything
– twice. What have I to fear from a roomful of strangers jabbering
in their own incomprehensible tongue?

Part of me had, I later realized, expected to find Thomas
there, sitting at a scratched old table, ale-mug in hand, or standing in some back room, discussing ships and trade with his
brother. But there was no sign of Thomas. Roland found Robert

Marlowe by asking one of the sailors for the landlord, and I handed him the letter.

He read it as I stood before him, Francesco in my arms. I wanted to laugh as I watched the expression his face change from curiosity, to confusion, to disbelief, and finally, gawping at Francesco, to credulity. He does not look in the least like Thomas, dear Robert: he is eight years the senior, and he is short and plump and balding. But he is the kindest man, truly the kindest.

After he had read the letter, he said nothing, but took me by the arm and led me into a back room. There was an enormous kitchen, hung with copper pots and pans, warmed by a blazing fire, busy with servants preparing food for the tavern. Robert's wife Anne was there, surrounded by four of their six children. The two eldest were at school, due to return home any moment. The baby, a boy a few months younger than Francesco, was lying in a cradle, a nursemaid rocking it with her foot.

It was after Anne Marlowe, too, had read the letter, that I knew that something was wrong. I could tell by the pity in their eyes, by the way they glanced at Francesco. I discovered, forcing myself to be patient through the agony of translation, that Thomas had never returned to England. That the *Kingfisher*, sailing from Pisa, had been sunk by Algerian corsairs off the Cape. That it was uncertain whether Thomas had lived or died. If he had lived, he was a prisoner of the corsairs.

I stayed that night in the Marlowes' tavern. The following day I rode to the Keanes' house in Blackfriars. John Keane spoke French and Italian, thank God, so I was able to learn the full story of the sinking of the *Kingfisher* from him without the need of an intermediary. Listening to John Keane, I began to believe that Thomas was alive. I could not accept that he would let the sea take him. So I began to plan again.

Even if I had not loved him, I could not have let him remain in Algiers. It would have destroyed him in a way that it was never able to destroy me. Thomas's nationality is stamped through him like dye through silk. Whereas I am a gypsy, a tinker, a pedlar of trinkets.

Robert Marlowe gave me the key to his brother's house in Greenwich. It is not a large house, but near enough to the docks to be useful to me. I went to the house after I had left the Keanes, and there I threw dust-covers off the furniture, lit fires in the chimneys to take the damp from the rooms, and engaged a few respectable and hardworking servants and clerks. Then I set to work.

A man – even one as valuable to the Turk as Thomas was – can be released from captivity if his relatives will pay sufficiently handsomely. I had gold in great store, salted away to secret places in Naples and Livorno after I had understood Galeazzo Merli's intentions against me in Pisa. And I still had friends in France and Italy. William Williams, Costanza, a few bankers and merchants who had desired me at first for my body, and had then come to respect me for my mind. Out of desire and respect can develop, occasionally, liking and loyalty. I knew the right people to talk to, and I was intimate with the languages of the bagnio, and of Islam. Because I knew that Thomas would never, like Kara Ali, take the turban, and because I knew how, ultimately, captivity would destroy him, I set about ransoming him.

To guarantee my stay in England, I became a Protestant. The change of religion meant little to me – after all, long ago, when I was still a child, I had ceased to believe in a benevolent God. I have believed for a long time that man creates a god to fulfil his own will, to stand between him and the terrors of the night. I sleep well at night now; I do not think that I have anything left to fear. A god imposes a pattern, yet there is no pattern, all that is an illusion.

Yet I will admit that I thought I saw a glimpse of some sort of order the day I received the letter telling me that Thomas was alive. The letter was sent to me by one of the Redemptionist Friars, and it explained that Thomas had not drowned, but was imprisoned in Algiers. I have received several more letters since, and all have stated that the conditions of Thomas's servitude are good, that he is treated well and encouraged to continue the trades he knows best. I have sent money, and I have written letters myself, though I do not know whether they have been delivered. Six months ago, I received a letter which said, *Messer Marlowe is building a ship* . . . I showed this letter to Edward Whitlock, who explained that the corsairs are eager to replace their galleys with the great galleons from the northern countries. Their captives will supply them with the vessels that will allow them to enslave other Christians.

When Thomas returns, he shall not sail the Mediterranean, he shall cross the oceans. He shall travel where his heart has always longed to go, and the corsairs, even with their fine Christian-built ships, will not dare to follow him. I will not tie him to me: I know now that the chains I acquired in Algiers were those of insecurity and lack of love, and I have severed them for ever.

It has taken me more than a year to grow used to the weather this island endures: a year of watching the skies change from sun to rain and to tempest by the hour. Now, approaching my second spring in England, I begin to see a beauty in it. At first, closing my eyes, I used to imagine myself back in Marseilles, or Pisa. I would paint grey skies blue, dry the rain-washed streets, calm the choppy waters. But I have begun to learn to live without deceit, and to see that there is, perhaps, a value in mutability.

I have also begun to see that the future belongs to the nations of the north. That in these times of change, the southern states are growing old. Spain has lost her great King, Philip II. And Italy is a fractured land, each state jealous of its neighbours, all states envious of the success of the northern nations. Last year the English were expelled from Tuscany, and now the two countries are no longer permitted to trade.

And my poor France is weary of civil war, its people tired of hunger and disorder. I learned of Angelo's death by accident, overhearing a fragment of conversation at the harbour one day. The sailor had been in Marseilles in the June of 1597, and had witnessed the rioting of the dispossessed. At first I found it impossible to believe that he had gone, that all that beauty and intelligence had been destroyed with the sort of arbitrariness that Angelo himself had once tried to counterfeit for me. Then I began to see a justice in it – that wretched desire for a pattern to make sense of our futile lives had overtaken me also.

But the days of Angelo and his like are gone. The days of the great empires – even that of the Turk – are over. With the death of the century we enter upon a new age: something different. The future – the new century – is the property of the north. England too will change; the English Queen grows old, and though she has not named her successor, she must bequeath her kingdom to the son of the dead Scots Queen. There is no one else.

The English are a crude, energetic nation. Immured in this island of grey mists and constant rain they are cut off from the miseries of the rest of the world, isolated from the burdens of history. The women are beautiful and strong-minded; the men I found discourteous at first, but I have since grown to like them. There is something of Thomas in so many of them – that stubborn refusal to accept what fate has offered, a pig-headed determination to wrest control of their lives from the disinterested gods.

For myself, although I know their philosophy to be incorrect, it suits me to adopt it. I am becoming English: I have an English religion and English friends. The Whitlocks and the Keanes, the Marlowes and the Stapers. Faith Whitlock and her three children are my and Francesco's friends. They call my child Francis, and soon he will no longer remember the colour of a Tuscan sky, the scent of oranges and lemons in a paved and fountained garden.

Through John Keane I have bought shares in the new East India Company. They are for Thomas, when he returns, and they are for myself. Men like Thomas, and the ships he will build, are needed here. They are the blood that pulses in England's veins, they will allow her to fulfil her worth. This is a young, vigorous nation, and it has been easy for me to become a part of it. English pirates may sail the Mediterranean and the Atlantic, but there are no slaves here. Unlike Algiers, unlike Livorno, every man and every woman is free.

I have shares in two ships now: they sail for the Indies in the autumn. Money uninvested is money put to waste, and I need money to finance both Thomas's ransoming and my child's future. But Thomas and Francesco are not the only reasons that

I have begun to trade again. From the parlour of Thomas's house I can see the docks, the harbour of the city of London, and I begin to grow hungry again, to feel the need to practise the crafts I was born to. It has brought me both happiness and sorrow, but it is all that I know, and it is necessary to my soul. I will have silk again, and spices and jewels and gold and silver. But mostly silk. Thomas will build me a ship when he comes home: I would not employ another shipbuilder. I have seen the *Kingfisher* spread her great sails ready to skim across the water, and I have stood on her bridge, the wind in my hair, feeling the movement of the waves through her wooden decks. These are not things I would ever forget.

So, you see, I have no regrets. I would not have one jot of it different, neither my life nor Thomas's. I did what I had to. I know that others would see it differently – Thomas himself, perhaps – but I know also that the course of my life was dictated the day my father said, *You are to marry Michele Corsini, Serafina.*

Thomas, too, I have realized, started the spinning of the circle that took him from the land of his birth six years ago. Soon, I hope, the wheel will cease to gyrate, and he will come home again. I also hope that by then he will have learnt to understand, and perhaps to forgive a little. To forgive the betrayal of him that was necessary for me to secure my freedom, and ultimately was meaningless. To understand that events are dictated by the characters of those drawn into the game, and by history. There is nothing else.

I am standing at the window of the first-floor parlour in the Greenwich house. The sun filters through the glass, making pools of light liquid with the colours of the rainbow on the polished wooden floor. It is midday, and the streets and the docks outside are busy. I can hear the calls of the street-sellers and the sailors shouting to each other on the harbourside, but their voices are muffled by the glass and by the breeze.

The sky is the light aquamarine blue that I have come to love, so different to the lapis and sapphires of the Mediterranean. It silvers the cobbled streets, still damp after a night's rain, it frosts the yards and spars of the ships anchored on the Thames. It filigrees the distant tracery of the galleon making its way carefully down the river, sailing from the open sea back into the embracing arms of the port.

The galleon is exquisite: strong and proud, possessing the grace and beauty of line that conveys both speed and agility. Her sails are all shortened now as she picks her cautious way through the tangle of barges and barques that litter the river. Her master, confident in his craft, guides her with courtesy around the obstacles. She is a living reflection of another ship: a ship that once flew pennants of blue and gold from her mastheads. She is a phoenix, a kingfisher reborn.

I rub my fingers on the pane, wiping the misted glass, needing to see more clearly. The tears in my eyes betray me, so that at first I cannot see the name inscribed on the galleon's bows.

Then the shadows fall away, and all is clear. I can read her name.

Serafina.